Run West
A Novel of the Civil War

Dan Wallace

Run West
A Novel of the Civil War
Dan Wallace

ISBN 9780828326759$16.00Trade Paperback
ISBN 9780828326742$9.95 E-Book
6 x 9, 369 pages
Publication Date: February 2018

Cover design by Molly A. Wallace
Cover photo by Jason P. O'Dell

Branden Books
PO Box 812094
Wellesley MA 02482

www.brandenbooks.com

To Molly and Conor
who make everything worthwhile.

Prologue

Daddy sat next to them both, wringing his hands when not wipingtheir brows with cold water. It didn't do any good, they both got sicker and sicker until they died. First, Ma, then Little Sister Bess, only a few minutes apart. As soon as they were gone, Daddy jumped up, told Billy to stay put, and ran off.

Billy sat in a chair facing the door so he wouldn't have to look at them. He expected that Daddy had gone off to get the preacher, though he wondered why he had to rush. Poor Ma and Little Sister wouldn't care one way or the other now.

Billy hated waiting by them alone. He wondered if he might get the sickness from being around their bodies for so long. Then he felt guilty for thinking only about himself. He wondered if the preacher when he arrived would know about his selfish sin just by looking at him. He could end up in the eternal flames, all alone because, of course, Ma and Little Sister wouldn't be there.

The hours went by until night fell, which made it worse. It shouldn't have taken this long to fetch the preacher. Maybe Daddy had gone on a drunk instead. Billy shook his head, that wasn't like him. Except Ma and Little Sister had died.

Early the next morning, Daddy hurried through the front door followed by a fellow wearing a coat and church pants with a round-brimmed hat on top of his head. But, he wasn't the preacher, Billy could see, and on his back he carried this jumble of boxes and long wooden legs with metal tips.

"Go outside, Billy, wait for me to call you," Daddy said.

Billy did as he was told, though he creased his forehead into a big furrow trying to understand what was going on. After an hour, his daddy told him to come back in the house.

He stepped inside, and stopped, nailed to the floor. Ma sat in the rocking chair wearing her Sunday dress, holding Little Sister in a white frock on her lap, their eyes open.

Billy turned to leave, but Daddy held him back gently. "Don't, Billy Boy, it's all right, Ma and our little sister Bess are fine, now, they with Jesus. They fine. Mr. Buckley, here, is gonna take a likeness of them with his box, there. Somethin' to remember them with. Come," he said.

Billy allowed himself to be maneuvered over to the bureau where Daddy picked up a brush. He did his best to tug it through Billy's thick red hair while telling him to get out of his coveralls. WhileDaddy helped Billy put on his Sunday shirt and pants, Mr. Buckley fidgeted with his box, sliding into it a strange, wooden rectangle with a shiny black surface. He looked under a black cloth at the back of the box pointed down from its wooden pegs toward Ma and Little Sister. Mr. Buckley straightened up and slid out another wooden frame from the box. He looked at his pocket watch for a long time, then slid the frame back into the box. He switched the other rectangle with another, then nodded at Daddy.

"Ready, Mr. McKinney. If you will," he said, gesturing over at Ma and Little Sister.

Daddy had combed his own hairand put on his Sunday jacket. He guided Billy over to the bodies in the rocker. Billy started shaking.

"Don't Billy," Daddy said softly. "Put your arm around Sister and your mother."

Billy stared up at Daddy, imploring.

"Go ahead, Billy. They fine, now."

Billy held his arm out behind Little Sister without touching her, and rested his hand lightly on his Ma's shoulder."

"That's good," said Mr. Buckley. "Please direct your gaze at me and hold still until I tell you."

Mr. Buckley removed the front rectangle on his box and began to look at his watch. Billy could feel Ma's shoulder through her dress, the knobby bone curving next to the top of her arm. He felt the linen of her dress and the bone.

Mr. Buckley sighed, and put the front piece back on his box. "Son, you're not staying still. I will have to start again. Mr. McKinney?" he said, gesturing with his head at Billy. While Mr. Buckley exchanged the shiny black frame in the back with another, Daddy reached over with his kerchief and wiped Billy's eyes and his cheeks.

Mr. Buckley waited, then said, "All right, gentlemen. Be still, please."

He counted with his watch, frowning now and then as he looked up at them. Finally, he said, "All right. You can move now."

"Okay, go ahead and change your clothes, Billy."

Billy watched them as he put his overalls back on. Mr. Buckley seemed unhappy, and whispered to Daddy while he packed up his gear. Billy could make out a few words, "Most possibly ruined," from Mr. Buckley, nodding in Billy's direction. Daddy whispered earnestly to Mr. Buckley, raising his voice enough for Billy to hear, "I'll pay for all of 'em. Just see what you can do, please."

Mr. Buckley nodded, and Daddy shook his hand. Only one image of the whole family turned out. Daddy kept it up on the mantel over the hearth so he could look at it once in a while when he smoked his pipe after dinner. Billy didn't like the picture much, though he had to admit, it did help him remember Ma and Bess better. Daddy did go for the preacher, too, who prayed some. Then, Daddy and the neighbors who had been able to come buried Ma and Little Sister in the back near the fence line of the corn field. Daddy put up some more fencingto close in a nice little family plot for Ma and Little Sister, leaving room enough for himself and Billy, and any family his son might have later. They didn't go to church so much after that, though.

Billy's ma and his sister died in 1851, when he was seven. After that, he and his daddy lived alone by themselves for the next eleven years.

Chapter 1. Cas-chrom

William "Billy" McKinney sat on a log in the hollow, dangling his bare feet in the small brook that coursed through the notch between the two hills on the north border. Heavy oaks and ash trees flanked the twin slopes covered by neighbor Jessup's brown wheat undulating slightly in the early morning breeze. The sight of the crop still standing in the field all the way at September's end puzzled Billy. He wondered why it hadn't been brought in yet this late in the year. Despite the hot days common to fall in Tennessee, one early frost could ruin the crop. Up here in the foothills, it seemed a more likely possibility than not.

Still, Billy welcomed the breeze on a day that, if just a tad hotter, would smother whatever relief the wind could bring. Billy already felt sapped from digging in the dirt all morning. He had pulled off his shirt, but he still felt the sweltering heat through his union suit and coveralls. His fair skin glowed red from the sun's rays, too, except for the lower parts of his arms that from daily exposure had turned a delicate light russet. He'd tossed off his stiff straw hat, too. For the most part, his thick, auburn hair protected his head from the rays, though his brow burned a bit.

The frigid water in the creek helped, but he knew he'd have to get out soon and put his boots on, get back to work. The old man could show up at any moment and bring down the wrath of Jesus. But, the water felt so good and Daddy really wasn't so hard.

A bluebird darted by and up the hill. He tracked it until it beat away beneath the trees. His eyes settled back on the wheat, a good crop. Even if the Jessups showed up in time to harvest, Billy wondered how they would do it. They couldn't use a reaper now that the Graybacks had taken all the horses and oxen. Even if they used cradles or even sickles to cut the wheat, how could they get it off and out of the hills down to market in Maryville? Billy shook his head.

He couldn't feel his feet. Sighing, he pulled them out of the stream and wiped them down with his wool socks. He pulled the damp socks on, then his boots, and stood up. His feet would be cool for five minutes, then quickly dry in the heat. As soon as he started digging a furrow, the socks would be sopping wet again from sweat.

Billy moved out into the small clearing down to the five furrows he'd opened up that morning. Just five, an hour for each. With no horse, he couldn't use their old plow, so Daddy had given him his granddaddy's cas-chrom to dig with, straight from the old country. Granddaddy had fashioned the crooked plow himself out of two hard pieces of wood, one a six-foot shaft that curved up and back for easier pushing. A shorter slab called the foot angled out from the lower end of the shaft. Thin squares of iron sheathed the foot for easier cutting into the soil. A round peg stuck out from the shaft so that the plowman could set his foot on it to push the iron blade into the ground. Then, he would bend to lever the plow back, causing the soil to break upwards.

Backbreaking work, Billy thought, sighing again. Daddy had sent him out here to dig up this little meadow with the idea that they could throw in some spuds and other root crops to carry them through the winter. "Keep the furrows low," he said quietly, "between some rows of grass or whatever, so no one sees them. If they do, the Rebel boys are sure to take them."

They would, too, never giving a bit about the folks around here. They'd yell "East Tennessee submissionists, serve y'all right to go hungry for not supporting the Cause." To blazes with them stinkin' Rebs, Billy thought, savagely shoving the cas-chrom into the dry, hard loam.

He pushed the foot of the plow into the dirt with surprising strength, given his small size and light weight. He pulled down and back on the shaft to loosen a clump. It would take a lot of this to get enough taters to sprout this late in the season or next spring. He looked at the rows next to him that he'd already dug up, then at the rest of the meadow. Just a tiny little clearing, now it seemed as big as the town green in Maryville when he thought about the furrows he still had to dig. Even if he could plow the whole meadow by hand, how the heck would anyone miss seeing the turned sod no matter how many grassy ridges he left between them? Whatever might grow would be scooped up by anyone who came along, no question. Maybe he and Daddy should just try to steal some provisions back from the Rebs, tuck them away in a good, safe hidey-hole for the winter.

He jammed the awkward blade into the ground and felt a jarring halt. Rock—gulldarn it. He yanked the crooked tool out and tossed it to the side. After a moment's hesitation, he made his way back across the glade to the stream. He took off his boots and soaked

5

socks, dropping them next to him as he collapsed onto the log and thrust his feet back into the stream.

"What-ho, McKinney," a voice called, coming from near the two hills.

Billy gazed aimlessly up, squinting in the sun's glare. He raised his hand above his eyes in what could have been mistaken as a desultory salute, and saw Trey Jessup amblingdown toward him.

"'Lo, Trey. What brings you up here?"

Seventeen like Billy, Trey Jessup seemed heartier, a taller fuller figure in his blue wool shirt and dungarees held up by a broad, black leather belt instead of braces. He wore a broad-brimmed hat and a checked red kerchief around his neck. Billy noted that Trey was dry as a bone, no sweat at all.

Trey stooped down and gave Billy's hand a strong shake like he was working a water pump, one, two, three. "Checkin' the wheat. Should be ready to bring in, soon."

"Looks ready to me now. Maybe past ready." Billy screwed up his face, "How you goin' to get it off this hill anyway?"

Trey smiled knowingly. "Chop it down, bale it, haul it out."

"That's a lot of work without oxes or hosses."

"Yup," said Trey, "but Daddy's got it figured out."

Billy raised his head, chin high. "That so? Your daddy gonna bring in some more help?"

"Why, you looking for a job?"

"No siree bob! I got plenty to do around our place."

Trey glanced around, "Yeah. What you doin' up here, Billy?"

Billy froze. He slowly pulled his feet out of the creek and began rubbing them. "Spottin'," he said, looking down at his feet.

"Spottin'?" said Trey, "Spottin' what, deer?"

"Whatever I see—deer, squirrel, possum, coon, whatever you can eat. Times are tough, you know?"

Trey nodded his head. Then, he said, "What's all the diggin' about?"

Billy said quickly, "Groundhog. They's a family in there somewhere, and I'm gonna dig 'em out."

Trey nodded again, distractedly.

Billy then said, "Where you sellin' your wheat anyway? Not much of a market around here nowadays, what with all the rails and roads cut by Johnny Reb or Billy Yank, one or the other. You're more likely to have it stolen by 'em either way. "

6

Trey grinned and said, "My daddy's got it all worked out. We'll be awright."

"So, you got somethin'already set? Your daddy sold it already?" asked Billy. He then cocked his head and said, "To which? The Yankees or the boys in gray?' He sat back. "My guess it's the good old boys. They closest, which makes it easiest. Why, they might even give you a hand cuttin', balin', and haulin'."

Trey said nothing, his face suddenly hardening. Billy went on, "Maybe they gonna get some of them black boys up here in the hills to cut for you. I hear they used to that kind of work."

"You don't know nothin', Billy," Trey said, his voice thin. "Like you said, times is hard. We're gonna sell this wheat all right, and it ain't none of your business who buys it. It our business how we get it out, too. So, good luck with your skunk hunt."

Trey turned and started back up the slope. About fifty feet up, he suddenly stopped and whipped around. "I will tell you one thing, McKinney. Some of Zollcoffer's boys rode into Maryville yesterday. The bustle is he lookin' for volunteers for the East Tennessee Cavalry. If you got the gumption, you might make a good stable boy."

Billy frowned and yelled, "Get the heck outta here 'fore I hit you with a stick."

Trey spat on the ground, and headed back up the hill, eventually drifting out of sight down the other side.

Billy spit, too, though he never chewed. Snooty son of a bitch.

Five furrows later, he'd had enough. The sun rode low on the tree line anyway. It was time to get on home. Rather than drag the cas-chrom back, since most likely he would be digging again tomorrow, he scanned the area for a hiding place. After a moment's thought, he pulled the hand plow into the trees growing nearest the newly turned earth. He searched around until he found a tree with low branches, and wedged the plow tight between one of them and the trunk. The foot hung above the ground to keep its iron shanks from rusting. Satisfied, Billy left to start the long walk home.

Just before dark, he reached the split-rail fence Daddy had put around the property twenty-five years ago. The house itself had been built with white-painted clapboard two stories high to please Ma. Daddy'd thrown up the fence the next spring to keep the livestock inside. No livestock now, Billy thought grimly. Johnston's boys had seen to that quick enough. After that, Daddy tried to keep a few hogs penned up out in the woods. But, other critters got to them, catamounts or wild dogs, maybe. That's why they were trying the tater patch, hoping to have something for the winter or at least next spring.

Billy walked through the fence at the gate, only there wasn't a gate anymore. Of course, no Ma, either, or Little Sister. Gone ten years, now, from the croup as it turned out. Daddy met him at the door, lanky like his son and even skinnier, if possible. His hair was red like his son's, but thinning and duller from stray strands of gray in the mix. His hands thrust into the top of his overalls, he asked "How'd it go?"

"Ten furrows," Billy said. Seeing just the slightest disappointment in his father's eyes, he went on, "It's tough work, Daddy. That crooked plow is like diggin' with a rock."

Daddy squinted, then laughed, "That what your granddaddy used to say."

Billy sighed with relief. Daddy clapped him on the back and said, "Come on in and have some tasty groundhog."

Billy stopped and looked to see if his daddy was pulling his leg.

"I spotted him in the back, ran him down, and kicked the livin' daylights out of him. We eat high off the hog tonight!" his father said, chuckling as they went inside.

Daddy had spitted and grilled the groundhog seasoning it with almost the last of the salt and pepper they had left. "Lord, it might be the last we get for a while, so why not cook it right?"

Billy tucked into it, tugging on the stringy meat as he chewed it, relishing every bite.

"I ran into Trey Jessup up on the hillside," he said between swallows.

His father stiffened slightly. "Oh? What'd he want? Did he see what you was up to?"

Billy shook his head, "No, I don't think so. I didn't get that much dug out for him to pay attention. At least, I don't think he figured it out." He grinned, "I told him I spotted a groundhog and was trying to dig 'im out. Funny, huh?"

He gestured at the roast on the table.

"So, what'd he want?" Daddy asked.

"He was checkin' on their wheat up there, seein' if it's ready to cut. It is," Billy said, chewing off another piece of meat. His daddy nodded. Billy said, "I think they gonna sell it to the Rebs."

His father gave him a questioning look, and he went on, "He was pretty cagey about it when I asked, but I do believe he's gettin' help harvestin' it and movin' it down to Maryville."

Daddy frowned, but said nothing.

"What I'd like to know is," Billy continued, "if they sellin' it to the Grays, how're they gonna get paid? With what, I mean? They can't take Union money, that's no good in these parts no more. But, what else is there?"

Daddy yanked a piece of meat off and stuck it into his mouth. He chewed, then pushed it to the side of his cheek. "Maybe they gonna give them I.O.U.s for when they print their own money."

"That don't feed the cows," said Billy.

"Nobody got cows nowadays. It's possible they get somethin' in kind. Perhaps beans to hold them over the winter."

"I don't think there's any more 'in kind' to get, either," said Billy.

"Yeah, well, then I don't know what they get," his father said shortly. "You can be sure that they won't be wastin' any gold buyin' wheat which they can take whenever they please. Maybe the Jessups are just true believers in their cause."

Billy pursed his lips skeptically, but let it go. He chewed thoughtfully for a while. "Trey did say one thing."

His father glanced up at him again.

"He said that the Graybacks were in town tryin' to sign some of our boys up. Fat lot of good it'll do 'em."

"They'll get some," his father said.

"You think so, Daddy? Everyone around here don't want a thing to do with them Rebs. All the boys I know want to join up with the Union, like in West Virginia."

"And theymost likely get hung for it, too. You stay away from them Union boys or you'll end up gettin' shot or stretched. Stay away from the Graybacks, too. Just because they askin' to join don't mean they won't use other ways to persuade them that say 'No thank you.' You just spend your time diggin' our potato patch so we can get through the winter. Stay away from all that other mess."

Billy looked at his father earnestly, "Okay, Daddy, I'll keep pushin' the rock through the dirt."

They both laughed at that.

The next day, Billy ate a little cold groundhog for breakfast and a cup of weak tea, waved to Daddy, and started back up toward the mountain. As soon as he was out of sight, he doubled back through the woods to the dirt road to Maryville. He had to go down and see for himself who from their part of the world would join up with the Johnny Rebs against the Union. The cas-chrom could wait another day, and he knew that Daddy wouldn't go up in the hills to check on him. Anyway, if he did find out, he might raise his voice a little bit when he said how disappointed he was. But, that was about it. He'd be over it as soon as Billy returned to the meadow to dig the next day. Today, though, Billy had to see what was going on in Maryville.

The walk would take him three hours each wayand Daddy would expect him back by sunset. So, he would not have a lot of time in town. If he was lucky, though, maybe he could beg a ride from a passing wagon or buggy. Sure enough, a mule skinner on his way through Maryville to Knoxville picked him up.

When they reached the outskirts of town, the clutter of wagons, surreys, and other carriages surprised Billy. Maryville was home to just a few hundred people, most of whom worked the fields outside of town. Laid out in a simple grid, the town looked pretty much like any small town with a courthouse, a few dry goods and hardware stores, some dress shops for the ladies, taverns on both sides of the street, and two liveries at opposite ends. On side streets, folks could find the Western and Southern Seminary and the Maryville schoolhouse. Old Isaac Anderson had started up the seminary, its enrollment totaling only about twenty or so.At the schoolhouse, Professor Milquist taught the children in those months between harvest and seeding. Even most winter days, though, attendance tended to be spotty, chores popping up the way they did all year round. Maryville normally just wasn't a busy place except on July Fourth. This jam-up of people and wagons today really had Billy befuddled.

"Must be some kinda big goin'-ons in town center," the driver said, the first words out of his mouth in an hour and a half. A gaunt man, no more than a hundred and a quarter pounds with arms and face dark brown from the sun, he rubbed the stubble on his chin, then pulled at the brim of his hat. "Don't look like I'll be makin' headway any time soon." He craned his head backwards, then looked forward again. "Can't even back up. Two more wagons right behind us."

Billy glanced back, then jumped down to the ground, throwing a "Thanks plenty for the ride," over his shoulder as he made his way forward.

He took to the sidewalk to get past the heavy wagons, buggies, and buckboards in the street, and slithered through the strings of people slowly winding toward the center square. The nearer he came to the square, the thicker the crowd and the slower the pace of those still thronging to get closer. Sightlines to the courthouse grew narrower due to the carriages parked smack in the middle of the thoroughfare. Around them stood groups of people, many arching their necks to see as best they could over those in front.

Billy managed to find a spot close to the cross street where he could stretch up and straddle a sign in front of the big, two-story brick building that housed thetown newspaper,the *Maryville Religious and Literary Intelligencer.* No doubt, its reporters sat right upnext to the stairs of the courthouse, ready to record every word of what was happening there today. Every day the newspaper devoted its entire front page to the conflict between the states, going back five months to South Carolina's bombardment of Fort Sumter. Even before that, since the abolitionists and the Society of Friends had been locking horns with the secessionists for years. Plenty of fodder for the daily rag.

Not for him, of course, Billy thought, since he couldn't read. He got his news from the neighbors. That meant he had to listen, wait, then listen again until the many different stories gradually became one, though still not necessarily true. He shrugged. The news from around here usually came out right.

He heard voices from the direction of the courthouse, and still couldn't see all that well. He looked around at the trees up and down the street, all full on both sides of the street. Finally, he put his boots beneath him and stood up on top of the sign, balancing awkwardly. Waving his arms around, he eventually steadied himself until he stood still. He enjoyed a perfect view of the top of the courthouse stairs across the square.

Facing the crowd stood maybe a dozen, twice as many as the town's residents. Billy recognized some of them onlookers, Mr. Jones who owned the shipping warehouse and Mr. Thomas, the owner of the produce store. In the middle toward the front stood a half-dozen men in uniforms, gray tunics with yellow trim on their collars, and gray slacks sporting a single stripedown each leg. They wore broad-brimmed gray hats with gold cords around their crowns tied into knots at the front. Two of them had swords hanging from gold sashes at their waists. Shined to a bright glare, their black boots climbed all the way up their legs cupping out at the top to allow movement of the men's knees.

Billy saw some other soldiers on the fringe holding horses for the men at the top of the steps. The trousers on these men appeared worn and their shirts dull, some of them more tan than gray. Instead of the big hats, they wore little caps with small brims, and not one of them had a sword.

He turned his eyes back to the stage when one of the men stepped forward. Sharp blue eyes peered out of his nut-tan face with long, red-haired sideburns growing down a lean jaw to join his beard. He wore a long, gray coat without any braid except for a gold bar on each shoulder. A leather belt and strap crossed his torso to join another belt around his waist with a sabre scabbard suspended on one side, and a pistol holster on the other. He tipped two fingers to the brim of his broad hat as he called out.

"Folks, I am Captain Benjamin M. Branner, Commander of the Fourth Tennessee Cavalry Battalion. You might know us better as the Peck Light Dragoons. We come from Mossy Creek in Jefferson County where we got together back in June to fight the Blue Bellies. Things are heatin' up, now, and we need your help for Tennessee. I'm no talker or preacher, but we have with us someone who will explain things better. Here is Henry Turner Dixon, folks, from Mississippi, now Colonel with the East Tennessee Cavalry Regiment."

Billy watched the most resplendently dressed man in the group sweep forward and doff his hat in a broad arc beneath his knees as he bowed low. He straightened up and struck a studied pose, one glistening black boot forward, the other set back at an angle as though he looked out over a full array of knights in gray armor. He sported no beard, but his long moustache curved out on either side under his nose like matching sabers, moving up and down as he spoke.

"Citizens of Maryville. We have organized to defend Tennessee's sovereignty and absolute right to secede from the Union. Our sacred mission is to cast back the northern oppressors in turmoil and confusion. At present, we number 250 able men, with another 250 or so unavailable due to illness and other misfortune. We are here, today, to call you to arms for the Cause. We hope to add another 200 or more brave young men to our force so that we can join up with General Zollicoffer. The good general has just won a glorious victory over Yankee forces at Travisville. He hopes to move on the Union fortifications in Cumberland to thwart any invasion plans that they might be hatching. We need to support him in this endeavor, and we need you all to stand up to do so."

The spiff bellowed the last line, but only a spattering of cheers emerged from the crowd. Billy wished he could get closer, and he noticed some kids abandoning an elm tree near the courthouse. He slid off the sign and worked his way to the tree, climbing up on a large limb jutting out to the right. Usually a lush tree, a good half of the leaves had already fallen, affording Billy clear sight of the pageant on display. Over to the right of the courthouse, he could see a small table manned by a contingent of grays. A fellow wearing spectacles sat at it, pen and paper at the ready. Then, to Billy's utter surprise, he spied Trey Jessup standing next to the table, decked out in a spanking, brand-new Johnny Reb uniform, gold epaulettes on his shoulders, shiny brass buttons down the front of his waist-length shell jacket, gold stripes bordering his trousers, his riding boots shined to a fare-thee-well. He preened, grasping his pistol holster and the hilt of his short sword several times as though harking to a series of summons. He pivoted repeatedly, thereby showing off his military grandeur at all angles. Every now and then, he'd call to one of the young girls on the periphery. If any of them looked in his direction, he would say, "Please support the Cause." Most of them ignored him simply because they knew him from school where he wore britches and flannels just like every other boy. A few schoolgirls giggled, however, blushing at the attention given by such a fine, brave cavalryman.

"Colonel Dixon," a stentorious voice called out from the crowd, "the people of East Tennessee have no interest in furthering the despicable institution of slavery in this nation."

The voice belonged to Dr. Robinson, the president of Maryville College who had suspended the seminary's classes after the bombardment of Fort Sumter. A tall, dark man, Presbyterian in the Scottish tradition, he commanded uniform respect from all of Maryville's citizens.

"We certainly do not wish to see our young men engage in war on the side of such evil. I advise you, Colonel, to withdraw now from our little town. Rather than trumpet through the countryside for young, impressionable lads to join your wicked cause, you might benefit from taking the time to examine your own commitment to this heinous path."

A murmur of approval coursed through the crowd, and Dixon slapped the side of his leg hard with his gloves. "The nation you speak of, sir, is not ours. Ours is Tennessee alone, joined with her southern sisters in a fight for freedom and our way of life. I refuse to leave, sir, and I demand the support of all in the service of this great state. Those who wish to serve, line up at the enlistment post. As for you, sirrah, and your other abolitionist cronies, let it be known that we shall have our 200 new recruits, one way or the other."

As he spun away, another scatter of cheers went up. Dixon headed directly down the steps to the enlistment table below, trailed by Captain Brenner and the rest of the officers. Billy found the entire event unsettling. He realized, too, that he had to leave for home right away if his daddy wasn't to find him out.

Billy dropped to the ground from the elm tree and glanced up to see Trey Jessup close in on Colonel Dixon, talking furtively. He raised his hand to point directly at Billy, who suddenly felt a cold spasm flash up his spine and through his legs. What could Trey Jessup be telling that fire and brimstone Grayback officer?

Billy quickly slipped aroundthe tree and loped down the street toward home.

Chapter 2. Rabbiting

Billy dug away as fast as he could with the foot plow, trying to make up for time lost on his gallivant into Maryville yesterday. When he arrived at his front door last night, Daddy had greeted him like a returning warrior.

"Sit, boy, right here while I get you a bite." He bent his lean frame over the stew pot suspended above a small cooking fire in the hearth. "Workin' into the dark like that, you must be all worn out. Here," he said, scooping up a bowlful from the pot, "have yourself some stew. You certainly earned it today."

Feeling utterly guilty, Billy sniffed at the bowl, and said, "What is it?"

"Groundhog, of course. We got to eat it before it goes off. I held back some salt last night so we could use before the meat went off. Salt it up, it's tasty."

Billy sprinkled some salt around and took a spoonful into his mouth. Mumbling around it, he said, "It's good, Daddy. Thank you."

"Eat away, there's a bit more. You need to keep your strength up, Billy Boy. You're doin' a good job. How much longer you think it'll take to finish diggin'?"

Billy gulped a big bite, almost painful as it went down. "Tomorrow, maybe. Not too much left."

"Well, that's good, Bill, very good. I'll get the tater chits ready for plantin'. You can pop them in as you go, and tomorrow we'll carry some water up there to get 'em growin'."

Billy started. "Uh, why don't we see how it goes tomorrow, Daddy? I might come up against some rocks that'll slow me down."

Daddy grinned, "Sure, but you can plant what's ready. Heck, I'll come up and help you put 'em in to get it all done."

"No, Daddy, we don't want to attract too much attention, do we? Let me work the rest of the furrows, first. I'll plant the chits tomorrow and bring water up the day after. No reason I can't do it all and, you know, keep it low."

Daddy scratched the stubble on his chin with his hand, big and stringy muscled from years of farm work. "I guess you're right. You do that, and I'll set some snares in the woods down here, see what we can catch."

Billy breathed easier, and dug into the rest of his stew.

He was hungry now, from no breakfast. The work seemed harder for it, but he had to get it done. He didn't want his daddy to suspect anything, although he wouldn't do much but look hurt in his eyes. He was a sweet old man, old before his time.

He jammed the plow head into the soil and pushed it forward with his boot. After a while, he figured he was getting better at it as he moved along. He started to think that he might finish the furrows today after all. Then, he'd hit another tough spot, or a rock, or some root of some kind, and wonder why Daddy had him doing this at all. Fall leaves had drifted down already, covering the ground in a thin carpet of rich earth colors. Most people plant their potatoes in the spring. Even if he dug all the furrows and planted the chits tomorrow, they were looking at four months passing before they could eat one spud. That is, if any number of freezes during the winter didn't kill them off first. And, what were they supposed to eat for four months while they waited? He shook his head and kept digging. If Daddy wanted him to do this, he would do it, he thought, still filling guilty about his holiday yesterday. He picked up his pace, determined to get the furrows finished that day.

Billy stopped. He heard a noise at the crest of the notch between the hills—voices. Grabbing up the foot plow, he put it on his shoulder and loped as quietly as he could into the woods. Dry fallen leaves lay everywhere, forcing him to slowly lift and lower his feet to keep from making too much noise as he walked deeper among the trees. He gently laid the plow on the floor behind one, and then tiptoed back to the trunk of an elm at the edge of the woods. He peered around the rough bark little by little.

A horse and rider worked deliberately down the slope of the notch, skidding a bit on a patch of loose stones. The rider pulled on the reins to slow the horse's descent. Trey Jessup sat astride the horse, wearing his new gray uniform with the gold braid. On his left side he wore his long, curved sword scabbard, and when he pivoted around, Billy could see a holster for a large pistol. A black leather flap pulled over and buttoned down kept the heavy gun from falling out, probably a good thing when Trey reared his horse up in some kind of showy way.

Trey called up to the top of the two hills, "I can see that someone's been diggin' down here, but I don't see him." He wheeled his horse around, back and forth while waiting for an answer.

"What kind of digging is it, Corporal? Perhaps a weapons cache?"

"I don't think so, sir, too shallow," Trey answered. "Theboy I wastalkin' about said he was huntin' groundhogs." Trey gazed back up the notch, waiting for orders.

Billy shifted deliberately around to the other side of the trunk to see better up the hill. Four more horsemen sat at the top, one of them the fancy dressed dandy in the big brimmed hat who had made the fiery speech in Maryville yesterday. From Mississippi, Billy remembered.

The decked-out officer yelled down, "All right, Corporal. Come on back up here. We'll run him down sooner or later."

"Yessir, Colonel, be right up."

Trey spurred his horse, which seemed reluctant to go up the hill, instead angling to the side. He spurred it again, this time harder, slapping his reins at the same time. The horse neighed in protest, but reluctantly began climbing the hill, Trey jabbing it all the way up.

They're after me, Billy realized. But, why? That blasted Jessup must have told tales, he thought sourly. That slimy snake!

Billy bolted into action, hanging the cas-crom back on a treelimb, then running through the woods straight down toward home. If the Graybacks were headed this way, he'd beat them to the house by a long shot running through the woods. The sun had dropped to the housetop when he burst in on Daddy stirring something in a pot over the fire.

"Daddy, I got troubles!" Billy blurted out.

Startled, his father turned around from the hearth and said, "What? Why? What's the matter?"

Billy pulled up short. He hesitated, then sighed. He had no choice, so he told his daddy all about slipping down to Maryville yesterday, and the rest.

Daddy listened, his features running througha series of contortions as Billy related each of the events that had happened. Billy watched him, feeling scared when he saw the color rising up his neck, then sorry when his daddy just looked sad, remembering how he had warned him. Finally, when Billy finished his story, his daddygazed at him in wonder, as if looking at a stranger. Billy saw deep pain in his eyes, too, as though he'd taken a knife and stuck it in his ribs.

"I'm disappointed in you, Billy. You didn't listen to me. I'm hurt by you, and now you could get hurt, too. Why didn't you stay here like I said?"

Billy had no answer.

After that, his daddy seemed to drift off. They ate their dinner in silence, Daddy just sitting there, not eating much. Every now and then he'd rub the graying bristle on his hollow cheeks, deep in thought. Billy cleared the table, stored the leftovers, and washed the plates and utensils. At length, he couldn't put it off any longer, so he sat down at the table again.

His daddy looked up at him as though seeing him for the first time. He pulled out his tobacco pouch, loaded up his pipe, and lit it. He puffed, his eyes fixed on Billy the whole time. Finally, he spoke.

"So, them Rebel boys are lookin' for you."

"Yes, Daddy," replied Billy, the flood gates open, "but why? I didn't do nothin', I didn't do a thing. Why do they want me, now?"

Daddy continued rubbing his beard. "I think it's pretty clear, Billy, they want you for their army."

"Me? Why me? I don't want to be a soldier. Daddy, I was just sittin' in a tree!"

"That may be, boy, but it don't matter to them. You say they want a couple hundred men? They be hard pressed to get them around here unless they force them into joinin'. I believe that's what they gonna do, and they want to do it startin' with you."

He looked up at Billy starkly. "You got to get out of here, Billy. You got to run."

"Run? Where? I don't know anyplace else but here. Where would I go?"

"It don't matter, but you can't stay. They probably on their way down the road right now. They be lookin' for you here soon enough."

Billy swallowed, thinking back to what the fancy Colonel had said up on the hill. Tears started coursing down his cheeks. "I don't wanna leave home, Daddy? Can't I just hide in the woods?"

Daddy shook his head, "No, Billy, they gonna search the woods, Trey will help them. No, you need to get far away from here for a while."

He left the hearth for the back room. Billy could hear him rattling around the can he hid under the floor boards beneath the bed. He returned and handed Billy a few bills and some coins.

"That's three dollars and two bits. Gather up anything you want from here, and head on down to Knoxville. Stay off the roads and travel at night. Try to stay out of sight as much as you can. Here, wear my hat." He pulled his old felt, broad-brimmed hat off the post near the door and stuck it on Billy's head.

"Daddy, I can wear my straw hat."

"Nah, I'll wear it. I'm a handsome feller in straw."

He pulled Billy's hat off a peg next to the door and thrust it on his head, grinning. Then, he reached out for the brim of his felt hat on Billy's head.

"Keep it pulled low over your face. ThemRebel press gangs're probably everywhere pickin' up all kinds of boys your age. Once you get to Knoxville, buy a ticket on the north branch toward Rogersville. That the end of the line up in the mountains. Then, head for Kentucky. The Yankees there will be keepin' them Rebs too busy to chase you down."

Knoxville? Kentucky? Billy thought. He'd never been farther from home than Maryville, and a couple of hunting trips in the mountains.

"Of course, the Union boys might want to grab you up, too, so don't hang around too long. Find a homestead in the hills, see if you can catch on to some work. Get as far north as you can, to Canada. That's the only place you be safe, there or out West. Here—" He rose up and went over to the fireplace.

Canada? Billy felt gut-wrenching fear in his heart. He might never see home again.

Daddy grabbed the squirrel rifle standing in the corner and came back to Billy. "Take this with you. Maybe you can shoot some critters up there."

"Daddy, I can't take your gun," Billy said as his father left the table to pick up the powder horn and shot bag. He brought them back and laid them down on the table in front of his son. "I can't take any of this, you need it for the winter."

"No, no," his father said, shaking his head, "I'll get by, don't you worry about that. There's plenty of game around for me to snare. I'll be fine. It's you Billy that's got to make it out of here. You're all I got left, I don't want to see you goin' off and gettin' killed in some stupid war that's none of our doin'. You take the rifle and make your way out of this mess. That's all I want."

Billy saw the emotion in his father's eyes, the past losses he'd endured and his fear of losing the last remaining loved one in his life. Billy pulled in a deep breath, and said, "Awright, Daddy. I'll go, but after the war is over, I'm comin' back. So, you better take care of yourself, because I'm gonna be back here really mad if you don't"

His father nodded, "Awright, son. It's near dark, so gather up everything, and be on your way."

The two men stood up and embraced quickly. Billy picked up his knapsack, loaded it with the powder horn and the shot bag, and turned to leave. His father stopped him with one arm while putting bread and some groundhog jerky in his bag. Billy quickly went out the door.

In the dark, he slowly picked his way down the side of the road in the shadow of the tree line. The light of thefull moon splashed into the woods enough for him to see his way to avoid rocks, logs, and other obstacles that might trip him. But, misery filled him, and worry that his daddy wouldn't make it alone through the coming winter. Daddy was good at hunting and snaring, but here Billy had his gun, while other hill folks would be out trapping anything they could find, too. Without his rifle, Daddy wouldn't be able to shoot a squirrel, never mind a deer. Daddy could starve this winter while Billy traipsed around trying to find his way to Canada.

He stopped and sat on a log. This plan was not good, he wanted to go home, even though Daddy was right about the Johnny Rebs. Billy knew himself that if he went back home, he wouldn't be staying one way or another. Maybe he'd be better off just joining the Tennessee cavalry. He might even get a horse.

Billy clenched his jaws and pushed his chin out. He'd made up his mind. He jumped to his feet and began tracing his way back home.

The new moon illuminated everything in an unworldly fashion, putting Billy on edge as the tree line on the roadside gave way to scrub bushes and tall grasses. In this light, he'd be easy prey for Trey and that Mississippi Colonel if they rode at night to hunt recruits. Billy swallowed and daintily stepped down to the fence leading to the house. Quietly, he opened the gate, slipped through, and closed it gently behind him.

He scrutinized the house. All the lights had been snuffed out, which probably meant that Daddy had been fast asleep for a few hours. Billy closed in on the front of the house and propped the rifle against the wall. He opened the front door silently, and holding it open with one hand, grabbed the barrel of the rifle and tiptoed inside. He carefully pulled the door in, leaving it slightly ajar to avoid making any noise.

Moonlight through the windows outlined the shapes of the table and chairs in front of the fireplace. Billy skirted around them, and softly laid his knapsack on the table. He propped the rifle in the corner next to the hearth and turned back to the knapsack. He opened it and deftly removed the powder horn and the shot bag, which he quietly hung on their pegs. Billy closed the knapsack and slung it over his shoulder as he moved to leave.

He stopped. After a moment's pause, he turned back to the hearth. He stared at the mourning picture of Ma, Sister, Daddy, and his younger self on the mantelpiece. An instant later, he plucked it off the mantel and slid it into his knapsack while making for the door. He slipped out and hurried up the road to disappear in the tree line.

Chapter 3. The North Branch

Billy made it to Knoxville in a day and a night. He walked into the town early in the morning amid the full bustle of wagons, carriages, and carts going back and forth with their goods. People walked to their jobs, and other folks in sharp duds headed to whatever rich place they worked in, maybe a bunch of banks. Women in fancy dresses strolled up the street with their parasols open, even though it wasn't raining and the sun had barely cracked the sky. Children trailed behind, young ones with sticks over their shoulders, their lunches hanging off the back wrapped in kerchiefs. Billy believed he'd never seen so many people, horses, mules, carriages, and wagons before, and not a cow in sight. Knoxville was the biggest city he'd ever seen in his life, maybe the biggest in all of Tennessee or the world.

He kept walking at a brisk pace toward what looked like the town center, though he really didn't know where he was going. After a few blocks, he turned into a general store and bought some beef jerky and two slices of bread for a nickel. The storeowner gave him some honey butter for free and let him fill his water skin from a barrel in the store. While Billy put his sandwich together, he asked the owner for directions to the train depot.

"Go out, left, and walk five blocks down the main street. You'll find it, can't miss it. There's a big sign, too."

Billy thanked him and left. Outside, he followed the storeowner's directions strictly, hoping that the activity around the depot would tip him off, since he couldn't read. He ambled down the street, using the wooden walkways when available, otherwise tramping in the dirt road trying to avoid the horse manure. After a few minutes, he saw an imposing brick structure, tall and stately, with a curved brick building behind it. The front displayed a wraparound porch, and uniformed blacks pushing big-wheeled carts told him that this was the station. Sure enough, as he drew closer, he saw tracks to the right of the depot. Behind it on the left, gigantic steam locomotives with huge, wide funnels on top stood in the roundhouse, ready to roll.

He also saw Rebels, three of them, lounging on the corner of the depot porch smoking pipes. Another bunch sat further down, jawing away at each other, probably telling one lie after another. Billy saw more soldiers, and by the number of them, figured that they were

22

waiting for a train. He frowned, shaking his head, and pulled Daddy's hat down lower over his eyes. Heading opposite from them, he walked down to the other side of the depot searching for another door. To his relief, he found another way in, a set of double doors with glass paned windows on top. He entered a vast, open room with rows and rows of wooden benches that looked like church pews. At the opposite end, he saw a bank of six windows apparently for buying tickets. In fact, there seemed to be several sets of doors at intervals up and down the station, beckoning travelers to the tracks from every direction. Between the doorways, vendors had set up their stands to sell whatever riders might need on their trip—food, drink, reading matter, trinkets for gifts back home, toiletries, comforters in case the weather turned cold, and other sundries. Billy would have loved to go exploring all of these new things, but he knew he didn't have time to dawdle. He hurried toward the nearest ticket window as he reached inside his pocket for the bills Daddy had given him.

"Where to, young feller?" the agent asked. He looked to be in his thirties, sporting a heavy, long dark beard without much hair on top of his head.

"The North Branch," Billy said, his voice a bit shrill despite his efforts to sound ordinary.

The agent's brow knit signing momentary puzzlement. "Rogersville?" he said.

Billy swallowed. "Yessir."

The agent nodded his head and said, "Round trip?"

Billy hesitated for an instant, and replied, "No, one way."

The agent said, "Oh. Okay, that's one-fifty."

Billy handed him two dollar bills, and the agent gave him two quarters as change.

"Nice to see a payin' customer for once," he said. He jerked his thumb toward the right, "Them Confederate boys commandeered a train ride. Said they'd pay after the war's over. I'm not holdin' my breath."

Billy nodded as he picked up the coins and the ticket. "When does it leave?"

"It boards in half an hour. They're hookin' up the engine now. The conductor will call you."

"How long will it take?"

"Three and a half hours, give or take. Change trains at Bull Gap."

Billy shook his head in thanks and turned to go.

"Have a good trip, young feller."

He nodded again, turning away. Slowly, he gazed around the station. With Rebs throwing their weight about, he wanted no part of them. He searched for the most remote place he could find in the big waiting room, now sun-splashed from the tall windows spaced all around the building. He saw a bench over in the back next to the farthest set of doors, the last ones. He ambled over and sat down in a corner seat to wait.

A conductor stepped into the waiting room after what seemed an eternity to Billy.

"Now boarding the 8:15 Chickasaw North Branch to Bristol, with stops at Strawberry Plains, Friend's Station, Morristown, Russellville, and Bull's Gap—change at Bull's Gap for the Cherokee Northeasterner to Rogersville, last stop at Bristol. The Chickasaw North Branch to Bristol now boardin'. All aboard! All aboard."

Billy stiffened, resisting the urge to jump up and run to the train. He waited until he saw a number of different people rise and gathertheir luggage. As they headed for the doors, he stood and sidled up to the back of a cluster of people going out the last exit. The conductor stood at the front of the train at the steps to the car just before the tender and engine. Quite a few soldiers started climbing into the first two cars. Billy spun and walked to the last car before the caboose. He stepped up and made his way to a seat in the back, where he sat slouched low as though he already had fallen asleep.

The engine bell rang loudly, and the steam whistle bellowed hollowly once. With the bell still ringing, the engine began its chuffing, staggered lurch away from the station. As the train gained speed, its rhythm and motion smoothed out and the regular clicks over the rails assumed a regular, soothing sound. After a day and a night of walking and worrying, Billy slowly slipped into sleep.

He dreamed. He walked again at the woods edge beneath a dark sea of a sky dotted by occasional blinking of a spatter of stars. He plodded along, tired, so tired, but he couldn't stop. Daddy moved next to him, "Go ahead, boy, keep your pace, keep on goin'." Then Ma appeared, tousling his head, "Be a good boy now, Billy." He heard voices behind him, far away, then closer. He tried to go faster, he tried to run, but he was tired and his legs felt numb, he couldn't make them go faster. The voices drew closer, calling out to each other. Panicky, he pumped his arms, stumbling with effort. The voices grew louder in his ear, until someone grabbed him, shaking him by the shoulder, "Wake up! Wake up!"

"Wake up, there, mountain boy, wake on up."

He felt his shoulder being shaken, for real, not in a dream. Billy squirmed, trying to brush the hand away.

"C'mon, now, Billy Boy, you can't fool me. Open your eyes."

Billy slowly opened his eyes and raised them. Still holding his shoulder, Trey Jessup grinned down at him. "Well, well, well, looky here, boys, a volunteer ready to join up."

Billy blanched and tried to stand up, but Trey immediately shoved him down. Four other Grays surrounded him.

"Leroy," Trey said without looking away from Billy, "go get the Colonel."

A gangly young fellow no older than Billy turned and quick stepped up the aisle toward the front of the train.

"You sit tight, Billy old boy, until the Colonel tells us what to do with you."

The fancy dressed officer from the rally in Maryville two days before sauntered down the aisle. He paused now and then to glance out the windows on either side of the car, taking in the scenery without a care in the world. Billy felt himself shaking uncontrollably.

At last, the Colonel arrived. The soldiers parted to allow him to step up to Billy. "Well, there, young man, you took us on a merry chase the other night. I am glad to see that you've reconsidered and have chosen the righteous thing to do, defend the autonomy of your sacred state. Corporal Jessup here will add your name to the roles." He stared at Trey, "The auxiliary foot, I think. No need to entrust a horse to a boy of such quixotic nature."

He leaned down close, the smell of his flowery toilet water now pungent in Billy's nostrils. "I'm keepin' an eye on you, boy," he whispered. "If you run again, I shall personally discharge your execution. That is the penalty for desertion."

The Colonel straightened up, rubbed his mustache with his thumb and forefinger. After nodding to Trey, he walked away.

The conductor brushed by the colonel as he strolled down the aisle, calling out, "Bull's Gap next stop in two minutes. Gather up your belongin's. Bull's Gap in two minutes, change trains for Rogersville."

The minutes passed like molasses running uphill to Billy, sitting crestfallen among the gray draped soldiers. He wanted to leap up and fly out the door or the window, anyway to get away. But, if he even twitched, all these eager Johnny Rebs would be all over him, not one of whom he recognized. Except for Trey, he was the only one from

Maryville. The recruitment drive there by the Colonel and Captain Branner had been a bust.

The train lurched. The hammering engine caused Billy's stomach to flip as he grasped that he'd missed his chance. The soldiers around him slouched or slept, bored with waiting for something to do. Billy could not sleep a wink, wondering where he was going and what he'd be doing now. He wished again and again that he had listened to Daddy.

"Men, I have bad news."

Captain Branner stood at one end of the car while the men gathered as close as the narrow space allowed. Some of them sat on top of the seatbacks to get a better view over the crowd jammed into the aisle.

The Captain paused, and said, "A cadre of Union sympathizers have destroyed the bridges to Bristol and Rogersville."

A series of breaths could be heard sucked in by the packed soldiers.

"These traitors have been rounded up and hung. Unfortunately, though, we can't ride the train to Union where General Zollicofer has set up camp. We'll have to walk, boys."

Unlike the Colonel from Mississippi, Branner wore only a worn, grey campaign coat with threadbare epaulets showing his rank. Beneath, he wore canvas trousers held up by braces, and a pair of black leather boots. Spurs hung from his belt next to a .44 caliber revolver in a cracked leather holster, with a Bowie knife secured to his belt on the opposite side instead of a sword. Shorn of any whiskers, his features were as long and straight-lined as his speech, a man whose simple manner drew other men to him like bees to honey. Despite his own state of alarm, Billy felt the man's plain power of attraction. In some way he reminded him of his daddy.

"We'll go as far as we can, then disembark from the train. We'll head up the line as necessary until either another train picks us up, or we reach Union on foot. So, pull your gear together, I don't know exactly where we get off. When the whistle blows, we'll all know."

Branner nodded, offered a semblance of a salute, and headed for the next car.

All the young fellows buzzed about the news. Some cursed those blue belly devils for their treachery, while others wondered if they'd be ambushed by some Union army waiting on them in the woods along the way. Billy felt even more miserable at this new development. He quaked inside at the prospect of either side shooting at each other with him in the middle. He had no dog in this fight, yet here he was.

Trey came back from a long sojourn with the Colonel, he happily reported, with direction to organize the men for debarcation and parade formation. The newly minted corporal beamed with pleasure in his station and ordered the other young men around as if born to it.

"Hicks, I want to see some regularity. Straighten out your pack and bedroll. You need to step to, boy."

Gangly awkward with his beard a scrub that barely covered his bad skin, Hicks glowered and said," You can step to yourself, Jessup, but not in my shit if you know what's good."

"That's insubordination, soldier, a court-martialin' offense."

Hicks stepped in close to Jessup, looming a foot over his head. "You want to get clobbered?"

Jessup paled and quickly turned to another young recruit. "What about you, Hoat, your pack in order?"

"Fuck off, Jessup," Hoat said without looking. The others all laughed.

Trey searched around and set his eyes on Billy. "McKinney. Follow me."

He turned and headed toward the back of the car. Billy sighed, rolled his eyes, and followed.

"Those men are in trouble," Trey said, without looking back. "I'm gonna report them all to the Colonel, each and every one of 'em."

"Even the ones that just laughed?" asked Billy.

"They the worst. Underminin' my authority."

"You think the Colonel wants to hear about it? You don't think he's too busy?"

"Gross insubordination!"

"Yeah, but ... maybe that's why they have corporals and sergeants and such, to take care of things like this."

Trey didn't answer, but Billy saw the back of his neck turning red. He smiled to himself, the first time in three days.

After crossing through several cars, Trey brought them into one filled with horses. "The officers's mounts," he said. "They're three more cars after this. Muck 'em all out."

Billy's furtive smile disappeared. "All of them?"

"That's right, son, clean 'em out. Keep you busy 'til we get off the train."

Billy frowned. He didn't like being called son by a boy from home just about the same age as he was. This fancy uniform with its extra stripes were going to his head.

"Go on, now, get to it."

Billy grabbed a pitch fork hanging from a hook on the side of the car. He looked at the fifteen stalls, each occupied by a horse, and pulled up. "How am I supposed to clean out the stalls if the horses are in them?"

Trey said, "This is what you do. Put a bridle on the horse, back it out, and hitch it to this ring over here." He leaned over to show an iron ring bolted into the wall. "You fork out the stall, get some clean straw at the end of the car, lay it in, then put the horse back. Do the same for all the horses here and move to the next car."

Billy figured that Trey's know-how came from personal experience before he'd earned his extra stripe. He wondered how many times Trey had been kicked by an unwilling horse. For that matter, Billy thought, a horse could crush him against the stall boards when he tried to move it out. What a sad way to go out, crumpled and crushed, his body found later by skinny, spot-faced Corporal Trey Jessup checking up on him.

"What do I do with the horse shit I dig out of the stall?"

"Just slide open the side door over there and toss it out."

Another way to get killed, thought Billy.

"All right, now, you asked enough questions. Get on it. I'll be back soon to make sure you're doin' it right."

Halfway through the first car, Billy wondered why he was doing this since they would be getting off the train soon anyhow. Must be the way armies work, he figured. As it was, his back ached from carrying shovelfuls of manure to the open doorway. He could have used a barrow, though maybe it wouldn't fit down the aisleway. His body was sore from banging against the wall when the train lurched, and from being pinned against the boards by a few cantankerous horses. Much more of this and he wouldn't be much for marching when they stopped.

He finished the stalls in the first car and was about to head through to the next one when the train shuddered, followed by a loud gasp of steam, then stopped. Billy leaned on the pitchfork, thinking about what to do. Maybe if he just stayed here they'd forget about him and he could steal away home. A horse neighed and he knew he was a fool. They had to unload the horses, of course, and of course they wouldn't forget him.

Sure enough, Trey entered the car trailed by Hicks, Hoat, and the other young soldiers in his troop.

"We've come to a wrecked bridge. Captain Branner has ordered us to get the horses ready for transit."

"That mean get 'em off the train, right?" said Hicks.

Trey's mouth tightened. "Just do it, okay?"

The men separated to attend to the horses in what seemed to be a well-worn routine. Trey turned to Billy and said, "I guess you're just in the way, boy. Stand over there 'til I say so."

Billy walked over to a corner of the car, hanging the pitchfork on its peg along the way.

"Parade rest, soldier," snapped Trey.

Uneasy, Billy said, "I don't know what that is."

Trey marched over, an exasperated look on his face. He kicked Billy's shoes apart, saying, "Spread your legs and put your hands behind you. Fold them together."

Billy did as he was told, and Trey went back to the others, who had saddled the horses and lined them up single file in the aisle that ran along the stalls. Each of them held the bridle of a horse close to them, standing attentively, if not at attention.

"Okay, the ramp should be set up any minute, now. So, we wait."

As they stood in the rail car, they could hear the noise of men stepping off the train, officers yelling out to them to form up. They heard a lot of banging in adjacent cars, too, and whinnying, which raised their expectations. But, nothing happened.

Hoat called up to Trey. "Jessup, my horse just dumped a load."

"Ignore it," said Trey, staring at the closed door of the car.

"But, it's a stinkin', steamin' mess."

"We'll be out of here soon enough. Just hold tight."

"Soon they all be shittin', Jessup," said Hicks. "Why don't'ya get the new recruit there to clean 'em out whilst we wait? He open the door and we all get a look at what's goin' on outside, there."

"Stand steady, private!" barked Trey.

"Yeah, up yours, too, Jessup."

The side door of the car rumbled open. A sergeant with long blond hair and a beard to match stuck his head in at floor level and said, "Secure your mounts, corporal. We're pushin' the ramp up now."

Without an order from Trey, the men stiffened and held their bridles with both hands. A heavy wooden ramp bumped up hard against the wooden flooring and one of the horses half-reared. Trey scowled at the man holding its bridle, who did his best to calm the horse down.

"Okay, boys, walk your hosses," said the sergeant.

In short order, they moved the horses off the train. A few stalled nervously at the top of the ramp, but slight nudges and slaps on their hindquarters encouraged them to descend. The locomotive produced a constant hiss of steam, the only sound heard near the track bed. Trees brown with fall leaves leaned overhead to create a canopy that blocked out most of the light around the rails. The underbrush left little room for anything but the tracks. Growth ran up the hillside on the left and down a slope on the right.

Trey joined an array of officers as they mounted the horses along with a good number of regulars. Once they all sat their horses, they formed a single line, with Trey at the end. From the vantage point of the rail car, Billy could see Captain Branner and the Mississippi Colonel at the head of a string of maybe fifty riders. Captain Branner stood in his stirrups and twisted around. Raising his arm, he motioned the horsemen forward. Billy looked toward the rear of the car and saw the long tail of the column, maybe a hundred riders or more altogether.

Next to the car, Trey pulled up his horse and twisted around in his saddle to shout, "McKinney, get the hell down from there. You can join Sergeant Burrow there with the support troops. You, too, Hoat, Hicks."

He turned back to the horse column, which started to move slowly ahead.

"Well," murmured Hicks, "Fuck you, too, Jessup."

Billy walked down the ramp and hopped off next to Hicks and Hoat. Once off the train, they all shivered from a passing, chilling breeze that whisked around them. Sergeant Burrow approached and said, "All right, boys, the rest of us are on the other side. Follow me."

A burly man of roughly thirty who looked like he enjoyed his mountain dew, the sergeant led them to the nearest end of the car. They clambered over the coupling, emerging to find a throng of soldiers crammed together next to the train, waiting. The number of them amazed Billy; he'd never seen so many men in one place before.

Some of them wore cadet gray uniforms and matching caps that sloped forward with little leather brims. Most of them dressed in ordinary butternut shirts and pants like Billy's. They wore an array of hats, straw, felt, and canvas, even a few made of home-tanned leather. All of them seemed to have bedrolls hanging from their shoulders or tied diagonally across their backs and chests. They all carried guns, too, some long-barreled hunting rifles, others old shotguns or muskets. The ones in gray uniforms looked to be armed with the same kind of weapon, standard army, maybe, thought Billy, shorter in length without the grace of a long rifle.

The soldiers milled about as officers tried to organize them into units. "Y'all can come join my squad," Sergeant Burrow said, "over here."

He led them to a group of about twenty, a mish-mash of different sorts. Some were dressed like neighbors of Billy's. They didn't have guns either. Others appeared to be from town, wearing factory-made shirts and breeches held up by suspenders. They were fully armed, too, with rifles and long knives. One of these townies smiled at Billy and the others as they approached.

"Hello, fellows, just arriving?" Despite the dark, scraggily beard covering his face, his eyes lit up with warmth as he greeted them. He looked older, too, closer to Sergeant Burrow's age. "Look to be a lively bunch there, don't they, Sergeant?"

Burrow smiled wryly, "They take up some space."

"Oh, I see bigger things in their future, Sergeant, I prophesize great successes for these sons of the South."

"Do tell," Burrow said. "Well, why don't you situate 'em, Murray, whilst I find out our marchin' orders."

The sergeant left, and the townie leaned toward them with his hand out. "Stewart Murray, gentlemen, from Memphis. Glad to know you," he said, shaking hands vigorously with each of them. Hicks and Hoat mumbled their names and stepped away. Billy stated his name and put out his hand, which Murray pulled up and down like a water pump handle.

"McKinney, you say? Another Scot among us?"
Billy grunted, "Scotch-Irish."

"Close enough. Welcome to the East Tennessee Cavalry Auxiliaries, Billy m'boy," pumping his hand again. Murray turned back to the others and surveyed them. "Looks like you boys are all set," he said to Hoat and Hicks, who had retrieved their bedrolls and other belongings from the railroad car where they had been sitting before they got off.

"You, though, Billy seem to be fresh up," Murray said. "Where you'd come from?"

"Knoxville—Marysville."

"Sure, just on board. Okay, you need a bedroll, canteen, and rations, I'd say. Well, when the sergeant gets back, I'll see if I can find the quartermaster wagon and fix you up."

He gazed down until he came to Billy's shoes, made of old worn-out leather cracking at the seams, the soles coming off after several re-sewings.

"That's all you have for footwear, son? I believe I see your big toes sticking out."

Billy laughed, embarrassed. "Haven't had a chance to get new boots, what with the war and all."

"Right. Well, I'll see if the quartermaster can rustle up a pair of brogans for you, nice pegged ones. What you're wearing now won't last a mile on a long march."

Murray disappeared, and the troops waited. The two hundred or so soldiers staged on the right of the train had little room to maneuver, barely enough between them to sit down. No matter, the officers started barking at them like dogs, getting the men to line up and ready to march. One horseman picked his way along the bed, his broad hat shadowing his features from afar. As he came closer, Billy gradually made out who it was, Colonel Dixon.

"Glad to see you soldiers poised to move. Remember," he said, slowly winding his head around to survey each man, "I have my eyes on you at all times. Do your duty, for the glory," he finished, trailing off as he rode on by. Billy pressed his lips together, clenching his teeth.

"Awright, let's go," said Sergeant Burrow as the men in line ahead of them slowly started to move. The men in Burrow's squad began to walk, passing the cars on their left until they came abreast of the engine. Suddenly, its whistle screamed shrilly, and a spout of smoke blossomed from the top of its stack. Its familiar huffing commenced, and the massive machine started to inch back from the makeshift railhead that had kept it from plunging into the ravine in front. Burrow's men reached the edge of the ravine just as the engine pulled back enough to reveal the wooden pilings that had supported the destroyed bridge. Hanging from broken beams jutting out at the top were the bodies of three men.

As Burrow's squad worked their way down the brushy hillside, Billy' eyes were fixed upon the corpses suspended above. They looked to be young like himself, though it was hard to tell, since it seemed crows had been picking at them for days. Billy saw an empty eye socket on one above a row of straight, shiny molars where a cheek had been. The absolute stillness of their bodies sent cold waves through Billy.

"Here you are, Billy," Murray said from behind. Billy looked back as Murray said, "A bedroll and a canteen was all I could get. No shoes to be had, sorry to say." He gazed up and said, "I see that some already availed themselves of them poor fellows's footwear. That's the way it is, these days. Socks, too."

Billy noticed their bare, bloodless feet just then, ivory white. He turned his head to the front and concentrated on going down the hill without taking a fall.

Chapter 4. Fishing Creek

They arrived at Zollicoffer's camp in Union, Tennessee, a week later. The march took its toll as the men tramped through the woods next to railways, up and down hills, over rocks concealed by beds of brown leaves, and through muddy gullies. As bad as Billy's shoes had been before, they came close to falling off by the time they arrived at the general's winter quarters.

Branner's company set up their tents in quick order, except for those men who had none. Burrow took his squad to the brigade's quartermaster wagons, where those who needed them were issued equipment and supplies according to what was on hand. Billy received a backpack with a knife and fork and a pan in it, along with a tin cup. Since the camp operated a general kitchen, no rations were included in the pack. He was, however, issued a weapon, an old flintlock the other men called a Brown Bess. Billy figured they called it that because of its long brown wooden stock, but he didn't know where the Bess part of the name came from. Along with the musket, he was given powder and some large lead balls. At first, he didn't think the Brown Bess weighed much, about ten pounds, until he started marching with it held over his shoulder. As the sergeant put them through their paces, the gun seemed to grow heavier and heavier. And, they marched.

They marched and they marched for hours at a time, back and forth, yelled at to keep in tight formation. At late afternoon, the drill sergeants dismissed them to tend to the horses. When the cooks struck the bar for mealtime, the men could barely sit up straight to eat, often falling asleep with their backs against a log, their tin plate in their laps.

After the first week of marching, the sergeants switched to maneuvers and other training. The men filed out in turn to a meadow where logs with paper targets tacked to them had been set up at varying distances. The closest stood fifty yards away; the furthest away looked to be about 200 yards out. When Billy's turn came up, he listened to Burrow instruct him the same as he had the rest of the men new to the squad.

"You have five balls," he said, "that's five shots. Follow the steps for loadin' your gun, and how you was taught to aim and fire. Take the first three shots from the standin' position, the next one kneelin', and the last lyin' down. Make sure you hit them targets so's you can go dig out the slugs. We'll need to use 'em again or give 'em to Requisitions to make new ones."

As miserable as Billy felt most of the time, he brightened a little at the prospect of shooting. Through many years hunting anything that moved at home in the hills, he'd become a pretty good shot. He liked the idea of plunkin' a few balls into the targets out there, show 'em all what he could do.

He stepped up to the firing line, deftly loaded his gun, primed the flint, and brought it up to his shoulder. Holding himself steady, he eyed the paper target on the 200-yard log. As smooth as a glassy sea, he fired.

He stepped back to keep his balance from the kick of the explosion. A voice called back from the target area, "Miss!"

Miss?

"Where were you aimin' at?" said Sergeant Burrow.

"Two hundred yards."

"Try fifty."

"How about the hundred?"

Burrow shrugged and said, "Go to it."

Billy loaded and fired again.

"Miss!"

"Blazes!"

"Look," said Burrow, "we need to retrieve the lead y'all shootin'. Go after the fifty target."

Darn, thought Billy, but he loaded up and bore down on the fifty yard target. He fired, and the voice called again, "Miss."

"What the—?"

"Kneel down and sight it in as tight as you can."

Billy reloaded and knelt down on one knee, holding the gun hard against his shoulder, aiming as carefully as he could. He breathed in and slowly exhaled, gently squeezing the trigger.

"Hit!" said the voice at the targets.

"All right then!" said Burrow. "Now, lyin' down."

Billy dropped to a prone position, cradling the gun. He squeezed off the shot.

"Miss!" yelled the spotter.

"B'god, if I shot like that at home, I'd starve."

He stood up, and Burrow clapped him on the shoulder, "It ain't you, McKinney, it's the gun. It's not rifled, it's a musket."

Billy stared at the sergeant as though he was insane. "A musket? How can anybody hit anything with an old musket?"

"Well, you did, which is pretty good. When we get the new rifles I'll be sure to tell the quartermaster you can shoot."

Billy gave him a skeptical look. "Does that go for shoes, too?"

Burrow grinned and said, "Sure enough. Things will get better, don't you worry."

In the last week of November, all of the men were called to assemble at the center of the camp. General Zollicoffer stood on a stump facing them. The general presented a proud figure of a man, tall, lean, with an impressive set of sculpted whiskers squared off on his chin, and a moustache. Word had it that he shot a rival newsman in a duel in Nashville over the disposition of a new bridge. A striking man, indeed, his voice rebounded among the men, full of volume and sincerity as he told them why he had brought them together.

"I have just received orders from Major General Crittenden. Now that we have secured the Cumberland Pass from Yankee incursion, the general wishes to make use of us in expelling them from Kentucky. Therefore, we shall strike our camp at once and march to deal those Blue Belly Devils what for."

The crowded men cheered heartily, and Billy thought he'd never get home.

In two days, Zollicoffer led his men out of the town of Union, a full brigade of nearly 5,000 men and horse, artillery, and supply wagons. They made their way west up the Cumberland River toward Somerset, Kentucky, doing their best to negotiate the hills, tree stands, and streams along the way that slowed their pace.

"Kentucky is split on secession and the war," Murray explained, "sort of like Tennessee was until Governor Harris called for another referendum. Yessir, a real politician—if the first one don't work out the way you want, do it again." He nodded down to Billy, "We have as many pro-Union folks and secessionists livin' in Tennessee as we did before the second vote, but now we're split off against the Union and a newly minted Confederate state. Kentucky voted to be neutral instead."

Billy's feet hurt from his shoes, which now were held together by leather laces. Murray's stories kept his mind off them, so he didn't mind the way the lanky fellow went on.

"Of course, neither the Yankees nor the Grays could let that stand. Therefore, Kentucky is infested with both of them on all sides."

Murray lapsed into some kind of reflection for a moment before continuing. "This means," he said, "that a big fuckin' battle is inevitable."

They kept walking silently for a while, until Billy said, "You don't seem to favor one side or the other."

"Naw," Murray answered, "I pretty much don't care one way or the other. I just as soon mind my own business."

Billy thought about that for a while. "Then," he asked, "how'd you end up here with the Rebs?"

Murray sighed, "Well, I was detained in Nashville, a little trouble with some long-term borrowing I did. They told me I could go upstate to their correctional institution or I could join the army. Since it is a Tennessee tradition, I volunteered.'"

He grinned.

"Oh," said Billy. He frowned a bit. "Have you been in any battles yet?"

Murray vigorously shook his head, "No sir. We rousted some Union sympathizers once, but I have never fired my rifle in conflict yet. To be honest, I'm hoping that this whole thing is resolved before we do have an occasion to fight."

"You better not let any officers hear you say that," Hicks said. "They got their hearts set on beatin' the shit outta the Yankees."

"Oh, I don't doubt that," Murray said. "And I shall speak carefully around our fearless leaders, if at all."

They reached the outskirts of Somerset in two weeks at a point where the Cumberland River wrapped itself around the small town of Mill Springs. On the southern banks of the river, tall bluffs dominated the landscape. The northern banks were flat and low, and nearer to the enemy's expected entry point.

"Where you think the general will set us up?" Hoat asked, resting with his crossed arms and head on the barrel of his rifle.

"Who knows?" said Hicks. "Who cares?"

"Most likely," Murray reflected, "he'll plant us right on top of that hill there, where we can shoot down on every Yankee that tries us."

"It's a hike," Sergeant Burrow said, gazing up at the steep hill, his hand over his brow to block the bright, winter sun from his eyes. "Once there, though, we have 'em all covered for sure."

Just then Captain Branner rode up with an entourage of other officers. Burrow walked quickly over to him, saluting as he arrived. Out of earshot, Branner spoke to Burrow, who craned his neck up at the Captain. Burrow nodded and turned around while Branner and his men galloped off further down the line of soldiers.

"We march, boys," Burrow said, "to the northern bank. That's where the general thinks the Yankees will be comin' from. That where he wants us to be. Get your packs and fall in."

The men stared at each other momentarily, then gathered up their gear along with the other members of their company. They formed a column four abreast, rifles on their shoulders, and strolled down the road toward Mill Spring. Despite the brightness of the day, it was cold, with wind whipping up dust and leaves along the way. Billy pulled his shoulders in close, trying to stay warm. His feet felt icy, almost numb, and he wondered how much longer he could go.

Two hours later, they came to the edge of the Cumberland River. Officers cantered aroundordering them to halt and fall out on both sides of the road. Billy sat down, immediately pulled off his shoes and started rubbing his feet, trying to get the blood flowing.

"Here," said Murray, "here's an extra pair of socks. You can give 'em back to me when you get some new shoes. And try this on," he said, handing over a short, gray jacket with dull brass buttons, two of which were missing. "It don't fit me, too small, and I got my old cowhide coat anyways."

Billy looked up Murray adoringly, like he was his mother.

The men surveyed the riverbank and saw boats of all sizes filled to the brim with soldiers working their way across the river. Some of the crafts were little more than rafts or fishing skiffs, others were rowboats and canoes. A few large flat-bottoms used to transport supplies were dragged up and down the river by mules and oxen on shore. These boats had been commandeered to carry the brigade's heavy equipment.

"That's why they pulled us off the road," Burrow said. "They got a lot of front units on the other side of the river already formed in line, I suppose. Now, they want to get the big guns over there as soon as possible to support them, followed by the rest of us."

Teams of horses pulling caissons and cannons that rolled up the road and clattered down the slope.One after another, in what seemed to Billy to be an endless stream. There, they waited in turn to be maneuvered onto the boats and secured. The horses balked on the decks of the unsteady riverboats, but their handlers had tied them down so that they had little room to move.

The men waiting on shore sat sanguinely and watched while eating and drinking. Most of them munched on molasses hardtack, though you needed hen's teeth, so the saying went, to bite through one. Others ate cold bacon bits mixed with cornmeal. All of them drank plenty of water from their canteens to soften up and wash down their food. While they chewed, they watched the artillery rigs fly by, followed by supply wagons, and other wheeled transport. Eventually, the flow slowed, and an officer rode back ordering the men to form up by the river bank for transport across. As they walked down, Billy glanced at the water, which flowed rapidly along its wide banks, frothing up over boulders in some spots, and whirling around in rapid-fire eddies in other rocky corners. To Billy, it looked deep, dark, and foreboding, though he realized he might feel that way because he couldn't swim all that well. He'd plunked himself in a few cold ponds back home when he was young, and learned to tread water. But, the wild water below scared him.

By midafternoon, they reached the position chosen by Zollicoffer for fortification. Officers instructed the men not to set up their tents or lean-tos in case the Yankees were close. The men did their best to stay warm bunching around each other for body heat. There wasn't much cover where they were, on a flat that ran from the river to the road.

Hicks twisted his head around and peered at the high bluff over his shoulder with an expression as though he saw a wolf pack in the distance closing fast.

"It would be bad," Murray said, "if the Yankees crossed the river higher up opposite us and marched down to take the hill. Then, we'd be the ones sited in on their bird guns."

Burrow glanced back and turned to his squad. "Well, they ain't up there yet, so don't go gettin' your drawers in a twist for no good reason. My guess is that our boys will find 'em first, and we'll surprise them before they get us. So, just be ready."

How? Billy wondered, his teeth chattering. He never felt more like the stranger in a strange land that the preacher spoke about back home. The way things were going, he couldn't see any way of getting to hear him preach everagain.

They sat on the river flats for two weeks without a thing happening. Jawing around the camp said that Thomas was coming down from

Lebanon to try and kick them out, but no one had seen anyone yet. The officers relented and allowed the men to pitch their tents, but the bad weather persisted. Some of the men came down with the flux, running back and forth from the latrines near the river to empty their bowels. The rest simply shivered all the time.

In mid-January, General Crittenden showed up and ordered Zollicoffer to move his men off the Cumberland flats toward Thomas and his troops. Billy saw Crittenden at Zollicoffer's headquarters, a tall, slender man in a long coat with a double row of gold buttons all the way down. His hair grew straight, cut hard at the neck, and he wore a thick moustache and a brush of a beard shaved away from both sideburns. His eyes were sharp but bloodshot and his manner seemed impatient. Zollicoffer acted deferential to his commanding officer, but as far as Billy could tell, little warmth passed between the two men.

"Hey, boy," a treacly voice called out to him, which suddenly harshened, "what the hell you doin' here?"

Billy followed the voice, and saw Colonel Dixon leaning over the neck of his horse, its head down as it grazed. Billy stuttered, with nothing cogent coming out.

"You spyin', boy?" The colonel sat back, his hands clasped together over the pommel of his saddle. "You plan on runnin' off to spill your guts to all your Yankee friends? That's espionage and desertion, boy, both capital offenses punishable by death."

He paused, watching Billy squirm, then laughed, saying, "Hell, boy, I wouldn't know whether to shoot you or hang you, maybe do both."

Just then Crittenden walked out of Zollicoffer's tent. Colonel Dixon straightened up and saluted as the general mounted his horse and rode off. Billy saluted and quickly scurried away, glancing over his shoulder at the colonel in his saddle watching him go.

Soon after, the junior officers and noncoms issued the new orders and the regular foot began to strike camp. The brigade would be marching on Thomas's force.

Rain fell, cold and steady. They marched up to where Fishing Creek intersected the roads leading to Somerset. Thick woods and mud turned the march into an exhausting ordeal. Billy's feet felt frozen by the cold rain, which made the extra socks given to him by Murray heavy and useless. The rest of Burrow's squad looked just as distressed, each man forced to lean against a tree for a while to regain enough strength to plod on.

After several days, they arrived below Logan's Crossroads where scouts had placed Thomas's brigade. Just above the creek, the Yankees' forward units advanced down three adjacent roads separated by thick woods.

"Scouts say the Yankees don't know we're here," said Burrow. "Orders are to line up at the edge of the woods before the creek and wait for the signal to attack." Burrow swallowed, "This is it, boys, what we been waitin' for."

Billy wondered how many of them really had been waiting for this.

"This is our chance to put them blue-belly bastards in their place. Check your weapons, make sure your powder is dry, and hold tight until the bugle sounds."

Billy felt an immediate need to pee. He shifted his sight from one fellow soldier to the next. Each suddenly looked pale and wide-eyed. There was no getting ready for this, he thought. They all had an idea of what lay ahead, though none of them really knew. He imagined that they all wondered if it would be as they'd imagined, or worse.

After relieving himself, he rejoined the men as their sergeants silently motioned them forward to close ranks among the trees at the creekbank. No one spoke; everyone stood still holding their rifles and muskets with both hands diagonally across their midsections. Rain poured down causing mist to rise up.

Zollicoffer rode across the line on the bank. Wearing a pure white raincoat, the general waved his hand over his head at the men, as if encouraging them silently to be stalwart. Then, the bugles sounded, and the men moved forward, down the bank and across the creek.

Billy's gut dropped as he walked through the stream and up the other side. He felt contractions that would have caused him to throw up, except he had nothing on his stomach to lose.

As the line of drenched, dun and brown-colored soldiers stepped forward, they nervously quickened their pace as though rushing to judgment. An ear-splitting screech sounded overhead, followed by the bass thunder of an explosion. More high-pitched screams blew through the sky above them, corresponding to a series of thunderclaps overlapping the flight of projectiles above. Zollicoffer's artillery pieces had opened up, sacrificing any surprise beyond this point. As one, the mottled gray throng stopped; the men looked back and forth at each other, and began to shriek and shout as they broke into a mad run toward the unseen enemy.

They flew through the woods, howling and screaming, shaking their guns over their heads. As Billy ran, he heard whistling sounds followed by crackling amongthe remaining leaves on the trees. The whizzing, buzzing noise increased, causing a few men to trip and fall. Billy and the rest didn't bother looking back, they simply charged ahead past the rain-drenched trees.

Suddenly, they burst out of the woods into a mist-covered meadow next to a road on their left. Vague shadows of men in black caps and dark jackets ran near them, clutching their guns by their sides as they sprinted wildly up the road. Burrow and his men slowed as they watched them pass.

"B'god, I believe them's Yankees!" Burrow shouted out. "Fire at 'em! Shoot!"

The massed Confederates wheeled around, leveled their rifles and let loose a ragged volley. Billy tried to shoot, but the soaked powder in the old flintlock refused to light. He could see Union soldiers close to them drop down from the panicked mass, some flat on their faces, instantly stilled. Others fell to their hands and knees, clutching at their torsos, coughing out spider webs of blood. The other Yankees fled furiously pursued by a large, drab gray body of men, some firing and loading, others racing toward the back of the blue soldiers with bayonets fixed.

The men around Billy reloaded hastily, some starting to raise their rifles. "Hold off!" cried out Burrow. "Our boys are in the line of fire. They chasin' 'em. Got 'em on the run, too."

They stood watching the ghostly blue forms fade into the woods at the other end of the road just as a single horseman rode up. Burrow and his men gazed at the closing rider, recognizing the white raincoat.

General Zollicoffer called out, "Sergeant, what's happening here? Are you firing into your own men?"

"No, sir! Yankees, we been shootin' at Yankees."

"I don't believe I see any of the enemy, Sergeant, just our men. Cease fire while I verify."

"Sir—," Burrow yelled out, but Zollicoffer galloped off into the fog.

They couldn't see him for a few moments until a breeze shifted the smoky mist apart. A tiny figure in white on a horse rode up the Mill Spring Road close to the woods where the Union soldiers had scattered. He stopped at the edge, his horse turning back and forth nervously. They saw a single puff of smoke travel from a dark figure standing in a straight line to the horseman. He stiffened in his saddle, threw his hands over his chest, and fell to the ground.

The men in the meadow below froze, their mouths open suspended in disbelief.

"Did you see that?" Murray said. "He rode right up to a Yankee and got shot down dead!"

"He maybe ain't dead," Burrow said. "We got to go get to him. He could still be alive," the sergeant said, the last part sounding more like a question than a statement.

Before any one of them could move, smoke and fire roared out of the woods directly in front of them. A dozen men acrossthe line crumpled and fell to the earth. More fire blasted from the trees, deafeningeven the sound of the steady rain. No one could see anything except soldiers falling around them. Hicks spun around and bellowed, "We gotta get out of here!" and a ball tore through his left shoulder into his chest. He seemed amazed before he collapsed in a heap.

Terrified, Billy jerked his head both ways, not knowing what to do. He saw a wave of bluecoats surge out of the woods, firing rifles at their hips and coming pell-mell at them, bayonets at the ready. Billy ducked low and swiveled. He ran, throwing his musket aside to go faster, feeling the air pass his head as shots whispered by. He raced for the woods as fast as he could, but others outpaced him. Murray's long legs carried him fifty feet further in no time. He soon disappeared as they closed on thetree line. Burrow loped by, too, still calling out for his men to form up. Billy started to fear that he'd be the last one, the only remaining target for every Yankee chasing him. He finally reached the woods's edge and bolted past the trees, trying to get as deep into the foliage as possible.

At last, he stopped, breathless. Cannon shot still screamed above, and minié balls continued to clip the last of the dangling brown leaves. Billy could hear the occasional thud as a slug slammed into a tree trunk. He hunkered down behind the biggest oak he could find and waited for the Union onslaught. But, they didn't come.

His heart swelling his throat, Billy stayed as still as he could. Still, the Yankees never showed, not even a slow, stealthy advance by skirmishers. Maybe they thought better of it, maybe they thought the Graybacks would turn the tables on them, too. Billy didn't know, but he felt relieved that they seemed to be gone.

He had regained his breath, but his feet ached. In the madness, his shoes had come apart, and he was utterly barefoot now. Blood seeped from a series of cuts on his soles, ripped somewhere along the way by stones and branches. He couldn't feel them, however, because his feet were frozen as well. He tried to rub some life into them, which caused sharp pain in the wounds. He shook his head, thinking that he was double lucky he wasn't being chased since he doubted that he could run very far now. But, he couldn't stay put, either. Sooner or later, someone would come along, Rebel or Yankee, and he wasn't eager to meet up with either one.

So, what to do? The artillery fire seemed to have shifted right, closer to the road. He decided then that it would be better to move away from it, keeping to the forest on his left. Slowly, he lifted himself up by holding on to the trunk of the oak. His feet throbbed with pain, but gingerly, he took a step, then a few more. If he moved very deliberately, he found that he could move away from the din of the battle. He also angled south, hoping to find Fishing Creek. Despite all of the rain, he was parched.

Careful to avoid the tumult to his right, Billy slipped back from tree to tree toward the creek. By the time he reached the fast-running stream, his feet pounded with pain. He threw himself on the ground and stuck his legs deep into the water. The freezing water at first shocked his lacerated feet with stabbing agony. The searing pain gradually resided, turning into a dull, almost distant ache. The numbing water relieved him, though he knew that he had to get out soon or risk freezing altogether.

Reluctantly, he pulled his legs back and pushed up to stand. Unsteady, he shifted his weight to regain his balance when he spotted something foreign out of the corner of his eye. He dropped to his knees and spied around the brush in a sweeping circle. He saw it, across the creek a few feet down stream. Billy hunched even lower as he looked closer. A body, half in the water, head face down on the bank.

Billy listened. Hearing nothing, he stepped into the stream and plowed through it to the downed soldier. Nearer, he could see that it was a Grayback who appeared to be dead. Billy stooped over, grabbed him beneath his shoulders and dragged him up the bank. After a few tries, he managed to flip him over. Milky eyes stared above at the missing sky. Billy couldn't find any wound, but the man definitely was dead. Billy closed the slain man's eyes.

As he rose, he glanced down at the body's feet. Sure enough, he wore a pair of brogans, muddy and wet, the soles somewhat worn, but without any major cracks in the topside leather. They were pegged, too. Billy bit his lip. After a moment's thought, he slid down to the body's feet, untied the right boot, and slipped it off. Gingerly, he pulled it onto his foot.

It was big. Better than too small, he thought. He untied the other and put it aside while he pulled off the dead man's socks. Drenched though they were, Billy knew that they would dry and be invaluable. He wrung them out and tucked them into his belt. He put the brogans on and tied them as tightly as he could.

Standing up felt strange, now, but he didn't have time to think about it. The din of the battle had faded off, though he still heard some noise behind him to his right. He wondered if the Yankees were pushing the Rebs all the way back to the Cumberland. His best bet might be to head north through the woods in hope of skirting both sides.

He checked his knapsack to be sure he hadn't lost anything in his mad run. Everything seemed to be there, especially the important items he'd brought from home, wrapped in soft leather. There wasn't much left to eat, though, just a few stale bacon biscuits. He realized then that his canteen was gone, probably lost the same time he tossed away the Brown Bess. After a moment of anguish, he turned his head and looked back at the body of the unlucky soldier. Sure enough, he had a canteen on one hip attached to a thin leather strap over one shoulder across his body. Billy took out his pen knife and cut the strap, grabbing the canteen before it fell into the creek. He tied it around his waist and started out.

After an hour struggling through the damp woods, he broke into the open next to a road. Which road, he didn't know. He gazed up at the sky and saw that the purple bruised clouds still churned, rolling around each other like writhing snakes. Billy looked up and down the road, recognizing that if he went south, he'd run into his own sooner or later. He decided right then and there that he wanted no part of the Cause anymore, as if he ever did. He wanted to go home. Maybe he could slip by them at some point, get back to Daddy and hide in the woods until it was all over. To do so, though, he would have to cross back over the Cumberland, which meant he needed to get to the bridge, since he didn't want to risk the frigid, roiling water. No, he said to himself, shaking his head, imagining the logjam of Grays there now. He'd have to wait.

He couldn't wait here out in the open near a road. If he went north, he'd meet up with Yankees, no question. They'd scoop him up and put him in chains, a prisoner of war, if they didn't pigstick him first. What to do, he thought, what to do?

He rubbed his chin, his eyes on the road, unfocused. His best chance, he decided, was to lay low and wait until the fighting had moved down the road. Then he could start back toward home. He wouldn't get caught again, he vowed to himself, he'd be as sly as a fox, sneaking around anyone he saw until he made it back. Daddy would be so surprised and glad, Billy hoped.

Nodding his head up and down, he surveyed the road again. North, he decided, away from Fishing Creek just to be sure that Captain Branner and his riders didn't come sweeping up the road. He'd go up a ways until he saw a nice little spot on high ground in the woods to rest a few days. After a good long while, he'd pick up and start home. The rain held off, but the clouds still threatened. Billy walked half a mile until he came to a field on his left between two stands of evergreens, each guarded by thick brush below. After thinking a bit, Billy picked the far woods to make his hidey hole.

He set out across the field, which the rain had turned into a muddy mess punctuated by cut-off, stubby stalks left from the fall harvest. He would have suffered stepping on them before he'd found the new brogans. Just then, a flight of crows cawing and cackling winged overhead in a southwest direction. Billy pressed his lips together, slowly swinging his head back and forth. The birds flew in the direction of the meadow strewn with crumpled bodies felled in the battle. He walked on.

At the edge of the dense brush leading to the pine woods, Billy heard a horse snort. He pulled up short and crouched down. Where could he go? Not back across the field, or over to the road. He had no idea of how many horses and riders occupied those woods.

Quickly, he moved as quietly as he could close to the brush but away from where he had heard the horse. After hugging the field edge for as long as he could, exposed as he was to anyone scanning the field, he decided it was safe to slip into the woods. He covered no more than thirty feet when he heard a voice behind him, "Hold it right there, boy."

Billy froze on the spot.

"Turn around and face me."

He held his open hands up by his shoulders and slowly turned around.

Colonel Dixon stood in front of Billy, trailing the reins of his horse in one hand while pointing a heavy revolver right at his face.

"Well, look it here, one of our hillbilly recruits. You pretty far afield from your unit, aren't ya, boy?"

The Colonel smiled, standing hatless, his immaculate uniform now splattered with mud.

Billy stuttered, "I lost my way, sir, in the mix up."

"Really? That's hard to believe, son, as close as we are to the roads." He put his left index finger up to his nose, saying slyly, "If I didn't know better, I'd say you might a been walkin' away from here, leavin' your fellah soldiers on the field. That true, boy?"

"No-no, sir!" Billy sputtered loudly, "I was lookin' for them just now, I swear!"

The Colonel lowered his pistol. "I see." He holstered it, saying as he turned to his horse, "I guess I got to take you at your word, if you swearin' to God."

"I am, sir, may God strike me down if I'm lyin'!" Billy flinched slightly after saying it.

"Well, okay, then," the Colonel said absentmindedly. He had started rummaging through his saddlebags, mumbling to himself, "Now, where is that—here it is."

Billy watched him, wondering how the Colonel had gotten so far from his troops, hatless, hiding in the woods. Billy at least still had his daddy's hat.

"Ah!" the Colonel said, then gestured to Billy, "C'mon over here, boy, you gonna wanna see this."

Billy clenched his teeth and forced himself to inch over to the Mississippi officer. "Look at this here," said the Colonel as he untied a cord around a leather cover wrapped around a bulky, oblongpackage. The unfolded leather revealed oil-soaked linen beneath, which Colonel Dixon quickly unwrapped to expose a handgun. It wasan odd-looking thing, thought Billy, with a wooden handlecurving down from a short, dull-grey metal barrel. Except for a site on its tip, the barrel ran level across the pistol's length. However, below it was missing the cylinder for its shot and powder. Instead, above the trigger,ahalf-inch thick metal disk satflat on top,like a heavypewter tea plate or maybe the iron eye off acookstove burner.The disk was divided by horizontal holes evenly spaced around its outside, each big enough to hold a lead ball.

"See that boy? What you think?"

Puzzled, Billy said, "Is it some kind a gun?"

"It is, indeed, son, a very special kind of gun. It's a .38 caliber Cochran turret, the latest in firearm innovation. See, it's easier to load it sideways," the Colonel said as he pulled a handful of balls out of his coat pocket. "I ordered this one special. See the engravin' on the barrel?"

He rapidly poured gunpowder into each horizontal hole in the pistol's cylinder plugging a lead ball into each chamber as he went along. To keep the powder from leaking out, he tamped the balls tight with some kind of slender rod flattened at the end.

"I keep a set of percussion caps on the pins," the Colonel went on, "so's all I gotta do is lay in powder 'n balls. Now it's loaded." He turned it in his hand and held it out by its barrel, "Care to fire off a shot?"

Billy stepped back, "No thank you, sir."

"Well," Colonel Dixon said, "I'm not surprised, boy, you holdin' an aversion to firearms." He slowly raised the Cochran up level with Billy's head. "After all, I saw right off that you fail to have your rifle with you."

Billy fell back more. "Colonel, I lost it in the confusion. There was so much goin' on!"

"Did you now? Jammed up did it? Shot out of your hands, maybe? Or, did you discard it like any other yellow-belly deserter on the run?"

Billy began to weep. "Colonel, I swear—"

"I believe you sworn enough today, boy. Instead of takin' his name in vain, you should probably be makin' peace with your Maker right now. As an officer of the Confederate States of America, it is my sworn duty to execute deserters on the spot. In this case, I believe it will be pleasurable."

He cocked the gun, and Billy covered his face with his hands, crying, "No, no, no!"

The gun exploded, and amid the staccato Billy felt a blow knock him to the ground. He screamed, "Oh, oh, oh!" terrified and in excruciating pain, his arms folded over his eyes. The report from the gun gradually faded away, spreading its morose message faintly across the field until complete quiet filled the air.

There was no pain, Billy thought. Was the wound too deep, too mortal for him to feel? He'd seen other men struck by fire falling to the ground, pulling their clothes apart, groping for the location of their wounds. They couldn't feel where they had been shot. Murray said that if a man didn't feel his wound at first, he was most likely shot deep, worse if it was in his belly, excruciating no matter how deep. If belly-shot, he was as good as dead. If not, he most likely would be gone later anyway.

Billy could feel some scratches and cuts on his face, but no big gaping hole. He moved his hands away from his face and opened his eyes. The uneven pewter sky still lurked, low and menacing. He could see.

He sat up, and realized that he had soiled himself. He grimaced, but ignored it as he slowly surveyed his surroundings. Colonel Dixon lay in a heap not ten feet away from Billy, his horse, too. Billy pulled himself to his feet and carefully stepped over to stare down at the officer.

Transfixed, the Colonel's eyes searched the heavens. He wore a crimson badge on his breast that slowly saturated the folds and creases of his tunic. His arms stretched out by his sides, as if imploring God to go gentle. In his right hand rested the Cochran pistol.

By God. He was dead, Billy realized.

He stepped over to the horse, clearly dead, too, from a ball in the brain. Billy snapped his head back and forth between the corpses, confounded by what had happened. He felt again around his own body for blood and a deadly hole. But, there were none.

He looked down at the Colonel again, shifting his attention to the gun in his hand. Billy stooped over and grasped it by its wooden grips and held it up close to his eyes. Every chamber was empty. The gun had misfired, sparking the powder of every other charge. One had killed the Colonel, another had dropped his horse. The other five had dispersed in a wide pattern around the field. The misfiredone aimed at Billy's head simply had missed.

My Lord, he thought. My Lord.

Billy stood stunned, his eyes fixed on Dixon's body. Still shocked by what had happened, he felt nailed to the ground. Dixon's face had frozen in a smirk as though unsurprised by the turn of events. Rain started to fall.

The freezing needles stung Billy and he shook all over. He pulled the brim of his daddy's old hat down to keep the stinging drops off his face. He didn't know what to do. If he stayed here, though, someone would be sure to see him in an open field, standing over the corpse of a dead officer. He had to hightail it out of there right away.

He turned to leave, then halted, thinking. He whirled around and stepped over to the Colonel's downed horse. He could only reach one saddlebag, the other was pinned beneath the still warm carcass. Billy opened the bag and began to pull out its contents. Biscuits, some beef jerky, and a big bag of nuts. Bacon. Three apples—where in Hades did he get them? Two pairs of drawers, a pair of wool socks, and a long-sleeve wool undershirt, all spotless and clean. A shaving kit and some soap, a brush, four combs, and a small pair of scissors.

Billy collected the food and clothing, and stuffed them into his knapsack. He grabbed the straight-edge razor, and slipped it into one of the socks, which he rolled, then put into his sack. He stood in a crouch and made his way back to the Colonel. Going through the pockets of his long coat, he found a pipe and a small leather bag containing tobacco, and a box of matches. All of that went into the sack. Billy rolled Dixon over and went through the other pockets. Nothing but a fine linen kerchief. He sat back for a moment, then jerked Dixon's body up and reached inside his coat. He groped around until he found a thick rectangular shape. He pulled it out, a beautifully worked leather billfold. Billy opened it to find a wad of paper money, all of it newly printed Confederate script. He threw it away and popped open the coin pouch. Inside, he found five gold dollars, U.S. He closed the purse and slipped the billfold into his knapsack.

He stood up and looked all around him, surveying the field, the woods at the far end, the road, and the grove near by. The clouds and the rain kept him from seeing anything, not the sun or the stars. Since he couldn't get his bearings, he decided it would be best to get as far into the forest as possible until the light failed, then bed down. He'd figure out where he was going the next morning.

The rain beat down and he had half a mind to take Dixon's greatcoat, but rejected the idea at once. If he was caught wearing it with a bloody bullet hole in the front, Grayback or Yankee would make sure he'd swing for it. Better off cold than dead.

He was about to set out, but turned back to Dixon. He rolled him over again to get to his holster. He unclasped the flap, pulled out the heavy .44, and checked its chambers. Empty, and the cylinder was jammed fast by a bent cap. The Mississippi son of a gun had bluffed him until he was able to pull out and load his other pistol. Billy tossed the Colt aside. He searched around and saw the odd-shaped revolver a few feet away from Dixon's remains. Hesitating at first, he walked over and picked it up. From the look of it, the gun fired smaller balls than the big Colt—that's right, the Colonel said it was a .38.

Billy went back to the dead horse and rifled through the saddlebag again. He found the linen bag where Dixon had stashed the strange handgun and groped inside. He pulled out an ornately decorated tin powder horn, a pouch full of brass caps, and a box of shot, .38 caliber as expected. Digging around some more, he locatedthe oiled cloth in which the gun had been wrapped. Billy carefully wound it back around the pistol and placed it and the rest of the paraphernalia back in the bag. Where he was headed, he thought as he thrust it down into the bottom of his own knapsack, he needed some kind of protection. The Brown Bess was gone, and the .44 jammed useless. The Colonel's sword would be a dead giveaway that he had taken it from an officer. The Cochran might be chancy and unreliable, but just pointing it might make some ne'er-do-well back down.

He straightened up and surveyed the scene of the carnage one more time to make sure he hadn't missed anything. Then, he set out, walking west away from the road and close to the edge of the woods, the rain causing the tall trees to loom dense and gray.

Chapter 5. The Wilderness

Beverly Bowman popped his head up above the bushes and looked down the tracks to the right, then the left. Nothing. So, he waited. A number of trains would come along soon enough. He and his fellows had sat at this curve for three days, scoping out what passed and when. By clocking each train, they would pick out one to run down that gave them the best chance to avoid slavecatchers from grabbing them up. They took turns scouting the trains during the day while the others fanned out at night searching farms or small towns for food and water. Three scavenged while one slept. During the day, the others wrapped themselves in their blankets and slept while the next man on watch markedthe passing trains. This fourth day, Bev hid in the nearby brush, monitoring the rail traffic. After four days of monitoring, they figured they knew the schedule as well as they could. If all went well, they'd make their try the next day at dusk,

While waiting, Bev thought again and again about how he had landed here. True enough, he'd been a lucky man compared to most every other black soul in the South. At six feet tall with broad shoulders and cinder dark skin, he had never picked a ball of cotton in his life. Master Kyle Bowman, son of Kentucky State Senator Wilson Bowman, had treated him more than fairly. Red-haired and raw-boned with permanent freckles on his face, the young sciongave straightforward orders in an even voice with never a curse word or a whip. Of course, it made some sense since they'd come up together, just like other white and black boys. When grown up, though, everything usually changed. White boys became masters, black boys learned their places as slaves. Until then, though, Kyle and Bev had been thick as thieves. Always at Kyle's prompting, they frequently ran off into the woods or to the creeks. Now and thenthey would trip on down to the cabins where the field slaves lived to play with their children. Kyle hated school lessons, and skipped out as often as he could. Running free was always worthwhile,no matter how many times his daddy gave him a licking, which was every time. Most times, he took off directly from the house classroom wearing his jacket, tie, jumper, and high laced boots, his school bag bouncing off his back. He and Bev would play until they were tuckered out, falling flat dead on a streambank tosleep for an hour or more. One time Kyle threw off his clothes and jumped into the water while Bev casually pulled out things from the young master's bag—books, charcoal stubs, and papers covered with rough dark marks.

"What's all this?" Bev asked Kyle, who had climbed up to dry himself off with his shirt.

"Writin'," he said.

"Writin'?" Bev repeated.

"Yeah. You know, readin', writin', 'rithmetic."

"You can do all that?" Bev said in wonder.

"Hell, no!" Kyle said. "They want me to do it, but I'd just as soon eat a live skunk. Why you think I'm out here with you? Daddy's gonna tan my hide good when we get back. You better stay out of sight yourself. But, it's worth it to me. I much rather be carryin' on like this than bury my head in a book."

"Huh," said Bev. He paged through a book, looking at the pictures amid the neat lines of tiny, black angles and curves all closely packed together. "You think I might do this?"

"What?"

"Read and write and such."

"I don't see how, Bev," Kyle said. "You a nigger, you know? They don't see a need for you all to learn that sort of thing, considerin' what y'all be doin' before too long."

"You could show me," Bev said.

Kyle rolled his eyes, "B'god, Bev, why would I do that? I hate all that horseshit, and besides, I'm terrible at it. How could I learn you?"

"C'mon, Kyle," Bev said, "Why don't you? Just a little bit."

And that's how Bev learned to read and write just a little bit.

By that time, Kyle began raising even more Cain by taking horses for wild rides. Bev couldn't go with him, or the young Bowman wouldn't be the only one getting a whipping. But, Bev ached to go, watching his white boy master with the pale skin and burning red hair bouncing around lanky-limbed on top of half a ton of wild-eyed, long-striding horseflesh. The stallion sped away at what seemed like a bullet, its smoke trail made of dust.

Bev thought he'd never ride a horse until Kyle took one and didn't return one day. Senator Bowman sent out a search party and found the horse grazing by a pond. His boy rider sat just a few paces away holding close to his chest an arm that he had broken in a fall. After that, the senator understood that his best chance to rein in Kyle was to schedule his riding time and the horses he rode. He also recognized that Kyle needed to have someone along that would slow him down or at least send out an alarm should the heir aplparent take another spill. So, once Kyle healed up, the senator allotted him riding time on select mounts. Bev served as his companion riding on mules and nags. In short time, though, Kyle realized that Bev possessed a natural harmony with quadrupeds and could ride like a comet.

When they grew into manhood, Kyle reluctantly acknowledged his adult role as master-in-training, assuming more and more responsibility in running the large farm and the 70-odd slaves that made it profitable. He conferred regularly with the overseer Evan Teal, a short, powerfully built man with a salt-and-pepper beard who brooked not even the slightest sign of cheek from any slave. Even the foreman, Meschach Bowman, brazenly brash and brutal to his fellow slaves, knew well to act unfailingly humble in the presence of Mr. Teal.

Still, the young master reserved special respect for Bev and his knowledge of the equine, as he liked to put it. He also still liked running around, though as a young swank, he ranged farther from the farm. "It's easy," Kyle told Bev, "just a short ride to Bowling Green. I get passage on one of them new trains they built to move cotton and the like north. I mostly take 'em south to Nashville, Memphis, and of course, Naw'lins. Aside from the expected delights of good food, good drink, and friendly women found there, I discovered in myself a previously unknown passion for playin' cards."

In fact, Kyle's substantial losses at the gaming tables compelled the senator to bar him altogether from trips to New Orleans. Such a mandate meant that Kyle's opportunities to slip away diminished significantly. He managed to get down there once in a while, but in the meantime, he fed his appetite for cards by teaching the boys in the stable bunkhouse to play for matchsticks.

Bev was drafted, of course, with Whit and a couple of other boys brought in to put five around the table. Eli played some, but mostly ran around getting food and drink to keep the games going, which often lasted through the night well into the morning. At sunrise, Kyle would stand up, stretch his arms and bend his back, then make his way to bed in the big house. At the same time, Bev and the other players started in on their morning chores. They moved fast, hoping to get the work done quickly so they could hide away in the barn and take a nap. If Mr. Teal or Meschach Bowman caught them at it, they could count on getting a few stripes on their backs.

They left Bev alone, though, and Eli, too, maybe because the boy was so young and also Bev's stepbrother. Rumors, too, had it that Eli was related to the young master. Long but slight, Eli had turned into a pretty good jockey, thought time would tell if he would gain too much weight to ride. For Bev it was simpler; he was Kyle's favorite since they were boys. When he grew up, his size and strength scared Meschach Bowman a little bit, too. Mr. Teal, however, never allowed any slave to intimidate him. That would be the end of him as far as he was concerned.

Eventually, Kyle grew up, too. He stopped stealing off to the southern towns so often. If he did go and play cards, he would stop before losing too much money. He married the young daughter of a next door neighbor, and proceeded to produce a good crop of offspringwith her at once.

Kyle lived in the big house with his wife and children, and his father the senator, who now occupied a wheelchair. Kyle obediently took over the patriarchal domestic and social duties at the Bowman Farm. A vast holding dependent upon tobacco and hemp,the farm distinguished itself throughout the county with itsfast horses, the favorite indulgence of the area landowners. Kyle worked at raising his sons to be gentlemen and his daughters to be ladies. In his white linen suit and broad straw hat, he regularly hosted the neighbors from around the Crackers Neck crossroads. Upon these occasions, he sipped tea and bourbon with his fellow farmers and planters on the long front porch. Bev knew, though, that the young master would just as soon be sitting in the bunkhouse with him and the other boys, talking about upcoming races, the spring foals, playing cards, drinking corn liquor, and telling big fat lies, one after the other. Kyle loved to watch his horses run, goading whatever young buck who sat astride to go faster, go like the wind.

A whistle blew in the distance, a rattling staccato of air and noise signaling that a big engine and its heavy rolling stock would soon be taking the curve, cows and pedestrians beware. Bev peered through the brush as the train appeared, slowing down as little as possible to avoid derailing while keeping to its timetable. He kept low below the incline of the tracks as it pounded by, a good twelve cars or so, some open for transporting wood, the resthouse cars. Bev buried his head until the train surged by, just a matter of minutes. He lifted up and checked the sun's position in the sky. Four, maybe five in the afternoon, just before twilight, the fourth straight day it had passed heading west at this time. He nodded, this was the train, slowing down enough for them to run and catch it with any kind of luck. Yes, he thought, he'd tell the boys tonight.

He drowsed off while he waited for the others to show up, hoping they had something to show for themselves, too. Water wasn't too hard to find, but hunger had turned almost into a way of life. Anyone near this war struggled to find enough to eat, worse if you were black. Scraping up food meant danger, from bounty men to militia searching for any soul at odds with their vision of how things should be. He remembered how late one night or early morning, Kyle, sitting opposite him,drunk, had said, "This world of ours, this way of life, it's all gonna go away. It will be gone. Sure, it seems like it'll last forever, nothin's gonna change. But, things change in a split second all the time. Splittin' off from the Union is a bad idea, bad for business. Those boys who think their fortune will protect them, they'rewrong. It could be gone like a flash fire."

With his ginger hair mussed over his brow and his cheeksglowing a richer red from the whiskey, Kyle stared earnestly into Bev's eyes as he spoke. He reached over and grabbed Bev by the shoulder, draping his arm around him to pull him in. "All your people will be free someday, and I don't mean later. You might live to see it, Bev. It's inevitable," he sighed, his breath heavy with the smell of corn. "We can't stop that. Ever'one around the world is freein' slaves. It cannot be stopped."

Considering his life on the Bowman farm, Bev might have believed that he would be his own man someday. His life was pretty good, raising and training horses shoulder to shoulder with Kyle. The old senator kept his distance on the rare occasions when he was wheeled down to the stables, usually to see the new fillies and the two-year-olds run. After that, though, he'd tell the overseer Mr. Teal to head out. Teal would push him from behind, rolling off to the fields to check on the real business, growing tobacco and hemp. Down there, people stepped to or got lashed. Some got worse than that.

Bev wasn't sure why they had him working with the horses, though among the dark folk,gossip had it that the old master was his father. Others said no, he was too black to be the master's son. He didn't know, since his mother died before she could tell him one way or another. The old master did pluck him out of all the rest and put him in the stables. Still, if the senator was his father, Bev thought, it wasn't like he showed it. Bev didn't care one way or another. He liked horses, and he liked to drink and play cards with Kyle just about every night.

Until that last night. Playing with Kyle, Eli, and Whit Mayo, the new whiskey brewer bought from a plantation in Louisiana, Bev made the mistake of winning. Old Josh was there, too. Short, stocky, and coal black, word had it that he was the strongest slave on the farm and maybe the oldest. Kyle remembered him from childhood, and liked to bring him in from the field to serve them cigars and whiskey. Old Josh watched, but never played.

As usual, Eli dropped out early, this time when the newcomer Whit beat his three queens with a straight. Kyle and Bev teased Eli a little bit when he lost, but the new man Whit never let up.

"Boy, you don't know a loserhand when you see one, never mind how you can't hold your whiskey. Why, y'all musta been struck by too many moonbeams, you so dumb. Explain why you so white, too."

Bev stopped dealing and stared.

"What?" said Whit. "Why you givin' me the evil eye?"

Bev remained still. He'd already had one run-in with the new brewer when he first arrived. Whit showed up to join them in the bunkhouse and announced that he was the boss, now. To prove it, he threw Eli out of his way onto the floor. That was when Bev laid him out. Now, he was at Eli again, the youngest and least likely to fight on the entire farm.

"Bev, deal the cards," Kyle said. Bev turned his cold stare on Kyle. "Don't look at me like that, son," Kyle said. "And leave my new brewmaster be. I got a big investment in him and his skills."

The evening didn't get any better. Bev started to win while everyone continued to drink without much conversation. Finally, they all watched Bev win the last hand. As he scooped up the coins, he could see that the young master's mood had turned ugly.

"You cheat me, Bev?"

"I didn't cheat you, Kyle, I just won this time."

"It must've been cheatin', Bev. How could you win every hand from me tonight?"

"Luck, Kyle."

"Yeah, dumb luck," Kyle said, drawing it out.

"Maybe so," Bev said, "but maybe you being drunk had something to do with it."

"What you mean by that?" Kyle said, his ruddy skin suddenly coloring a deep, crimson.

"I'm sayin' you too drunk to see straight. Who knows what cards you tossed in that cost you some hands."

"Horseshit! I could be a firewater breathin' Injun and still beat a dumbass nigger like you blindfolded. You cheated me, you black bastard."

He lurched to his feet and swung a roundhouse at Bev, who hit him straight on with a fist to his face. Blood exploded from Kyle's nose and he sat down on his chair, tipping back in it a bit before it righted itself.

Bev stood over him, fists curled, waiting for him to get up. Old Josh and Whit stared slack-jawed at the carnage done to the young master's face, his nose gushing like a new oil well. Eli slipped up behind Bev and pulled gently on his arm. Bev brusquely shrugged him off.

Holding his hand to his nose, Kyle gazed up at Bev from the chair. "You made a big mistake, I think, Bev." He looked down and pulled out a handkerchief from his pants pocket and wiped his nose. Just then, a pile of other men burst into the room and stopped short as they took in the scene. All of them were black except for the overseer Teal. He spread his stance and held the stump of an old bull whip in front of him.

"Mr. Teal, if you please," said Kyle, "take Bev here and lock him up in the tack shop. I shall deliberate with my father on the proper chastisement for such disobedience and gross violence against my person."

Teal, a half-foot shorter than Bev, but solid and muscular with long experience in dealing with incalcitrant slaves, nodded his black-bearded head and motioned with it to Bev. Bev slowly walked out of the bunkhouse followed by Teal smacking his bullwhip handle in his other hand. After Bev entered the small wooden shed, the overseer slammed the door shut and barred it on the outside.

In the dark, Bev stumbled over harnesses and yokes pil edon the floor. He could picture the saddles hanging from pegs on the wall along with bridles, halters, and other equipment used with horses, mules, oxen, and other beasts of burden. He groped around searching for particular items that he knew from memory were stored in the shop. After a few false steps, he found them, a pile of woolen blankets stacked in a corner. He grabbed two and pulled them out. He kicked around to clear a space, and laid one blanket on the floor. Then, he wrapped the second around his shoulders and sat down cross-legged Indian style. He pulled the edges of the blanket over his chest. Spring might be on its way, but Kentucky still froze in January.

He shivered, too, about what he had done. No matter the reason, hitting his master would get his back laid open, or get him hanged, or both. No matter which or what, he was as good as dead. Why he could do such a thing, forget that he was their property, that they thought of him less than a man and maybe even a prize horse, amazed him in a horrible way. He'd gotten too cocky, out of touch with the real world. Tonight might be his last day alive on earth. He wondered if God would welcome him with open arms, or if there was some other set of rules for black folks. If the Lord loved them, how could He make life for most of them so miserable, so unfair? As good as he had it working in the stable and living in the bunkhouse, it took just a second of lost self-control to destroy a black man.

And, what would become of his brother Eli? Who would look after him now?

"Did you know Mama?" Eli had asked him when he was just seven years old.

"I did. I was about twelve when she passed. After that, they sent me up to the stable."

"Did I really cause her to die?" Eli said.

Bev remembered looking at him and saying, "Naw, Eli, she died of a fever when you was two. It didn't have nothin' to do with you."

"Folks say she caught the sickness from me," Eli said mournfully.

"Now, there's no way of knowin' that. Even so, I don't believe the Lord works in those ways, Eli. True, you was sick, too, but only Mama died. The Lord loved her so much, he wanted her with him right away is all. And, to ease our sadness, he let us keep you."

He still could see the smile breaking out on Eli's face. So, were the Bowman masters so furious that they would punish Eli, too, Bev's only real family? Would they kick his little brother out of the bunkhouse, make him work hemp until he shriveled up and died?

Old Josh worked the hemp, and he'd lived a long time, a lot longer than most other men had, the senior field slave owned by the Bowmans. Maybe Old Josh would take care of Eli, teach him how to survive, if he could. He might die anyway, though, Bev thought, shaking his head. What have I done?

In misery, he rolled over on the blanket on the floor as he covered himself with the other from head to toe.

A clumsy thumping outside the shop door roused Bev out of a troubled sleep. He heard another thud, and sat up. The door was pulled open, which allowed the full moon's light to illuminate the entranceway. Kyle Bowman stood in the doorframe.

Bev drew back. The young master was just a few inches shorter than Bev, but he filled the open space completely, his legs spread in a solid stance. He held something in his hands, but his silhouette blocked the light, making it hard for Bev to see.

Bev swallowed and said, "You here for a reason, Kyle?"

Kyle emitted a cough and said, "I am."

"You decide to finish me yourself?"

"I have not come to do that," the young master said.

"Well, then, what? It pretty easy for a man who's all-powerful to gloat."

"I didn't come here for that either."

Silence took hold of the tack shop. Kyle eased himself inside, out of the moonlight. He didn't speak. Eventually, Bev said, "You been drinkin' again?"

"I had a glass with Daddy, but not too much. I'm pretty much myself, now."

Bev grunted. "So, what did Massuh Bowman have to say about all our tusslin'?"

Kyle crouched low, just inches away from Bev so that he could see his face.

"He says,Bev, you need to hang for what you did. If he had his way, he'd use fence wire."

Bev nodded, "I suppose rope is good enough for you, Kyle."

"No, no it's not. I don't really want to see you hung, Bev. I don't want to see you die in any way." He sat down. "I feel responsible, some, for what happened. I was out of line, and if we'd been in a gentlemen's club in Franklin, the subject of my insults would have called for satisfaction and rightly so. But, you, Bev, you can't expect satisfaction, not here. You crossed the line. And, by doin' so, you put me in a tough spot."

Bev laughed coarsely, "How's that, Kyle?"

"I don't want you to die for this, but you can't live neither—"

"That is a tough spot, Kyle."

"—'round here, anyways."

Bev suddenly snapped alert.

"That's right. I can't let this go, after all them boys saw what you did, but I don't feel right about it either. So, you gonna have to run, Bev."

60

Bev stared sharply at the dark place from where Kyle spoke. "Someone must'a dropped the bar wrong on the tack shop door. It didn't take but a shake or two to loosen it. That boy Bev didn't wait around, he run off right away."

"Yes he did," Bev said.

Kyle rose up and stood in the doorway again. Before leaving, he turned sideways and said in Bev's direction, "It's out of my hands, now, Bev. You go, go like the wind. They just had a shootin' match down near Fishing Creek. Maybe you can catch up with some of them Yankees, go north, I don't know," he said, his features hardening. "'Cause, if you get caught, Bev, I can't help you. It's on you, now. It's all up to you."

Kyle faced the moon again and left.

Yes sir, Bev thought, it's all up to me. And, I will indeed run like the wind.

After ten minutes or so, he stole out of the tack shop, keeping close to the shadow of the wood-planked wall. Instead of heading straight to the fields and the trees, though, he stayed low and slipped back up the hill toward the stable and the bunkhouse. He sneaked into the long wooden building and slipped down the row of bunks to one near the far end. Curled into an s-shape under a blanket, the figure beneath lay still, not breathing heavily like the others in the long hall.

"Eli," Bev whispered.

He could feel the stiffening of the body on the bunk. "Who that?"

"It's me, your brother."

Eli sat up and said into the dark, "Bev? How'd you get here?"

"Never mind that, we gotta go."

"What? Go? Go where?"

"Outta here. Off the Bowman Farm."

"Off the—you mean run?"

Bev shook his head up and down, then realized that Eli couldn't see him. "Yes," he whispered hoarsely, "and keep it down. We don't need to wake nobody else about this."

"Too late," a voice in an opposite bed said.

Bev immediately recognized the speaker as Whit. "You don't want no part of this, Whit, dogs and guns, hangin' if we're lucky."

"You run, I'm runnin' with you."

"Blazes, Whit."

"That's it."

Bev had no time to argue. "Grab your coats, hats, everything you need and let's go. Bring your blankets, too. It's mighty cold."

Crouching low, the three tip-toed out of the bunkhouse. They straightened up as soon as they emerged, and Whit said, "Which way? North?"

Bev shook his head. "North is where the bounty hunters look first. Follow me."

Bev led them back to the tack shop. He took them inside. "Each you all, grab a saddle, blanket, and bridle."

They did as he instructed, and he peeked out of the tack shop door, and held up one hand behind him. Evan Teal stalked by, a jug under his arm, on his way to his quarters. Once he was gone, Bev gestured to them to follow.

They worked their way quietly back to the stables. Bev quietly cracked open one barn door and squeezed inside. He grabbed a lantern and lit it with a match from a box on the wall. Quickly, he found an empty burlap bag, and slipped it around three sides of the lantern to cut the light. Then, he walked down between the stalls until he came to one housing a big bay stallion.
"Bottle Lightnin'. This one's for you, Eli."

He proceeded to another stall nearby. "Revolutionary Colors," he said, gazing at a pure black horse. "Go ahead, Whit, saddle him up. Eli will help you if you don't know how."

He stopped at the last stall in the building on the right. "Mighty Beau. One fast stud," he said wondrously.
"He's pretty ornery, too," Eli said.

Bev shook his head slowly, "Not with me, he ain't." The horse rumbled in his throat and put his head over the stall door. Bev caressed his left cheek, and opened the door. In a matter of minutes he had the horse bridled and saddled. He walked it out of its stall to join the others, who also had their horses ready to ride.
"Walk 'em out as quietly as you can," Bev said.

They emerged from the stable into brilliant moonlight. No one stirred anywhere that they could see.

"So," said Whit, "which way? We go north, we can outrun them ridin' these boys."

Again, Bev shook his head. "We'll never outride them in the long run. We got to outfox them."

"We could hamstring the other horses. That'd slow 'em down good."

Bev stared at him, a cold cast to his eyes.

"We go southwest for starters."

Slowly, deliberately, they walked their horses down toward the cabins opposite the fields. A service road between them led out of the farm on the southern side. They picked their way down to the road and started passing between the cabins and the fields. Just as they reached the last one before the gates, a voice rasped out.

"Who that? What you doin'?"

The three men froze. Silence filled the air for a time, until the voice spoke again, much closer this time. "Y'all are runnin', ain't you."

Bev knew who it was, now. "It's me, Josh. I'm runnin', yes, I got to, now."

"Oh," Old Josh said, "it's you, Bev. I guess you right. Who that with you?"

"Eli and Whit," Bev said, his voice low.

"Oh. They don't got to run."

"No, but we want to," said Whit, on edge.

"Oh. Okay, then. Good luck," said Old Josh.

Without a word, the other three started leading their horses to the gate. They made it twenty paces away when they heard Old Josh's voice again. "I wanna go. I wanna run, too," he said, too loudly, Bev thought. He peered around to see if anyone was coming when Whit put his face close to his.

"He can't come, we only got three hosses. We can't go back for another now. And, he's old!" Whit said.

Bev stared at Whit, a tall, lean whipsnap of a man. Perhaps he was stringy tough, skinny though he was. Still, Bev didn't like him.

"Josh ain't that old, and he's strong as any of us. Good lord, Whit, he been workin' hemp all his life and he's still here. If he wants to run, he can run."

Whit stepped back, then whispered, "What about the hoss?"

Bev thought for an instant. "He can ride behind me. Beau's up to it. And, we don't need to ride for long."

He turned toward Old Josh, who held up a hand palm out and said, "That awright, boys, if y'all don't want me to go, I won't slow you down. You better go on now, I be fine."

Bev stepped up and into his saddle. "C'mon, Josh, let's go," he said, reaching down a hand. Josh ran up and climbed up behind Bev, and the four rode off on three prize Bowman steeds.

By the break of dawn, they had covered twenty miles. They crossed the White Oak Creek four times, the Sputter and Coplin branches, Faubush and Alligator creeks, and a host of other rivulets too small to be named. They finally halted at the east bank of Caney Creek. Bev led them down the side of the stream searching for exactly the right spot for what he had in mind. At last, they came to a small inlet called Jack Hollow. Bev reined his horse to a stop and surveyed the horizon on all sides. To his left, he could see the edge of the sun's aura just peeking above ground. This was the place, he decided.

He dug his heels into his horse's sides. He led them down and around Jack Hollow until they came upon a small grove of beech trees with thick clumps of grass all around them. Bev dismounted, and the others followed suit. He used a pen knife to cut some brown branches into stakes and handed them out to the other men.

"Unsaddle the hosses and stake them apart so they can reach the water but can't be seen right off. Should be good a few days 'til they're found. Throw the tack into the Hollow."

The others gazed at him, stunned. Whit said, "We leavin' the hosses? Why we doin' that? We can cover a hell of a lot of ground on a hoss."

Bev said, "Hosses are big and easy to see, too. They need water and food, and they leave a good size trail. Bowman's men will run us down quick if we keep 'em, never mind slavecatchers and regulators. Anyway, there are four of us and only three hosses. That will slow us down, too."

"That was your idea. With us on foot they probably catch us just as quick," Whit spat.

Bev shook his head, "Not right away, not if they don't know where we goin'." The others looked even more perplexed and unsure. "Okay," Bev said, "Where do runaways run when they take off?"
Eli answered slowly, "North."

"That's right, Eli, they head north. Sooner or later they set out for the North even if they started in another direction first. And, that where the slavecatchers and the rest look for them. Unless they blessed by God, they get rounded up and sent back, if they lucky. So, first thing, we rode southwest instead of north. That'll take them time to figure out when they don't catch us right off. Ridin' the hosses through the creeks should throw their dogs off some, too. Eventually, they'll spread out lookin' for us tryin' to escape on hossback. So, they should be slowed down until someone finds these hosses with the Bowman mark on them. They will be angry about that. By that time, we will be long gone away to a place they won't think to look."

"On foot?" Whit scowled, "No matter how long they take lookin' in the wrong place, we can't get far enough away just walkin'."

"Oh, we'll do a little walkin'," Bev replied, "but I have in mind ridin' another kind of hoss before long."

That had brought them this far. Traveling at night and foraging just before daybreak, in eight days they managed to work their way the 85 miles from the Hollow to the outskirts of Bowling Green. Listening to Kyle talk about trips to trade horses and deliver freshly harvested tobacco and hemp, Bev knew that a train depot operated out of the small town. Before the war, the rails carried King Cotton, of course, and other goods past Louisville up north for sale. On return trips, the trains brought back fortunes for the crop owners. Now, with the war, much of the trade had ended. But the railroad still ran, serving the Southern Cause all the way down to New Orleans, and also as far west as Memphis. Bev planned on jumping the train to Memphis, which would bring them to the Big River and that much closer to their final haven, Indian Territory.

After Bev explained it all to them, Whit's upper lip curled into that sneer of his. He cocked his head back as he said, "How you know all this stuff about Bowlin' Green, Bev? You ain't never been on a train. Where you get this from?"

Bev stared at Whit, his face stony. "Massah Kyle told me. He told me all about Bowlin' Green, catchin' the train, and where it went."

Whit still looked skeptical, almost disdainfully. But the look on Bev's face kept him from saying anything else. Begrudgingly, he nodded and walked away.

They spent a few more days scouting the railroad tracks until they decided on a steep bend that slowed the train down just a few miles below town. A dense wood flanked the inside embankment beneath the rails curving around the bend. Though mostly leafless, the tree stand seemed to Bev the best place to track the trains for the right time to steal aboard with the least risk. Twilight would be best, he thought. Slavecatchers and regulators would see this as an ideal spot for runaways and deserters to try jumping on. Some darkness would help.

"We'll be here for a few more days figurin' this out," he said to the others. "We been lucky so far because we moved fast before people can man a hunt. Now we in one spot, we got to be more careful about where we get food. We need to find enough to carry us for a couple of days, but they can't miss it. If you find a root cellar, don't grab all their taters, take just a couple of different things. Don't take baked goods coolin'on windowsills."

Eli moaned at that, and Bev sent him a scowl. He resumed, "Never mind chickens and such, we can't cook 'em anyway. If you see any jerky, get some, and anything else like that. I calculate we'll be off and on the train for maybe two, three days and nights. We'll be jumpin' when we see a good size town ahead, skirt around it at dark 'til we find a good place to catchanother train the next day. My guess is we won't get near Memphis for three-four days best."

"Why we goin' to Memphis?" Eli asked.

"It's where the train gets nearest to the Mississippi. We cross the Big River, we in Arkansas. Next to that isInjunTerritory, wild and free. We make it there, see how the war goes. If the South wins, we keep going west, then north to Canada. If the Yankees win, we can live pretty much where we want."

Bev hoped it would work out that way, but he really didn't know. He had no idea what Indian Territory was like, how it would be for four runaway slaves. He was betting it all on one cut of the deck. But he knew that whatever came up had to be better than going north right now. So, they waited on the late afternoon freight train heading down to Memphis.

Chapter 6. The Memphis-Ohio

Pouring rain obscured the last daylight just above the horizon opposite to the rail embankment. Bev and the rest of the men crouched, their heaving breath in the cold air visibly cut down by the driving rain. The only relief from their misery came from the thought that the downpour would slow the train down further and offermore cover to them racing in the open. Poised to make a rush when they saw the train appear at the bend, everyone knew that the first on board needed to help the next man, and so on. After they'd made it, they would look for an open box car where they could hide. Glancing back and forth from each of the men next to him, Bev could see tension and fear in them all. This didn't surprise him; he himself never had felt so afraid in his entire life.

The slow chug of the locomotive pulling around the steep curve heightened their anxiety. So many things could go wrong, Bev thought. They could lose someone from a fall, and all of them could be lost trying to help. He steeled himself. This is better no matter what.

Two sets of tracks wound around the tree bank, wooden rails with thin steel sheathing attached by spikes on top. Because of constant wear and tear, the metal casingsfrequently loosened and caused derailments.As a precaution, the trains operated at speeds much lower than the capabilities of the big, smoking engines. Usually averaging twenty miles per hour, when rounding pronounced curves even on graded embankments, they reduced their speed to ten miles, sometimes even five. The raging rainstorm dictated the lowest rate of speed. An easy trot would bring them abreast of the train, and they could pick their car. Of course, the railroad guards knew the same and would be extra vigilant at these bends and curves on the railway.

The southbound train had the inside track on this trip, another benefit of running for it from the treeline. The engine still seemed formidable in its powerful, shaking appearance, even if it was slowing down. Its broad stack blew out heavypuffs of black smoke guttering against the torrent of water as its pistons adjusted to less momentum of the massive weight. It was a good hundred yards away and closing when the four runaways saw him.

"What the—?" uttered Whit.

"What's that?" Eli said at the same time.

A small white figure wearing a felt hat, gray jacket, and brown canvas slacks, ran along the railway. Bowed over with a knapsack belted across his back, he hurried down the tracks just seventy-five yards in front of the train, losing ground with every step as he looked back over his shoulder.

"God-damn," spat Bev, seeing it all in an instant.

Horses neighed and snorted, and the four fugitives could hear thin voices in the distance.

"He here, boys, we got 'im now."

The scrawny white man looked back again and seemed to know that he wasn't going to outrun the riders. The train's whistle wailed its breathless high pitch in warning as the engine came up on the drenched fugitive. It passed him, blocking the view of Bev and his party. Amid the third long shriek of the whistle, they heard the riders shouting in alarm, and from beneath the undercarriage of the moving train out came the scrawny white man rolling, twisting, and spinning to a stop.

They heard the horsemen yelling in consternation on the other side even as their prey pulled himself up and darted toward the moving train, halfway past him now. He ran on his short, little legs and jumped up for an iron rung on a boxcar. He missed and fell hard to the ground. Without hesitation, Bev barked, "Let's go!"

He dashed out straight at the crumpled heap in front of him and grabbed an arm. Old Josh grabbed the other one, and they pulled him alongside a car. Whit had clambered up first, Eli on his heels and they both grabbed the side of a door open acrack and shoved it wide. Almost simultaneously, Bev and Josh tossed the flailing white man up onto the floor of the car, then hoisted themselves up and in.

"Shut the door!" Bev cried out. Whit and Eli slammed it shut and dropped a bar to lock it. Bev leaped to his feet, leaned against the wooden side of the car and peered through a gap between the planks. Sure enough, the riders galloped around the train from both sides, converging in front of his eyes. They milled about as the train moved past them, causing Bev to shift to look back down the line. Even as his sightline narrowed, he could see them suddenly rein about and head into the small woods where he and the others had been hiding.

He collapsed on the floor, his back propped against the closed door, which jiggled as the train picked up speed. "They ran off into the trees still lookin'," he said. "Musta lost him in the rain, didn't think he got on board."

The other three stared at Bev for a second in wonder, and started to laugh. All three of them were laughing out loud bent over, their hands on their knees. But, Bev wasn't laughing. He motioned with his head at the limp figure on the floor.

"He alive?" Bev said.

The other men stopped abruptly, and Whit turned to see. Just then, the scrawny little white man crumpled on the floorpopped up to a sitting position.

"Well, I'll be," said Whit.

"Baby Jesus in heaven," Old Josh said, while Eli just stared.

"God-damn it, white boy, you almost got us caught!" Bev strode over to the small man before him and kicked him squarely in the chest. He fell back, and Bev kicked him again and again, saying with each blow, "You almost got us caught, you jackass, you almost got us caught. You almost got us caught!"

Bev pulled back to take a breath, and Whit came over and slammed his shoe into the cowering man's side. "Look at him, he wearin' gray!" He kicked him again. Eli took the other side, hammering the toe of his boot into the figure, now curled up on the floor like a baby. Only Old Josh stood back, staring starkly at the terrible beating happening before his eyes. Now easy to see him as not much more than a boy, the curled up body on the floor stopped moving altogether. Blood pinked the rainwater around him.

Bev saw Old Josh shudder, and he stepped between Whit and Eli. "Awright, awright," he said, "enough."

He spread his stanceas the accelerating train shook more and more.

"Enough?" Whit snapped. "For a cracker like him? What you think he do to us if he could?"

Strangely, Bev thought of Kyle letting him go. Maybe the senator's son was just throwing him a bone to ease his own conscience, thinking the slavecatchers would round Bev up in short order. But, Kyle had given him a chance. Of course, once they stole the horses, they guaranteed that they all would swing from a rope if captured. He looked down at the still body on the car floor.

"We don't know what this boy's like," Bev said, "and even if he is a Reb, we don't want to be like them."

"You said it yourself," Whit muttered, "he almost got us caught."

"Yeah, except he didn't know we was there. He was runnin' himself. Those riders was after him, not us."

"So, he a yellow dog coward, he still a Reb."

Eli said, "We ride down the rails a bit, why not just drop him off the train?"

Bev shook his head, "It'd probably kill him."

"We could look for another bend, slow down some again," Old Josh ventured.

"He probably live and talk," Whit said, "tell them other white trackers all about us to save his own white skin!"

He drew closer to the figure on the floor, reached behind the small of his back and pulled out a skinning knife. Running his thumb across its edge, he said, "Let's kill him now and be done with it."

Bev drew his head back. "Where'd you get that?"

"Tannin' shop," Whit said, smiling slowly, "just in case."

"Yeah, well, put it away," Bev said.

Whit frowned. "You tellin' me to put it away?"

Bev turned his head and gave him a look. Whit tucked the knife behind his back. He looked back at the battered white boy below him. Skinny as a starving cat, the boy had a shock of burning red hair and freckles all over that did nothing to hide how truly white he was. Bev then realized that he was awake. The lurching movement of the cattle car probably shook him until he came to.

Bev loomed over him, spreading his feet even further to keep his balance, his fists curled at his hips.

"Who are you, boy?" Bev asked harshly, "What's your name? Why you runnin' away?"

The red-faced boy gazed up wide-eyed at Bev standing over him. He managed to squeak out his answer, "William. William McKinney. Folks call me Billy."

"Where you from?"

"Maryville, Tennessee."

"Maryville. Where the blazes is that?"

"In the mountains. In the east."

"Well, what the hell you doin' in Kentucky?"

Billy sighed. "It's a long story."

"You better start tellin' it, boy," barked Whit, "and it better be good, since you wearin' the colors of the crackers that want to keep us black folk down."

"We don't believe that where I come from. Our preacher says slavery's wrong. Just like the pharaoh with the Israelites, a sin against God."

"Oh, you go to church, do you?"

Billy shook his head sadly, "Not much. But we believe in what the preacher says."

Whit pulled his hand back and moved upon Billy again. "Why I ought to smack you again, boy. Sayin' you believe but don't go to church."

Billy said, "Too busy tryin' to get by. Farmin', huntin'...," he trailed off. "I didn't like it too much, though, the times I been to services. But," he went on in a guilty voice, "we do believe in God and we don't believe in slavery. Not in East Tennessee."

"Then why you wearin' that gray jacket?" Whit said, pointing his finger at Billy as though he had caught him in a lie.

"To stay warm in the cold," Billy said loudly. Softer, he said, "I got forced into the Reb army. I didn't want to, but I was stuck. Then there was this battle and the Rebel boys got whipped good—our general got shot dead!"

"Your general," Whit said acidly.

Billy grimaced, holding his ribs. "The Grayback general. So, everyone skedaddled. I had enough of that, I was ready to go back home. But, I got into trouble."

"Yeah?" said Whit. "How's that?"

"I started goin' the other way from where the Rebs were runnin'."

"Oh, you plan on joinin' the Union boys, did you? Gonna free all us darkies?"

Billy shook his head no, "I don't want no more part of this war at all."

"You're lucky about that, boy," Bev said. "Them boys in blue see that gray coat, they might shoot you on sight."

Billy turned to him, startled.

"So, what was this terrible trouble you get into?" Whit said.

Billy said, "I, uh, I killed this colonel."

"A Yankee colonel?"

Billy slowly shook his head, "No. One from Mississipppi."

"You killed a southern colonel," Whit said, hand on his hip, elbow out. "Now you my hero. You all us's hero."

"He hounded me the whole time I was in with the Johnnies! Kept sayin' he knew I wanted to quit, that he would shoot me on sight for desertin'. Darned if I didn't run smack into him when I was tryin' to get away."

"And, so, he shot you on sight?" Whit said.

Billy nodded up and down, "Yes, he did!"

"He shot you. Where you been shot?"

"It didn't work out that way. He got killed instead."

Whit lifted his boot and shoved Billy back flat. "You so full of it, boy."

Bev noticed the knapsack strapped across Billy's back. He stooped down and pulled it off. "Let's take a look, see what you got."

As the other men closed in, Bev began digging through the damp sack, pulling out one object after another, laying each aside in turn. He seemed to go through his things, Billy thought, like he was already dead.

"Some pone, hardtack, a bit of jerky—put them with the rest of the food, Josh. A grub kit. One raggedy shirt; a sock. No tobacco. What's this?" Bev said as he pulled out a small leather case. He opened and pulled out a beat-up, thin piece of cardboard stained brown from food and other ointments of time. He turned it around to the other side.

"Well, look at this." He held it up for the others to see. "One of them dead-people pictures."

He passed it to Eli, who nodded, then gave it to Old Josh. Josh gazed at it solemnly, his lips pressed together. "Him and his family, I'm guessin'. He's young there, but that him. Must be his daddy and mammy. His sister with the angels, maybe his mammy, too."

He handed it to Whit, who took a look and said, "White folks is so creepy."

Bev shrugged, "Somethin' to remember 'em by."

Whit dropped the picture at Billy's feet, who grabbed it with both hands and pressed it against his breast. Bev reached into the sack again. Extracting a round bundle covered with thick, oily muslin, he said, "This got some heft to it."

He unrolled the muslin by rotating the bundle until he exposed the dull metallic color of a pistol. "Another surprise," he said.

He uncovered it completely, holding it in both hands.

"He got a gun," Eli said, "why he don't keep it out, ready to use?"

"Must be broke," Whit said, grabbing it up. "Look at it, it's all messed up. I seen Mr. Teal's pistol, how he load it up in a cylinder in the middle. This one all flat, like it been squashed."

"Maybe that why he had it tucked away in his sack," Eli suggested.

"Carry that extra weight? On the run?" Whit said scornfully.

Eli shrugged his shoulders, "Maybe it belong to his daddy."

Whit looked at Billy and said, "This the gun you use to kill you colonel with?"

Billy stuttered, "He was shootin' at me and it didn't work right. Killed him instead."

"So, it don't work, why you still carryin' it?"

Billy shrugged, "I thought I maybe could fix it later. It was the only gun I could get."

"Huh." Whit handed the pistol to Bev, who rewrapped it and shoved it back down in the sack. He tossed the knapsack back to Billy.

Billy hesitated, then said in a low voice, "Are y'all gonna throw me off the train?"

Listening to the question, Bev realized that the white boy must have heard them the whole time talking about whether to throw him off or knife him, cold as could be. He frowned, and said, "We ain't doin' nothin' for now. You act up, though, for sure you will be tossed from this train, no matter it movin' fast or slow."

He watched the boy turn paler than he already was, if that was possible. Bev turned away and said to Eli, "Break out some of the grub. Give Rebel boy there a little water and some of that pone he was carryin'. Might as well let him eat for now anyway."

Whit started to voice a complaint until he saw Bev glance at him, which caused him to think again. Bev said, "Let's find ourselves as many burlap bags as we can, soak up the water. It's getting cold in here."

The car shook wickedly as its speed picked up, causing the men to lurch one way and the other. They stooped lower to keep from falling, putting their hands down on the planks to steady themselves as the car bounced up and down. Josh and Eli crawled around gathering the bags and brought them back to the others. Bev threw a couple of bags at Billy, "Wrap youself up boy, it's gonna be a cold night."

The cold seized hold of them brutally, so much so that none of them spent any amount of time sleeping. The jarring ride disrupted the few times their eyes did close. But every mile covered extended their patience as they felt closer to reaching their final destination.

In the middle of the night, in the dark, a dissembling quiet among the men was finally pierced by a disembodied voice.

"You always sayin' you don't like church, Whit," Eli said.

Whit replied, "I don't like bein' forced to go to church by the 'Massah.'"

No one said anything for a time. Then, Eli said in a hushed voice, "Yeah, but you also say you don't believe in God."

"How can any black man believe in God?" Whit asked.

"God works in mysterious ways," said Old Josh.

"All right, old man, go ahead and believe in the white man's god if you want."

"Baby Jesus is every man's savior."

"Sure enough, brother," said Whit.

"Whit," said Bev, "all of us deal with the same problems, so why're you such a sourpuss all the time?"

"I ain't white."

"You think that makes a difference? The white boy don't go to church neither, and he don't seem like a sourpuss. Why don't you go to church, white boy?"

The crashing of the wheels against the metal-sheathed rails presided again. At length, a tiny weak voice said, "I don't know."

Bev thought he sounded like a kid caught stealing apples when asked why he was a thief—"I don't know" said in a tone like that was going to get him off, like he was saying, "I didn't do nothin'."

A screeching sound that had them all covering their ears filled the car, which buckled and started dipping to the right. Tearing metal sounds could be heard and the car started slowly heeling over. The men inside began clawing for a hold as the floor slanted down at an ever increasing angle.

"What the hell is goin' on?" yelled Whit.

"Train's runnin' off the tracks," said Bev, "we got to get out quick!"

They all scrambled up toward the side door just as the car heeled back and slammed upright into the ground, sending them all flying to the floor. The car moved beneath them, pushed forward by other cars colliding behind from the momentum of the crash. At last, everything stilled.

Bev sat up. "Eli, you okay?"

"I'm okay. My arm hurts a little."

"Josh? Whit?"

"He's knocked out,"Billy said.

Bev clambered over to where he had heard the voice.Light suddenly swept through the car in a constrained beam. Bev wheeled around to see Josh and Eli at the open car door. Distant flames sputtered, flickering back and forth in the rain, casting an erratic hallway of orange light in the doorway. Bev turned back and saw Billy crouched over Whit's rumpled form.

"What happened?" said Bev.

"Don't know," said Billy, "musta hit his head."

Bev drew closer and Billy held out his hand. In it, haft first, lay the knife Whit had been carrying. Billy held it out further, gesturing with his head.

"What the—? What did you do to him?" Bev barked.

"Nothin'! I found him this way. The knife was next to him on the floor."

"You didn't take it? You weren't gonna cut him?"

"No!" cried Billy.

"Psst! Lower!" whispered Josh.

Bev leaned in and grabbed the knife. "Then, what happened to him?"

"I tell you, I don't know, he was like this when I found him," said Billy, almost pleading.

Whit moved, sat up, and said, "What the hell!" He shook his head vigorously, and said, "Where am I?"

Bev grasped his arm and said, "You okay, Whit?"

"I fell in the dark and smacked my head. Blindin'! Where are we?"

Bev said, "Still on the train, but we gettin' off right away if you can move."

"I can move."

Bev and Billy helped the tall man to his feet and started to inch him to the door. Abruptly, he stopped, leaned over, and threw up. Both hands pressed against his temples, he said, "My head hurts bad."

"Yeah, well, looks like you got your bell rung. We gotta go, though."

Whit nodded, and the two men helped him to the door. Josh and Eli already had jumped out, and stood poised ready to ease Whit down to the ground. In the distance, they heard voices of men shouting, yelling back and forth in an indiscernible code. While the railway men tried to sort out the mess, Bev saw other passengers leaving the train.

Torchlight showed that the train had slid off a curve of the wet tracks without any cars turning over. Crouched down next to their car, the fugitive men saw trees inside the bend, with nothing but harvested fields spread into the distance on the opposite side. They ran off as fast and as quietly as they could, hunched down in the smallest silhouettes possible. Just out from the disabled train, they dropped into a rut between low mounds left from last spring's plowing.

"What we gonna do now?" asked Eli in a tiny whisper.

Bev gestured with his head for the boy to keep quiet. Then, he muttered back, "Wait. See if they get the train movin'. Then, we catch it again, or get on the next one. Right now, we got to get to the other side, hide in the trees."

Bev started crawling parallel to the train, and the others followed. They made their way a hundred yards down past the train, then quickly crept across the tracks. Behind the tree line inside the banked rails, they moved carefully back toward the boxcar they originally had climbed aboard.

Bev peered out from behind an oak trunk and saw men with side arms walking back and forth, calling to each other about track damage and other matters. He worked his way back to the others.

"Too busy," he said. "They all over the train. We can't get back on this one, we'll have to hop another."

Glumly, they backed away from the trees and melted into the countryside before daybreak. Now of biblical proportions, the deluge made dawn hard to distinguish.

The cold cut through them in shivering waves. They huddled together as closely as possible, clinging to each other as life itself. Billy was left alone, chattering in his thin gray tunic. If they took him along to make sure he didn't sound the alarm, he wondered, then why didn't they kill him outright? Maybe they wanted him to suffer as much as possible the way they had all their lives at the hands of white men.

A voice from the intertwined men called out, "Hey, white boy, we don't want you runnin' off to tell your friends where we are. Get your ass over here so's we can keep an eye on you."

Billy scooted over and wedged himself among the pile of shaking bodies, and soon fell asleep.

A day and a night passed since the train ran off its track. The rain had stopped, but the low temperature caused vapor to rise from the half-frozen ground. Bev decided that their best chance was to head south of the wreck as far as possible and as long as it took to catch another slow line of cars. He recognized the heavy risk, that they might see no trains at all if the derailment blocked the southern bound tracks. Of course, they also might watch the train they had quit rolling again right past them. No matter, he thought, they still had to stay ahead of any slavecatchers, which meant they for now had to continue south.

They moved at night, and slept during the day, in tree lines if possible, taking turns on watch. Even though the paddy rollers and slavecatchers would expect them to move during the dark, they at least could avoid running into other white people. They covered ground slowly due to these precautions and also because Whit wasn't himself yet. At the end of two nights, Bev figured they had walked barely ten miles from the train wreck. At this rate, food and water would be a serious problem. Despite all the rain, drinking water proved hard to find.

During the middle of the third night, they saw lights down the track. Bev told the others to lay low while he scouted ahead. He kept as close to the ground as possible, gliding as silently as he could just below the rail bed to hide his outline. Without the others, he managed a much faster pace, drawing nearer to the town lights in what seemed like no time at all. Before he could reach the outskirts, voices in the night stopped him cold.

"Pack it up, boys, let's ride."

Slavecatchers, thought Bev, as he heard them bustle around gathering their gear.

"Lester, you take Jim and Wilmer here down the tracks. The rest of us will pan out above 'em."

They walked their horses off, three of them passing just a few yards by Bev. Tense, he waited until the sound of the hooves faded away. He waited some more. Finally, he crept up to their campground to see if they had left anything behind.

He found the embers of a small fire kicked apart. He also saw a darker shadow of something looming above him near the railroad tracks. He stepped slowly toward it until he could make out its shape. A water tower for the engines, he realized. He could see the outline of the spout suspended above the tracks next to the girth of the giant wooden barrel.

Water, he thought, and a place where the trains would come to a full stop. This was their chance.

Bev backed away and slipped out of the camp into the field next to the tracks. He scurried as fast as he could through the ruts and mounds, halting now and then to see if he could hear the slavecatchers or their horses. Then, he would start again, hoping that he wouldn't bump into them, hoping that they wouldn't hear the hammering of his heart.

At last, he reached their hiding place for the night, a small stretch of locust trees. He whispered and heard one in response.

"That you, Bev?" Eli said softly.

"Yes. How's everyone here? They're paddy rollerson the lookout. We have to be quiet and move."

"Whit's not so good, he threw up a couple of times. His head hurts bad, he say."

"They see you, Bev?" Josh asked.

Bev shook his head in the dark, just then realizing that they couldn't see him. "I don't think so," he murmured. "What about Johnny Reb, he here, right?"

"I'm here. I don't want no part of them hunters."

"Okay, let's go. We have to move fast and quiet."

"I don't think Whit can walk, Bev," Eli said. "We're gonna have to carry him, I think."

Bev's mouth tightened. Long and lean as he was, Whit was all muscle, too. He would be a load and would slow them down. He shook his head like a dog, and said, "Okay, we'll carry him."

"I got 'im," said Josh. "No problem for me."

"He'll drag you down, Josh, with his long legs and feet. Better two of us should carry him."

"I'll get 'im up, don't you worry."

"I can help with his feet," said Billy softly.

"No need," said Josh, "I got 'im."

Josh moved away, and returned with Whit on his back, moaning. "Let's go," said Josh.

He started walking as if he wascarrying nothing. Bev squinted, slack-jawed, amazed at the strength of the old black man. "Okay," he said softly, "Let's go."

The sun started its arching climb soon after they left their hiding place. Bev guessed that they had an hour before it would light the morning up fully. But, he frowned, worried. The slavecatchers might not be an immediate threat. Most likely they were sleeping now after a night of fruitless searching. But catching a train at rest in broad daylightpresented a different level of danger. White men would be passengers on the train no doubt, but several brakemen also were sure to be inspecting it, up and down its length. The only good thing about daylight was the hint of warmth they felt.

Bev positioned them down below the water tank on the other side of the tracks. "When it stops, we wait for them to hook up the water spout. While it's fillin' up the boiler, I'll scout for a good car. As soon as they start unlimberin' the spout, we run for it. Y'all follow me to the car."

They all nodded silently at him except for Whit. He groaned, and Bev leaned over him. "Whit, you got to keep quiet."

Whit nodded his head, "My head hurts bad, somethin' terrible."

"I know, Whit, but you need to shut up."

Whit nodded again, grimacing with pain, this time in silence.

Hours passed without any sight or sound of an approaching train. The tranquility of the day, sunny and the warmest since they'd left the Bowman farm, did nothing to relieve the tension among them. Instead, each passing moment strummed their nerves as they imagined a host of gun-carrying crackers suddenly riding out of the trees on top of them. In turn, each could feel the shots tearing into his body, or worse a rope around hisneck strangling him as he was hoisted in the air, flaming torches burning his feet before he died. Picturing such horrors made them each want to stand and run away madly.Common sense told them that doing so most likely would bring such terrors down on all of them sooner rather than later. So, they waited silently instead as they shrieked silently inside.

In the middle of the afternoon, Eli heard a distant train whistle. At first, its ragged wail sounded so far away he couldn't be sure which way the train was traveling. Bev strained to hear where it was; he abruptly popped up.

"It's comin' from the north, headed south."

Eli and Josh beamed.

"Get ready to move," whispered Bev.

He set himself on all fours, waiting for the train to arrive, hoping that it would stop for water rather than blow right through. Another day like this one, he thought, and every one of them would go crazy and run directly into the arms of the catchers.

The woofing locomotive appeared down the track, blasting black swells of smoke accompanied by a guttural sound as though straining over every yard of track. As it drew closer, he could see two day coaches, an open coal car, and two boxcars, one ventilated. To his surprise, they all seemed to be empty. That could be good luck, he thought, working hard to stifle his excitement.

The train slowed as it approached the water tank, its bell ringing. Now at a crawl, it blasted its whistle once more, stopping at the same time as the engine eased to a halt next to the tank. Bev turned his head back to the others, grinning broadly. He waved his hand, and they all took off, Eli first, Billy between him and Joshhumped over carrying Whit on his back.

Bev dashed to the end of the train and raced ahead, staying close in on the sides of the cars. The door on the end boxcar was shut. So was the second, their luck running out. He came abreast of the open freight car and hiked himself up to look over its side, just about five feet high. Empty.

He waved the rest of them to hurry over. Eli sprinted up first and Bev motioned for him to climb inside. Billy followed him up and in, sliding to the bottom. When Josh came up, Bev leaned down to help him with Whit. The ropey muscled black man ignored him and scampered up onto the car side as though Whit didn't exist. Josh swiveled Whit around and gently lowered him like a basket of eggs to the upraised arms of Eli and Billy. Then, he jumped into the car himself, followed by Bev.

Bev signaled for them all to lay low next to the side of the car closest to the tank. He quickly slithered up to the front and peered cautiously over the edge at the water tank.

Two men at the top stood by the spout, which they had maneuvered to the center of the boiler just behind the broad stack of the engine. Water poured into the boiler in the middle, causing steam to rise in a cloud until its temperature had reached a state of equilibrium.

The men on top worried Bev. If they looked this way, they would see them hiding in the open car. He stared at them, ready to yell for everyone to run for it if they were spotted. When the boiler was full, however, the two men pulled on the ropes attached to the overhead block and raised the spout into an upright position. They tied it off and started to climb down the ladder as the engine began building steam.

Bev turned away and allowed himself to slide on his back down the side of the car. They were on a southbound train again without being found out. It would be dark, soon, and cold. Yet,with any luck they would be close to Memphis and the great Mississippi River in a few hours less than a day. Once they got that far, he thought, any slavecatchers or paddy rollers sent out by the Bowmans would be left a long way behind. Then, they'd only have the rest of the bounty hunters   to   worry   about.

Chapter 7. Clarksville

They had been on the train for less than an hour when it pulled into the station at Russellville. Rain began to fall again, and they did their best to pull their clothes close in to try to keep warm. In the dimming light at the depot, they could see that it was a middling size town, probably supported by tobacco and cotton coming in to be sent north by rail. Surprisingly, though, this sleepy little town of maybe a thousand or so residents buzzed with activity. When they heard a band strike up, Bev and Eli stared at each other as strains of soulful music wafted through the night.

"What the hell is that noise?" Whit said.

"Glad to see you back from the dead, Whit," said Bev. He continued over his shoulder as he stood halfway up to sneak a peek, "I don't know what that is, some white folks' song maybe."

"It's Darlin' Nelly Gray," Billy said, "a favorite old tune. Lots of people sing it around where I come from." He started singing softly.

> There's a low green valley on the old Kentucky shore
> there I've whiled many happy hours away
> a sittin' and a singin' by the little cottage door
> where lived my darlin' Nelly Gray.
> Oh, my poor Nelly Gray
> they have taken you away,
> and I'll never see my darlin' any more,
> I'm sittin' by the river and I'm weepin' all the day—

"That's enough—" said Bev,

"That plenty," Eli chimed in.

"—you'll bring every Rebel in these parts down on us."

"What are you talkin' about? There ain't nobody else on this train, you said so yourself. Who' gonna hear me?"

"Them," said Bev in a hoarse whisper. He pointed over the side.

The other four men sidled up the car side to see a host of Confederate soldiers falling in, rifles across their shoulders, facing the train, ready to board.

"M'God, there must be a hundred out there!" Eli rasped.

"More," said Whit.

An officer in a broad-brimmed hat stepped up and yelled an order. The assembled men immediately began to swarm into the two coach cars.

"What if they don't all fit in them coaches?" Eli said.

"Let's hope they do," Bev said solemnly. "If any of 'em come this way, we go over the other side and scatter."

The tide of men slowed as the passenger cars filled up. Slowly but surely, however, they all managed to shove their way inside.

The five fugitive men relaxed. Eli kept watch over the top, reporting quietly whatever he saw.

"A few of 'em in short jackets pryin' open the last car door. They puttin' up a ramp. Now, they pullin' horses up the ramp."

"Officers's rides," said Whit.

"They pullin' up the ramp, shuttin' the door."

The engine expelled steam on either side and uttered a single, large snort. Another followed, repeated in close order as the train lurched forward. The whistle blasted as the train picked up speed at a painfully slow pace. In what seemed like an hour, it finally chugged past the depot and through the small town.

They all slipped down to the floor of the open car, momentarily relieved. Bev brooded, then turned to Billy.

"You know anything about this? About what they doin'?"

Startled, Billy said, "No! They never told us nothin', just 'Get on the train,' 'Get off the train.' They stopped now and then, and more men got on. One time, we was so crowded, men were sittin' on top of the house cars."

Bev nodded at the scrawny redhead. More men, headed south. He looked at Eli, almost asleep from his tiredness. Such a young reed, with smooth, cocoa skin like a woman's. Nothing like his own black elm skin, Bev thought, or his mother's. She'd loved Eli the most despite who his father was. Maybe because he was the youngest, her last baby boy. Now, here he sat, in the middle of hundreds of white men who would kill him as soon as look at him. Bev wondered how many more towns they would pass through, and how many more Graybacks would climb on board to ride the car tops, and discover the runaways in their midst. He shook his head, thinking that he should have left Eli back on the farm. But, Mama would never forgive him wherever she was.

The train rolled along, covering miles quickly. The cars reeled wildly back and forth, scaring them to death. They held on as best they could, filled with dread at the possibility of another derailment.

Someone seemed to be flogging the engineer to push the locomotive to its limit, in a hurry to get somewhere fast.

The rain slowed and stopped, allowing sunrise to spread morning daylight, a bright yellow tint cast over the wet landscape. The cold had not abated, however, and the men in the open car clung shivering together trying to stay warm. The train roared on, and they shared the last of their food and water. Wondering where to find more provisions joined the threat of discovery by the Rebel troops as uppermost concerns in their minds.

"We can't jump off without them cuttin' the speed," Whit said. He mostly had recovered from his injury except for a throbbing headache. "We need another bend in the road to slow us down."

"Either that or stop in another town," replied Bev.

"Or the train could crash again," said Eli.

"No sir," said Whit, "no more of that."

"The train seem to be goin' faster than ever," said Josh.

Bev nodded, mulling things over. "Stoppin' at a town's our best chance. At night, stoppin' at night."

"Day or night, at this point we got no choice," Whitsaid.

Within an hour they slowed, closing in on another town, smaller than the last one. But, the train did not stop, blasting through the one-street burg in less than five minutes.

"Why didn't it stop?" asked Eli.

Bev moved his head back and forth slowly, his mouth flattened tight. "No troops," he said, "not big enough. Don't matter, ain't nowhere near dark. Nighttime is best."

They traveled along for nearly another half hour when they felt the train's speed ease.

Whit looked at Bev and said, "What you think?"

Bev shrugged. "Could be anything."

"Think they'll stop?"

"I don't know. I'd take a gander, exceptin' the brakemen or some of them Rebs might be climbin' about."

"How about him?" Whit said, jerking his thumb in Billy's direction. "He's wearin'gray. If them others are about, they won't think twice about him stickin' his head out."

Billy glanced at them wide eyed.

"I'll stay with him, just below, make sure he don't send a signal to them other white boys." Whit had pulled out his skinning knife and ran his thumb over its edge as he spoke.

Bev hated it when Whit did that sort of stuff, always with the knowing, evil eye. Sometimes he felt liked boxing Whit's ears until he heard bells. But, it wasn't a bad idea.

He turned to Billy, "Go on up and stick your head out, see if you can see somethin'."

"And, no funny stuff," Whit said, still caressing his blade.

"Why me?" Billy said. "They gonna want to know what I'm doin' here. They don't know me, I'm not in their outfit. They gonna think I'm a deserter!"

"You are, boy," said Whit.

Bev shook his head impatiently, "They won't think a thing. If you quick enough, they most likely won't see you. Just stick your head over and take a fast look and get back down."

Billy's face filled with panic.

"Go ahead, now," Bev said, shooing him toward the front of the car.

Reluctantly, Billy made his way to the front end. He carefully worked his way up to the top edge and peered over. The train bucked and the engine spewed a glut of black ash and sparks up and back over the train. Billy shriekedand tumbled back into the well of the car carrying Whit with him.

Billy screamed and screamed, "My eyes, my eyes!" He cried out louder and louder, until Whit backhanded him, saying in rhythm with each blow, "Shut the hell up!"

Grabbing his eyes, his fingers spread like claws around his face, Billy moaned and moaned, twisting and writhing with pain. Whit pulled him up by his shoulders and threw him against the hardwood planks of the car. He raised his eyes to Bev and snapped, "If they didn't know we was here before, they sure do now. Let me cut him," he said, freeing one hand to pull his knife.

Billy struggled furiously, shouting, "No, no, no—oh, oh, oh!" crying out with fear and pain. Whit slammed him down on his back and brought the knife to his throat.

"Hold it!" yelled Bev, lurching forward toward Whit. Whit pulled up and said, "What you doin'? We got to be rid of this no account cracker!"

Bev knocked his arm away, then shoved his chest, sending him back into the side of the car. "Give me the knife." Whit handed it over to him, unsure of what was happening, what Bev meant to do with it. "Josh, hold him down."

Josh flew over and pinned Billy to the floorboards. Bev turned to the side of the car and used the knife to cut a sliver of wood. He held it up and sliced off a long, thin splinter. He motioned to Eli, "Sit on his legs so he can't move. Josh, get his arms down to his side. Now, sit on his chest and hold his head between your hands so it don't move."

Billy redoubled his efforts, bucking and shaking, but Josh held him perfectly still. Bev moved in front of Billy's head as Whit called to him, "We don't have to kill him, Bev, we can just slip him over the side of the car. He probably be okay, we can be done with him, Bev. He gonna bring the whole Confederate army down on us!"

Bev peeled open Billy's right eyelid. "Nothin' there. Lucky boy, Billy." He raised the left lid, and Billy howled. "There it is. You lucky, Billy boy, it's a cinder, just one, that's all, but nasty all the same." He glanced up at Josh and Eli. "Keep him steady, boys." Josh and Eli bore down.

Carefully, deftly, Bev inserted the point of the splinter into Billy's eye just below the cinder. Billy screeched, but couldn't move. Bev gradually moved the splinter point beneath the cinder. Painstakingly, he worked the cinder out of Billy's eye.

"Okay, that's it. You can let him be, now."

Billy lay whimpering on the floor. Bev asked Eli, "We got any water left?"

"Just a cupful," he replied.

"Okay, bring it over here."

Eli left to retrieve the water bag and gave it to Bev. Bev held Billy's head on his thigh and gingerly opened his sore eye. He poured the water onto the red welt, which caused Billy to cry out in pain.

"Jesus, Bev," Whit said, "I tell you, he gonna get us caught!"

"Be quiet, Whit." He dabbed Billy's wounded eye with the edge of the boy's shirt. Then, he tore a strip off its tail and wrapped it diagonally around his head, covering the hurt eye while leaving the good one free to see. "It should feel better in a couple of hours. Eyes heal fast."

Billy groaned, exhausted. He soon fell asleep.

"That's good, white boy, sleep," said Bev quietly.

As he rose, he sensed a change in the train's motion.

"We pickin' up speed again," he said.

Josh nodded, "We goin' faster."

"Huh," said Bev, "guess they backed it off 'cause of a bump in the road."

Billy awoke, his eye pulsing with pain. Still, it felt so much better, he thought. He gazed around to see the other men sprawled close together in the car. Tired, cold, hungry, and thirsty, they coped as best as they could by trying to sleep. Billy was wide awake, alert, and alive. With every throe of agony he had felt, he also was terrified that his screaming would cause Whit to slit his throat or send him tumbling off the train. Instead, they had saved him, using the last of their water to wash out his eye. Billy barely believed such a thing could happen. Yet, here he sat.

The whistle on the old engine blasted, stirring the black men out of their drowsing for a moment. They settled down, and Billy noticed that the train's speed had fallen off again. Screwing up his nerve, he twisted around and lifted himself up to the edge of the car. This time he hung on with one hand and shielded his eyes with the other as he scanned the area out front.

The train crossed a small wooden bridge over a river and braked, this time to enter a town, big, almost a city. Coming into the station, they passed a sign, illegible to Billy. The engine's bell rang, and its chugging slowed to a stop as the train halted. Only the steam blowing out of the sides of the big iron workhorse signaled its recent heavy labor.

Voices called from the day coaches and horns blew. The soldiers inside started evacuating the cars, forming up as best as they could, given the number of them on the station platform. Billy looked back and saw the ramps already positioned on the boxcars, the adjutants ready to guide the horses down. He quickly glanced down into the car. The four runaway slaves stared up at him, petrified. Without a moment's hesitation, Billy hiked himself over the side, climbed down, and took off in a jog on the train platform.

Bev managed to leap to the side of the car just in time to see Billy disappear between two buildings next to the station. Bev pivoted and collapsed down the side of the car.

"Gone," he whispered, "he's gone. Run off."

"Son of a bitch! I knew we should a got rid of him," Whit snapped, staring hard at Bev.

"Maybe so," Bev said, "but it's too late to do anything about it now."

"What are we gonna do?" Eli said in a high voice.

"Don't know," Bev said. "I don't know. We can't move, it's broad daylight. All we can do is sit still for now, hope they don't catch us."

"That all?" Whit said, his words dripping venom.

"You got a better idea? No? Then, shut up and sit down. If we lucky, the train starts moving before ole Billy Reb mouths off to all them other soldier friends of his. We just have to sit still."

"Sit still," Whit said acidly.

Fury flashed across Bev's features. "Boy, if you don't be quiet, I'm gonna beat you to death, never mind gettin' caught!"

Whit tightened his lips and said nothing.

Hours passed. The men sat in silence, their eyes occasionally fearful, but otherwise almost resigned. They heard a commotion, and Josh slid up to take a look. More wood was being loaded into the tender. The engine had cooled off enough for water to be poured into its boiler. The engineer and his fireman returned to the cab, and the brakemen began to walk up and down the track, inspecting each car. They seemed to be preparing to get under way, again. If not, darkness would soon envelop the town, Clarksville, Bev had learned, from a sign on an abandoned baggage cart pushed to one side on the platform. If they could keep out of sight for just a little longer, they could make a run for it.

A bag sailed over the side into the car, making a soft thumping sound. Immediately, Bev and Whit jumped to their feet. His fists balled, Bev stared at the spot where the bag had landed. Whit held his knife low, at belly height. He kept his eyes on the high edge of the car's side where the bag had been thrown, facing away from the station. Whit quickly glanced over to the other side to check if any others were around. He dropped back and joined Bev. The muzzle of a rifle appeared at the top.

The two black men quickly moved up the side of the car, full of menace.

"Hey," Josh said, "they's food in this bag."

Bev and Whit stopped and looked back. A clattering brought their attention to the car's bulwark. Two large canteens bounced together against the wooden wall, suspended by a jangle of canvas straps. A head appeared over the side, covered by a brimmed felt hat.

Whit snapped out, "Hold it, Rebel boy, or I cut your heart out." He waved his knife blade in a ballet beneath the chest of the figure looming above him.

"It's me, Billy. Can you give me a hand with all this?" He threw his other hand over the car, and another two canteens banged against its side.

Whit and Bev exchanged glances, stunned. They helped Billy clamber into the car, careful of the rifle on his back, and gently brought him down to the floor. Just then, the engine barked, and steam hissed. The cars lurched, then again.

"Thanks, that's a help," Billy said, unlimbering the canteens and the rifle. He stretched, then turned and addressed Whit curtly, "Like I said, I ain't no damn Rebel."

Once off the train, Billy headed for a large camp he had seen a few miles back north of the town just before the train pulled in. He crested a small rise and looked out at the crosspatch of tents, lean-tos, and other bivouacs. By their number, he estimated three times as many men assembled here as those that fought at Fishing Creek. He whistled beneath his breath. Something big must be in the wind.

He took a knee and perused the jumble of men, wagons, horses, carts, and mules jockeying for a path to get to where they were supposed to be. Officers shouted back and forth at the foot soldiers and drivers telling them to get the devil out of the way. Some argued with each other, closing in to face off as the heat rose around them. Then, soldiers from their respective units separated them, guiding them away. Over on the far side away from town, smoke billowed out of a makeshift chimney above a large canvas tent. The mess, Billy checked off in his mind. He rotated his view with deliberation, scouring one end of the camp to the other. The hospital tent, he noted. Makeshift stalls for horses. There it was, he thought at last, the quartermaster's depot. Without looking further, he stood up and left the rise to work his way down around the perimeter of the camp. Even so, he hardly could expect to march around alone without some interference.

"Where y'all headed, soldier?" a Captain asked. Sandy hair fell from his campaign cap, blue in color, which might have alarmed some new recruits except for his splendid long gray coat. The Captain cinched his waist tightly with a black leather belt secured by a brass buckle ornamented with the raised letters CSA. As blue as the fabric of his cap, the Captain's eyes twinkled as he waited for Billy to answer.

"Trying to find my outfit, Captain. Lost track of 'em when I got wounded."

The Captain squinted, leaning down to look under the brim of Billy's hat. Seeing the red-stained rag covering one eye, he squinted and said, "What happened to you, son?"

"Cinder, sir, while riding the train here."

The Captain raised up. "That's gotta hurt some."

"It sure did when they dug it out at the hospital tent."

The Captain nodded. "What's your company, soldier?"

"The Fourth Tennessee Cavalry Battalion, Foot Auxiliary."

The captain scratched his beard. "I don't believe I'm familiar with them."

"We just arrived on the train. I hightailed it over to the surgeon for my eye. Now, I'm going back to my unit."

"I see," the captain said. "Well, the new contingents is up closer to town. You seem to be goin' the wrong way. You should be headed back that way," he said, pointing with his gloved hand.

"My mistake, sir. I guess my eye's led me astray."

"Yes, well, take care of yourself, son. Get well and stay outta trouble. We got a big one comin' up and we need every man."

"Yessir," Billy said, saluting.

After the captain returned his salute, Billy started back toward town. He went about fifty yards until he came upon a logjam of two wagons and a cart, the horses pushed close together, making them nervous and unruly. Billy stepped left between two tents as though searching for another route. As soon as he was out of sight, he crouched down and edged his way to the end of the tent. He sneaked a peek down the path and sure enough, the captain stood in the middle, his gaze directly in line with the place where Billy had disappeared.

Billy quickly moved to the other side of the tent, looked down the path next to it. As soon as he had made sure that the captain was nowhere in sight, he scurried across to an opposite row of tents. He would have to be very careful, now, not to run into the blue-eyed officer again. With this in mind, he picked his way back down to the lower end of camp, constantly darting his one good eye around to see if anyone was watching. Finally, he reached his objective, the depot. He stood up straight and walked quickly to the front of the tent and pushed the flaps back to enter.

A dozen men worked in the depot, some with pencils and paper pads inventorying, others hauling various materials to and from different locations in the long, broad pavilion. A sergeant stood at the head of a table made from planks and hobby horses, counting shirts and pants on top. He stood well over six feet, his canvas pants held up beneath an enormous belly by braces and a belt for good measure. His beard came down to the middle of his chest, still spotted with crumbs from his last meal. On top of his crown sat a beat-up old felt hat, full of holes from marauding moths.

"Sir," said Billy trying to get his attention.

"I ain't no sir, boy. What you want?"

"Sir—I mean, Sergeant, I'm sent here by Colonel Dixon of the East Tennessee Calvary Regiment, Foot Auxiliary, for supplies."

"You want supplies? Where yo' requisition order?"

Hellfire, thought Billy. "I lost it on the way, uh, Sergeant. Caught a cinder on the train, and left the order in the hospital tent whilst they dug out my eye."

The sergeant raised his eyes for the first time. He stared at Billy for a second, then dropped his head to the pile of clothing in front of him.

"Well, then, boy, you best toddle on back there and get it. No order, no goods."

"Please, I'm late already. It's ain't a lot, just a few things."

"No order, no nothin'," said the sergeant.

"Sergeant, Colonel Dixon is a jackass and he gonna kill me if I don't bring some stuff back to him quickstep."

The sergeant's eyes snapped back up. He stood still, watching for a while. Then, he said, "What he want?"

"Canteens, four canteens, that's all."

A sneer formed on the big quartermaster's face. After another long wait, he yelled back behind him, "Obadiah, help this boy find some canteens."

A bony man ambled up to the front and jerked his thumb at Billy, "Follow me."

He walked Billy to the back out of the long tent's rear flaps. "Oveh theya," he said, pointing. He turned and stepped back into the tent.

This is good, thought Billy, very good. He raced through the piles and piles of materials until he came upon an enormous stock of canteens.He grabbed four and hung them diagonally over his shoulders, two to a side. Then, he searched for foodstuff. Working his way from one heap to another, he found a good size sack of Johnnie cakes, a slab of salted bacon, dried peas in a bag, and a small jar of molasses. He put them all in an empty flour bag, taking care to cushion the molasses, and hoisted it over his shoulder. Glancing back and forth at the tent flaps and the supply yard, Billy walked stealthily toward a path behind the depot.

He stopped. Stacked in triangles, five rifles each in four rows, twenty in all stood before him. Billy lowered the sack on his back to the ground and moved to the first pyramid of rifles. Brown Besses, he realized, not worth their weight even as clubs. He learned that lesson back in Union town trying to hit something just fifty yards away.

Billy turned back to pick up the sack of food when he saw one against a stack of wood next to the tent flaps. He glided over and picked it up, holding it in both hands, admiring the clean lines of the steel glistening with oil and the burnished wooden stock. He took aim with it; straight as an arrow. Lowering it to his feet, he peered down the barrel and saw the spiral grooves of its rifling disappearing all the way down its length. Without a doubt, he was holding a new Enfield from England. Sergeant Burrow had promised him one back at camp in Union. Now, he had one in his hands.

Billy did a quick search around the logs and found a canvas bag containing a powder flask and some shiny new minié balls. He quickly hung the bag across his chest next to the canteens on his left and slung the Enfield over his right shoulder. He stooped down and picked up the food bag. As soon as he found his balance, he hurried down to the path perpendicular to the depot and walked away.

The trip back to the station seemed to take longer due to his ungainly cargo. But no one stopped him either, maybe thinking that he carried all these things for a purpose. He did, too, he knew exactly what he was doing and where he was going.

Just on the corner of the station fronting the town street, he came to a water pump next to a fountain. Still wearing his most purposeful expression, he unloaded the flour bag, rifle, the powder horn, and the ball box. He took off the four canteens and proceeded to fill each of them at the water pump. Once full, he hung them back over his shoulders, followed by the food bag, ball box, and the rifle.

The added weight of the full canteens created an even greater challenge to maintain his balance. He slowly made his way to the back of the station, careful not to topple over and attract any attention. He managed to traverse the back side of the building without a tumble. When he reached the corner adjacent to the platform, he scanned the area up and down for anyone who might show an interest in his unwieldy load and where he was going. He saw no one, but happened to notice a folded newspaper on an empty bench next to him. After a moment's thought, he stooped down gingerly, taking care not to shift any of the weight on his body, and scooped it up with one hand. He tucked it inside his jacket and continued on toward the train.

The engineer and his fireman suddenly appeared on the far side next to the locomotive. Brakemen emerged from the middle doors of the train depot, wiping crumbs from their mouths as they headed toward the coaches. Seeing them, Billy realized that the train would soon be leaving.

He picked up his pace, swaying dangerously as he worked his way around the back of the cars. On that side, they blocked any view of him from the platform. He hurried past the two cattle cars to the open box car, stopped, took a breath as he leaned the Enfield against it, and slipped the flour bag down to the track bed. He pulled open the drawstrings, took out the molasses jar and gently put it into his tunic. Then, he tied the drawstrings closed and tossed the bag over the side of the car.

Billy unlimbered the canteens from his torso and hung them from his shoulders. He climbed up the coupling and stretched out a foot for the steel wheel, finally reaching the top side of the car. Holding on with one hand, he grabbed the straps of the two canteens dangling from his left shoulder and swung them up over the wooden edge. They clattered against the planks, and he boosted himself up to peer inside. Bev and Whit stood ready to fight, Whit waving his tanning knife menacingly, back and forth.

"It's me, Billy," he said. "Can you give me a hand with all this?" he asked as he threw the other canteens over the side with his right hand.

Billy slipped the jar of molasses out of his tunic and handed it to Josh.

"Molasses!" uttered Josh, "A genuine miracle. The Lord is good. So are you, Billy."

They all sat around, swaying in time to the movement of the cars as the trainaccelerated over the tracks. The light was starting to fade, though they still could see a good deal of countryside around them. Josh passed around Johnnie Cakes with a smear of molasses, courtesy of Whit's tanning knife. Eli followed with two of the water canteens.

Bev took a bite. He chewed and stopped. "Give it back to him, Whit."

Whit frowned, holding his hard cracker in his hands. "Why would I do that?" he asked.

"'Cause it's his."

"So what?" Whit said.

Bev, a sleepy eyed look on his face, said calmly, "Give it back."

Whit scowled, then reached behind himself and pulled out Billy's knapsack and tossed it to him. "Don't get any ideas you part of us now, white boy."

Billy let a tiny smile slip across his face.

Bev stood at the front of the car, looking out. "This train seems empty. I don't see a thing movin', nothin'."

"They didn't put no more soldiers on it," said Billy. "They was all camped back outside of town. Lots of 'em, thousands."

Bev grimaced briefly. "It'd be good to know what they doin' there."

Billy brightened up, "Hey, maybe I got somethin' that'll tell us."

He pulled the newspaper out of his jacket and held it up.

"Why you get that, boy?" Whit sneered, "You can't read."

"No, I can't," Billy said in a formal tone, "but, I believe Bev can. That right, Bev?"

"Lemme see it," Bev said, stepping down on the car bed. He took the paper and opened it up.

"I ain't sure it's today's. I found it on the platform. Maybe it's too old."

"The Clarksville Chronicle," Bev read out loud, "February 7, 1862. Could be today's." He glanced up at the attentive faces circled around him. "It does tell us why the train's empty goin' south." He returned to the paper and read aloud, "'Enemy Forces Overwhelm Fort Henry.' 'Gunboats Reduce Ramparts, 99 Casualties.'" Bev looked up, trailing off with "'Floyd Bolsters Fort Donelson Defense,' 'Vital River Crossings at Risk.'"

He laid the paper down, "That says it. The Yankees have come down south."

The four other men gazed at Bev, utterly surprised. Eli and Josh broke into smiles while Whit simply sat back numb-faced. Billy stared, his mouth curled open. Just then, the train approached an iron trestle bridge above a wide, flowing river, completely brown from the past rain and brimming at the top of its banks.

"This might be the crossin' they worried about."

The train rolled sluggishly over the high bridge just at twilight. In the disappearing light to the west, they saw billows of smoke rising leisurely in the north. Without a word, they watched the plumes join with the darkening sky, even as a small flotilla of gunboats passed through the brown waters below. The men looked down to see on their flagstaffs Union flags gently undulating in an inconsistent breeze.

"Well, that's it," said Bev. They turned around and sat down against the car's wooden bulwark. Josh handed out more food and passed around canteens.

The men ate and drank, rested, and talked.

"You know," Bev said, "this train is empty exceptin' us runaways."

The others smiled at that, including Billy.

"Know what that means?" Bev asked. No one answered, and he went on, "Two things. First, we might see about gettin' inside one of them cattle cars, stay out of the cold and the rain."

Everyone laughed, nodding their heads.

"Second," Bev said, "if they gettin' ready for another big battle, could be no more trains runnin' south past the river. This might be the last one."

"Maybe so," said Whit, "but what if they stop this one down the line to pick up more Graybacks, turn around and go back to fight?"

Bev grimaced, a pained expression quickly crossing his face. "Could be, but it might be quicker to load up trains already headed north. The little towns might not be able to switch the engines around. They could run the engine backwards, but it'd have to move a lot slower, way too slow for any battle. Lord be, we might make it all the way to Memphis without stoppin'! It's only a day or so away."

Whit moved his head up and down thoughtfully.

"We'll keep a look out when the train slows down," Bev continued, "see if any Johnny boys are waitin' in town. If so, we'll jump. But, I'm bettin' we got ourselves a free ride."

The others agreed silently, and Josh climbed up to see if they could get into one of the cars. Sure enough, both were empty, so they gathered everything and crawled up to the top of the boxcar behind them. Keeping low, they scurried along the top of the train to the last house car and slipped inside. Once in, the men scooted together on the floor to keep warm while the train heaved and rolled on.

Chapter 8. The Memphis Stockyards

When Bev and the others recognized this, they held their breath and pulled together their gear, ready to run if discovered. A few tense sentries stood watch at the corners of the platform, but otherwise the station was quiet, with just replenishment of wood and water for the engine the only activity. In fact, the town seemed deserted for the most part, perhaps because of the reports from Fort Henry and Clarksville. In just twenty minutes, the train was underway again.

Once inside a car again, with the temperature outside rising somewhat as well, the men felt relatively comfortable for the first time in days, maybe even weeks. They sprawled on the floorboards, naturally adjusting to bumps in the ride, relaxing finally for a few precious moments from the ever-present stress, the constant fear ofbeing on the run. For the longest time, they simply drowsed, spinning their own thoughts.

Eli spoke softly. "You ever wonder what it gonna be like to be free?"

No one said anything at first. Whit said, "It gonna be great! We can do anything we want to, go anywhere we want, pester any women, make our own money, buy our own things."

"True?" said Eli. "How can we do that? How we gonna make money?"

"We take it, we have to," Whit replied, almost harshly.

"Don't be more a fool than you already are," said Bev quickly. "You do that, you hang for bein' a thief 'stead of a runaway. Why trade one for the other?"

"You don't think they owe us?" Whit snapped back.

"I don't think they gonna give us anything, and they don't need excuses to do any worse to us. So, why give 'em more?"

"Then, what are we gonna do in your free world, Bev? How we gonna get by?"

Bev hesitated, "I don't know yet. Right now, I want to put miles between us and them. Once I'm sure they won't catch us, I'll start thinkin' about gettin' by."

An uneasy lull took hold of them. Again, they retreated to their own thoughts, this time almost begrudgingly. Then, Billy said, "You can always hunt in the hills. Fish, too. We use to plant some crops, though they didn't grow much. Still, we got a few snap peas. We got by."

"Unhuh," Whit said, "that's why you skinny as a skinned squirrel."

Everyone laughed, including Billy. "I can't help it, I eat, still can't keep meat on my bones."

Whit said, "Looks like we won't be eatin' the white boy when we run out of grub," which caused them all to laugh again. "Have to go for the marrow," said Bev, and the laughter continued. "I best start huntin' and fishin' for y'all soon," said Billy, and they joined in again.

The laughter trailed off. They rolled around until they found a more comfortable position. They dozed, half-awakened now and then by a lurch of the train. Only the gradual drop in the train's speed brought them all back to full attention.

Bev sprung up and peeked through the crack of the slightly open side door.

"We're comin' into a town." The train rolled past a sign just in front of the station. "Brownsville," Bev said. "Gather our things," he said, "be ready to roll."

He saw bales of cotton piled high on the platform, and more stacked on the side of the depot. He wondered if the train would stop, if their brothers would be hoisting the cotton up into the cars, men unable to run with all the overseers and paddy rollersand their dogs strolling around.Maybe they should jump now, he thought. But they surely would be rounded up if they did.

The train did not stop, instead pacing quicker once it had cleared the station, passing one massive mansion after another, each fronted by elaborately fashioned, wrought-iron fences. A small town, Bev observed, yet still full of wealthy cotton raisers and dealers. Different from Kentucky, a place that bundled as much tobacco and hemp as the great cotton kings. More proof that they traveled further south than west at this point.

The fact that the train pushed hard ahead relieved him. As soon as it hit top velocity, signified by further creaking and bumping, he dropped to the floor again. As he had hoped, the train hadn't stopped, and maybe it wouldn't again before it traveled all the way to Memphis. Then, they would have to figure out when to leave the train, and what to do next.

Mary Louise Smalls mucked out the bull stalls at the Memphis stockyards every day, no matter what weather. In the summer, great beads of sweat blossomed around her forehead, coursing down her face like a mountain spring barely glazing an outcropping of black mica. In the winter, she layered every piece of tattered cloth she could find on her to keep the chill, wet air from freezing her. Just two blocks off of the Big River, plantation-owner Jacob Burkle handled all livestock passing in and out of Memphis. To do so, he employed scores of slaves, some he owned, others contracted out by planters in the off season. Mary Louise had come to Burkle from Davies Manor, before that the Smalls plantation where she had been born. On the Smalls place, at age five her morning started with collecting eggs from the chicken coop. She did her best to nestle them into the basket, but it was so big and she was so tiny that accidents happened. For every egg she broke, Master Smalls gave her a lash. By the time she was eleven, she carried a filigree of scars on her back that would never go away. When she was eleven, Master Smalls started bothering her. Every Sunday after services, he would take her to his office for a special lesson on the Bible. He covered her there, and sent her back to the cabins. During the week, she picked cotton.

Mary Louise hated Master Smalls and what he did to her on Sundays, but there was nothing she could do. Her only consolation came from the farm animals, innocents in her mind. She loved them all—ducks, chickens, sheep, pigs, even goats, stubborn and ornery as they were. All of them were cute when newborn, but she even liked all of the grown critters, even steers and horses. She had a way with them, too, which the overseer, Everett Dubois noticed. He suggested to Master Smalls that she could be put to good use taking care of them, more useful to the plantation than the little bit of cotton she managed to gather in a day. Master Smalls agreed, which sent her spirits soaring, until the following Sunday. But, that Sunday turned out to be different, too.

Mistress Smalls had been appointed the head of the Memphis Christian Women's Guild in charge of the annual drive for charitable contributions to the city's impoverished and unclothed. The Mistress conducted several meetings about the campaign, but of course, she found them difficult to schedule due to the distances between the many big houses. As a bridge to continuity, she turned to letter writing in which she summarized the decisions made during the last meeting, including designated tasks and proposed dates for the next face-to-face gatherings. She had posted the vast majority in the past week, but ran out of stamps to send the final few. Determined to have them in the mail on Monday, Mistress Smalls made her way to

Master Smalls's office to appropriate postal stamps that Sunday. That Sunday, she knocked on the closed door and without waiting for a response, walked in to find Master Smalls mauling Mary Louise spread-eagle on his desk.

On Monday, Master Smalls contracted with the Davies for Mary Louise to work on the Manor. At first, the Davies sent her into the fields to work the cotton, where she again proved to be a significant disappointment. However, the Smalls overseer Dubois spoke to his Davies counterpart about her ability with animals, and soon she found herself working in the barn and paddocks.

She missed Smalls to some extent, especially her mama, who cried and cried when her little girl was sent off. She missed some of the other folks there, too, even Mr. Dubois, who was a mostly decent overseer, except when he had to mete out punishment. Then, as wicked as any paddy roller, he laid in into her as he would any slave said to be out of line. She didn't miss Sundays at the Smalls. To her surprise, the Davies and their overseer left her alone as long as she did her work. She felt lonely at the Davies Manor plantation, but otherwise better off than at the Smalls.

At the age of sixteen, she met John Tunney at the local slaves'sChristmas celebration. Tall, lithe, and cocoa black like other folks from the islands, he offered her a sweet smile that disguised surprising shyness in such a formidable man. A drover at the Kildare farm, he too enjoyed the company of animals. He asked her to dance, and they did for the rest of the night. The following Sunday he appeared after hours, given permission to see her. After a goodly amount of time, he asked for her hand, and one Sunday they jumped over the broom. Embracing her in his arms felt like being on the other side of the world from Sundays with Master Smalls.

After a year, Mary Louise birthed a beautiful girl child whom they named Ruth. She nursed her and loved her more than any being in the world, and the Smalls came and took her away. When John heard, he ran off to steal baby Ruth back. The paddy rollers caught him quick, lashed him into unconsciousness, and with the Kildares' go-ahead, sent him to the Memphis slave market. He was bought by a Louisiana planter who took him and four others down on a riverboat to work sugar cane. Mary Louise never saw him again.

She cared for the animals as carefully as usual, but seldom said a word to anyone. The Davies saw her as sullen and unanimated, which upset their model of a closely knit village of people, masters, and slaves, dedicated to creating and maintaining a thriving farming enterprise. In time, her dour mood moved them to send her back to the Smalls, who did not want her. So, they approached the strange German stockyard and bakery owner, Jacob Burkle, who took one look at her, grunted, and in a thick guttural said he would take her, but only at a lower rate.

Mary Louise walked ten miles to the Burkle place and immediately found herself mucking out the mule stalls, scores of them. When darkness fell, she and a half dozen other slaves marched up the hill toward Burkle Manor, a single-story clapboard house with a few half-grown maples in front. The slave quarters were lower on the hill on either side. Four men slogged to the left, the women to the right. Mary Louise followed them, and the oldest, a tall, sturdy middle-age woman named Rachel, turned to her and with cool eyes said, "You get the corner near the door. You'll be sweeping the floor and washing the dishes after dinner."

Mary Louise said nothing. She dropped her burlap bag carrying her few belongings on top of a tick mattress and some blankets near the door. Without a word, she sat down and ate, a good hunk of black bread with some soup, all washed down with a cup of water. Taking a spoonful of the soup, her eyes widened.

"This is good! What kinda soup is this?" she asked.

"Oxtail," another girl said, young and willowy with light almond-shaped eyes. "Old man Burkle brung it with him when he first get here long time ago."

"It's that old?" asked Mary Louise ingenuously, and the others laughed.

"Naw, girl, he brung the recipe, not the soup! You funny!" she said. Alice was her name. Mary Louise dropped her head without saying anything, a little smile passing across her face.

After they all finished eating, Rachel and Alice stood up. Rachel said, "It's time for prayer service at the big house."

Prayer service. At the big house. Mary Louise shifted a bit on her stool.

"You stay here and clean up," said Rachel. "When you finish, go to the men's cabin and clean up after them. Then, come back and go to bed."

"You be back?" Mary Louise asked.

"That's none of you business. Just do as I say."

As the two women were leaving the cabin, Alice whispered, "It don't matter. You new. You work hard and show the right spirit, you be comin' to prayer service soon enough."

They went out the door, Mary Louise watching them join the men. They hiked up the hill and knocked on the door. The door opened, they entered, and it closed behind them.

Mary Louise sighed, and began cleaning up. She carried the wooden bowls and spoons out to a big tub next to a water pump. On the edge of the tub she found a big bar of soap and an old sponge. She placed the dirty dishes into the tub, then walked to the men's cabin to fetch theirs. The cabin looked pretty much the same as the women's, a low porch in front with two plain benches and a roof covered with wood shingles to keep out the rain. Behind each cabin she saw a wooden outhouse with a quarter moon carved into the door.

Inside, she inventoried a few slat chairs and a plank table, a potbelly stove, burlap curtains on the windows with shutters to cut the winter wind. She saw some candles on a makeshift mantle near the stove. A picture of the Lord Jesus hung above another shelf stacked with dishes on the back wall. The men's mattresses and blankets lay spread out on the floor, with just a narrow passage left to get around the room. The women rolled theirs up during the day, unfolding them only when going to bed for the night. The other difference she noticed were long scythes stacked in the back corner of the men's cabin. The women's had a just few hand sickles hanging from hooks, some brooms in a corner, and a spinning wheel.

After finishing her chores, she made a trip to the outhouse, washed her hands and face at the pump, and took herself to bed inside. She found it hard to sleep, though, in a new place. She tossed and turned for hours it seemed, drowsing now and then, yet easily awakened by the slightest noises. Near morning, the return of Rachel and Alice stirred her again.

Their late return surprised Mary Louise. How long could they sleep before Burkle or his overseer rousted them? Even as she wondered, a voice called out harshly for them to rise and report for work. Grabbing a crust of dark brown bread as she went out the cabin door, Mary Louise followed the command to head directly to the stockyards. Rachel and Alice hurried close on her heels out of the cabin, then headed in the opposite direction toward the big house. By day's end, they reconvened in the cabin, exhausted, with dinner waiting to be made.

Alice chopped, Rachel cooked, and Mary Louise delivered the meal to the men. The women then ate, and Mary Louise cleaned up while her companions left for services. Again, they returned in the small hours of the morning, looking more worn out with every passing day. What was going on? Mary Louise wondered.

On Sunday, Mary Louise woke up to light pouring through the window between the gingham curtains. Someone outside pounded on a steel ring with a hammer, the call to Sunday prayer meeting. Mary Louise felt hollow inside from fatigue. She couldn't imagine how done in Rachel and Alice must feel, groggily pulling themselves out of deep sleep and up from their bedclothes.

They dressed in their cleanest, whitest dresses and went outside to wash their faces, necks, and arms at the pump. The men did the same at a trough close to their quarters. They joined together and walked down the hill to a large magnolia looming over a half-circle of wooden benches. Facing them at a makeshift wooden lectern, Master Burkle stood waiting.

He wore a tweed suit, a pristine white shirt, and a lavish purple bowtie. Big suspenders curved over his substantial stomach hiking up his pants above his high-tied shoes. His hair had been slicked back, and his beard trimmed and combed. Set beneath wild thatched eyebrows, his piercing blue eyes startled Mary Louise with their intensity. Sitting on wooden chairs on either side behind him were his wife and two daughters, and the overseer William Stewart, all wearing fine Sunday clothes.

Burkle spoke in a thick German accent, "Willkommen, children, Gott bless you all. Ve vill pray."

And they prayed, for two hours. Burkle launched into a long sermon, almost unintelligible due to his accent. He talked something about angels of mercy and the path to heaven, as far as Mary Louise could tell. As he ended, he thanked them all for coming.

Mistress Burkle, a tall, angular woman with dingy brown hair and freckled skin stood and invited everyone to lunch under the magnolia below. They all made their way down to several tables and benches covered with fresh bread, butter, fruit, hard-boiled eggs, and thick cuts of bacon. As they ate, the two Burkle daughters carried pitchers of buttermilk from table to table, filling tin cups that quickly sweated streams of chilled moisture.

The slaves ate with unrestrained relish, and Mary Louise realized that this was not right. What owners treated their slaves so lavishly, even on Sundays unless it was Christmas? She recognized from their ardent manner during the meeting that the Burkles were very devout. And why wouldn't they be, considering their lives compared to that of their property? But, masters and mistresses treating slaves like guests on a regular basis? Mary Louise knew that something was wrong.

After the lunch, both the men and women returned to their quarters and slept until nightfall. In the evening, they ate lightly and performed a few personal tasks, mending and washing clothes, tending to the vegetable garden, whittling, smoking, and singing Gospel. At midnight, they went back to bed.

Lying beneath her blanket, her arms folded under her head, Mary Louise marveled at the personal time wasted sleeping on their only day off.

Days passed, a week, a month. She did her work, cleaned up after dinner, and went to bed. Before long, she slept through the early morning returns of Rachel and Alice. At the same time, curiosity ate at her every day, growing more intolerable as every day went by. Finally, she could ignore the abnormal no longer.

Her chance came when Rachel was called back to the big house one Sunday afternoon. As soon as she left, Mary Louise cornered Alice by the pump.

"Alice, what goin' on in this here place?"

"What you mean, Mary Louise? Everything goin' on as usual."

Mary Louise noted that Alice looked wary and guilty after her answer.

"Everything as usual? Work all day, pray all night, sleep never? That usual?"

Alice started to squirm uncomfortably. "We sleep, on Sundays."

"That ain't enough! Y'all look like a litter of dead cats! You never got time to do what you want—your precious time on your only day off. Why does Master Burkle have all these prayer sessions anyway?"

"He religious," Alice stammered, "he believe in God, praise Jesus!"

"That ain't enough!" barked Mary Louise. Lower, she said, "Tell me, Alice. Tell me what goin' on up there when you pray so much."

Alice searched around frantically for something to do, someplace else to be. "I can't," she said plaintively.

"You can and you will, or I start askin' Rachel, tell her that you led me to it."

"No!"

"I will, Alice, I swear on Baby Jesus I will, unless you tell her first."

Panicked, Alice's eyes darted everywhere for an escape.

102

"On Baby Jesus, I swear!" shrilled Mary Louise.

"Don't you be swearin' on the Baby Jesus!" Alice cried out. "We all go to hellfire, you do that!" She covered her mouth just for saying the evil thing.

"Then, go tell Rachel this night."

Looking miserable, Alice shook her head yes.

Rachel came over to Mary Louise immediately after talking with Alice.

"How'd you come here, Mary Louise?" she asked forcefully. "Tell me you story."

They stood under an oak tree in front of the cabins, pretending to beat some braided rag rugs against its trunk.

"I came here from the Smalls plantation. They beat me and old man Smalls bother me until the mistress catch us. They sent me to Davies where I got married. My baby girl was born and the Smalls took her as theirs. When my man try to stop them, they lashed him a hundred times, cut off his ears, and sold him to work sugar cane deep down south. Master Burkle took me because no one else would."

Rachel stared at her with slit eyes. She pressed her lips together, weighing her options. "So, you don't love the southern gentlemen too much?"

Fury filled Mary Louise's face, but her words seemed calm. "I do not. I hate 'em, pretty much all of 'em all the time."

Rachel nodded her head. "Awright. We talk again on Tuesday.

On Monday, everything proceeded as usual. On Tuesday, the day unfolded routinely until dinner. After they had eaten, Mary Louise rose to do her chores when Rachel said, "Wait. Leave them be and come with us."

The three women started up the small rise to the big house, hardly typical of the broad, two-story manses favored by the landed gentry of the South. The Burkle home stood just one story high with a low profile, no steps or wraparound porches. To reach the modest single front door, visitors ascended two wooden steps, opened a screen door, and knocked on white-painted planks.

When Rachel reached the door, however, it swung open, held by Master Burkle himself.

"Enter, ladies, always gudt to see you."

They passed under his arm into a long, dark pine paneled hallway that ran to the far end of the house. Burkle nodded at Rachel and Alice, who walked all the way back toward the kitchen. When Mary

Louise made to follow, Burkle raised his hand, "Vait, young lady. Please come vit me first."

She trailed him into a sitting room immediately to the left of the front door. Inside, she noticed two French loveseats facing each other on a far Eastern rug, exquisite wooden side furniture, brass kerosene lamps topped by fabric, tasseled shades in the corners, and a stunning, carved mahogany fireplace standing at least six feet high.Burkle gestured for her to sit down on one of the loveseats. In just her plain linen skirt, she felt extremely awkward, hoping fiercely that no dirt would be left behind when she arose.

Burkle sat opposite her, and said, "Tea? Lemonade?"

Solemnly, Mary Louise gave an almost imperceptible nod of her head. She began to stand to go fetch the refreshments from the kitchen, when Lydia Burkle stepped in with a tray of both. She placed it on a small table between the loveseats, smiled broadly at Mary Louise, and left.

Burkle poured out a glass of lemonade and a cup of tea for himself. They both took a sip, and when the master lowered his cup back down on the tray, Mary Louise matched his action with her glass.

He sat back. "Mary Louise Smalls, moved around from one farm to another, finally deposited here."

She listened without moving, without expression.

"You are told to have caused some consternation by your former employers," he went on, "all happy to see you go avay."

Avay. She drew back her head slightly. What had happened to the rest of his German accent?

"Beaten relentlessly as a child, you married only to see your own little girl taken from you, your husband savagely whipped and unceremoniously sent off to toil to death in the sugar cane."

She remained still.

"Do you hate white people, Mary Louise?"

She said nothing.

"I do," Burkle said. He paused, his eyes down as he reached for his tea. "At least, I hate what many of them do. God doesn't allow men to hate other men and have them expect to reach heaven."

He lifted his eyes to hers and said, "I came to this country in 1849, vhen our war for independence in Germany collapsed, back before you were born, I believe. For freedom, I came here, to pray to God in my own way, only to find a deeper abomination occurring in this, the land of liberty, freedom." He shook his head, "I prospered, but I could not live properly, contentedly. As long as these horrors went on and I did nothing, I was not enriched."

Slowly, Mary Louise felt a strange sensation creeping into her.

"So, I left Stuttgart, Arkansas—a German city in America, funny no?" he said, laughing broadly. "Anyway, I moved to Memphis in 1856 and bought the stockyards. I also started a bakery—mygrandfather baked bread," he smiled. "I own many slaves and buy many slaves. How do you feel about that, Mary Louise?"

She did not answer.

"Mary Louise?"

"I feel nothin'," she said.

He sat back. "Of course you don't. You despise me, of course. I despise me, or I would. Except for one thing."

Burkle stood up and beckoned her to follow him. They walked all the way back to the kitchen at the end of the long hall, passing Rachel and Alice, who started, startled by their appearance. Burkle led Mary Louise to a door secured by a padlock. He unlocked it with a key in his vest pocket and opened the door to a stairway leading downward. He ushered Mary Louise before him and they descended below.

Halfway down the stairway Mary Louise stopped, stunned by what she saw. In the basement, at least twenty black people stood, sat, or lay reclining in various places on the floor. The three slaves who lived next to her cabin stooped whispering in earnest conversation with the others, obviously slaves, too. Shelves all along the walls hung full of provisions, water bags, blankets, candles, and other sundries. Two massive wooden doors reinforced by iron bands stood at either end of the broad cellar. Taking all of it in at once, Mary Louise didn't notice that the quiet activity had come to a halt; all eyes were on her and Jacob Burkle.

"That's fine, brothers and sisters," Burkle said softly. "Go on with your business."

He motioned for Mary Louise to follow him. They walked a different way to another door, which led to a set of stairs near the front of the house. After climbing them, Burkle pushed up on the ceiling planks. Joined together as a door, it turned out to be part of the floor in an alcove next to the parlor. Burkle stepped up first and held it open for Mary Louise. When she emerged, he lowered the door and pulled a rug over top of it. Then, he went into the parlor and sat down in front of the table again. He took a sip of his tea, now lukewarm, she imagined. She sat down across from him and waited quietly.

"So," he said, "now you know. I do buy slaves, many, and many of them disappear. I am enraged, of course, but somehow they are never caught. Now, you know why."

He sat silently, waiting. She gazed at him wide-eyed, not knowing what to say or do next.

"You, too, can disappear, Mary Louise Smalls, if you like. I can buy you, and somehow lose track of you. I am proven very careless that vay."

Emotion flooded through her, nearly sweeping her away.

"You see, you have me at your mercy. Now that you know, you could take this to the authorities. They would hang me, and I don't know what they might do to my family. Throw them out on the street, anyway. But, you, they might reward with your manumission papers. Or, they might just send you to some other plantation to work. For me, I cannot take a chance. Faced with the former possibility, I would have no choice but to escort you out one of those doors downstairs to freedom."

He paused, then said, "Or, you could stay here, working in the stockyards all day for no pay. And, also for no pay, every night you could help other enslaved Christian brothers and sisters escape. Either way, Miss Mary Louise, sooner or later, one way or another, you will be free."

That all occurred two years ago, she remembered. Once she decided, Jacob Burkle immediately offered to buy her from the Smalls due to her excellent ability with livestock. He tried to buy her child, too, but she was gone, sold at age six by the Smalls to an itinerant slaver on the Memphis slave block. In her sorrowful memory, Mary Louise helped usher scores of slaves out of the iron-cased doors through tunnels that led to the Gayoso Bayou. There, they hid low in boats that took them out to the Mississippi and on up to other friendly stopping places, Ohio and Illinois, all on their way to Canada and free lives.

She relished doing it, every bittersweet taste of it. The Burkles realized that her quick mind and steel will armed her perfectly to captain the entire operation. Rachel, Alice, and the other conductors soon looked at her with undisguised awe. Her successes and expansion of their enterprise embellished her own confidence. Mary Louise almost felt that she could do anything. No challenge seemed too great.

Until she watched a scrawny Johnny Reb coming up the road between the magnolias towing a slave by a rope around his neck. What could all this be about?

Chapter 9. Lighting Out

Hopping off the train turned out to be little trouble for the men. The engineer slowed it down for another water tank just outside of Memphis, and the men slipped out of the cattle car on the opposite side as planned. They melted into the pines surrounding the track and waited until the big stack gradually powered its way down toward the city.

The winter chill had returned, though not as bad as the long day they spent in the open car. Once the train passed, Eli scaled the water tower and replenished their canteens. He dropped each of them down to Josh, who handed them out to Whit, Billy, and Bev. Eli quickly scampered down the tower, and the troupe moved into a grove of pines to eat and plan.

"We have to figure out how to get around Memphis and how to cross the Big River," Bev said.

"We could wait until night," Whit suggested, "work our way around then."

"Still, how we gonna cross the river?"

"Steal a boat, make a raft," said Eli.

Bev shook his head, "Too many chances to get caught. Buildin' a raft'd take too long, and we out there, sittin' on it, four black men on the loose. Who wouldn't put a halt to that?"

They fell silent in thought, chewing on the last of the dried peas and bacon. After a time, it was Josh who spoke.

"They's people in this town who help us," he said quietly.

The others looked at him in surprise. "Who?" said Whit. "How you know that?"

In a whisper, Josh said, "People back on the farm tell me. People runnin' to the river come here, folks help 'em out, white folks. Get 'em to the river, hide 'em in boats, move 'em up north to meet others who do the same. Go all the way to Canada."

"What you talkin' about, boy?" Whit snapped. "Ain't no white people on earth gonna help four niggers run away."

Josh flinched. "I know it true. Lots a folks know it, tells us with magic—whirls and swirls. They show the way. That why I come here with you all."

"You so full of—" Whit snapped.

"Hold on, Whit, hold it," Bev said, pressing his hand down in front of him to keep the noise down. Then, he said to Josh, "If this is true, old man, how do we know them white folk who help us? How we find that out?"

"Whirls and swirls," Josh said, almost in a sing-song.

"Whirls and swirls," mocked Whit, "my ass!"

Bev turned his palms up in the air. "I don't know what you're sayin' Josh. I don't know how we can find these folk."

Again, they all became quiet.

Billy said, "We could reconnoiter."

Everyone turned their attention to him, then to Bev.

"Scout," said Bev.

Whit looked back at Billy and said disdainfully, "What that, one of them army words?"

Billy shrugged sheepishly. He went on. "We could go down, see if Josh finds them whirls and swirls and such."

"Now, how we gonna do that? The slavecatchers be all over us before we put one foot down in Memphis."

Again, they all lapsed into thought. Then, Bev said, "Not if we's already caught." Once more puzzled, they waited for Bev to explain. "Who gonna pay any attention to us if we led into town on a rope by a Grayback?"

The men seemed confounded. Whit pointed at Billy, "Him? Who gonna believe that scrawny cracker caught all of us? Why, we stretch him with his own rope first! Anyway, I ain't gonna take my chance with him in front. What you thinkin', Bev?"

Bev rubbed his beard. "You right. Billy too small to hold onto all of us."

"I could take one," Billy said. "Old Josh. He know the whirls and swirls. We could look around for some, come back if we find any."

Josh nodded up and down, "That right, I know 'em when I see 'em. We find 'em, come back for y'all at night. People help us get to the Big River."

Bev's face scrunched up as if in pain. "Seem like a long shot, Josh. Maybe we better off just findin' our own way."

Josh shook his head vigorously back and forth, "No, no, folks will help us! I know!"

"But, what if they get stopped?" Eli asked, flicking his head at Josh and Billy.

After a short pause, Billy said, "I say I'm takin' Josh to town to sell him."

They stared at Billy in disgust. Gradually, though, the idea took hold.

"They won't pay much attention, Josh so old," said Eli.

Abruptly, they all laughed, including Josh. Whit said, "That right, Josh, you ain't gonna bring much at market," and they laughed again.

Bev said, "That okay, make it more likely this poor white boy sellin' the last of the family Negros to get through the winter. That's the story. I like it."

They didn't have any rope with them, so they fashioned one out of the drawstrings on their sacks. Woven together, the makeshift rope looked all right as long as it wasn't given a close look. After eyeing them up and down once more, Bev leaned in and whispered into Josh's ear, "You don't have to do this. We can work our way around, find the river ourselves."

Josh looked directly into Bev's eyes and said, "It worth a try. If we lucky, it make it better for us. If not, y'all can still search out the river youselfs."

Bev nodded. He stepped close to Billy and said in a low voice, "Don't get jumpy, now. Stay out the way of other whites, but don't look like you tryin' to stay away. They ask you, tell 'em they can come to the market tomorrow, you lookin' for a place to bed down for the night. If they ask where your unit is, you on leave."

Billy whipped his head up and down quickly, his eyes wide open with attention.

"Awright, then. Get back here tomorrow at twilight. We movin' tomorrow night one way or other."

Memphis was a big, stinking town, thought Billy. The sight of all those tall, brick buildings looming everywhere overhead scared him, causing his throat to tighten with a lump of anxiety. How was he supposed to find anybody in this confounding pile of rocks? He pressed his lips together while holding his nostrils closed from the stench, and gave the tether a yank.

"Hey!" Josh said.

Billy quickly said, "Sorry, Josh. I just don't know where to go first."

Josh said, "We got to find some place where they got the whirls up where people can see 'em."

"Yeah, but where's that?"

They wandered some more, up and down one street after another, sometimes passing by huge mansions with castle-like towers and white latticed porches at the end of tree-lined carriageways. They also walked by great stone structures with ornate molding at the top broken by busts of important looking men, maybe ancient gods. The more they walked, the more confused and demoralized Billy felt. He glanced behind at Josh, who seemed unaffected by the daunting magnitude of a real city, a place that could eat them up altogether.

"You lost, boy?"

Billy whipped his eyes back in front. A big burly man wearing a large beaver hat and a thick woolen coat open at the front stood opposite them on the street. He had one thumb stuck in his belt, and the other hand resting on the butt of a large revolver in a holster on his left. His belly stuck out above the belt. His face was covered with mutton chop whiskers, and his nose shone a vivid red, probably from drinking, Billy thought.

"No sir," Billy stammered, "I am not lost. I'm takin' my Negro here to market to sell him."

"Well, y'all look lost, boy. That nigger looks all used up, too. Anyway, which market you talkin' about? Memphis has fo' markets fo' tradin' slaves."

Billy hesitated, scratching his chin. "I don't rightly know. The closest one, I guess. I'm in a hurry, I'm on furlough 'til I can sell him and get the money back to my pap."

The mutton-chopped man lifted his head a bit, towering even higher over Billy. "That so? I'm surprised they let you go now, with everythin' that's happenin' and all. That blue devil Grant and his boys are makin' life mighty hard fo' the folks up around Clarksville. The mayor has called up all local militia to defend the city. What outfit you with, boy?"

"I'm from the East Tennessee Cavalry Regiment, Auxiliaries. Colonel Dixon gave me special leave because my mama and baby sister died of the fever. My pappy's sick, too, and we ain't got a corncob left to chew. Here, want to see the picture of my dead mama and sister?"

Billy reached into his knapsack and started to pull out the photograph, but the large man in front of him held out his arm to stop him. "Fever you say? That awright, I unnerstan' now, son. I believe you. Best you be on your way, get that nigger sold, n' take the money lickety-split back to yo' daddy. The nearest slave market is down that street right theye, then left on the next street, just off Second near the train station. That'll be Auction Street, you cain't miss it. Second and Auction, son, be on yo' way and good luck to y'all."

Billy flashed a grin and pulled on the tether. Josh and he quickly walked up the street, turned right on Main, and started looking for ways out. Before they knew it, though, they had reached the square with a large stone slab situated in front of an open, brick building. All manner of black people huddled outside the building, while a line of young men waited to take their turn up on the slab. A sinewy, young man stood at the top, stripped to a loin cloth, his legs a patchwork of crisscrossed welts and scars. The auctioneer had him turn around to show his otherwise sound body, calling out what a fine field hand he was. Below the line of men next to the slab sat women and children, waiting their turns to be sold. The children seemed oblivious to the strange goings-on about them. The women held the youngest of them closely, cloaking behind blank expressionsimmeasurable feelings of anguish and heartbreak.

He stared at them, open-mouthed, stunned. Never in his life had he seen so many black people, such utterly hopeless, miserable people. The preachers was right, he thought.

"Billy," Josh whispered, "we got to move."

Billy shook himself out of his reverie and said, "Yeah—where?"

"Outta here somewhere!" urged Josh quietly.

"Okay," Billy said. He saw a large, long building past the marketplace next to the slave block that displayed foodstuffs also for sale. The long brick building looked to be flanked by several sets of rails. The train station, Billy recognized. His attention soon shifted, however, to the scores and scores of gray and butternut clad men lounging around the shaded platform.

"M'god, Josh, look it all them Rebel boys. What'll we do now?"

"Work around 'em," Josh said, "down that alley on our right, up the next street, and out the city."

Billy nodded, and they started up the block. They came to the alley, which looked to run all the way through to the next street. Peering out from a building corner, Billy saw behind them a half dozen Confederate soldiers lounging beneath a giant magnolia covering another smaller town square. He turned and pointed in the opposite direction. They slipped out of the alley and,without running,hurried as fast as they could up the street beneath the gallery.

They kept a quick pace for several blocks, leaving the large city buildings behind and fewer and fewer of the showcase residences. As they moved, the city opened up, farmhouses replacing town

112

dwellings, with more cropland and evidence of livestock. At length, they came upon a one-story house on a rise shaded by three sprawling magnolia trees and two young oaks higher up on the slope.. In the middle of the trees, they saw slave cabins. A road led down from the hill on the far left past other cabins and outbuildings, crossing the main street and disappearing down below the slope. They saw truck gardens, livestock pens, and plenty of chickens and ducks ranging over the entire farm.

"This is more like it," Billy said. "Let's keep goin'."

He turned to continue on the road when Josh said, "Wait!"

Josh slipped off the tether around his neck and dashed up the hill toward the slave quarters just below the house.

"Josh!" Billy hissed loudly, "where you goin'? You gonna get us found out!" He scrambled after Josh, who veered right of the nearest cabin. Once next to it, he stopped.

Billy came up to him, whispering madly, "You crazy, we'all gonna get killed, maybe hung!"

"Look," said Josh, pointing to the side of the cabin. Billy looked, and saw a clothesline running from the cabin to an old pine tree about thirty feet away. He saw a bunch of linen quilts hanging from the line, dead still in the windless cold. Taking in a rug beater leaning against the pine, Billy said, "It's quilts. They cleanin' 'em is all. Let's go."

"This time of year, why ain't the quilts inside on the beds?"

Billy glanced at Josh, then back at the quilts. They were wet and dirty, the middle ones almost drooping to the ground as though they had been hanging for a long time. "That is strange," said Billy.

Josh approached the quilts and grabbed one by its edge to hold it closer. "Looky this," he said. Billy came up and squinted his eyes at the piece Josh held out. "Whirls," said Josh, "lots of whirls. Whirls and swirls," he said quietly, almost solemnly.

The black woman stared at them with unveiled hostility, one hand on a hip. Short, Billy noticed, shorter than himself even, by maybe three inches. Skinny, too, he thought, though her upper womanly parts filled out the canvas apron she wore over her brown gingham dress. Not very scary in size, she still scared the daylights out of him.

"Can I help you?" she asked, coldly. "If you want water, the pump's right there."

"No, ma'm, I'm just on my way to take my Negro here to the—" said Billy starting in on his story. Josh cut him off.

"You got swirls here in yo' quilts. I know what they mean," he said, urgency filling his voice.

Mary Louise froze. She glanced back and forth from the Grayback and his coal-black slave, thinking to herself, now what? She began again.

"Most likely you hungry. I can put somethin' on the table."

"Ma'm," Josh said, "I know what them marks are, but I don't know what they say. Please help us, show us the way."

Mary Louise's expression hardened again. She looked directly at Josh, her voice all flint, "What yo' doin' with this Johnny Reb? You crazy? How you supposed to get anywhere with him?"

"He not a Johnny Reb, he a good man, helped us get away more 'n one time. He is righteous before the Lord's eyes!"

Mary Louise turned her attention to Billy and said scathingly, "If you not a Grayback, why you wearin' a Grayback jacket?"

Imploringly, Billy said, "I ain't a Grayback, I'm from east Tennessee! The preachers learned us slavery is wrong. But, them Rebs grabbed me up anyway, stuck me in their army and their darn Rebel skins. I hate 'em, so I run. I fell in with this boy and his friends, now we all runnin' together."

She didn't know whether to believe them or not. The Rebel lovers in Memphis suspected that Mr. Burkle was freeing slaves, they'd been all over his house more than once. Maybe this was another one of their devilish tricks. This shiny black man might be getting a nice reward out of this, maybe even freedom. How terrible would that be, selling out his own people? At the same time, Mary Louise understood it somewhat, what any slave might do to get free.

She sighed. "Wait here."

In ten minutes, she returned with a tall, red-bearded man behind her, puffing on a pipe held in one hand, his other hand's thumb thrust into his belt. He wore a big, straw hat with a wide brim, almost like my old one, Billy thought. The tall man spoke.

"I am Jacob Burkle, proprietor of dese premises. You are?"

"Billy McKinney, late of the East Tennessee Cavalry Regiment, Auxiliaries, 'til I quit."

"And, vhere are you from?"

"Maryville, Tennessee, in Blount County. Actually, my daddy and me live in the foothills of the Three Sisters, south of Maryville."

Burkle then turned to Josh. "And, your name? Your home?"

114

"They call me Old Josh. Don't know my last name. I come from Bowman Farm just down from Nancy, Kentucky. I don't know where I was born."

Burkle nodded, and said, "You haf others vit you?"

Billy looked at Josh, who said, "Yessir. Three other men still in the wood."

"Und, you all vish to run away."

Josh moved his head up and down vigorously, "We will do anything to get outta here."

Burkle pressed his lips together. He faced Mary Louise and said, "I believe them. Haf dem come inside—you are hungry, yes? Haf them come inside and feed them."

"Massah, Sir, we need to get back to our other men. We on a schedule, time is runnin' out 'fore they leave out on us."

"Yes, but first you must fortify yourselves. Come in, eat quickly, then go find your friends. Bring them here at nightfall."

Amazed, Billy stared at the tall German, now speaking with no accent. He glanced at the short Negress, who did not look happy at all. But, she gestured them to get into the house, and Billy realized suddenly how hungry he was.

Bev surveyed the two of them skeptically. "So, the first house you stop at turns out to be full of folk ready to help?"

"That is the God's truth," said Billy reverently. "I kinda don't believe it myself."

"Some cracker with a funny way of talkin' and a little black girl all uppity and shit," said Whit.

"She was fiery for sure," said Josh. "Her and the white man talk like they was equals."

Bev sighed. "How can we believe this true?"

"They fed us!" Billy blurted. "Real good, chicken, grits, gravy, even some dried peas. Awful good, it was, best I ate in weeks, months!"

"Yeah, all that could be a trap," Whit said. "Slavecatchers use every trick known to Satan hisself."

"Maybe we better off keepin' on our own," Eli offered.

Again, Bev's face tightened. "We could use some help."

They all thought for some time in silence. Finally, Bev spoke.

"All right, we ain't sure we can trust them. So, we cut our risks. When dark comes, we all sneak onto the place. I go in, the rest of you wait nearby. If they get me proof, I call you in. If they don't, we scatter, do what we planned all along."

They all agreed solemnly, and at sunset they started for town. Billy and Josh led the way. In the dark of the night, they hid behind one of the outbuildings within shouting distance of the big house. Bev breathed in, stood, and started walking down to the front door.

"Yes?"

Sure enough, a tall, white man stood in the doorway. A pipe extending from his beard sent slow spiraling ribbbons of cherry smoke into the air.

"You Massah Burkle?" Bev asked.

Burkle dipped his head yes.

"I'm Beverly Bowman. Friend of Billy McKinney and Josh."

"I see," Burkle said guardedly. "What brings you here alone, Mr. Bowman? Where are your companions?"

"They're around, not too far."

"Why are they not here with you, Mr. Bowman? We expected all of you this evening."

Just then, a tiny black woman came from the back hallway up to Burkle. Bev took her in, lively almond eyes, handsome features, and a sturdy frame despite her small size. That all came together for him as a solid, strong woman, yet somehow she struck him as being more than that.

"My assistant, Mary Louise Smalls."

Bev bowed his head to her, but her expression didn't change.
"Mr. Bowman," Burkle said, "where are your friends?"

Bev set his eyes on the white planter again. Where was that funny accent the boys heard? He settled himself and said, "Out there, waitin'. Beggin' your pardon, Massah Burkle, but we need more proof that you really help us 'fore we come in. That's why I'm here now."

"I see," Burkle replied. He looked at Mary Louise behind him, and she frowned, clearly not in favor of this development. But Burkle shrugged and faced Bev again.

"I take it, Mr. Bowman, that you will signal to the boys to run if you find us to be dissemblers?"

Bev nodded, figuring he had gotten the gist of the man's statement.

"And, you'll call them in if we are to help you."

"That right.

"Tell me," Burkle said, "what do you call to make them run?"

116

Bev weighed the question. He lifted and dropped his shoulders, "Get goin'."

Burkle smiled, "Didn't have a lot of time to think of something, no?"

Bev smiled back in spite of himself.

"Very well," Burkle said, "I will give you proof that we are honest and willing to help you in five minutes. Can you wait that long?"

Again, Bev mulled over the proposal. "Awright."

Burkle twisted his head back to Mary Louise and whispered something to her. She immediately disappeared down the hall into the back.

Burkle gestured to Bev, "Come into the parlor. We'll sit while we wait."

"Thatawright, I stay next to the door."

"Of course," said Burkle. "Open it, if it will make you feel more comfortable."

Just then, another black woman came up the hall, taller and somewhat older than Mary Louise. She approached them smiling, carrying a silver tray with two glasses on top.

"Another believer, Rachel Fisher."

"Pleased't meet y'all," she said, a glassy smile lighting up her face.

"Likewise, ma'm."

Burkle lifted a glass off of the tray and handed it to Bev, then took the other and sipped while Rachel returned to the back. Bev simply waited with him silently.

Mary Louise appeared from a parlor directly adjacent to the front door, surprising Bev.

"It's done," she said to Burkle, again frowning at Bev.

"Very well. If you will come with me, Mr. Bowman." When he saw Bev hold back, he added, "This is the only way."

Reluctantly, Bev followed Burkle into the parlor, inventorying as he went possible escape routes, at least to warn the others. Burkle entered an alcove next to the sitting room and pivoted to face Bev.

"What I show you is damning. If you are a southern agent deceiving us and we are besieged, understand that I will shoot you dead before everything else." As he spoke, he raised a single-shot pistol in his hand. Bev pulled back.

"I ain't a southern agent."

Burkle nodded his head at Mary Louise, who then leaned down and pulled a throw rug back from the center of the alcove floor. Just as Bev noticed the outline of a door in the floor, Mary Louise raised it up to reveal a steep set of stairs leading into the dark below. Burkle started to descend, and Mary Louise looked Bev directly in his face, her piercing expression challenging him to go down. Bev hesitated, then tripped down the stairs.

Surprisingly, the flight was short and the ceiling low. A single candle illuminated the room, longer than wide with a dirt floor. Sets of neatly piled blankets covered benches along the walls, with more stored on shelves at the room's end built with brick from floor to ceiling. Whitewashed wooden planks supported stacks of canned beans, preserves in blue glass jars, burlap sacks of potatoes, thick loaves of bread peeking out of linen sacks, and a good pile of water skins. In the middle, a pot hung from a tripod over a circle of hearthstones around a small coal fire. A stew in the caldron hanging above bubbled from the heat of the coals, just enough to cook without producing much in the way of smoke.

Bev turned his attention to Burkle. "People just left from here."

"Mary Louise sent them to hide," Burkle said, "a precaution in case you are an agent." He spread his hands out, "So, now you know. If you tell anyone, all of us will be executed."

"Hanged," Mary Louise said. "That'd happen last, though."

Bev gazed around again, and said, "If okay with you, I'll go fetch Josh and the others."

Burkle lifted his head, "Gudt. If you come with other than your friends, remember, I shoot you first."

Bev headed up the stairs, crossed the parlor to the hallway, and looked out one of the narrow windows on either side of the doorway. Seeing no unusual movement, he slipped out and dashed to where the rest hid. In a matter of minutes, all of them sat on the benches in the secret cellar, spooning hot stew from clay bowls on their laps. Another few minutes passed, and nine black men, women, and children appeared through another door in the back. They took their places on the open benches and began eating.

"I'm standin' out like a sore thumb," Billy said between deep slurps of stew.

"You look like a sore thumb," Whit said, and everyone laughed. Mary Louise passed out cups and poured water into them. When she reached Bev, she filled his cup, then motioned to sit down next to him. He quickly scurried over to make room.

"So, where you from?" Mary Louise asked.

He told her the story of their travel from eastern Kentucky and how they had come to be in Memphis. As he spoke, he noticed her brown eyes moving alertly at every juncture of his tale, how alive she was, and sharp. He realized, too, that as he talked, her initial hard skepticism seemed to soften. She appeared more sympathetic about events so common to others who had passed by this way running for their lives. Her newfound warmth warmed him, too.

"What about you?" he asked. "You ready to run?"

The set of her jaw stiffened again. "I'm not runnin' yet, not while others can't. Besides, I come from these parts. I got family I can't leave behind."

Bev sunk a little on the bench. "Oh. You have a man, a child?"

Mary Louise looked down at her feet, "My husband long gone to Louisiana, workin' sugar cane. I made up my mind he gone for good. My baby girl, though, lives just a few miles from here. I can't leave without her. So, I help here for now, 'til the Graybacks go belly up. Then, things change for everyone."

"That could be a long time comin'," Bev said. "They whup up pretty good on the Yankees so far."

She shook her head, "Naw, they losin'. Lost Fort Henry a while ago, then Fort Donelson just a couple days ago. Mr. Burkle say they in big trouble, the Yankees breathin' down their necks. Say a big bunch of Rebs comin' up from 'Bama by train totry and stop 'em. Meantime, Memphis is gettin' every soldier they can in the city. Things are changin' for sure," she said, nodding her head up and down with conviction.

"Maybe so," Bev said, "but I'm still leavin'." He thought for a moment. "You say Fort Donelson is Yankee now?"

"That right, bluer than blue."

"Really? You think Massah Burkle gotta a newspaper 'bout it I might read?"

"That's Mr. Burkle. We don't call anybody massah 'round here. Anyway, what you want a newspaper for? You can read?"

"Yes," said Bev, "I read. You get me a newspaper?"

Mary Louise looked up at this big, dark, black man, his hair all burry, hands gnarly, his clothes dirty and ripped. But, he seemed smart, smart enough to get himself and his friends this far without knowing anything about where they'd been and where they were going. And he could read. At that very moment, Mary Louise resolved to learn how to read and how to write.

Smoking an ornate meerschaum pipe, Burkle sat opposite the four men. Of them, only Billy smoked, a corncob pipe offered to him by

Burkle. The bittersweet waft of cherry tobacco drifted above them, its fragrance pleasant to all.

"We could get you up the Ohio River on your way to Canada. There, you would be completely safe."

Bev replied, "Too far. That law lettin' slavecatchers run us down in Free states ..." he shook his head. "I like our chances out west in wide open country."

"You still will have to go through Arkansas," Burkle said, "that is, if we can get you across the Mississippi."

"We'll cross it if we gotta swim," Bev said.

"If we gotta learn how to swim," Eli added. They all glanced his way and laughed. Still smiling, Burkle said, "All right. You must do what you think is right."

He tamped his pipe down and relit it. "We have two parties leaving, one this night, and another soon after. I don't like to marshal too many at once, it makes for suspicious eyes. Activity around the river must seem part of the natural flow. Thus, I think you will have to wait a little bit."

Burkle stood up, "In the meantime, you can help out with the chores. Our ladies work very hard day and night. Anything to lighten their labor would be very useful. I will issue you papers that state you are new here. I am buying and losing slaves all the time." He glanced at Mary Louise and said, "Please divide them up, thank you," and left by the back stairway.

Mary Louise looked them over. "What can you do?" she asked Eli. He scrunched up his face, embarrassed, "Housework?"

She nodded and said, "Go with Rachel. She cooks for the family." She turned to Josh, "And you?"

Josh shrugged, "Hemp."

Mary Louise's expression softened somewhat. "You go with Alice. She works the vegetable garden. And you?" she said to Whit.

"I distill bourbon whiskey, top quality!"

Mary Louise smirked, "We don't do that here. Mr. Burkle likes his beer." She placed her hands on her hips, sighed, and said, "Awright, y'all come with me to the stockyards tomorrow. We got plenty of horse and mule shit to shovel out, more than you can dream of. Go on out to the cabin next to ours. Deke will show you where to bed down."

As they left, Bev said as he passed by her, "I try not to dream of mule manure tonight, just you." She smiled slightly following him up the back stairs.

Chapter 10. The Crossing

Down at the stockyards, Bev shoveled out the stalls of a dozen mules before the bell sounded to break for something to eat. The work warmed him in the cold morning, but the day almost became too hot by noon. Spring definitely had started its tease, he thought, though bad weather still crept around. As he headed out to the tree where the midday meal was served, he marveled at the number of mules housed in these yards. There must be hundreds, he thought, maybe more considering the size of the stables.

"They use the mules to haul cotton up and down from the levees," Mary Louise told him. "Burkle owns all the animals. Got a little gold mine goin' here."

She amazed him. As strong as he was, as fit as he felt now that he'drested and eaten regularly for a week, she still finished twice as many stalls as he did in the same time. He determined to pick up his pace so that she wouldn't think he was a slacker.

"What you do on that farm in Kentucky?" she asked while they ate. They sat in the sunlight just outside of the tree's shade to soak up the warmth of the day.

"I worked with the hosses."

She eyed him skeptically. "How many?"

"Four, five." Seeing her hiding a little smile, he quickly said, "Racers, some Araby, high-strung."

"Must be so, take up all your time like that," she giggled.

"I do other things, too."

"Don't matter," she said, "whatever gets you by. No need to kill yourself for the white man. They take care of that for you, give 'em a chance."

They laughed together ruefully. Man, I like this girl, he thought. He remembered a conversation he and the others had on their travel one evening, sleepless in the cold. Whit and Josh lay close together, trying to settle in somewhat before sunset when they would start walking again.

"Josh, you one stinkin', bony man," Whit said. "I wish you was a fine-smellin' woman," he said. "Then, you really keep me warm!"

Eli and Bev had been holding on to each other until Bev stood up to relieve himself.

"You ever marry, Whit?" Eli asked.

"Once or twice, when it suited me."

"How the women feel 'bout that?" Josh asked.

Whit waved a hand in the air, "Sometimes it don't suit them."

They all laughed quietly.

Eli lay on the forest floor, his arms on top of his head resting on a log, oblivious to the chill while he thought. "I would like to marry someday, have a good woman be my wife, raise us some babies. That would be nice."

"I'm sure the Massah would be tickled with your li'l pickaninnies runnin' 'round the farm," said Whit. "I'm sure he could find somethin' fo' them to do."

"Maybe so," Eli said, "but they still be God's children."

They lapsed into silence. Then, Eli rolled over and said, "Why you never jump the broom, Bev?"

"Too many pretty girls to do that," Bev said.

"So? Why you let that stop you?"

Bev gave a shrug. "Might as well go after 'em all since they all there."

He had lied. He never married for fear of the pain of inevitable loss, of his wife, his children, just like Mary Louise. Only ten miles away, she might never see her baby girl again. Yet, here she stood, moving Bev in a way that he'd never felt before. In just a matter of days, too, he thought. A few broken conversations countered by the heavy weight of her yearning for her lost husband and child. Why should he take a chance with his feelings when she could not in any way? Yet, here he was, torn suddenly by hopeless hope.

In the evening, Burkle counseled them about their run.

"We use row boats deep in the night, low profile to make them hard to see. Slavecatchers are on to us, generally speaking, patrolling with dogs in the dark as much as during the day. We push out from the shore, but not too far, heading up river until we are away from any kind of settlements. At prearranged destinations, friends will be waiting. They take our passengers to the next safe place, either continuing on water, or sometimes over land. It all depends on where and how the patrols have been most active. From these points, we execute another leg, and so on, up to Ohio. There, other conductors will route you to Canada."

"I said before, we ain't going to Canada. Too dangerous with the slave hunters up north. We headin' west for the territories."

Burkle frowned. "I see I cannot change your mind." He started tamping the bowl of his pipe. "It is your decision, of course, though

122

I'm not sure it is the best one." He held a match stick over his pipe, then blew out a massive plume of smoke. "This close to the levees we tend to move up the side of the river rather than across it. The militia are out in force to protect the trade, of course. No matter, we will prepare to see you safely across to Arkansas. Our friends there will supply you then for your trip."

Bev dipped his head, "Thank you, Mr. Burkle. Thank you so much."

Burkle reached over and put a hand on Bev's shoulder, "Thank the Lord, Bev. And, please, I am not Mister, I am just Jacob to you and your companions, always."

Until the night of their leavetaking, Bev spent as much time as he could with Mary Louise. She seemed to brighten up when he came around, but not in the way he wanted. He found himself pining for her like a youngster when he thought about leaving her behind. Yet, what would going with him gain her? He sighed when she wasn't looking.

Mary Louise looked forward to seeing Bev each day, which troubled her. God would not approve of her straying from her marriage vows, her lost husband, and her daughter. God had given her a calling at the Burkle house to help others find freedom. Despite her growing attraction to this new man who soon would be off in the wind, her mission was here until all were free. Yet, she missed him now even before he had left.

The night arrived, and the five men gathered in the basement of the big house. Eli and Billy shared a bench, each looking nervous. Billy held onto his Enfield with both hands, standing it barrel up between his knees. On the opposite bench, Whit glowered, sitting next to Josh, who wore an implacable expression on his face. Bev paced between the benches, ready and waiting to go.

Burkle descended the stairs from the kitchen and gave each of them an oilcloth sack. "To keep your provisions dry. There will be more for you once you reach the west bank, enough to see you through a week." Mary Louise came downstairs, wearing a black scarf over her head and a black shawl and dress. It almost seemed as though she had outfitted herself for a funeral, Bev thought.

"Mary Louise has volunteered," Burkle said, "to escort you to your point of embarkation. Because of your number, we had to engage two boats. Mary Louise will introduce you to our agents who will row you across. You will be hidden beneath tarps at the bottom of each craft. It will be somewhat crowded for three, so I recommend that the two largest men occupy one boat, and the three slightest take cover in the other."

Burkle shook hands solemnly with each of them in turn. Rachel and Alice took turns hugging them all, which startled Billy. He hadn't expected the women to hug him, something he wasn't used to under any circumstance. Mary Louise dropped her head, and the men lined up to follow her lead.

Once outside, she waited until their eyes adjusted to the dark. There was no moon that night, though the stars blinked above like a river of candle flames. Billy pulled the collar of his jacket close around his neck to dull the cold air, thankful that no breeze stirred. Without a word, Mary Louise set out, slipping down the path quietly, the men behind her doing their best to mimic her stealth.

They traveled north along a tree line on the right of the road to hide their silhouettes against the starlight. Billy could see just a few lights at this time of night, and not a one in what he thought was the direction of the river. The serenity surrounding him did little to ease his inner turmoil. He felt stark fear at what they would be doing soon. He couldn't swim well, and the idea of drowning in the cold river water petrified him. The prospect of meeting up with the notoriously vicious slavecatchers or paddy rollers and their dogs horrified him just as much. So many, many things could go wrong, he thought. And, here he was, thrown in with a bunch of black slaves, renegades to almost everyone, who all seemed to take such danger in stride. He shook his head, he was a coward, no doubt about it, scared for only his own skin. God help me for being such a yellowbelly weakling, he thought ruefully.

They had been walking for nearly an hour when Mary Louise held up. She whispered to Bev, "We need to cross the road now. Crouch down low and follow me. Pass it on," she said. Bev repeated the message to Whit, who relayed it to the rest of them. When Mary Louise was sure that they all had their instructions, she stooped down and scurried quickly to the other side, the rest following one by one.

Again, she waited. She moved her eyes back and forth along the road, listening intently. Finally, she breathed, "Okay. Let's go."

She led them down a gentle slope through a stand of sassafras into a hollow flanked by black locust trees. At the bottom, they came upon a small inlet of the river, where two white men stood next to two rowboats pulled up on the bank.

Both men wore slouch hats and dungarees held up by suspenders. One fellow with dark brown hair and a mangy beard wore an old wool jacket, threadbare and not much use against the winter cold. He seemed oblivious to the elements anyway. The other man wore a sweater and a mackinaw on top of his overalls, and ear muffs beneath his hat. His long, bony face sported a well-waxed mustache, and he wore thick, wire-rim glasses. He stepped forward and, ignoring Mary Louise, said to the men in a low voice," You fellas our cargo for across the river?"

Billy nodded, and Bev said quietly, "We are. And you are?"

"I'm Colt, this here is Remington. Best get into the boats, then, and get goin' with it."

Billy clambered in first into a heavy wooden row boat with a high prow and a flat stern. It looked to be made of oak, he thought, as Eli climbed in after him, with Josh crawling in last.

"Get yourselves under the cover there," Remington said.

Bev turned to Mary Louise and grasped her by the hand. "Thank you, Mary Louise, for seein' us on our way."

She smiled faintly, though her eyes searched around warily. "Stay well, Bev Bowman, and safe."

Whit tugged on Bev's shoulder, and he let her hand slide out of his. "I'll write to Mr. Burkle about our whereabouts."

"C'mon now, Mr. Bowman," Colt said, "we need to push off."

Bev threw a leg over the high side of the next rowboat and stepped in gingerly. Whit gave him a hand, and they both dropped to their knees and pulled a canvas tarp over their heads. Colt pushed the boat off the bank and jumped in as it drifted away.

Mary Louise turned and hurried up the hollow to the hilltop and stood next to a pin oak where she could look out over the river. It was too dark to see much, but she could hear a dull scraping sound as the two white men used their oars to pivot the rowboats around to face the far bank. Pointed in the right direction, the men took their seats in the middle of the boats and unlimbered their oars. In short order, they emerged from a line of bald cypresses on the bank out onto the river.

Mary Louise could see them faintly outlined in the starlight as they started moving toward the far side of the river. A flash of light from down river followed by a muffled report startled her. She watched as one rower slowly folded up and fell into the bottom of the boat. More gunshots sounded, and a cacophony of howls from the shore suddenly shattered the silence. A canoe raced from below toward the rowboats as distant shouts and cries sounded over the water. Dear God, she said to herself, Dear God!

Billy pushed the body of the stricken Remington off of him as though he carried the plague. Terrified, he peered over the transom and saw canoes skimming across the river toward them while a string of gnashing hounds barked fiercely from the riverbank. "B'god!" he said, "they comin' for us!"

"Who?" cried out Eli, "Who?"

"The slavers! They firin' at us!"

A flight of buckshot hit the side of the boat, causing it to rock.

"Dammit! We gotta get out of here, we gotta get off this boat!"

"Hold on," said Josh, jumping up to the seat. "Stay low!" He grabbed the oars andstarted pulling, heavy cuts into the water that sent the heavy rowboat forward in sudden, swiftsurges. Bullets whizzed above them and thudded into the side of the boat, shaking it again.

Billy heard voices float across the river from the location of the other rowboat. Josh yanked on the right oar twice, turning toward the sound of the calls. Another round of shot flew into the boat and Josh suddenly jerked forward.

Horrified, Billy shouted out, "Josh! You hit, Josh?"

Josh sat up and twisted around, showing his left hand holding the shattered end of the oar.

"Oh, no!" cried Billy.

Eli glanced up, then back at the canoes. "They comin' up on us!" he screeched, "We gotta get outta here!"

"No, no, no!" bellowed Josh. "Billy, fire yo' gun!"

Billy reached behind to unsling the Enfield and stopped. "It ain't loaded!"

Another barrage of shot hammered the wooden boat. Eli jumped off into the water and started flailing.

"That boy cain't swim," Josh said.

"You runaways ready to give up?" The voice was close in. One of the canoes bobbed up near the rowboat. A man stood in the canoe, his foot raised up on the bow, a shotgun resting on his knee. "We'll shoot you if you don't," he said.

Josh and Billy stood up. "Awright," said Josh, "but help us fish that po' boy out the water right now or he'll drown."

"We'll get him," the man said. The other canoe coasted up next to the first one, carrying four men with rifles and shotguns.

"Lemme get you a rope for the little muskrat." The other men joined in laughter, cut short by a rifle shot flying close between the canoes.

"What the hell?" The man on the bow dove down back into the canoe while the others ducked low. "They got guns!"

Josh immediately turned to Billy. "Rock the boat hard, tip it over."

Another shot was heard, followed by a different blast. The men in the canoes sat up and started paddling backwards. Those not paddling fired off a few wild shots, not knowing where to aim in the dark.

Billy and Josh managed to flip the rowboat over, sending them both into the river along with the lifeless body of Remington. The freezing water immediately numbed Billy to the bone. He started to flounder, the Enfield dragging him down, when he felt a steel trap on his shoulder pulling him up. His head broke the surface and he gasped for air, Josh's thumb and fingers dug deep around his clavicle. Josh said urgently, "Grab hold of the edge of that seat and stay still."

They were beneath the capsized boat, holding on to the seats out of sight of the patrollers. They could hear muffled gunshots as they floated. Then, something thudded hard against the outside of the boat. They felt their boat shift away from the contact, followed by a smaller thumping against the side near the stern.

Billy shuddered uncontrollably, wondering in terror how much longer he could hold on. In the dark, he felt something round, cold and soft against his lips which caused him to snap his head back. The cold cylinder pressed on again until he recognized it as one of Josh's fingers, warning him to keep silent.

The water splashed next to them, and they felt a surge as another form broke the surface beneath the boat. "Eli? Is that you? You there?"

Billy recognized Bev's voice, but he was too scared to say anything. Josh said, "That you, Bev?"

"Josh, thank Lord, you okay? Where's Eli?"

"I am—Eli in the water, Bev."

"In the water?" Bev repeated. "He can't swim! We got to find him! Where he'd go in?"

Josh hesitated. "He jump in back yonder."

Just then, they heard rapid knocking on the outside of the boat. The dull crack of a distant rifle sounded at the same time. They could hear muffled voices above them.

Bev said, "We gotta get outta here. Billy here?"

"I'm here, Bev," Billy rasped.

"Remington?"

"Shot dead," said Josh. "Gone."

"Okay, feel your way out to the other boat. Go under it to the opposite side so Whit and Colt can pull you up. Let's go!"

Billy heard the sound of Bev submerge followed by a similar sound that must have been Josh diving under. Terror filled Billy and he couldn't bring himself to let go. The others could leave him, he'd take his chances with the Rebs even though he knew they'd hang him for sure now.

A powerful grip pulled him by the leg and he felt himself being dragged under the water. Before he could cry out, he found himself bumping his head on the bulkhead of the capsized boat. He suffered several more skull cracks on the bottom of the other boat until he breeched the water next to it, gulping for air. Josh had let go of his leg and now grabbed the Enfield and thrust it up to other waiting hands. They pulled Billy up into the rowboat, almost strangling him with the rifle belt.

Billy collapsed in the bottom of the boat, followed quickly by Josh. Everyone immediately went quiet as Colt pushed off from the overturned craft. Silently, he slipped his oars into place and pulled away from the other boat and the closing canoes. With studied, strong strokes, he maneuvered them away from the area of the melee out to the main part of the river, allowing the current to take them downstream away from the lanterns held out in front of the canoes. Once out of earshot, he reversed the boat and began rowing up and across the water. In forty-five minutes, they had covered the width of the immense river, arriving at the planned rendezvous where two waiting men met them and spirited them away.

Bev sat on a log alone, inconsolable. Billy and the others occasionally approached him gingerly, fully shocked themselves at the loss of Eli. But the big black man ignored them. Instead, head down, eyes fixed in the direction of his feet, he grieved.

Billy imagined the loop of thoughts going through Bev's head hating himselfand going over and over what he could have done, should have done. Thinking about this brought his daddy tomind, which momentarily drove Billy's spirits deeper into his own dark place. But Bev's state distracted Billy from his own pain, as it did with Josh and even Whit.

"Think the boy still alive?" Whit said in a low voice.

Josh replied, "The water not that cold. Spring comin' around, now." Then he shrugged, "Eli don't swim."

They each mulled in silence.

"Maybe Eli grabbed on to somethin' out there," Billy mumbled. "They's a lot of junk floatin' in that river."

"Yeah, and maybe them cracker slavecatchers grabbed him up!" Whit added bitingly. "If that true, he wish he drowned first."

Bev strode forward. "That's it. I'm goin' back for him."

Whit looked at him and said disdainfully, "You what?"

"I'm gonna find him. Dead or alive, I'm gettin' him back."

"You crazy, he dead! Next, you be dead!"

"He's my brother."

"He old man Bowman's half breed by your mama! She favor Eli, let you goalone on your own. But, don't you dare leave Eli behind! Now, you gonnabe a hero, save him even if he dead. What about us? You get caught, you die, what we do? It was you started us runnin', you tellin' us how to go, now you leavin'?"

Josh stepped up, "Whit right about you gettin' caught. I cain't let that happen."

"See?" said Whit triumphantly. "You gonna try Josh?"

Billy didn't know what to do. He felt bad about losing Eli, but the idea of Bev leaving froze him with panic. Maybe he should try stopping Bev, too, but he was afraid of him. Instead, he stood, rocking back and forth, one foot to the other.

Colt and the other two white men walked up to them. "We've been talkin' it over, and we decided to row downstream, see if we can find Willard's remains—sorry, that's Remington to y'all. I'm Leon, by the way, Leon Hutch. This here's Evan Willberry and Christopher Teague. We glad to meet you boys."

Even as he spoke his eyes gazed far away, shocked and full of anquish. They all shook hands awkwardly, acknowledging each other with a nod of the head.

Leon continued, "We're awful sorry about your lost man, too. If'n we find him and he's still alive, we'll get him back to Mr. Burkle's for another try. If he's dead, we vow to give him a proper Christian burial. That's all we can do."

The four fugitive men gazed at their three guides without replying. Finally, Bev said, "Thank you, Mr. Hutch. We thank you all for what you done for us this day. We pray that you find Mr. Remington—"

"Willard. Willard McLeod."

"—Mr. McLeod, may he rest in Jesus's arms. I personally thank you for lookin' out for my brother Eli. He's good boy, I hope God blesses him one way or the other."

Hutch nodded. "We'll do our best." He gestured to a tall, blond whiskered man as lean as a sapling. "Christopher will guide you to the foothills so's you can get goin'. We have some goods tucked away that should keep you for a few weeks. Chris knows where they are. Other than that, God bless you all."

"And you as well," said Bev. They shook hands all around again, and the guides melted into the woods. Teague followed them, saying he would return after he saw them push off down the river.

Bev glanced at Josh, Whit, and Billy staring at him. "All right," he said. "I guess we move on."

The others slowly lowered their heads. While they waited for Teague to return, they watched Bev go back to the log and sit down. His back shook as he silently wept.

Mary Louise stood behind the tree straining her eyes, hoping to see something, anything that might show her what had happened. Had they all been killed? Had any of them been captured by the slavecatchers? She didn't know, she couldn't tell. She kept searching, hoping.

Dawn slowly crawled up behind her. The big river gradually turned from black ink into gray wash water. She scanned up and down the bank, but saw nothing. As the light grew, she peered across the water but the other side was too far away to see. After another hour of fruitless searching, she scrunched her head close to her shoulders and started walking back.

After slipping out of the tree stand on the riverbank, Mary Louise plodded down the road toward the Burkle homestead, her eyes on the ground. No matter what, they were gone, Bev and the rest of them. If she had been someone else, she would have cried her way home.

"Hey, there, Negress, what you doin' out here all by yo'self?"

Startled, she looked up to see five white men riding horses, and a sixth on foot holding the leashes of a half-dozen dogs. The man in front spoke again, his hands resting on his saddlehorn. "You got a pass?" he said, "Or is you a runaway, too?"

Mary Louise didn't say a word.

"If you be, we happy to tie you up with our other runaway nigger. Y'know, the more the merrier?" A smarmy smile passed across his face. He turned in his saddle, "That one there, he gave us a merry chase on the river last night. His dirty ab'litionist friends threw some shots at us, but we ran 'em off. They skunked away with them others niggers, but we pulled this one out of the drink. Don't look like much, do he?"

Mary Louise peered past the lead rider at a slight figure on foot being towed by a rope around his neck. Without changing expression, she realized it was Eli, Bev's brother. He had been beaten so badly, she almost hadn't recognizedhim.

"Normally, we string him right up, 'specially since he give us so much trouble. But, times is hard and a few hunner' dollars is a few hunner' dollars. The boy tells us he belong to some fat planter up in Tennessee. So, he go back just as soon as we get a wire off.

"Now," he said, leaning further over toward her, "about yo' pass. You got one, or you want to join our boy, heah, be his galfriend?"

Without a word, she reached into the pocket of her apron and produced a rectangle of paper. She thrust it up at the horseman. He grasped it and held it back away from his eyes.

"Jacob Burkle. And you Mary Louise Smalls."

She nodded her head quickly.

Begrudgingly, he handed the paper back. "I heah he some kinda Yankee sympathizah. That so?"

She shrugged her shoulders.

"Well, then, off you go." He called back to the other men, "Okay, let's ride."

When Mary Louise arrived back at the big house, she told the Burkles everything. Jacob Burkle's expression turned darker and sadder with each detail. He sighed, saying, "Well, maybe the others escaped. We will know when Mr. Hutch and his friends come back, God willing."

"We should try to get word to them about Eli," Mary Louise said urgently.

Burkle sighed again. "If they eluded capture, they are well into the Arkansas brush by now. We can do nothing at this time."

"Maybe you could write a letter. That Bev, he can read, he told me!"

"But, where would I send it?" Burkle said, raising his hands. "We have no idea where they will be. We may never know."

Mary Louise slumped slightly and Burkle placed his hand on her arm. "All we can do is pray to God for their safety."

She nodded.

"In the meantime, I will find out about this Tennessee planter and if possible try to make sure that Eli isn't harmed. Then, we will pray to the Lord that someday they are allunited in freedom. This I promise."

Again, Mary Louise moved her head in agreement. She would pray to Jesus to save them. She also would learn to read and write as fast as she could. Someday, she would write to Bev Bowman telling him what had happened to his lost brother.

Chapter 11. Mountain Spring

Billy had the deer lined up, ready to go down as soon as he squeezed the trigger. Instead, he quietly pushed the rifle toward Whit, lying next to him on the rise behind the fallen oak.

He whispered, "Wet the sight, hold the stock hard against your shoulder, look down the barrel and aim at its middle, right behind the front shoulder."

Whit followed Billy's instructions deliberately, and waited, blowing quick breaths in and out in the frigid air. Billy murmured, "Now, squeeze—"

The blast nearly took his ear off, the stock of the rifle jumping up from Whit's shoulder.

"Shit," said Whit.

Billy shook his head. "Whit, you got to be patient, slow it down."

"Awright, cracker," Whit snarled, "next time."

Billy grabbed the Enfield, "Yeah, well, we ain't got enough shot for you to keep next-timin' it. Not to mention we all are hungry."

"Listen, just shut the hell up, will you? You shoot the damn thing if you so hungry."

"Too late," Billy said, his mouth scrunched up in exasperation. "That deer and all its kinfolk beatin' it over the next mountain by now."

"Well, then, why don't you go over it, too, maybe don't come back!"

Whit stood up and trudged back down the snow-covered hill, leaving Billy sighing to himself. They all want to learn how to shoot, he thought. He got to his feet and started down the slope, shivering from the brutal cold. But none of them seem to know that it takes time. Billy figured he had been shooting since he was nine, while the rest hadn't been allowed to come anywhere near a gun. He'd done his fair share of scrabbling in the ground, but he felt sorry for the others, working all day into the dark with nothing to show for it. Just by being around them, he saw how the preacher was right. No man should have to go through what they did, do what they were forced to do. He shuddered, remembering them all down in the lower farmland, scrubbing up by a stream with cold, cold water. Josh stood in his trousers with his shirt off. When Josh turned away, Billy saw his back covered with thick, round scars. It looked as though someone had sewn lengths of rough, black rope in a crisscross pattern like a quilt over his shoulders and down his spine.

Josh saw Billy staring, his mouth wide open. He grinned wide at Billy and said, "Oh, it ain't nothin'. It don't hurt, I'm used to it. When I's younger, I got into a spot of trouble with the overseer. But, I got over it, it just fine, now."

Billy remembered bobbing his head slowly up and down. He had been lucky to be white, even poor white, raised in the mountains as a righteous man, thank the Lord. Here was a grown man apologizing for the permanent massive welts inflicted upon his back because he was black. He amazed Billy with his good nature, how he always managed to adjust with great humor to whatever faced him. Yet, when the chance came, he had run from a slave's life.

After leaving the Big River, they moved at night through the low country heading northwest toward the mountains. At night, they secretly skirted past small farmsteads in the valleys, stealing what food they could along the way. The countryside started to show signs of life. Green shoots peeked out of the damp, dark loam between diminishing knolls of snow. Saplings started showing early seeds and birds began to sing.

Spring had yet to take hold of Arkansas in the foothills of the Ozarks. At the higher altitude, a freezing snowstorm two weeks ago had them clinging together closer than ever during the night. Since then, some of the snow had melted off, and Billy saw some green signs around his feet where the withering wind had swept aside the icy snow. Despite the vicious change of the daily weather, he knew that soon everything would be coming up and all the critters would be afoot with their little ones.

But not yet. Billy wondered if the freezing temperatures would kill off the early greenery that ordinarily brought out the small famishedanimalsafter their winter ordeal. If so, the animals would be gone, too. They had been lucky to see any deer at all on this cold day.

Josh tried to trap rabbits and squirrels and the like, but the group kept moving, which didn't give the snares any time at all to work. They gathered hickory nuts, chestnuts, anything they could find beneath the snow to keep from starving. But, Billy was determined to bring back game. They needed something that they could roast and tuck into, the best meal they'd had since leaving Memphis. That would be good, he thought, smacking his lips. He knew he could do it if the rest of them just stayed in camp. Trying to teach them to shoot was a waste of powder, shot,and any number of chances to bring down any meat. So, in a way, he was glad Whit had steamed off.

He climbed up and down two more hills before he found a good spot, two trees tumbled over onto each other, forming a notch with their trunks. He slung the Enfield over his back and scaled the tree trunk using the easiest path up to the notch. He sat down, not very comfortable, he thought, and rested the length of the rifle over the trunk in front. From there, he had a good line of sight of any animal that might appear over the farther hill. He waited.

Despite the cold, he enjoyed being back in the mountains even if it wasn't home. The thought sent waves of sadness through him wondering how Daddy was doingand if the potatoes had come up at all. He wondered if he was making it through the winter. Billy felt so far away from home. Every now and then he would pull out the photograph of his family and miss them all over again, his dead mama, his little sister, and now his daddy, maybe dying or dead. The only one he could be sure about was the boy in the picture, alive but inside maybe a little dead, too.

He heard something in the hollow below, a ruffling sound. Peering down over the trunk, he saw a young boar using its snout to shovel snow and earth away from the base of a locust tree. A hog, Billy thought, one he could carry back himself. He inched out onto the log in front of him, pointed his rifle down and honed in on the boar. It snuffled some more, Billy shot, and the wild pig smacked up against the locust and fell on its side, its legs kicking, trying to run in the air.

Perdition's fire! Billy thought, got it! He slung his rifle over his shoulder and deliberately worked his way down from the entwined tree trunks. As soon as he hit the earth, he hurried, scrambling down the hillside toward the locust tree and his prize.

When he arrived the boar lay still, already dead. Billy whistled at the size of the hole in the wild pig. The slug had cleared its heart and nearly all its lungs out the other side, a gory mess slapped up against the trunk of the tree, staining the remaining snow below. After that, there wasn't much left to gut.

He showed up with the small boar over his shoulderand the the other three gawked, open-mouthed. Even Bev came out of his fixed state of misery. He looked at Billy as though he was seeing him through new eyes. The rest of them did the same, appearing slightly shocked at the notion of Billy as a new man.

Billy dropped the boar at their feet, unslung the Enfield, and placed it against a tree. He rolled his shoulders as if to loosen them up, then said, "We do it now, they won't be much of a flame or smoke cookin' it."

Again, they gazed at him, speechless, as though he had come from a foreign land. "Okay, I'll roast 'er up."

He proceeded to clear away caked snow from a spot in the middle of the small meadow where they were camped. He brushed off frozen leaves and branches to sculpt a shallow depression in the frozen ground.

"Josh, can you fetch some dried wood out there? We need enough for a couple hours."

Josh went off, trailed by Whit. Billy walked to an overhanging rocky slab that they slept beneath and began to rummage around for pieces of stone. He brought them to the shallow pit and started piling the rocks around the perimeter. Bev followed Billy to the outcropping and brought a pile of rocks that he added to the makeshift wall circling the shallow pit. After they finished, Billy cut two long saplings, halved them, and tied them together with hog gut to fashion two off-center crosses. He dug and drove them into the half-frozen ground at either end of the pit, angling the two forks up and even to each other. Then, he cut another, thicker sapling and sharpened it at one end. "Hold up the pig for me, will ya?"

Bev grabbed the boar and held it up. "Snout down, ass in the air," Billy said. Bev did as he said. "Hold him steady," Billy said and drove the stake through the carcass's anus and out its mouth. Just then, Josh and Whit returned with two large piles of dead tree limbs.

"Okay, then, that'll do fine," said Billy. "Let's grill it."

Whit started turning the pig and Billy said, "We'll likely be eatin' in an hour or so. But, first, I gotta another little thing to add." He stepped over to his knapsack. From it he pulled out a smaller leather bag, which he beat a few times against a rock outcrop. He returned to the pit, opened the small bag, and proceeded to sprinkle tiny, white granules on the boar as it slowly rolled over. When they looked at him questioningly, he said, "Salt. I took a little side trip to a lick I spotted a ways back. Figured, if we gonna eat big, it might as well taste as good as it can."

His companions again viewed him with new respect. "That's right, boys, we eatin' high on the hog today!" Grinning, he sat down to await his turn at the spit.

All of them laid around the campsite coals in stupors, blankets wrapped around them, but with their waistbands lowered to free their distended bellies. Each had eaten almost past their capacity to hold it all in, and they fought to keep it down. They all were in some discomfort, but none of them would admit it in deference to the pleasure of the feast.

"That's the best I ate since Christmas," Josh murmured. "You was right about the salt, Billy boy. I ain't never eat no pork that good before."

"I'd eat it all over again, if I could," said Bev.

They all mumbled grunts of agreement. "Where'd you learn to cook like that, Billy boy?" Whit asked. "How you do that?"

Billy stared up at the sky, watching the sun fade, waiting for the moon to show. "My daddy. He learned me to cook all sorts of critters—birds, fish, deer, beef once in a while, small stock like squirrels, chipmunks, mice, polecats—you got to carve out the smelly sacs first, without poking a hole in them, else you pay for sure. They taste good without the smell. We even boiled a snake now and then. We cooked up and ate everything we could. We even roasted corn and other greens like we done the pig. We didn't have pork all that often, but when we did it was good, just like the late Mister Boar, here."

"Well, I say we make you chief cook of the party from here on," said Whit. "Chief Cook Billy Boy!"

Everyone laughed except for Bev. He had dropped into that dark place of his again, where he resided ever since Eli had disappeared. Billy appreciated all of the compliments, but Bev's misery made him sad and brought to mind his own homesickness. He recalled times like this that he and Daddy had shared together, well-fed and sitting by the fire, whittling while talking about the day or telling some story or another. Once in a while they would sing a song together, not good, but not too bad. The memory almost caused Billy to cry, which he wouldn't, of course, in front of the other men. But, he could sing.

Let us pause in life's pleasures and count the many tears
While we all sup sorrow with the poor;
There's a song that will linger forever in our ears
Oh, hard times come again no more.

Tis' the song, a sigh of the weary,
Hard times, hard times come again no more

Many days you have lingered around my cabin door;
Oh, hard times come again no more.

Though a bit thin, his emotion-filled voice stilled the other men as they listened. When he finished, no one said anything at first. Then, Bev said, "I surprised at you, Billy. You can't sing much, but you got spirit in your singin'. Where you learn that song?"

"My mama, just before she died. My daddy sung it once in a while...." He said no more, and the other men exchanged silent glances. Then, Whit began to sing.

> There is a balm in Gilead
> To make the wounded whole;
> There is a balm in Gilead
> To heal the sin-sick soul.
> Sometimes I feel discouraged,
> And think my work's in vain,
> But then the Holy Spirit
> Revives my soul again.
>
> If you cannot sing like angels,
> If you can't preach like Paul,
> You can tell the love of Jesus,
> And say He died for all.

Billy found himself moved by the pure baritone coming from Whit, not a false note struck. More amazing, the man everyone thought of as a hard case was singing a gospel song like the angels themselves. He looked around and by the expressions on their faces saw that Whit's voice amazed the others just as much.

By then, darkness cloaked the camp. Bev said, "Better cover them coals in the pit. No need to let people know we're here."

"Lord, man, can't we let 'em be for tonight?" said Whit. "We ain't seen a soul for two weeks. Another night like this, I'm gonna be a block of black ice."

Bev jerked his head back and forth, "No sir. No need to take chances. One mistake and we cooked for good."

Reluctantly, Billy and Josh arose to start scooping dirt back into the pit. As he helped smother the fire, knowing that they would be cold again that night, Billy still silently celebrated the realization that, for the first time in three weeks, Bev had taken charge.

The four deprived men picked the boar carcass clean in less than two days. Josh went off to check his traps while the rest hunted for more nuts, edible roots, and whatever else they could find. When they came back to their campsite mostly empty handed, all eyes turned to Billy. He sighed, hiked up his rifle, and started to head out.

Whit came up to him, "How 'bout I go along again?"

A pained expression flashed across Billy's face, quickly gone when he saw Whit's cold glare.

"Yeah, sure, c'mon with," Billy said, then whispering under his breath, "waste some more shot."

Billy led them to a vantage point on a low, flat promontory above the saltlick he had found before. There wasn't much in the way of cover on the cliff, but if they moved a log over to hide behind, they would have trouble shooting over it down into the hollow. Instead, they did their best to pile some branches and fallen leaves in front of them.

They waited in silence. True, thought Billy, it was a good idea to hold off talking to keep from scaring away any game. But, he felt there was more to it than that.

Daylight faded away. After hours stretched out on the cold ground, they took turns crawling away to relieve themselves. Just before sunset, they drank the last of the water out of Billy's canteen.

"Let's go," said Whit. "There ain't nothin' showin' up."

Billy frantically gestured for him to lower his voice, "Shh!" he said, barely audible. "Deer mostly eat at night. We wait 'til dark, they might come."

"Then, why we come out here so early?"

Billy shrugged.

"I ain't waitin' 'til dark! Next thing, you wanna wait all night! I'm gettin' outta here now, go back, see if Bev and the others found anything to eat."

"Just wait 'til nightfall. If nothin' shows, we'll go."

"What the hell can you shoot in the dark?" Whit rasped.

"Wait. We'll see."

Whit blew out air and stretched out on the icy ledge again.

The sun dropped below the horizon, causing bright orange beams of light to flash between the tree trunks, nearly blinding them. Soon, the orange dulled to a scarlet haze, then disappeared. The stars and a slice of moon cast a pale glow on the meadow below. Sure enough, a deer stepped daintily through the trees to the saltlick. Two tiny fawns followed in single file. As their mother stood gazing around, the fawns took tentative licks at the barely visible salt deposit in a patchwork of late snow.

Whit hit Billy with his elbow hard in the ribs. Billy managed to stay still after absorbing the blow. He lifted the Enfield, wet the sight, and slowly drew it down to target the doe. Calm, he rested his finger on the trigger, gently putting pressure on it despite Whit's nervous fidgeting next to him. Billy triggered the rifle, controlling the recoil just as another shot rang out. The doe looked up and collapsed in a heap, all four legs splayed apart. The fawns jumped involuntarily, then froze, not knowing what to do, their mother motionless at their hooves.

Billy had just raised his rifle, ready to climb down to the deer when he heard the second shot. One of the fawns collapsed, and the other ran off, bouncing up and down as fast as it could. Halfway up to his feet, Whit dove down next to Billy. They heard voices coming from the other side of the woods.

"Beau you see that? Somebody else shot that doe."

"Hell no, I plunked it."

"No, no, it went down 'afore you shot. They's somebody up in them rocks up theya."

"Where? Who, Yankees?"

"I told you it was smoke we saw comin' up over them hills."
Another voice.

"Never mind, pull back. Tell all the boys to hold their posts, keep they guard up."

Whit repeatedly hit Billy on his bicep, motioning for them to leave. Billy nodded, putting his index finger to his lips. Carefully, they eased themselves backwards away from the lip of the cliff. They gradually turned and wiggled on all fours back away from the scarp down to the lower hollow. Getting to their feet, they felt their way through the trees back toward their camp, Billy leading the way.

When they were sure they were out of earshot, Whit said sharply, "Damn Rebels!"

"You sure? We ain't seen anybody up here for weeks."

"One asked if Yankees here. Who else ask that but Johnny Reb?"

Billy replied, "We got to get back to the others lickety-split!"

They thrashed their way through the woods, all stealth left by the wayside. Just before daybreak, they heard voices coming from ahead. They burst through the forest into the small clearing where Bev and Josh sat talking quietly. Both men whisked around at the noise.

"Graybacks!" Whit called out, "Behind us, a few hills back!"

Bev and Josh looked up at them from the log where they were sitting. Theyleaped up. Bev asked, "They comin' for us?"

Whit nodded as he gulped for air, and sputtered, "Soon as they can, my guess."

"How many?"

Whit shook his head, "Don't know. We heard three, but they sounded like they's more."

Billy said, "The one feller talked about all the boys. They gotta be more than them we heard."

Bev rubbed his hand back and forth across his mouth. "Okay," he said, "then, we gotta move. Grab your stuff, let's get goin'."

They scurried around picking up canteens, blankets, and the rest of their gear. Bev waved to the others to move, and plunged in among the trees heading oppositefrom where Billy and Whit had come.

Something whizzed by them at eye height followed by the crack of a rifle. They all dropped to the ground.

"Hey, boys," a voice called out from the trees to their rear, "looky what we got. A bunch a niggers on the run."

"I spy a white boy, too," said another, "a ghost nigger, I guess."

"Well, if'n they don't get up and raise their hands in the air," the first speaker said loudly, "they all gonna be ghosts."

The voice behind yelled, "Awright, boys, give it up or we'll plug you in yo' guts. We got the drop on you, so get 'em up."

Bev waved for the rest to follow him as he rolled around and started crawling on his belly up a stony bluff to the cliff hanging above the camp clearing. Josh and Whit quickly scrambled after him, Billy taking up the rear. Bev and Josh crouched behind a large boulder some yards away. Whit and Billy dropped down on the top of the crag, turning just in time to see someone working his way through the stand of trees. Wearing a beehive hat pulled down to his eyes, the Rebel held a squirrel gun up against his cheek. Pointing it ahead of him, he inched forward from tree to tree. He looked to be in his mid-twenties, gaunt and hunched over, dressed in a dirty, dark-wool jacket with a red-checked shirt underneath. His rough, serge trousers were torn at the knees, and in tatters at his ankles. His feet were bare.

An elbow stuck Billy in the ribs. Whit whispered to him fiercely, "Load yo' gun and get ready to shoot that Rebel rat cracker!"

Startled, Billy whipped his rifle around and pulled loose its ramrod. He dug around in his pouch for a wad, a ball, and his powder horn. In a matter of a seconds, he loaded the Enfield and trained it on the Rebel stepping further out from the forest.

The Rebel stopped and wheeled his gun slowly around as he surveyed the small clearing.

"What you see, Robbie?"

"A nigger. One nigger and one nigger lover." He called out loudly again, "You best come down from theya or we gonna blow you apart."

Whit seized Billy's bicep, gripping it fiercely, "Shoot!"

Billy took aim. Only thirty yards away, he had the Grayback dead to rights. Shoot him now, he thought, and he'd see his heart and lungs splattered all over a tree trunk. He started to squeeze the trigger and the rifle suddenly started shaking. He pulled off, took a breath and tried again, but the shaking worsened. Finally, he laid his head down beside the stock.

"What the hell!"

Whit grabbed the gun and shot. The Rebel out front dropped to the ground, startled, his eyes round disks. He raised his squirrel gun without looking and fired, then scurried back into the woods.

"Shit," Whit spit.

"You hit, Robbie?"

"No, they missed. But they shot at me! A nigger shot at me! Let's go boys, let's get 'em, clear 'em out!"

A volley of gunfire filled the air and Billy could hear minié balls whizzing by. Whit pushed the rifle at Billy. "Reload this."

Billy frantically reloaded the Enfield as Whit whipped out the tanning knife from the back of his belt. Jamming the shot down the barrel, Billy saw Bev holding a knife low and Josh gripping a thick wooden limb in both hands like a club.

"Gimme that gun," Whit snapped. He held it in one hand, the knife in the other. Looking over the ridge, he said, "You still got that pistol in your sack?"

Billy nodded, "But I don't know if it works."

"Now's the time to find out!" said Whit.

Another round of fire winged past them, some thudding into the cliff, others hitting tree trunks and branches. Billy worked the bundled revolver out of his haversack, and started to unwrap it.

"Let's finish 'em, boys!" bellowed Robbie, and a dozen Rebel soldiers broke from the woods, some with fixed bayonets. They screamed chillingly like cats in a fight, rushing toward the slope up to the cliff.

"Never you mind," Whit said, "too late for that now." He tossed the rifle down next to Billy's side. Billy clutched it in both hands, wondering if he should start running.

"Let's go!" shouted Bev. He turned around and ranaway with Josh close behind him. Whit took off. Billy grabbed the rifle and sped after them. As he bolted, he could hear the Rebels closing in, huffing and blowing as they clawed their way up the short cliff face. After a few yards, Billy let go of the Enfield and ran as fast as he could.

The runners had opened up a hundred-yard gap between themselves and the Rebels, thought an occasional shot flew by above them. In time, even those ceased, since every time the pursuers stopped to shoot, they lost some ground reloading. Their yells faded, too, as the Rebel chasers saved their breath while running, climbing over rocks, through brush and fallen trees, negotiating slants and slopes on the difficult terrain of the Ozark plateau.

Bev and the others managed to maintain some distance from the pursuing Rebels. Recognizing that their lead had increased, Billy prayed to God in thanksfor letting them eat that pig. Maybe they could keep running until nightfall, hide away in the dark. But, it was only morning, they would have to run for hours.

The Rebels began to close the gap. Billy couldn't figure out how, and he tried to pump his legs harder. But, the terrain slowed them down, too. He could see Whit beginning to labor, losing distance between himself and Josh. Josh trailed Bev, and he, too, looked to be struggling to keep up. How could those Rebs be getting closer? Billy wondered. Still running with their heavy guns?

"We gotch you, boy, we gonna string you up first, you yellow coward."

Closer yet, Billy realized with alarm. What could they do now? A shot rang out, and Billy blanched. They were shooting again? Another rifle went off without any whizzing balls cutting through the woods. They must be firing in the air to scare him.

"I see you, now, boy, you dead!"

They were near enough to aim now. Billy started to zigzag up a rise, close to Whit and the others. They rolled over the rim out of his sight, and suddenly he heard them crying out in loud shouts. The Rebs had gotten in front of them? Billy crested the hill, three shots passed him on either side, and he dropped to roll down the slope.

"Stop him, hold him down."

Held to the ground in the iron grip of two men, Billy figured the Rebels must have dealt with the devil to get around in front of them.

"Be quiet, lay still," said a low raspy voice.

Clutched close to them, Billy's face was thrust into one man's chest. All Billy could see was dark blue wool and one gold button. He lay still, and heard the Rebels' shrill war cry just above them as they crestedthe rise. A tremendous din of rifle fire caused Billy to flinch, after which he heard a stentorian voice call out forcefully.

"Drop your weapons, we have you in our sights. Hands up, you Confederate sons of bitches, or we'll shoot you down where you stand."

The men holding Billy relaxed and stood him up. He looked around to see a host of soldiers in blue, maybe fifty, half of which had the Rebels surrounded, their rifles trained directly on them. The Rebels had their hands in the air, a dozen of them, bone thin and raggedy, most of them barefooted. One stood out in their midst, a stunned, glum expression on his face. Robbie, their point man, Billy figured.

At the head of the Union troops stood a tall man in a long, blue coat with gold epaulets on his shoulders and a gold tassel on his wide brimmed hat. He also wore a sword and pistol at his side. Dark-haired with a fine set of sculpted whiskers, his eyes flashed blue in contrast to thecalm, even voice he used to address his new prisoners.

"We've been looking for you fellows for quite some time," he said. "Glad you got careless chasing these contraband. What a racket you put up, just like a duck call. Tell me, are you deserters, too? Did you plan on selling these men, or just murdering them? No matter, you're ours, now. Sergeant Hampstead, secure these Johnnies for transport. And, get them something to eat."

"Yessir."

"Lieutenant, sir," said one of the soldiers with Billy, "we got one here, too."

Billy struggled in their grasp, astonished. "I ain't no Grayback!" he said. "The Rebs made me join up with them. I run off as soon as I could. I come from East Tennessee, where God Almighty hisself tells us slavery is wrong!"

The tall offcer looked skeptically at Billy. "Are you sure you're not just saying this to stay out of a prison camp?"

"M' Lord, yes! I was runnin' from them Rebs, not with them!"

"He's tellin' the truth, sir," Bev said. He had stepped up during the exchange. "He'sbeen runnin' with us a long time now. We

144

thought he was a Johnny Reb, too, at first. But he did right by us, even fed us. Saved our bacon a few times, too." Josh joined in, "That God's truth, Massah, Billy boy a good boy."

The lieutenant stood observing them, weighing their words. At length, he said, "Well, that beats all. I've never seen anything like it. It appears that you are on the up and up, feller. Let the young man go."

The two men oneither side of Billy moved away and he walked over to Bev and Josh who patted him on the back with big grins on their faces. Even Whit smiled and Billy figured he was grinning just as big himself.

"I'm First Lieutenant John Simmons of the Fourth Iowa Volunteer Infantry Regiment under the command of Colonel J. A. Williamson. We just gave the Grays a good whipping at Pea Ridge up north near Leetown, Missou. General Curtis ordered us to root out any Confederate stragglers. We weren't having any luck until you ran this bunch right into us. So, I thank you for that." The lieutenant leaned over in a slight bow. "Now, where do you men hail from?"

"We from Kentucky," said Bev, "and our white friend here is from Tennessee like he say."

"I see. You've come a long piece. You're a bit far west to be heading to Ohio."

"We not goin' there, we goin' to open territory."

Simmons pulled back, "That's a surprise. Nothing much out there but Injuns. I thought you would want to head to Canada."

Bev shook his head, "Too dangerous. Even if we tried and got caught there in the North, the law says you got to send us back."

Simmons frowned, "Not really, with the new confiscation act. You fellers are now considered contraband of war. We don't want you working for Johnny Reb so he can fight longer. We'll be taking these prisoners east to St. Helena to join up with the rest of our company. You're welcome to accompany us. From there, I can send you to a camp that will keep you safe from being returned to your oppressors."

Bev looked at Whit and Josh, then turned back to Simmons. "We don't want to go to no camp. We free now, we want to stay that way."

Simmons nodded his head slowly. "Very well. In my opinion, you men can do what you want, free or not. Sergeant Hamptead, please see that these men are provided with plenty of rations and blankets." He twisted his head around to the captive Confederates and said," Allow them to have their pick of any armament and supplies possessed by the prisoners. If they need powder and balls, give them a good stock."

Bev moved over to the pile of arms taken from the Rebels. He picked out a rifle and a pistol, then stared at the Confederate prisoners a moment before falling back. Josh picked up Robbie's squirrel gun while saying to Billy, "You show me how to shoot, huh Billy? It be easier than catchin' 'em in a trap."

"I'll show you," Billy said as he stepped over and grabbed a rifle, a Brown Bess, not an Enfield. Whit selected four knives, and handed them out to each of them. He saw an Army colt, and stuffed it into his waistband.

Just then, the sergeant returned weighed down by four full canteens, followed by four privates each holding a full haversack. "Here you go, boys, food and drink, blankets and coats. You can thank the Rebel boys over there for the ratty coats."

Billy saw them in their thread-worn shirtsleeves, wrapped in blankets but still shivering in the cold. One of the privates holding their other gear said quietly as he handed it over, "You and your Negra friends can thank us for you being able just to mosey on down the road. This war's cost a hell of a lotta good men's blood for the likes of you."

Billy kept silent. He walked over to the cluster of shivering Rebels and dropped his coat on the ground. "We got better ones on us." Bev, Josh, and Whit followed suit. Whit spit on the ground after throwing down his coat. Without looking at them, the captured Confederates picked up their coats and put them on.

Simmons watched Billy and his friends hoist the haversacks onto their shoulders. "If you're heading west to the Injun Territory, you might want to talk to our scout, Abraham Bowlegs over there." He jerked his head in the direction of a man sitting on a boulder, watching the Union soldiers regrouping for their march. "He's a Seminole Negro from thataways. Knows the Territory pretty well, I believe."

They looked closer at the man lounging on the rock. Sitting there, he seemed to be of average height, with a deep, dark complexion, a thin, curving moustache, and a narrow strip of whiskers following his jawline. He wore doeskin moccasins laced up to his knees and resplendent red, patterned leggings, topped off by an embroidered deerskin coat tanned gold in color. Belted with a sea-blue sash at the waist, the coat ended just above his knees. A cream-colored shirt peeked out from his coat's lapels, and around his neck he wore a cravat seemingly made of blue silk. On his head sat a broad brimmed leather hat decorated by two long, exotic bird feathers, green and yellow. Propped against his left armpit rested the barrel of an old Kentucky long rifle. They also noticed a sizable Bowie knife tucked into his sash.

"How we miss seein' him before now?" Bev uttered.

"He do stand out," said Whit.

Lieutenant Simmons had stepped over to the Seminole. They spoke for a moment, and the Seminole unfolded himself from the rock and meandered over. He must have stood six feet tall, Billy thought, not ordinary at all.

Once he reached them, the tall Indian stuck out his hand, "Abraham Bowlegs," he said.

Bev took his hand, and the scout shook it vigorously, then worked his way around to the other men. Billy thought he would crush his hand, his grip was so strong.

"I hoid from de Lieutenant dat you all wantuh go tuh Injun Territ'ry. Um headed dat way, so uh'll tek you."

Billy and the rest exchanged glances, confounded and amazed.

Chapter 12. Indian Country

"I bin seventeen when de war end."

They huddled around the embers of a fire, listening to Abraham Bowlegs tell his story.

"We never give in to dem white soldiers, but de Seminole Chiefs Osceola, King Philip, and Micanope, dey all put in de jailhouse in South Carolina; dey soon die. But we nevuh give up. De Black Freedman Chiefs John Horse, Billy Bowlegs, and muh father Abraham, dey fight on. Many tuk tuh de swamps where de white soldiers could not find dem. Dem dey find, dey send tuh de Injun Territ'ry. De white chief promise us pardons; dey call us Seminole Negroes. But we de Estelusti, de Black Seminoles. John Horse believe de white chief, and many of us join 'n followde other Seminoles tuh Injun Territ'ry. De travel been hard, de land harder. I loin how tuh live wid de old enemies, de Cherokees, Choctaws, Chickasaws, and de Creeks. De white chief, 'e put us wid de Creeks, very bad.

"We wus not lucky; I wus not lucky. The white chief tuk our guns and de slavers hunt us. We Black Seminoles, Black Freedmun, but dey tuk us anyway. I wus put in a boat tuh N'awlins where dey sold me. I wus a slave 'til de whites' war with each other, north 'gainst south. Many slaves ran away tuh de Yankees in de north. I run.

"I return tuh de Territ'ry tuh fight on de blue side wid de Creek Chief Opothelyahola. We fight t'ree big battles, lose de last very bad, so de old Chief tuk his people out'uh de Territ'ry. I went east tuh fight more. I bin a scout fo' General Curtis n' he won a great battle ovuh de gray soldiers. We chase dem heah, n' I find ya'll."

He took a bite and chewed. The others sat ruminating while he ate.

Whit said, "Lemme understand this: you a free black man, and you a Injun, too? That right?" Abraham nodded. "But you also a slave in N'awlins?"

Again, Abraham shook his head yes.

"And, they a lot more of you up north of Injun country fightin' for the Yankees."

Abraham munched.

"That gotta be the tallest story I ever heard."

Abraham had led them out of the Boston Mountains north toward Bentonville near where the Pea Ridge battle had been fought. For the first time in weeks, they all felt like they might not freeze to death. They also found it easier to forge for food, whether for nuts or small game just out of hibernation that they captured with Josh's traps. For water, streams provided plenty. Except for Fort Gibson south of the mountains, very few people lived in this far reach of the country, which allowed the fugitive men to relax somewhat in the wilderness. This late night, after feasting on a small nest of young rabbits, they sat back waiting to hear Abraham tell more outrageous tales. Instead, he talked about plans.

"We cyan't keep goin' north neah Missou, Rebels theya. Bettuh follow de Spring Rivuh, light out fas' fo' de Territ'ry neah Wyandotte land," Abraham said. "But, we cyan't stay theya, Injuns fight fo' de Grays. Dem Injuns slavers, too." Seeing their incredulous looks, Abraham went on. "De Cherokees 'n de Creeks, dey have plantations wid slaves, same as de buckruhs." Seeing their puzzled looks, he said, "Ya know, de buckruhs, de whites."

They all nodded their heads knowingly.

"Dat why dese Injuns get wid de gray buckruhs. Dat 'n hatin' what de blue whites done, force 'um out heah in des cold land. Lef'um all tuh die. De Graybacks, dey promise dem Injuns land 'n freedom ef dey fight fo' de South. All dem do fight fo' dem gray bucks. Chief Opothelyahola of de Creek, he don' fight fo' de gray bucks, he fight fo' de blue soldiers 'gainst slavery. De Delaware 'n de Wyandot also fight fo' de Blues. Dey run, too, but mebbe some friendlies still theya. Das why we goin' through dey land tuh Kansas."

Bev and the others shook their heads solemnly up and down in agreement.

"Chief Opothelyahola, he be en Fort Belmont wid de Yankess. Dat long way frum heah."

"So, if we goin' into Injun Territory, how we gettin' outta there fast if Kansas is all that far away?" Whit asked.

Abraham rubbed his face, "Uh hav uh plan."

During the days that followed, they shadowed the White River north up to Sequoyah Lake, rounding it to pick up the West Fork. Below Fayetteville, the river turned into the Town Branch, where it petered out. They then crossed country to pick up Goose Creek, which fed into the Illinois River. They traced the Illinois north and west where it bent south, just seven miles from Indian Territory. Heading west from the bend along Spring Creek, in a matter of hours they found themselves in Indian Territory.

They trailed after Abraham as he told them about the host of tribes forced to move here from their ancestral lands more than three decades ago. Traditional enemies living "up on top each othur," Abraham put it, "bad fo'um all."

He was careful to keep them close to cover as much as possible, for the first time camping at night. During the day, they stayed low around streambanks flanked by stands of hickories and walnuts just leafing. Now the end of March, spring showed more signs of new life, though frigid air blown by fierce gusts of wind still chilled them now and then. It was as though they still journeyed during winter days. Also, by moving further up the valleys, food became harder to find. The seemingly endless march through the elements took its toll.

"Why in God's name we followin' this here Jim Dandy?" Whit complained. "We ain't gotten any closer to bein' free with him than when we was on our own."

Bev lowered his head. "You might be right," he said. "Maybe we shoulda gone north directly, like most other runaways, 'stead of sideways."

The statement shocked Whit, used to being slapped down by Bev whenever he complained. But, the big horseman seemed brought down, worn out by the endless march across the wilderness. He hadn't been the same since his little brother had gone missing. Probably drowned, thought Whit.

"Hey, now," he said, "it ain't all on you. We all say this be the way to go. I just ain't sure 'bout the way that popinjay pointin' us now is all."

Billy joined in, "That's right, Bev. He knows Injun Territory, I guess, but he's crazy, too."

Bev swung his eyes to Josh. "What you think, Josh?"

Josh closed in on himself somewhat, uncomfortable with the attention. He hesitated, then said, "Either way's good fo' me. I don't much care where we go as long as we don't run into any slavecatchers or militia, crackers or Injuns. It all the same to me."

"Awright, then," Bev said.

They sat in a small grove of trees a mile or so above the river crossing. Daylight had arrived, but they lit no fire, wary of any Indian militia sniffing around. Abraham had told them that the Cherokees and most of the other tribes of the Five Nations had allied themselves with the Confederates, but only if they could stay to fight in their own land. Formed up as Indian militia, they actively patrolled the border between Oklahoma and Kansas on horseback, posing a serious threat to any slaves on the run.

On that cold day, the five fugitives and their guide kept warm in their coats and blankets. Josh had passed around some old beef jerky left over from the Yankee supplies. It didn't taste like much, but no one complained as they sat chewing away.

Whit paused, his head cocked as he looked up at Abraham sitting on a stump. "You sure look purdy, Abraham. Why you dress so purdy, stick out in a crowd like that?"

In fact, Abraham's finery did not seem so fine up close. Greasy dirt stained his deerskin coat, and his colorful cravat was darkened with dried sweat stains, the same as the brim of his hat. His leggings had been torn in a few spots, and his moccasins appeared worn at the toes. Even the fancy feathers on his hat looked to have suffered some wear and tear. Nonetheless, Whit told the truth when he noted that Abraham would stand out in any gathering.

"How do you sneak around scoutin' purdy like that, never get caught?"

"Uh stay low," Abraham replied. "Uh know muh way, too."

Whit still seemed skeptical, but he let it go.

That night, Abraham called them together. "We not too far frum Kansas," he said, "but it dang'rous heah, too. Injuns on hossesheahafta us north 'n south. We got tuh cross de Elk Rivuh."

"What, another river? Now we gotta cross it?"

Abraham dipped his head rapidly, "Right naw."

Bev's eyes widened. "How we gonna do that? How we gettin' over?" asked Bev, "We can't swim."

"We mek uh coonoo."

"A coonoo? What a coonoo?" Whit said.

"Yuh know, fo' duh rivuh, tuh float in de watah."

"Coonoo?" Whit asked.

"A canoe!" said Bev.

"Lord, I can't understand this man most times," Whit muttered.

"A canoe? How we goin' to build a canoe anytime fast?" said Bev, his voice edgy. "And, we gonna need more than one, we need two, maybe three with all our stuff."

Abraham shrugged, "We use logs, tie 'em in 'n float ovuh."

"So, rafts. What about our sacks and guns?"

"Tie 'em upontop."

"Lord have mercy," Bev mumbled, and the others shifted around uncomfortably.

Once Abraham Bowlegs made a decision he jumped into action. He led them up to the river, moving along the bank until he found a thick forest stand. He searched around for trees that had fallen recently enough so that they had very little rot, roughly twenty feet tall and six inches in diameter. Using a tomahawk from his haversack, he stripped a trunk of its branches and cut off its top and roots. The others watched long enough to see what he was doing, then located trunks of their own to work. In the meantime, Abraham cut down mid-thick grape vines to use as rope.

They built the rafts according to Abraham's instructions. He hovered over each one as they worked, tying the vines tight in some places, loosening them in others, "tuh let de limbs float free so dey don' flip."

By the end of the day, they had lashed nine trunks together in threes using grapevines. Abraham weaved more vines together into several lengths of rope. Billy and Josh copied his technique to fashion more while Bev and Whit stood watch with their rifles at opposite ends of the hastily roughed-out clearing. Once Abraham felt that they had enough rope, he began to tie the men's gear to the rafts. He divided the sacks and rifles, positioning them as equally as he could on the rafts to keep them from swamping. He then tied lengths of the makeshift ropes into loops at either ends of the rafts, two apiece. In the water, the men would use the ropes to keep them safely in contact while they kicked their legs to push the rafts across.

"But, I told you, Abraham," said Bev, "we'all can't swim. None of us. If we in the water, we go under."

Abraham said, "Cyan't swim? Nun 'um?"

"Nun'um," repeated Bev.

Abraham held his hands out, palms up, and said, "Den, you git upontop de rafts. De sacks 'n guns, you put dem upontop of you'um."

They looked and realized immediately that the rafts were too narrow to fit everyone and their supplies on top. Even if they could manage it, trying to propel the rafts across the river would be much more awkward and difficult. The men's extra weight would cause the trunks to bob up and down in the water, most likely soaking their goods through and through.

Sighing, Billy pulled Bev away. "You really want to do this, Bev? We lost Eli on the Big River, the water flat as a flapjack. This river's movin'."

He watched the life leave Bev's face when he mentioned Eli. Bev quickly hid the expression and replied, "What choice we got, Billy? Abraham says the militia's hard on our heels."

"Yeah, but you believe him? He's crazy, Bev!"

Bev's shoulders dropped. "What choice we got?"

Finally, they seemed to be ready. Their goods and guns were securely tied to cross logs that raised them higher on the rafts. Grape vines lashed to the long trunk sides floated loosely, waiting for the men to tie them around their waists. Abraham put them in position in the shallow water, then lashed them to the rafts. Once they seemed secure, he took up his own position in the middle of one next to Josh and pushed off. Whit, Bev, and Billy followed suit with their raft.

The water chilled them and the wind kicked up a chop as well, making progress across the moving river frighteningly slow. Nowhere near the breadth of the Mississippi, the Elk called for twice as much effort to cross. In midstream, Bev pictured a row of slavecatchers lining up on the bank behind, leveling their rifles to take careful aim at them as though they were sitting ducks. He cringed, and shrank even further behind the raft's silhouette. Then, he wondered if they were on the opposite bank waiting to scoop them all up.

He hung on to the vines knotted to the logs, kicking his legs to keep moving. He realized that he preferred being shot or hanged rather than dying like Eli had, deep in a dark river suffocating while trying to breathe water.

The far shore closed in on them, and Bev lifted his head up. The bank seemed quiet, not necessarily a sure sign that no one waited for them. Then, he heard peepers croaks, proof that they felt no threat from unknown intruders. They suddenly ceased, aware now of a new potential danger from the arrivaling fugitive party.

Abraham and Josh touched first, and the black Freeman agilely leaped up over the raft onto the rocky riverside. He slipped into the woods along the bank, and reappeared quickly, waving his hand to urge the others ashore. Josh already stood on one side pulling his raft up out of the water. Bev and the others soon joined them, yanking the heavy wooden rafts halfway out of the river. They hastened to unload their gear, and melted into the woods. They had made it across.

"Frum heah, we wan tuh falla de Neosho Rivah north tuh whey it joins de Spring Rivuh agin," Abraham told them the next day. "Dat lead us all de way tuh Kansas. Uh know a road neah heah, tek us whey we wantuh go."

Bev exchanged tense lookswith Whit until the distiller shrugged his shoulders. Bev said, "This road, how far from here, and where it gonna take us?"

"It close," said Abraham, "Tek us next tuh de rivuh neah plenty uh trees. Easy tuh hide theyah lickety-split. Frum heah on out we'um sleep nights, walk nights."

"Awright. Then, we go," said Bev.

The rutted path that Abraham led them to consisted of two rugged tracks formed by heavy wagons rumbling close to the Neosho, the main river running north and south in this part of the Indian Territory. Traveling at night, the fugitives found it easier to hike next to the rough uneven ruts rather than in them. Tired and hungry, they shared a couple of small catfish that Josh pulled in from a trot line he had put out early the morning before. Abraham said they would reach Fort Scott in a couple of days. The brisk evenings and uncertain roadway slowed them down, but during the day warmer temperatures allowed them to sleep deep, each with their own dreams.

Bev couldn't sleep that night. With Fort Scott and safety only twenty miles away, he could not keep from crowding his thoughts with the loss of Eli. It seemed so long ago, yet it was less than two months. Memories assaulted him of when he was a boy and Eli just born. His mama held that baby so close to her breast, it was almost hard to see him within her arms. Everyone knew who had fathered that light-skinned child, but it didn't matter to his mother; she loved that baby completely, more than her other son. Bev couldn't understand it, he loved his mama so much. When he looked at his reflection in a pond, seeing his own black skin, he figured his pappy had been another slave. Maybe that was the reason Eli seemed to count for more to Mama. On her deathbed, she begged Bev to take care of Eli like he was his own child. Amid his tears as she faded away, he promised he would.

He might have forgotten that promise, except that Eli turned out to be the sweetest boy he had ever known, so innocent and full of wonder. Long and thin, with blue eyes in his long face and slender fingers, he seemed better suited for playing an instrument instead of toiling in a cotton field. Eventually, Bev began to think that perhaps his mother had loved Eli because he was so good, not that he was the Master's son. The idea caused Bev to rue his jealousy and resentment, thinking that maybe his mamamostly left him on his own because he was stronger, capable of taking care of himself. If so, it was natural for her to ask him to take care of Eli. She trusted him with his half-brother's protection. The consideration did not make his hurt feelings disappear, he still missed having his mama close to him. It did allow him to feel better about Eli and to love him more simply because he was so lovable. Now he was gone.

"You awake, Bev?" The soft voice spoke disembodied in the dark night. Bev recognized it as Billy's.

"I'm up," replied Bev. "Can't seem to sleep."

"Me neither."

The night quieted again for a moment.

"Here I lie," said Billy, "maybe a day or two from being saved, ready to breathe easy, and I can't sleep a wink." Bev didn't reply. Billy went on, "I been away from my daddy for five months, almost half a year, and I don't have no idea if he's alive or dead." He waited to see if Bev would talk, then went on. "I left him just 'afore winter when times was so hard, I don't know if he had enough to eat to get through it." He paused, remembering, and said, "He sent me out to plant some 'taters in the woods so's the Johnny Rebs or Yankees couldn't steal them. I planted 'em, though I was mad about it. I planted 'em, and I left home without tellin' him where they was planted. For all I know, he may a starved to death from hunger while them spuds came right up in the first good weather. Here I am hundreds of miles away and I just don't know.

"I miss my daddy," he said, his voice full at the end.

Bev lay near him, listening, a bit bitter yet recognizing the young white boy's sorrow. At length, he said, "Your daddy might be awright. He's been livin' in the hills a long time, right? He know enough to find them taters. He probably gettin' by well enough."

"You think so?" Billy asked. Then, he said morosely, "I feel so guilty for gettin' into this fix. If I'd just stayed home, do what he told me to do, I'd still be there instead of here in the wild, Injun Rebs and regulators all around."

"You might get home yet," Bev said. He followed softly with, "I doubt I'll be goin' back ever."

His last sentence floated in the air alone for a while until Billy said in a rush, "Gosh darn, I'm sorry, Bev, you ain't got no home to go back to and you lost your brother Eli. Here I am complainin'. Please, I'm sorry, please forgive me."

Bev smiled, hearing Billy sounding so earnest. "That's awright, Billy, I'm awright. I ain't alone, I got you, and Josh." He paused, and said, "I got Whit, too."

Billy listened, and stifled a laugh, "Whit!"

Bev rumbled a low chuckle, "He can be hard to like for sure. I remember when he first showed up at the farm. Old man Bowman bought him to cook up whiskey to sell. He wanted him close, so's he put him in the stable quarters with us, me and Eli. I got the youngBowman to let Eli work with the hosses with me, and we in the bunkhouse next to them. Well, Whit start in right away, talkin' 'bout how big he is, goin' to take over the farm, and we might as well get used to it. I laughed and nodded like'okay, if you say so.' But then, he go over to Eli's bunk, grab him, and toss him on the floor like a sack of oats. I jump to my feet, and Whit say, 'So we gonna go now?' but before he finish, I so mad I lift him off his feet by his neck and drop him on the floor. I jump him, my arm 'cross his throat, he chokin', can barely give in. That the end of it. Oh, he still mouths off now and then, but that's all."

"So, why you let him go with you all?" Billy said.

"I didn't have a choice, he threaten to holler about us runnin'. Still, the past few months he's shown he back us up in a tussle."

"And Josh?"

"We lucky Josh ain't Whit. Josh the strongest man on the farm, maybe anyplace. He's also the gentlest. When we gettin' ready to run, he up and say he wants to go, surprise the devil out of me. He like a statue at that farm, always there, never change. But, he wants to run with us, so he run."

"And now you all are real close to bein' free."

"Not yet. And not Eli."

Billy said nothing, and they fell silent until they slept.

"Git down!" rasped Abraham, pushing his hands low through the air. Without a word, all five of them dove to the ground. They hid behind a line of hickory trees bordering a broad, brown field. The trees bore fresh leaflets peeking from their branches, the only foliage showing at Baxter Springs this early in April. As they lay gripping the twigs and leaves on the damp ground, they could hear the thumping of hooves, many of them. Lying just in front of them, Abraham waved his hand behind his flanks, gesturing for them to go back

156

further among the trees. They faded into the woods stealthily, hiding behind large tree trunks, chancing quick glances now and then back at lamplight flashing over the road. A large group of men on horses churned up the ruts, thirty riders or more, Bev figured. As far as he could tell in the low light at this distance, they looked like they were outfitted like Indians. He noted some in deerskin shirts with long feathers in their broad hats. Then again, they might be Ruffians disguised as Indians to take the blame for any Kansas settlers they massacred. The leader, though was black. No Ruffians would have a black man ride with them, never mind having one giving them orders.

Abraham stood further out front behind an oak, staring at the riders. He abruptly stood straight up behind the trunk and began loading his Kentucky rifle. Then, slowly he raised the rifle above his head, pivoted, and swung it around the trunk leveled in the direction of the horsemen.

Bev froze, his head whipping back and forth, moaning to himself, don't, they'll all come after us. Just then, the black headman dropped from his mount and stepped toward the woods. He moved into the trees gingerly, unholstering a large handgun as he walked. As he approached, Bev jerked his head over to see Abraham silently pull back the hammer on his long rifle. No, no, shouted Bev silently, there are thirty of them, they will kill us all!

The black headman halted, hesitating. He wore a black suit with a vest and a broad silk tie pinned to his blue-striped shirt. His pants appeared dusty, probably from the ride, cuffed over a set of chiseled boots. He seemed to be listening, his head cocked to one side. Finally, he lowered his pistol and turned around. He headed back to the road, holstering his gun on the way, and climbed onto his horse. Wheeling around, he shouted words that Bev couldn't make out. Then, he took off, followed by the rest of them in quick order. Bev exhaled and relaxed, noting that Abraham had eased the hammer down and lowered his rifle.

They waited silently for a good fifteen minutes. Then, Abraham stalked out to the road. He looked left and right, then turned back to face the other men and waved them forward. Once they reached the road and were sure that the riders had gone, they set out again without speaking a word. They covered several miles without incident, until daytime approached. Abraham led them into a thicket of locust near a small rivulet. They drank their fill and began settling in to rest. But, Whit faced Abraham.

"Who was that nigger you damn near shot?" he demanded angrily. "If you bring him down, all them riders be on us 'n we all dead!"

"'E comin' towad us in de trees. Uh had tuh git ready tuh fight."

"You ready to drop him before he do anything. Why is that? What he got to do with you anyhow?"

Abraham sat down. "'E uh Freemun. 'E uh overseer fuh Stand Watie, Cherokee Chief. Watie big soldier wid de Graybacks. Watie uh slaver, tuh. Dat mun wid de hawsemens, uh know 'um frum befo'. 'E beat slaves, kill slaves. Uh kill 'um fo' dat."

"Maybe so," snapped Whit, "but you would 'a got us killed the same time!"

Abraham dropped his head. "Dat true. Uh sorry." Then, he raised his eyes to Whit's. "Uh wait 'til uh come back. Wen uh do, uh kill 'em den."

Abraham guided them north, tracing their way from Spring Creek along Cow Creek and other streams that led to Fort Scott. The hilly hike along the Nesho River among leafing trees gradually transformed into open land covered by tall grasses and wild blue flowers as far as they could see. Fewer trees occupied the landscape, and the air breezed cooler. They had made it to the high plains plateau, just miles from Fort Scott, Abraham assured them. They had made it into the Free State of Kansas.

They all felt hollow from hunger, and their water swished lightly at the bottoms of their canteens. The walking was not easy in the thick vegetation in the dark, but their pace seemed to quicken the closer they drew to the fort. At dawn, they finally came to a point where two flowing streams joined, one a creek coursing from the northwest, the other a larger river running east to west. Situated on a bluff above the tributaries stood a town.

"TheyaFort Scott," Abraham pointed, "on dat hill. Dat de Marmaton Rivuh. Mills Crik de othuh."

The men gazed up at the buildings, wondering where the fort walls were, and the Bluecoats.

"Over there in front," Billy said. "White tents, lots of 'em."

Bev lowered his sight and saw the tents beneath some trees with trickles of smoke rising between them in the cool air.

"We git op theya, dey give us food 'n watah. We dicker wid dem fo mo, hawses, mebbe."

The tired men hiked up the last half-mile nearer to the tents, hundreds of them. They drew closer, and a sentry wearing a blue tunic and a broad-brimmed hat halted them, holding diagonally across his torso a Springfield rifle topped by a bayonet. He hesitated for an instant, then addressed Billy, whose gray shell jacket lay hidden beneath his winter coat.

"You in charge, here? Where you goin' with these boys here?"

Billy swallowed and said, "I'm not in charge, I'm with them." He turned his head to Bev.

"We on de run frum de Rebs," said Abraham. "We ravish 'n need uh place tuh stay."

The guard scrunched up his face. "The Rebs? You runnin'?" He looked back at the others and said, "I can barely make out a word this fellow says."

"Neither can us," said Billy.

"I don't know how the sergeant is going to understand him," the soldier said, shaking his head.

"I know what he say," Josh piped in. Bev and the rest stared at him with amazed expressions, and he said, "I unnerstan' what he mean. He say we' runnin' from the Johnny Rebs, that we're real hungry and we need someplace to stay."

The guard hesitated for a second, then said, "All right, I'll take you to the sergeant, but I can't leave my post 'til I'm relieved of duty." He gazed up at the morning sky, "That's about an hour from now. You boys might as well get comfortable until then."

He stepped back and assumed his stance, while Josh, Bev, and the others took a seat in the grass.

After an hour, another soldier in blue meandered up to the first guard and said, "I'm here, Victor, you can go back to camp."

"About time, Evan, you're late."

"A couple minutes, bully for me." The new soldier, small and compact, and sporting a tiny French moustache and beard, also wore a broad riding hat with tassels. He noticed the five men lounging on the ground.

"Who are those niggers?'" he said, "And the scrawny muggins with them? They all look like bags of bones."

Stewart shrugged, "Contrabands, my guess. I'm taking them to the sergeant for orders."

The little soldier nodded indifferently. Victor faced them and said, "You boys will have to leave the firearms behind. Strict orders."

Each of them clutched their rifles and pistols harder, causing Victor to say, "You can get them back later if the sergeant says okay."

Reluctantly, they laid their rifles and pistols in a pile. "Knives, too," said Evan. Whit scowled at him and dropped his knife near the guns, followed by Bev and the others.

"Okay, follow me," said Victor.

He led them on a serpentine march into the camp, walking them left, then right, and left again through the parallel rows of white tents. They reached a larger space where the tents faced each other, and strolled down the center toward the middle of the camp. All around them, blue-dressed soldiers ate breakfast, smoked, and scratched their backs and buttocks through their union suits without giving the passersby more than a glance.

Victor brought them to a larger tent and told them to wait. Another guard stood at the flaps, and he, too, ignored them after quickly sizing them up. In no more than half a minute, the tent flap was pushed aside as a sergeant emerged. He stood six feet tall in a blue fatigue jacket closed by a row of brass buttons, one of them missing in the middle. Blond-haired, he bore a straggly goateethat hardly showed against his light tan skin. His trousers sagged at the knee and his boots were scuffed and scratched from hard wear. A leather belt at his waist supported a heavy pistol in its holster that hung low on his hip. Still and all, Bev saw something in the man's searing blue eyes, something solid.

"Contraband?" he said.

Bev and Whit exchanged glances, puzzled.

"Contraband, contraband," the sergeant said impatiently, "runaway slaves from the South."

Abraham said, "We lit out, but uh not a slave, only dem." He pointed at Billy, "Dat un, 'e uh Reb, but 'e run away, too."

The officer blinked, and said, "What was that, again?"

Josh moved forward and said, "He say we all run, but he ain't a slave, only us," gesturing to Bev and the others, then at Billy,"'ceptin' him, he run from the Rebels."

The officer confronted Billy, "Are you a Rebel deserter, boy?"

"Yessir," Billy stammered, "I'm an ab'listionist. The Rebs made me join up, so I run."

The officer pulled back. "Oh." Then, he addressed them all. "I'm First Sergeant Porter of the Third Wisconsin Cavalry. We're ordered to defend Fort Scott from any Rebel attacks, so right now we're building fortifications around the fort and town. Since you are escaped slaves from the South, you have been declared contraband of war. What that means is you cannot be returned to the Rebels to help them in their war efforts. So, you will be allowed to stay here and assist our regular infantry men with fort construction. In time, you will be reassigned to a contraband camp with others of your race for future dispersal."

The men appeared taken aback. Whit said, "We get paid for workin'?"

"Shelter and board, clothing if necessary," replied Sergeant Porter. "You will be helping in the war effort."

"So, now we have new blue-dressed massahs," Whit uttered.

"It is better than being sent back to the Johnnies, I'm sure you'll agree."

"We'd just soon keep movin' on," said Bev. "That's why we run west, so none of us be sent back 'cause of them fugitive laws."

"I'm afraid that's out of the question,"the Sergeant replied. "You are under our authority, now. We can use your help."

Abraham spoke up, "Yo' hav othuh slaves heah?"

Porter listened blankly, then turned to Josh.

"You got other slaves here?"

The Sergeant said, "Yes, all at work save the children."

"Wha 'bout Injuns? Yo' hav Injuns, tuh?"

"Ya'all have Injuns here, too?" echoed Josh.

Porter nodded, "We do, many of them."

"Dey not slaves, dey woik?"

Josh started to speak, and Porter cut him off, "No, they do not work. They are refugees who will be sent to Fort Belmont to reunite with others of their people. They are loyal bound to the Union."

"Muscogee Creeks, some Cherokee, Seminoles, Estelusti," Abraham said, "Chief Opothleyahola people."

"That's right."

"Who tek dem tuh Belmont?"

"We are organizing a wagon train to leave soon, now that spring has arrived. We have guides returning from Belmont to take them. They should be here in a month or so."

"Fuh now, yo' gotta feed dem, house dem, protek dem. Dey git north, yo' save all dat."

Josh translated, and Porter mulled the Freedman's suggestion. At length, he said, "I'll have to bring this up to my superior. He'll have to check with his, which means it'll probably continue to go up the line." He examined the runaways as he spoke, and said, "For now, you can get yourselves situated, get something to eat and drink. If we put you to work now, it'd probably kill you. Private, lead them to the mess tent."

Victor maneuvered them further around the camp until they came to a long tent with trestle tables and benches inside. He told them to take a seat, then walked to the end of the tent. At the end, a row of black men and women washed and dried tin plates used for breakfast, stacking clean ones on shelves in a long cabinet on a cart. Victor glanced back furtively at the sitting men as he spoke to a round, bearded man wearing an apron up to his chest. Victor ducked out of a nearby entrance, and the bearded man approached.

"I heah you niggers want vittles without havin' to woik. That so, we'll get you what's left of the pigs we et for supper last night." He sneered, and turned to go.

"Ham hocks 'n 'pone, pulees," said Billy, "'maybe some grits?'"

The others burst into laughter, and Bev said, "Maybe we oughta retrieve our guns, now, scrape up somethin' to eat later."

They arrived at the sentry post just in time to see a couple of soldiers looking over the rifles, one holding a handgun straight out with an eye closed to check the sight. Whit stepped up to the one holding the pistol and said menacingly, "Those our weapons. I hope you jus' takin' a look."

The soldier, barely eighteen, paled and quickly placed the pistol on the ground. The other one, older looking, said, "What makes you boys think we're gonna hand these weapons over to a bunch of contraband Negras?"

Bev stepped up, "'Cause they ours. We just walked five hundred miles to get here, takin' down plenty of men on our way. A few more ain't gonna make no difference to us, no matter what color their coats. We movin' on one way or another. So, if you want to try all five of us, we ready."

The sentry Evan continued to stare ahead out at the plain as though no one else was there. The young soldier backed away slowly toward camp. The older man looked around, then dropped the rifle. He took a few steps away toward the tents, saying as he retreated, "Regularly, I'd teach you a lesson myself, but why should I have all the fun? I'll go get me some of my lads, show you we fight for the Union, not a bunch of no-account niggers."

Whit brandished his fist, and the soldier broke into a run.

"Now what we do?" Billy asked as each of them gathered up their weapons.

"Get into town, see if we can get somethin' to eat."

162

They wandered up to the fort, a crowd of buildings surrounding a parade ground. Various military structures stood on the grassy square's immediate perimeter, some old and some just under construction. They saw an old hospital, two floors with wraparound porches on each level that had allowed convalescents to cool off in hot weather. It served now as the officers headquarters and bivouac while new command centers were being built, clapboard buildings with rows of dormers across the roofs. A number of tents had been set up for the infantry, also waiting for barracks to be finished. At the far end of the ground, they could see a large, long, single-story stockhouse with wagons lined up beside it being loaded by other black men.

The men wandered around the fort buildings up to the private commercial edifices, the Western Hotel, a hardware store, livery stable, cafés, a barbershop, and several saloons. Beyond them were cabins and other domiciles for common folks.

They headed out behind a café and found a stout black man standing on a short set of steps smoking. When he saw them coming up, he slowly pulled his head back.

Josh moved up in front. "You spare anythin' to eat? We been on the road a long time and we near starvin.'"

The black man looked them over, then said, "Wait heah."

He soon returned with a few loaves of bread, a jar of molasses, and a block of cheese. Tossing them down, he said, "Y'all best get movin' outta heah, o' they gonna scoop yo' up and put y'all to woik."

"Yessir, thank you brother, we obliged."

They ran around the side of the building into the alley and began devouring big slices of bread covered with molasses and cheese. In less than five minutes, they had consumed everything. They were still hungry.

"Des north folk en't been all dat good fo' us so fah."

Josh said, "Maybe so, Abraham, but they ain't much we can do 'bout it right now."

Sitting with their backs against the wall, they were surprised by Sergeant Porter and a contingent of soldiers.

"I've been looking all over for you," he said. "The Great Sultan of the whole shebang wants to see you boys."

"Who?" asked Billy.

"General Denver," Porter replied, "he's in charge of every man jack at this post, including you."

163

Porter led them to the officers' quarters, walked them up the stairs to the long front porch and inside the main hallway. He told them to wait, then knocked on a heavy wooden door just in front of the stairway. Told to enter, Porter straightened himself up, and went inside. He returned within a minute and beckoned for the party of black men and the one white stray to step inside.

Various officers crowded the room, furnished with a table covered with maps, several bar chairs, and a few kerosene lamps. A large walnut desk stood at the back under a tall sash window. There, a clean-shaven man of imposing girth sat leaning back, puffing furiously on a long cigar. Engaged in lively conversation with a couple of officers standing opposite him, as soon as he saw the fugitive men enter the room, he waved his subordinates away and gave the newcomers his complete attention.

"I'm General James Denver. I run this place. The good sergeant, here, tells me you boys can lead Indians to Fort Belmont. He tells me you have a Freeman scout that knows how."

Abraham stepped forward. "Uh be 'im."

The General propped his elbows on the desktop and said, "Well, all right then. Let's talk turkey."

Chapter 13. Fort Row

They had hoped to cover ten miles each day on their way west to Fort Belmont, but the string of men, women, and children straggling behind slowed them down. Mostly refugees from the Indian Territory, they had left Fort Scott with just the clothes on their backs. General Denver had given Bev and the other men a sutler wagon full of supplies, two old mules to pull it, and one horse for scouting. Bev complained that they needed more horses, but Denver swore that he couldn't spare any more, that they were lucky to have anything at all.

Everyone knew that the general was stretching the truth; if he hadn't come up with supplies, the five of them would have lit out on their own, never mind guiding refugees to Fort Scott. Now they were on the trail with sixty Indians in tow who were making quite a dent in their goods just in the first week of the march. Bev and his men wondered if they wouldn't have been better off on their own. In doing a quick inventory, at their present traveling speed he figured they would run out of food at about the halfway mark. Then, what?

For starters, he divided up the remaining supplies he could and doled them out for men and women to carry. Then, he put nine children and two older Indians into the wagon. This helped some, but they still had a definite chance of starving to death before they arrived at Fort Belmont. A stray thought crossed his mind, that if matters really became tough, they could push on themselves without the Indians. He quickly shook his head as if he could toss out such a horrible idea once it had occurred. Instead, he pictured them heading fast to Belmont to bring help back to the rest. Even as he entertained the notion, he understood immediately that it was an excuse to run, that all of these people would be lost if they were left behind. But, the trip to Belmont was going to take a month at least, and if they didn't come up with something, many would die before getting there.

The realization caused Bev to divert the party to Fort Row, roughly a third of the way to Belmont, though further south. He knew that they were taking a huge chance. Word had it that Chief Opothelayahola led his people to Row from Fort Scott. Because his group of refugees numbered in the thousands, the men at Fort Row faced enormous difficulties providing for the Indians. The Creek chief soon moved them on to Belmont in hope of finding more food and shelter.

At least the land was mostly flat, thought Bev, plenty of trees, grass, and bushes. But, an actual road mostly didn't exist. General Denver had given them some maps, all of which proved to be confusing, wrong, and contradictory to the others. Bev and his companions did their best to match landmarks with points on the maps. Rather than depend on them, they relied more on rough calculations using the sun and the stars. Abraham scouted ahead, too, but a big surprise to Bev was that he wasn't much of a horseman. Instead, he struck out on foot ahead of the caravan, covering ten miles or so, then returned to tell them what he had seen. It helped in finding water and shelter for setting up camp, but his forays weren't of muchuse in determining their distance from either fort or if they were traveling in the right direction at all. The damnable flat land afforded them no high ground to look far out, either. And, though the end of April was near, the nights on the grassland remained cold, causing them all to cling together to sleep.

The Indians never complained. Mostly Creek and Cherokee, only a handful spoke English. The rest remained silent, or talked softly among themselves, never causing any commotion. As far as Bev could tell, even the two tribes' warriors got along. Without being asked, they all pitched in to set camp, scavenged for firewood, and brought back water no matter how far they had to go. Even the children chopped any nearby new grass for the mules and the horse to eat. They also treated the strange men leading them as though they were royalty. Like Josh and Billy, Bev felt awkward at being considered some kind of duke or earl, something he never expected at any time in his life. Abraham came and went from dawn to dusk, so he had nothing to say about being spoiled. Only Whit took it in stride. In fact, he loved it, especially if it was the little Creek girl Nila.

Nila spoke English, which made it easier for Whit to come closer to her. A tiny, dark woman, she wore a plain dress deep blue in color that covered her all the way from her neck to the laces of her hobnail boots. She wore a short jacket on top and a scarf in her long raven hair. A simple beaded necklace Robin-egg blue in color fell from her neck. Except for her dark skin and black opal eyes, she could have been mistaken for a local farm girl instead of an Indian maiden. Even her English was flawless, far better than Bev's and the rest. When they needed to tell the entire group something, they spoke to Nila or a Cherokee named Degotoga, which meant "standing together," an apt name for a wise old man. Degotoga spoke English also, but not nearly as well as Nila, whom they turned to most often.

Whit took to her for other reasons, though. Every chance he could, he tried to sweet talk her, saying how pretty she was, smart, too, the way she spoke all sorts of languages. Nila smiled plenty, but seemed to keep her distance. Whit never gave up, trying different things, telling her how much he admired the Indian ways, giving her little presents, like a small wooden animal whittled out of a stick he'd found. At first, he never seemed to make any ground. Then, he started sharing his food with her. After that, Nila warmed up to him right quick, Bev observed.

He wasn't happy about Whit fancying her. Nila was young, too young for the likes of Whit. She could be hurt or ruined. Suppose Whit took advantage of her, Bev thought to himself. The rest of the Indians might take offense, cut all their throats. No, he thought, silently shaking his head, this was not good. He fretted for a while, then decided to talk to Nila's father, Chekilli. To do that, he would need Degotoga to translate.

That evening, Bev took Degotoga aside to talk.

"I'm worried, Deg, 'bout Whit and Nila. If he keeps on wooin' her, he just might make her daddy mad. That could be bad for everyone."

Degotoga's grey hair hung long from his wide-brimmed hat. He stood tall and lean, wearing an old suede jacket with a tie and a high-collared shirt underneath. His britches were dark-blue dungaree, and his boots were scuffed leather, pointed at the toe like horsemen wore. He stared down at Bev and said, "Don't you care 'bout this," he said. "Nila good woman, know what she do."

"Maybe," Bev said, exercising patience, "but I ain't sure Whit's all that good a man. He might bother Nila too much, you understand? He's a rollin' stone."

Degotoga rubbed the grey stubble on his chin, then said, "No matter. Nila good."

Bev sighed. "Maybe so, but I want to talk to her daddy, make sure nothin' bad happens."

Degotoga sighed heavily then, and grunted, "Huh. You want to talk Chekilli, okay. You waste his time, okay."

Degotoga led the way to the spot in the camp where Chekilli and his family rested. Chekilli was slightly shorter than Bev and thick in the middle. His hair was gray, too, but close-cropped and slicked back. He wore a black suit with a vest and a red silk tie, and black boots, also with pointed toes. On top of his head sat a black, narrow-brimmed hat with a crease in the middle of the crown. When they approached him, he stood up and smiled broadly. He rattled off words in his language that Degotoga translated.

"Mr. Bowman. Nice you visit. Sit down, have tea."

"Thank you, no, Mr. Chekilli," Bev said, crouching down on his haunches. "I just want to let you know about a situation. It looks like my man Whit has struck up a friendship with your daughter, Nila. I ain't sure this is a good notion, thinkin' about her age and all."

After Degotoga translated, Chekilli gestured to a woman wearing a deep scarlet skirt, a blue field jacket, and ankle-high tanned moccasins. Chekilli's squaw, thought Bev. Without a word, she turned to the fire where a kettle hung from a branch and poured out a cup of thick, black liquid. She returned and handed it to Bev. He nodded his thanks and took a sip. The hot tea tasted sugary, with a tang of chicory and herbs he couldn't recognize. He knew, then, that it wasn't tea, it was soup, something they could hardly spare.

"Nila grown woman," Degotoga said, Chekilli's words in English. "She know the way of men."

"That maybetrue," Bev said, "but sometimes Whit don't act like a man, a gentle-man."

Chekilli shook his head and spoke to Degotoga, who said, "No matter. It is for Nila to decide." Seeing that Bev still looked skeptical, the old Creek spoke again, and Degotoga said, "Do you know what Nila mean in white manwords? It mean 'wide awake.' Nila take care of herself. If she need help, she will call."

The elderly man sipped his soup. Bev drank his and said, "Okay, Mr. Chekilli, I just thought you should know. We don't want no problems to jump up between us and your people."

Chekilli reeled off another round of Creek, and Degotoga said, "We grateful for what you do for us, Mr. Bowman. No matter what happen, we treat you and your friends with respect always."

Bev nodded, stood up, and started back toward the wagon. A high-walled, thick wooden crate on wheels, it was a wonder that the mules could pull it at all. Whenever they came to an incline of any sort, they would join the horse with the mules in the traces while every able-bodied man would push from behind. Even though the distribution of supplies lightened the load, the heavy war wagon always posed a challenge moving over rough terrain.

When Bev reached the wagon, the supplies for the day had been distributed, a bit of bread and some water for each soul. They all sat around a row of campfires, trying to keep warm, their paltry food and drink already consumed. Bev expected them to reach Fort Row the next day. There, he hoped that its soldiers would be able to spare more provisions for such a small group. If not, the trip to Belmont would be brutal, costing at least some lives if not most of them.

Bev moved around to the other side of the wagon and stopped. Whit handed a thick piece of bread to Nila, who then leaned over and kissed him quickly on the mouth.

"Son of a ..." Bev said. "What the hell you doin'? You wanna get us all killed?"

Nila quickly looked around and saw Bev. She jumped to her feet and bolted around to the other side of the wagon.

Whit stared up at Bev. "What, you spyin' on me, nigger?"

Bev bounded over to Whit, who pulled out his Bowie knife and said, "What now, big fella?"

Bev held up. "You know that don't scare me, I take it away from you and stick it in your gizzard. Why you bother that girl? She a chief medicine man's daughter, you know that? If he find out, he get all his braves to skin us alive!"

Whit lowered his knife. Sullenly, he said, "She won't say nothin'."

"Then, why you givin' her food? The others find out, they might kill her. That food for you, not for that Injun girl."

"What I do with my share, that my business," replied Whit.

Bev shook his head back and forth. "You one dumb black bastard. You run outta food, don't think she'll tell Daddy then? Meantime, you get weaker, what good you to me and everyone else?" He kicked at Whit's foot, "Don't do it no more, hear me? Now, I gotta find her and straighten her out. You stay away!"

Without waiting for another word from Whit, Bev pivoted and stalked back to Chekilli's campfire.

He came upon it and saw Nila sitting close, her back to him. As he drew nearer, he saw over her birdlike shoulders three little, big-eyed Indian children sitting in a row. Nila broke the piece of bread she'd received from Whit into three pieces and handed one to each child. They nodded gratefully at her as they pushed the bread into their mouths, then scrambled away. Nila sat back, and looked around her until she saw Bev standing behind her. He raised his head, nodded slowly, and walked back to the wagon.

The gently undulating land gradually flattened out as they closed in on the Verdigris River. Fort Row had been built on the south side bank near a fork in the river. Its stockade walls faced the direction from which any hostile forces might attack, and the flat grassland allowed defenders to see enemy troops from a good distance. A line of trees along the riverbank flanked the fort on either side. Coming at the fort from the rear across the river, it was too distant for Bev to see much. Even though he sat high on the horse, he could make out just a few wooden structures. He would just have to wait until Abraham returned with news.

While he sat, the wagon pulled up with Josh and Billy on its seat. Most likely, Whit was on foot with Nila. Soon, they arrived at the head of the train of other people who fanned out around the big wooden cart. After some time had passed, Bev climbed off the horse and staked it out to graze. Then, Billy called.

"Here he come, Bev, direct at us through the grass."

Bev stepped up on a wheel hub and sat on the wagon side. He looked out and, sure enough, Abraham trotted toward them through the newly sprouted waves of bluestem grass. When out scouting, Abraham often returned with a critter on his shoulder, a rabbit or a groundhog that he caught along the way. Since the Freeman was coming back from the fort, Bev hoped to see some kind of animal or supply sack on his shoulder. But, he was carrying nothing and he looked to be in a hurry.

Uneasy, Bev said to Billy, "Tell the folks to stay put while I go out to meet him."

He jumped off the wagon and up on his horse, heeled her lightly, and she moved forward at a slow walk. Bev reached Abraham about a hundred yards from the rest of the waiting people. The Estelusti scout stood in front of them, wet from crossing the river.

"Well, Abraham, what'd you find?"

Abraham wore a solemn expression, almost starkly unsettled. "We cyan't go' dey, Boss, e' uh bone yaad."

"Say what?"

"Uh bone yaad, full uh bones. Dead people's bones, haws bones, dog bones, all kinds uh bones."

Confused, Bev gazed down at Abraham. "Bones?" he said. "Bones? What about the soldiers? Ain't they there?"

Abraham vigorously shook his head back and forth, "No soldahs. Dey gone. Nun uh'um theya, dey all gone 'cept duh bones."

Bev grimaced, pressing his lips together. "Climb up on back. We goin' back over there."

The Freeman grabbed Bev's arm and rose up, throwing a leg over the horse's haunches. The mare shifted forward involuntarily from the extra weight. Bev spurred her, and she broke into a rapid canter

170

toward the riverbank. When they reached it, Bev kicked her hard as she moved back and forth from side to side, trying to avoid the steep bank and river. He kept prodding her until she finally took the plunge.

The water was cold, freezing, thought Bev as he felt it seep up his legs to his waist. Abraham had abandoned the horse, swimming sideways instead, his right arm straight in the air holding up his rifle. Bev held on to the horse's neck for dear life, petrified by the cold water and terrified of drowning if he let go. The mare worked hard to reach the far bank, some seventy yards away. For what seemed like an eternity, the horse changed her motion as her hooves felt hard ground. She rose up out of the water with Bev still astride, clutching her sides fiercely with his knees. When she gained level land, she stopped and shook her head, spraying water everywhere. Abraham emerged from the river soon after, and Bev dismounted to walk the horse as he followed the scout's lead.

"Over theya," said Abraham, motioning with his rifle. He stepped through sprouting bluestem toward the fort, its wooden walls and three blockhouses clearly visible in the near distance, backed up against the southern bank of the Verdigris. As they walked, Bev noticed low white mounds around them. When he stopped to look at them more closely, he realized that Abraham had been telling the truth. There were piles of bones, many of them horses, with some smaller animal skeletons intermingled. He stopped and kicked apart one heap. Among the pony's larger bones and skulls, he spied the skull of a dog.

"Good Lord," he said. He lifted his eyes and saw piles of them everywhere, whitened in the sunlight. As he stepped quickly, he began to see what he had feared he would. Human skulls smiled up at him amid the jumble of the rest of their bones. Large, smaller, and very small—men, women, and children, many of them. He stooped low and pulled his knife out, using it to push a pile apart. He saw remnants of clothing, mostly rotted away from the winter moisture. But, after examining various scraps, he understood who had made them. He stood up and rejoined Abraham.

"They Injuns," Bev said

Abraham nodded, "Creeks, Choctaw, Cherokee, and some Estelusti, muh bruthers. Nuh buckruhs dat uh cyan see."

Bev squinted. "No whites? No soldiers?"

"Nun uh cud find."

"So, there weren't no battle. How you think they died?"

Abraham shrugged, "Uh dun't see no cuts, 'ceptin' some skeletin's missin' legs n' feet. Most a' dem look peaceable."

Bev couldn't figure it out. What had happened to all these people? He asked, "How many are there, you think?"

Abraham took a deep breath, "Dey all over. I find dem everwheya. Some I find in holla logs neah duh rivuh, uthurs in tree hollas."

"Like they was buried?" Bev uttered. He refocused on Abraham. "So, you don't think Johnny Rebs killed them?"

"Uh dun't tink so. Look like dey all jus' die."

"Then, where did all them Bluecoats go?" Abraham shrugged, and Bev said, "Let's go in the fort."

They walked through the hillocks of bones to the front gate, double wooden doors wide open. Two blockhouses, each sixteen by twenty-four feet, stood at the opposite ends of a six-foot high wall that enclosed three sides. In the rear, the steep riverbank provided a natural barrier, though a third blockhouse centered on its slope provided a clear line of fire in the event of an attack from canoes. Bev and Abraham searched around, but the fort had been picked clean. Since they found no wreckage or other evidence of a fight, they guessed that the regiment simply had abandoned the fort, most likely under orders.

On top of the east side of the stockade, Bev stood thinking. He scanned the horizon, realizing that these dead people, their children, even their animals must number in the hundreds, maybe thousands. After a long time, he saw Abraham approaching from the west wall. Bev said, "We can't let the others see this. They get a look at all their people dead like this, they be brought so low, we might lose 'em. We get back, we tell 'em the fort's empty, no one there, nothin' for us there. We tell 'em we got to move on. You hear me?"

Abraham shook his head briskly, "Too late. Luk out yonder."

Bev followed Abraham over to the west wall, and looked down below to see a half-dozen men picking through the mounds, holding up thigh bones, ribs, and skulls.

"Great Jesus in heaven," he expelled.

It was too late. Chekilli had sent his own men over to the far side of the fort where they had found the same evidence of mass death. When they reported back to the chief, he would tell everyone. Sure enough, one of them saw Bev at the top of the wooden wall and shouted to his companions. They quickly broke into a run and headed for the river. As they disappeared down the bank, he idly noted to himself that all the Injuns could swim.

The Indians sat in camp, women crying and tearing at their clothes, men sullenly gathering their bows, arrows, axes, and knives with a purpose. When Bev saw them all in a bunch, ready to fight, he went immediately to Chekilli.

"With respect, Chief, we can't go back and bury all them people. They too many. We runnin' out of goods now. Now, we gotta get movin' west to Fort Belmont. If we stop here for any time, we all gonna die."

Degotoga translated and Bev could see Chekilli's jaw harden in fury as he listened silently. Then, he spoke, Degotoga relaying in English, "If we runnin' outta supplies now, Mr. Bowman, we no make it to Fort Belmont no how. Better to honor our lost prople, let them join the Great Spirit. They speak for us when our time come."

Bev shook his head furiously, "No, Chief, we can eat off the land 'til we get to Fort Belmont. I feel your loss, Chief, I lost my little brother to slavecatchers along the way. I gotta survive for him, like you gotta for your lost folks, so that we can make them damnable crackers pay for what they done. You got to survive, Chief, and your people. The Lord will see us through, but we gotta help ourselves, too. Think of them children your daughter been feedin'. You want to see their bones whitenin' under the sun like across the river? That what you want? 'Cause that what's gonna happen if we stay here."

Chekilli's features softened. Bev implored him, "Ain't there some ceremony we can do tonight to honor your people? Maybe a bonfire to the Great Spirit or somethin'?"

Chekilli eyed him angrily, but also appeared deeply downcast. He spoke softly, and Degotoga interpreted. "The Chief speak with the elders. Our people honor the fallen tonight, and be ready to leave tomorrow."

Bev expelled an audible sigh. "Thank you, Chief Chekilli. I promise to get us all to Fort Belmont."

Chekilli lowered his head in acknowledgment, while Bev immediately wondered how in the Lord's name he would be able to keep his promise.

Late that night, the sixty Indians assembled around a large fire. Warriors had crossed the river earlier to bring back the remains of one man, one woman, a child, and the skeletons of a pony and a dog. Laid out in front of the dappling fire, the bones received the blessings and prayers of the living. Bev watched the women cry inconsolably as the men smoked. They then waved smoking wands over the dead to send them on their way to the sky above. He thought it to be a strange mix, all of these people dressed like whites howling and moaning like any other Indians. They could be "civilized" only so much, he guessed.

Eventually, the young warriors gathered up the bones, gently wrapping them in blankets to take to resting places back with the others around the fort. Poor Nila cried and cried near the skeleton of the child until Whit wrapped her up in his arms and led her away. She buried her head into his chest as Bev watched in surprise.

In the morning, they would leave for Fort Belmont without gathering anything but soul-wrenching sorrow from the abandoned boneyard of Fort Row.

Chapter 14. Fort Belmont

On top of the bluff, Billy peeked down at the vast plain of grass waving in the distance all the way to the horizon. Below the hill's crest, Josh slept, his squirrel rifle gently held next to his body, the barrel just beneath his chin. Billy hoped it wasn't loaded.

He turned his attention back to the vista below and the objects of interest standing in stark, dark contrast to the endless field of grass surrounding them, buffalo. Abraham had seen them on his last outing, and also this small cluster of hillocks. After talking it over, they decided to send out their two best shots, Billy and Josh, to position themselves on the hills. Bev, Whit, and Abraham would ride the mare and the two mules around to drive the buffalo to the foot of the rise. Then, they would peel off so that the big animals might settle down to give Billy and Josh good chances for clear shots. Now, there they were, several hundred dotting the plain, including a small constellation of six or seven within rifle range.

Billy had never shot such a big animal before. He'd plunked plenty of deer, but that was all. Never bagged a bear, a cougar, or a wolf, and he'd never evenseen a moose. The best he'd done was popp a ten-point buck. Just twelve years old,he remembered, firing Daddy's hunting rifle, a decent caliber for deer and small game. He'd hit that buck square in the heart, collapsed it in a heap like a felled tree. What he saw in front of him now, however, were hairy beasts the size of mountain boulders, with mean pink eyes darting about and thick pointy horns on top, both males and females. He wasn't sure about the Enfield's range, either. The gun had a heck of a kick, and he'd never fired it at more than a hundred yards. These critters were at least that far away, probably further. If he missed, he wondered if all the beasts would charge up the hilltop to gouge him and Josh to death. Heck, just looking at them, he thought, he could hit one and it still might make it up here to kill them. He better not miss, he thought, and he better shoot dead straight, a singlekillshot.

Billy slid back down the hilltop and gently prodded Josh awake. "They in range, Josh. We got to take our shot."

Josh nodded as he rubbed his eyes with his fists. He quickly rolled over and, holding his rifle in his right hand, started creeping up the hillside. Loaded, thought Billy, giving his head a nervous shake. He followed Josh up to the crest and looked over again.

The buffalo were still there. If anything, Billy thought, they'd browsed themselves closer. No matter, he had to bring one down. The party had run out of food a few days ago. No one complained, except the smallest children, who cried their empty bellies. The rest just marched on as best as they could, filling themselves up with the Verdigris's water. But, a lot of them were walking slower, too, and some children were starting to eat prairie grass. He had to bring one of these big critters down.

Billy put his head next to Josh. "There's a mother, I think, just to the right. She's got a calf grazin' with her. That's our mark."

Agreeing, Josh said, "I shoot at the calf. I think that all I can get with this gun."

Billy shook his head briskly, "No, no. We both shoot at the mother. We can't afford to miss and we have a better chance if we fire at the same target."

Josh seemed skeptical, but he whispered, "Okay."

"All right. I fire first, then you right after me."

He clambered up to the hilltop and slowly brought the Enfield up over, raising it to his shoulder. Slowly, he pulled the hammer back and cocked it as quietly as he could. He glanced over to his right and saw that Josh had his rifle ready to fire, his eyes directly on the game in front of them. Billy returned to the mother buffalo.

He estimated a hundred-yard shot right above her front leg and back maybe six inches. That should be her heart. Once he bore down on her he breathed in slowly, and out. Gently, he depressed the trigger with his finger, gradually bringing it back, holding the rifle stock tight to his shoulder.

Josh shot. Startled, Billy pulled his finger out as he watched the calf's legs fold under, collapsing the young buffalo to the ground. The mother stared at the calf's body, then turned her head to look up the hill. She roared a high-pitch whining cry and the other buffalo scrambled, some running away, some toward her, big bulls.

Billy quickly lined up his shot, relaxed his breathing, and fired. The mother buffalo staggered, bellowed again, her head pointing to the sky, and fell forward on her front knees. The massive bull buffalos started pounding up the hill.

Billy twisted around, groping in his shot bag while yelling at Josh, "Reload!"

Josh shot again, dropped below the ridge and started reloading. Billy jerked his rifle up over the top and saw that the bulls had slowed. He took a shot right away, missing. Getting to his knees, he started reloading when he saw the bulls stop, then go back down the hillside to stand with other buffalo around the fallen mother and calf.

Billy fired again, hitting one in the flank, causing it to moan loudly and run away. The others in the herd watched her run, and trotted off behind. Josh shot and missed, but the noise caused the big animals to quicken their pace.

Billy sat down on the hillside, away from the sight on the plain. "Good Lord, that was close. I figured for sure they was gonna gut us or trample us, kill us some terrible way."

"That right, Billy, they almost get us," said Josh. "But, we got 'em, too, two of them. We're gonna eat tonight!" He grinned broadly, and Billy smiled.

"All right, then, let's go down and start skinnin' anddressin' 'em. Bev and the others should be along soon. They musta heard the shots."

Bev and Whit arrived soon afterwards on foot and began to help butcher the carcasses. After a few hours, Josh drove the wagon up with the Indians strung out behind him. As soon as they arrived, the women started searching for firewood while the men joined in quartering the carcasses. Before long, several fires were roaring with bison meat above roasting on spits. After weeks of deprivation, they would eat well.

Billy and Josh were given the hearts of the animals, though in the fashion of the "Civilized Tribes," both had been cooked beforehand. With his mouth full, Billy leaned over and said to Josh, "That's a heck of a shot you made with that little peashooter. Right through the eye."

Josh replied, "I aimed for the heart."

The two men looked at each other, chewing quietly for a moment, then burst out laughing, each spraying a red mist of little buffalo bits.

Bev watched them, smiling. They were about a week out of Fort Belmont and dried buffalo jerky should last them until they got there. It looked like they would get all of the Indians back with their people, while the boys in blue would keep the runaways safe from the Graybacks. Soon, they all could start thinking about their new lives. Except for me and Eli, he thought, sighing.

Fort Belmont looked to be laid out more like Fort Scott, a large expanse of land occupied by a tent camp and four wooden cabins, probably for the officers. A redoubt constructed of earth walls topped by four layers of logs stood north of the camp, approximately sixty by twenty yards in size. Inside, a blockhouse loomed over the tall walls, commanding a broad field of fire. A mile to the right of the entire complex, the engineers had staked out a parade ground. It possessed that wide-open feel of Fort Scott, but without the adjacent bustling town. Instead, Indian wigwams, stick lean-tos, and other makeshift shelters covered every square inch of soil not taken up by fortifications. Rising up in his saddle, Bev looked out over the grounds. He figured that this must be where Chief Opotheleyahola and his people had ended up.

A horse soldier rode up to the wagon and said, "You in charge here?"

Bev gazed up at him, taking note of his long, curling moustache and dark hair flowing out of his kepi. He said, "Me and my friends are guidin' this group. We from Fort Scott under orders of General Denver to bring these people to Chief Opotheleyahola and their fellow tribe men."

"More Injun runners," the soldier said, "and contraband to boot. Shit." He glanced around and said, "You come to the right place. This is Fort Belmont under the command of Captain Joe Gunby, Companies C and G of the 16th Kansas militia. Chief Opothle's quarters is over thataway on the parade ground. I'll send some dragoons over to escort you there whilst I report to Captain Gunby."

"What about all these folks with us? What they supposed to do?"

"They're gonna want to inspect them before they can join up with the other Injuns. Make sure no Confederate agents snuck in with you to spy on our fortifications and such. Tell them to rest here until a detail comes over to check them out. Then, I suppose they'll be told to join up with the others on the grounds."

"And, what about food and water for them?"

"The Injun Super is in camp, a fella named Coffin. I'll let him know you and yours are here and in need. He'll see what he can do, I suppose, but there's a mess of other folk here already."

The soldier offered a casual salute and wheeled his horse around to leave when Bev called out, "Hey! What your name?"

The horseman turned back and said, "Lieutenant Wilcox. Benjamin Wilcox from Wichita, Kansas." He rode off.

Bev dismounted, tied the reins to the wagon, and started working his way back to tell everyone what was going on. Eventually, they moved to the periphery of the Indian camp and put up temporary lodging. While they worked, other Indians came out of the camp with food and water. At the same time, Abraham sauntered into the large campground to find other Estelustli and maybe even Chief Opotheleyahola himself.

Bev worked with Josh to attach some canvas to the side of the wagon, which he stretched across to two poles on either end. Once they had that secured, Josh stood in the wagon and threw sleeping blankets down to Bev. When everything had been situated, the men fell into their blankets and slept.

Bev woke up an hour or two later and realized that the promised dragoons never arrived. He sighed, put his shoes back on, and stood up, looking around to see where the Indian superintendent's quarters might be. Josh still slept, so Bev gestured to Billy to follow him, and they trudged up to the cluster of cabins to the left of the redoubt. When they finally reached them, they asked a soldier where they might find Superintendent Coffin. The soldier pointed off to the west at the Indian encampment.

Bev and Billy traipsed back down toward the hodgepodge of lean-tos and makeshift tents that housed the Indians, picking their way through them. As they walked, they searched for some more formal structure that might serve as an office. Sure enough, they saw a larger rectangular tent clearly the product of a northern mill rather than Indian handiwork. Bev knocked on a supporting two-by-four, and a private pulled back a door flap from inside.

"Yes?" said the private, wearing an impeccable uniform. Clean-shaven, his brown hair newly cut and neatly combed, his fresh face called up to Bev a young master on his way to school.

"We here to see the Injun superintendent," said Bev. "This his place?"

"These are his headquarters. Can I ask who you are?"

"I'm Bev Bowman, recent freeman. This here is Billy McKinney, who run away from the Johnny Rebs. He's an ab'litionist, now. We brung a tussle of Injuns here from Fort Scott. They need food, water, and a place to stay."

The private slowly nodded. "I'll see if the superintendent can see you."

"You do that," Bev said, "quick as you can."

The private dropped the flap, leaving Bev and Billy outside to wait. Bev looked up at the midday sky, crowded with dark, heavily-inflated clouds threatening rain.

The private returned and ushered them inside. Standing to the side of a small campaign table stood a tall, slender man of about fifty, wearing a heavy wool suit and a vest with wide lapels. His hair was a mottled black and gray, but his full beard was a cascade of white. His brow seemed crinkled from age, while his sorrowful, soft brown eyes peered out at them from deep, overlapping bags of fatigue.

"Gentlemen, I am William G. Coffin, Superintendent of Indian Affairs for the U.S. government in this region. This is my son, Oliver," he said, dipping his head toward a young version of himself, though with a full head of black hair and an equally robust black beard. He wore a suit very similar to the superintendent's, including the gold watch chain draped across his waist. The young man murmured, "Gentlemen," slightly bowing his head.

"Private Hayes said you have conveyed Indians here from Fort Scott?" asked the superintendent.

Bev scratched his head, "We brung 'em here, anyhow."

"You escorted them, of course," Coffin said, "and how many in your party?"

"Sixty or so," said Bev. "Creek, Muscogee mostly, Choctaw, and Cherokee. Our scout is a Black Seminole. They in need of food, water, and cover."

The superintendent pressed his lips together. "Sixty. Not a huge number, but ...," he trailed off. "Has anyone told you how many Indians are quartered here now, Mr., uh, Mr.—"

"Bowman. Bev Bowman." He jerked his thumb back, "Billy McKinney. And, no, we don't know how many Injuns you got here. Looks like a lot."

"More than six thousand."

Bev drew his head back. "That's plenty."

"Yes it is, Coffin replied. He paused, and said, "We have sufficient water, but securing food is an ongoing challenge. And, you can see," he gestured with his arm outstretched in a half-circle as if they were outside, "that accommodations are barely serviceable." His eyes suddenly seemed even sadder. "It has been very hard on them."

"Why that?" Bev said. Then, he squinted. "You know what happen at Fort Row."

Coffin paled, and his son reached out to touch his shoulder. The superintendent drew in a breath and said, "I do. I was there, as was Oliver."

Bev's hand instinctively rested on the haft of his knife. "What happen? We found folks' bones wherever we went when we was there."

Coffin's eyes sharpened. "You were there?"

180

"We was. Thought we could get help, maybe some food for the trip here. But, everybody gone exceptin' all them dead people. You know what happen to 'em?"

Coffin shifted his head down deliberately as he reached behind him for a camp chair. He sat down, and Oliver moved closer, appearing concerned.

"What happened," Coffin said, "was a tragedy. You are aware of the battles fought by the Indians in the Territory?"

"Our scout Abraham, he a Black Seminole, he told us somethin' about the Injuns fightin'. Chief Opotheleyahola won some, then lost."

Collins nodded, "The Five Civilized Tribes sided with the Confederates, all except the Muscogee Creeks under Chief Opotheleyahola. A few others, the Delawares, and some other tribes, too. The Rebel Indians tried to persuade them to join them. But, when they refused, the renegades attacked, led by their chief Stand Watie. The Union supporters won twice, but the last battle at Chustenahlah was a disaster for them. Opotheleyahola and his people were forced to flee the Oklahoma territory with barely the clothes on their backs. They had no food, no blankets, some were near naked, and they had to travel 150 miles north here to Kansas. This was in late December, a brutal month in a brutal winter. More than a thousand died on the march from exposure.

"When they arrived at Fort Row, they still numbered more than nine thousand. They were starving. Only eighty men were posted at Fort Row. They possessed nowhere near enough supplies for thousands of famished, freezing Indians. The troopers gave them what little they could spare and sent for help. Oliver and I came down from Fort Scott with some supplies, but they were soon exhausted. I tried to get more, but it was hopeless. The Indians hunted to eat, but there was little game that time of year. So, they turned to their ponies and dogs. I did everything I could to find them food, but failed. One thousand more souls expired at Fort Row. At first, their surviving family members entombed those they lost in hollow logs or trees. Soon, though, conditions grew so desperate that the dead were left where they fell."

Coffin paused, looking down at his boots. "The company received orders in March to assemble at Fort Leavenworth for a new expedition back into the Territory. By then, we had started relocating the survivors here at Fort Belmont. But, the winter was so hard, and they had so little shelter. Sickness took many off here as well.

Another 250 perished. We've started moving many of them to Fort Leroy and other posts, but we still have plenty here who need help."

Coffin stopped then, gazing somewhere far off in the distance just in front of him. Again, his son Oliver grasped his shoulders to console him.

Stunnedby the account, Bev turned to Billy, open-mouthed and frozen still by what he had heard.

"You have brought us sixty more Indians loyal to the Union to house and feed. We are very grateful for their loyalty, but it will be a struggle to provide for them. Frankly, gentlemen, we never know where the next meal will come for any one of those already here."

As Coffin spoke the words, Bev found it difficult to grasp them. After traversing a hundred and twenty miles from Fort Scott under extremely harrowing circumstances, they were no better off than if they had stayed put, probably worse for it. He started to stammer something, but he could not for the life of him think of anything to say.

Seeing Bev's discomfort, Coffin said, "Well, you're here, now. Hayes will tell you where your people can set up. We'll add them to the lists, though what we have for them to eat isn't much."

He nodded at Hayes, who gestured to Bev and Billy to follow. Once they left the big tent, he walked them over toward the east perimeter of the sprawling compound, speaking in a low voice.

"Coffin isn't bullshittin' you. The Injuns at Row overwhelmed him. Him and his son used their own pay to buy more supplies, but it was just a drop in the bucket. Losing all those folks stills lives with him." He fixed his eyes directly on Bev. "He will do his level best by you and yours, but don't expect much."

They reached the edge of the campgrounds. "I see you're already set up here. That's fine. I'll be around with rations later. By the way, they're going to want the mules and the horse, the wagon for that matter. They're mobilizin' to go back into the Territory in force."

He left before Bev could protest. He and Billy returned to the others. The women started fires while the men finished up whatever shelter they could around the wagon. In the meantime, Bev filled in Josh and Whit about their meeting with Coffin.

"It don't look like this place is gonna be any better, maybe worse. Now, they got thousands here to feed."

"Then, maybe it's time to move on our own selves," said Whit.

182

Bev grimaced, "I don't know. Somehow I feel we part of these folks some way. We got them this far, seem wrong to just leave 'em here."

"Damn, Bev, we don't owe 'em a thing. We did what we said, they here at Fort Belmont. It's time to take care of us."

"That right?" snapped Bev. "We don't owe Chekilli anything? You don't owe Nila a thing?"

Whit scowled silently, dropping his eyes.

"Okay, then."

"So, what're we gonna do, Bev?" Billy asked.

Bev didn't reply, thinking. Just then, Nila and some other women came around to pass out some of the remaining buffalo jerky and gourds of water. The men ate quietly, mulling over what to do.

"This jerky ain't half bad. I come to like buffalo, the taste of it. Be nice to go back and get some more."

Bev chewed, thinking that Billy was right, it did taste pretty good, even dried out.

"Hey, you know," Billy said, "we could go see if any still they'. It only a few days ride, and there were an awful lot of 'em in that field."

Suddenly, Bev felt as though a light had splashed over his thoughts. "B'damn, Billy, that's a good idea! They's plenty of buffalo out there, plenty to eat! Coffin and the captain runnin' this show'd be real happy if we carted back a wagon full. Let's go see 'em, see if they buy in."

Private Hayes was surprised to find them back at Coffin's tent so soon. When Bev told him why they wanted to see Coffin again, Hayes carried the message, and soon they were face-to-face.

"How many buffalo did you see?"

"Hundreds," Bev said, and Billy chimed in, "Maybe thousands!"

"Anyway, hundreds," said Bev.

Coffin ran his thumb and index finger down either side of his nose and rubbed his moustache. "And, you're sure they're still there?"

Bev hesitated, and said, "We ain't sure, but it only been a few days. They can't be that hard to find."

Coffin glanced at Oliver, who shrugged his shoulders and nodded almost imperceptibly. The superintendent turned back and said, "I'll take it to Captain Gunby. I'm not sure how receptive he will be, he's completely focused on preparing for the campaign. What will you need to do this?"

"We're gonna need powder and shot. We also need to keep our horse and mules for starters, and the wagon to bring back the meat. Matter of fact, when we find the herd, we're gonna need more horses and mules, enough to pull maybe ten wagons. That feed everyone for a week or more."

Coffin shook his head, "Gunby won't provide that kind of support unless he's assured that you can track the buffalo successfully. I'll persuade him to let you keep your mules and wagon for the hunt. Once you find them, you can send for more wagons and men."

Bev agreed, and he and Billy headed back to their campsite.

"Well, we got as little as we wanted," Bev said on the way back. "If nothin' come of it, we can just keep on goin' with the critters we got. If we lucky and find all them buffalo, we're set. Maybe we become the fort's hunters for a good long time. Right now, though, we need to find Abraham. He's our best chance to dig up them buffalo in a hurry."

Back at the camp, Bev filled in Whit and Josh. He told them to keep an eye on things here while he and Billy searched for Abraham. Bev had checked with Chief Chekilli about Creek hunters he could bring along. The Chief told him that most of them were farmers or plantation owners who might have hunted deer now and then but knew little about buffalo. He recommended talking to Opotheyelahola, see if any of the Creeks or Choctaw had experience, maybe the Cherokees, too. Bev thanked him and left.

"Perhaps Abraham knowssome Seminole brethren who hunt buffalo. All them Civilized Tribe members know is how to get black folk to slave for them growin' cotton and such."

As they wandered among the Indian dwellings, they asked where they could find the Estelusti. They learned that the Black Seminoles camped out on the southwest part of the compound. Sure enough, they found a cluster of shelters highly decorated with feathers and beads, populated by splendidly dressed people in a fashion much akin to Abraham's. They located him soon enough in a long hut where the head of the Estelusti presided.

Abraham introduced them to the chief, Sonuk Mikko, and he invited them for a smoke and some home-brewed liquor. A gray-haired, stout man in a pair of striped pants and a vivid red shirt, Chief Mikko was delighted to see them and to hear their stories of escape from the Grayback slavecatchers. However, when Bev asked about buffalo hunters, Chief Mikko said that his people knew of the marshes in the deep South and now the Oklahoma Territory where they farmed. He'd heard that Apaches and other Indians liked those hunted buffalo to live, but he and his people hadn't met any here at Fort Belmont. Bev thanked him profusely, and gestured to Billy and Abraham that it was time to leave.

"Amazin' how we come across them bison while no one else seem ever to see 'em."

"We gwine see Chief Opotheyelahola," said Abraham, "'E know 'bout buffalo, mebbe."

They found Chief Opotheyelahola quartered in a modest oilcloth military tent, typical of those shared by small corps of men. Two Creek warriors guarded the door, both wearing dark-blue serge suits with colorful, ornate scarves wrapped around their heads. They both had rifles slung from their shoulders and large knives stuck in their belts. On their feet were high ankle deerskin moccasins decorated with ornate, colorful beaded patterns. Abraham approached them and identified himself and his companions. Without hesitation, one of the guards raised a triangular flap and ushered them inside.

Opotheyelahola sat on a small folding chair to one side of a wooden card table. The table was covered with a beautifully woven cloth made of brightly dyed linen. An oil lamp stood in the middle, with various pipes and beaded objects scattered on top. When they entered, he looked up, then over to a black man sitting in the far corner of the tent. The Chief stood up, at least six feet tall, and the black man, somewhat shorter, arose and made his way over.

Unlike the other chiefs they had met, Opotheyelahola wore deerskin boots and pants, a hand-sewn linen shirt with tribal runes on the front, and a silk white tie around his collar, the only concession to the white man's style of gentlemanly dress. Over all this, he draped a long, beautifully woven blanket gracefully over his shoulders, and displayed a bright patterned red scarf wrapped around his head like an eastern potentate's turbin. His hair was long and brown with a few strands of grey denoting his age. His face, however, was drawn and wan, with deep lines traveling down his cheeks. Opotheyelahola's eyes were black and sad, and though he was massive and imposing, he stooped somewhat when standing.He spoke to them in a hardy voice, thoughthey could not understand anything he said.

"Is that Injun speak?" asked Billy.

"I'm guessin' it is," said Bev. He turned to Abraham, "You know this lingo?"
Abraham shook his head no.

The black man stepped forward, "It Creek. The Chief does not speak the white man's language, ever. But I can tell you what he say. He welcome you into his dwelling and asked for your names."

"I'm Bev Bowman, this here Billy McKinney of Tennessee and Abraham Bowlegs, Black Seminole."

The black man quickly translated, and the Chief replied. The black man said, "The Chief says he's glad to make your acquaintance."

"And you?" asked Bev.

"I am James, former slave to the Chief until he decide to stick to the Union. He free me then, and hired me to be his man servant."

"Huh," said Bev, sizing James up. The former slave seemed ordinary in appearance in a white linen shirt and black slacks held up by braces. He wore heavy boots, and his sleeves were rolled up and gartered at his biceps. He didn't look particularly imposing physically, not like a field hand, but he carried some heft with a flat belly. Bev guessed him to be maybe ten years younger than the Chief, though that was hard to tell under the circumstances.

"Tell the Chief we're glad to meet him," Bev said, "please."

James whirled around and spat out a string of words to the Chief. The Chief bowed his head, smiling. He spoke, and James asked, "He would like to know why you all have come to grace his home?"

Bev paused, then continued, "Please tell him we are honored to be here, and thank him for his kind hospitality. We goin' on a hunt for buffalo that we saw. We shot a couple not too far off from here. We want to shoot plenty more to feed his people here. We was wonderin' if the Chief can lend us some buffalo hunters."

James relayed the request to the Chief, who shook his head sorrowfully as he replied.

"The Chief ask you to forgive him, but none of his people hunt buffalo. They all mostly farmers and herders, only know how to hunt and trap small critters in the woods or meadows near their land. They don't know 'bout the buffalo, never saw much of them in their country."

Bev frowned, "That too bad. No hunters and no scouts?"

"What you should know," James said in a quiet voice, "is that most of the folks in this fort are starvin' and sick, a lot of them just about dyin'. If any of them could help you, they just ain't up to it." He whispered as though the chief might hear and understand him, "The Chief hisself just lost his daughter to cholera."

Bev pulled his head back reflexively. He faced the chief head on and said solemnly, "Tell the chief we sorry for his people and his loss.

Tell him we hope to bring food back soon for all. Thank him for seein' us."

After James finished, the chief flashed a brilliant smile and patted them all on the back as they turned to leave. As they passed through the tent doorway, they heard one more phrase from the Chief. "He pray that the Great Spirit will guide you and protect you," said James.

"Thank you," said Bev. "I see why all the folks follow him," he said, gazing hard into James's eyes. James tightend his lips in a grim smile of his own.

Outside the tent, Billy said, "Now what?"

Bev answered, "I guess we're goin' huntin.' You need to find us them buffalo again, Abraham."

Abraham nodded, "Uh find dem soon enuf."

It didn't surprise Bev, of course, that the bison weren't as easy to find as they had hoped. When they returned to the field where they had shot the mother and her calf, the herd was nowhere in sight. Abraham spent some time circling around the area until he figured out which direction they had taken.

"Dey gwine west," he said.

"More grass," Bev imagined. "Okay, you and I head that way, leave markers for the boys with the wagon."

They covered a good twenty miles before finally packing in for the night. Lying on a blanket while chewing buffalo jerky, Bev stared up at the stars above. As he gazed at the random spangling amid the dark cloak over head, it came to him again that he was as close as he had ever been in his life to being free. The surrounding endless sky and wide open land signaled enormous possibilities still unknown to him, what he could do on his own.

His thoughts strayed back to the Bowman farm, the place and people he knew, the memories, Eli now with the stars in the heaven above. Memories of Mary Louise Smalls also surfaced. He imagined some future in which he would go back to Memphis, woo her, and make a home with her somewhere that they both liked, someplace free. Wild thinking, he sighed to himself, lonely thinking.

In the morning, they set out again, soon coming upon the Chikaskia River. They moved northwest along its banks looking for a good place to ford. As they traveled, they passed through wooded stretches where hackberry trees grew and all sorts of birds flew. The trees gave way to the bluestem grass interspersed with bush clusters, which was where they found the buffalo.

Abraham crouched low and motioned with his hand for Bev to move out of sight with the horse. The freeman retreated with stealth, joining Bev and the horse backing as far away as possible.

"Buffalo," whispered Abraham.

Bev rapidly shook his head, "Okay," he said, "stay with 'em. Leave a trail. I ride back for the wagon and bring 'em up quick."

He rode as fast as he could, retracing their path to intercept the wagon. He came upon them just before nightfall. As soon as they set up camp, everyone brought out their rifles and began to clean them. They laid the rifles in the bed of the wagon, then tried to sleep as best as they could. In the morning, they pushed the mules forward to close in on the herd as quickly as possible. By midafternoon, they arrived.

Abraham had used the time waiting to find a ford across the river a few miles north of the meeting place. With Abraham leading the way on the horse, the others doubled up on the mules and headed quickly to the ford. After they crossed,   Bev split them up into two parties.

The best shots Billy, Josh, and Abrahamrode off on the horse and mules, taking awide path around so as not to spook the herd. After they left, Bev and Whit back moved out onto the open ground and searched for a good hiding place in the middle of the plain. They crouched low behind a clump of tall grass and scrub brush and waited, expecting the riders to take an hour or so to work their way around to the rear of the herd. The plan called for Abraham and the others to open fire first on the grazing animals, driving the rest straight at Bev and Whit poised directly in their path. Once the bison came upon them, Bev and Whit could shoot at nearly point blank range to bring down more of the panicked, bunched beasts. In the meantime, they sat and waited.

When Abraham felt that they couldn't be far off from the herd, he silently signaled to Billy and Josh to dismount and quietly stakeout their animals. With Abraham in the lead, the three men gingerly slipped up close to the buffalo on foot as quietly as they could. Abraham stopped when he thought that trying to get closer would risk stampeding the herd. They were in range. He checked to make sure that Billy and Josh were ready, rifles raised and lined up. Then, Abraham slowly lifted his long rifle, took aim, and fired. Two loud reports followed at once, and the Eestuli watched as three buffalo hit the ground. The rest of the herd turned and thundered away.

Bev and Whit heard the three gunshots, and almost immediately they spotted a host of terrified, massive beasts thudding at high speed directly at them. Startled, Bev fired his rifle and missed. Whit shot fast after him, and the herd split, pounding by them through the growing bluestem.

Lying on the ground, Bev lowered his arms from covering his head. He slowly rose up on his hands to look back in the herd's direction. Nothing. He glanced over to see Whit also gingerly rising for a peek over the brush.

"Boy, we missed them all," Whit said, amazed.

"They run past us pretty fast," said Bev. "I hope they done better down where they shot."

The two got to their feet and started ambling down toward the others. No need to hurry, thought Bev, Abraham and the boys either got some or they didn't. He drew closer and saw three piles of brownish black fur in separate heaps down on the grassy field. Three shots, three kills, he thought.

The five men all converged upon the buffalo carcasses, big ones, two males and an adult female. Without a word, they grinned at each other, resting on their rifles.

Bev said, "That's darn good shootin', friends."

"How you do, Bev?" asked Billy. "Got any up river?"

Bev shook his head, "No, Billy, they jump us too fast. We barely pulled our triggers."

Billy frowned, "Too bad."

"Yassir," nodded Josh, appearing sympathetic. "Guess we picked the right men to shoot last."

Everyone stared at the gnarly black man as he casually leaned on his squirrel gun next to one of the big bison bodies. They all burst out laughing.

"Why Old Josh!" Bev said laughing, "I didn't know you had it in you!"

"Guess I'm just feelin' extra special good right now," he said, smiling.

"That be three outta five," said Billy, and they all laughed again.

"Not bad," said Bev, "not too bad t'all. Well, we better skin and butcher 'em before some wild critters come around. I don't suppose you want me and Whit on guard duty?"

They laughed again as they started in on the dead buffalo.

In the morning, they managed to drag themselves up for a quick breakfast before heading for Fort Belmont. Abraham would go the other way to keep track of the bison herd, while Bev would ride the horse back to let Gunby know of their success and to get help. Before they left, they all shook hands. Across the river, vultures circled above the buffalo entrails being pulled apart by coyotes.

Bev worked his way back by intermittently riding hard, then walking the horse to keep it from fagging out. He felt good about the hunt's success. Captain Gunby would see that they could be valuable to the fort. However, the Blues were planning an invasion of Indian Territory again, which meant that they would pay greater attention to their army rather than feeding the refugees. Even if they continued to care for Opotheyelahola's people, once they learned where the buffalo were and how easy they were to hunt, they wouldn't need Bev and his gang anymore. Bev understood that if they were to survive and stay free in Union territory, they had to become more than contrabands. They had to provide a service that no one else could, one that the Bluecoats couldn't do without. But what?

He came to a small creek coming from the direction of the Chikaskia River. He lowered himself from the saddle and started to wade into the stream, leading the horse behind him. The creek was cloaked by a number of oaks and hickories, so that Bev couldn't see what lay before him. Once the horse had reached dry ground, he mounted her and started forward. They hadn't crossed this creek on the way out, he thought. He must have wandered off track some ways back. He pressed his lips together, angry at himself, more time wasted.

As he emerged from the trees, he found himself some distance away from a gentle hollow between a few low knolls. Definitely off track, he thought.

He heard something. A whinny, he thought, maybe someone riding close by. Rather than take the chance that they were Graybacks or Rebel Indians, he pulled up on the reins and eased the mare back into the trees by the creek. He waited, and heard another whinny and some snorts.

A horse burst out from the hollow, a pinto, followed by a dozen more. Without another sound, they galloped down the southern side of the creek away from him.

Horses, he realized, wild horses. Armies always need horses, as many as they could get. And they'd pay money. He smiled to himself and turned the mare around toward the northwest.

Chapter 15. The Indian Expedition

The entire business of catching wild horses sapped Billy's energy, both physical and mental. It usually took days, sometimes weeks to locate a herd. Then, they likely had to trail the horses for more days to find a good spot to try and run them down. Maybe a watering hole near the Flint Hills or a gully in the Red Hills where they could hem them in. Figuring out and perfecting their methods had taken some time, and they failed plenty. Many times they had to run the herd's stallion down in the open, and often it just ran away from them. At the start, Bev took the lead, since he was the only one who could toss a rope. Josh caught on pretty fast, but the best that Billy and Whit could do was to try flanking the horses to keep them from veering off. Still, with Bev out front they had managed to bring more than fifty horses back to the fort by the end of May.

That was fine, thought Billy, but it still meant long days eating hardtack, lots of hardtack, and cold nights sleeping on the Kansas prairie. After six months living out in the open, Billythoroughly enjoyed slumbering on the cot and tick mattress supplied by the army. That didn't lasted long, thought Billy, just enough to miss it deeply while out in the countryside. But, he knew that the alternatives were even less inviting—Bev and the others sent off to a contraband camp, while he volunteered, this time in the Union army. Such looping thoughts blunted his complaints until he tried biting into his next piece of hardtack. They didn't call them worm castles for nothing, he lamented, or tooth-dullers. No meat out here, either, just tack or beans, many beans. Life was full of little miseries.

Billy and Whit watched from a copse of cottonwoods as Bev raced after a stallion, angling his quarter horse back and forth to keep his prey going toward them. Behind him, Josh spurred his horse to keep up, pounding the prairie grass from behind,swerving opposite to Bev's moves as best as he could. Together, they kept the strawberry roan heading in a more or less straight line toward the wooded hollow. As they plunged in amid the trees, Whit and Billy emerged from either side. The stallion pulled up abruptly, allowing Bev to ride close enough to toss his rope. To Billy's relief and satisfaction, the loop settled over the snorting horse's head. Bev pulled hard and quickly wrapped the rope around his saddlehorn. The horse tried to rear up, but the rope restricted it and its front hooves came back to the ground. Josh slipped his mount to the stallion's side and draped his rope around its neck. He backed away opposite to Bev, and they had the horse caught, jerking and wrenching at the two ropes while kicking its hind legs into the air.

Billy and Whit moved up and tossed their ropes onto the stallion, pulling back in opposite directions to further immobilize it. While the other three maneuvered to keep their ropes tense at triangular points, Bev unwound his rope from his horn and dismounted. The big roan eyed him wildly while he headed toward a tree and wrapped his rope around the trunk. He tied it off, and Billy and the rest loosened their ropes and let them drop to the ground.

"Good enough," Bev said. "Y'all got the gate ready?"

"Yup," said Billy, "right over there in the woods near the front."

"All right, we'll camp near it 'til he starts whinnying."

They rode to the head of the hollow and set up camp. By sunup the next morning, the stallion was neighing and nickering loudly, snorting as it tried to pull free from the rope. Soon, his herd showed up, mostly mares and a few young colts and fillies. They all came up to the big horse, trying to urge him free, whickering in empathy. At the same time, the four men in the woods near the entrance to the hollow pulled a rough brush gate across it, blocking the horses from bolting. The next day, they roped the mares and tethered them next to the stallion. The colts and fillies stayed close to their mams. The following day, they had them all tied together in a string and gave them oats and water. With the stallion tethered close between Bev and Josh, and Billy herding the mares behind, they made their way back to Fort Belmont.

They had been lucky this time, thought Billy, finding the small herd close enough to a hollow to pen them in after staking out the stallion. Even so, it was hard work.

"I gotta say," Billy said, "buffalo huntin's a lot easier than this."

"Sure, but the buffalo moved on west," replied Bev, "and shootin' buffalo don't pay."

Upon their arrival back at Fort Belmont, their old pal Lieutenant Wilcox greeted them. Twirling one strand of his scimitar moustache, he said, "Looks like you boys hit the jackpot again. I count ten, twenty—twenty-one, including the stallion. Another nice little payday. Half-price for the little ones, of course."

Billy grinned broadly. The money sounded good, ten dollars a horse, five each for the colts and fillies. That came to about ..."Hey, Whit, how much does that amount to?"

Whit eyed him and said, "You ain't got enough fingers and toes?"

"No, I don't. So, how much?"

"Somethin' over two hunnert dollars, two thirty-five, I think."

Billy smiled with respect, "That's good, Whit, real good. So, how much for each of us?"

"Just under fifty. No, wait, Bev takes out the half for savin'. That leave a little bit more than twenty-five each."

"Twenty-five! That ain't bad, that's purdy good!" Billy said. They never complained when, once paid, Bev doled out five dollars per man. He tucked the rest of the money into a hidey-hole near their quarters for safekeeping. Everyone had agreed to put most of the money aside as a hedge against the war's end. Billy figured that without Bev, they wouldn't have a cent. Even if Bev decided to keep the rest of the money all to himself, Billy and the others knew that they still had more money by far than they would without Bev. Without him, they wouldn't be able to catch even one horse.

Whit gave a slightly begrudging nod of his head. "Yup, a man can buy some whiskey with that, maybe even get some honey on the side."

Billy frowned at Whit's last remark, thinking about Nila waiting in their tent.

"We still gotta break them nags in, though," Whit continued. "That kinda makes the pay low."

Billy winced at the thought. Nothing was easy, even back at the fort. For the next several days, they would be working with some of the Union cavalry men to break in the wild mares. He could feel the welts and bruises on his butt just thinking about it. Bev and Josh did most of it, but Whit and Billy would take their turns, too, and end up in the dirt for their trouble. No matter, the idea was to wear the horses out until they eased up, eventually turning docile.

Both Billy and Whit rode better now, though neither could be called a natural. Josh again proved himself to be a wonder. In a matter of a month, he matched Bev himself in maneuvering around a wild horse to box it in. Billy wouldn't be surprised if Josh turned out to be Bev's equal in gentling them, either. In some ways—in most ways— Josh was good at anything he wanted to do.

Stallions were another story. Bev always took on the stallion, the lethal mount requiring the best rider of all. The real skill came from Bev's special talent in quieting the horse. He approached it with complete empathy, sympathy really, conveying to the animal how he understood that any kind of enslavement was intolerable. Somehow, it worked. Aside from the bruised tailbone and hips he suffered too during the riding stage, horses learned to trust him. Sometimes, though, the horse could not be gentled. Then, Bev would take it out a day's ride from the fort and let it go. If it returned for its mares, the soldiers would shoot it.

Billy put the roundup out of his mind, instead thinking of the good things the money would bring him. Pork and molasses and other delicacies from the commissary. For once, Fort Belmont enjoyed a surfeit of supplies. After much back and forth, the Union brass had decided to build a force at Baxter Springs just above the Oklahoma border. From there, they would stage their campaign to take back the Indian Territory. Infantry and cavalry units from Fort Belmont, Fort Scott, and many other Kansas posts received orders to mobilize at Baxter Creek. Indians who had survived the massacre by Stand Watie at Chustenahlah formed the First Regiment of the Indian Home Guard, which also marched. Abraham Bowlegs left with the regiment "ta fight duh wickity Injuns in duh territ'ry."

Chief Opothleyahola left, too. At first, he resisted putting his people on the trail again. But, after receiving firm promises of more food and better shelter, he relented, and watched as groups of them were sent to Quenemo, Le Roy, even as far as Fort Leavenworth in northern Kansas. Once the wealthiest Creek in the Indian Territory, the lean old Chief joined his people moving to Quenemo, his only possessions being the clothes on his back. By the end of May, Fort Belmont stood emptyexcept for a skeletal company left behind.

Chief Chekilli and his party had left with Opothleyahola, except for Nila, who stayed with Whit. They had set up house in an old tent that Nila had sewn back together. She lived in it, waiting for Whit to return from his regular trips searching for horses. Whit would have preferred to remain at the fort fulltime, but just the four of them were barely able to bring back any sizeable drove of stallion and mares. He fidgeted, antsy while Lieutenant Wilcox did his head count as the band was maneuvered into the corral.

"Another fine bunch of hosses, boys," Wilcox said as he swung open the gate to one of the fort's corrals. "I suspect you're probably getting rich off of this trade."

"It better than pickin' cotton," said Whit. "We was tired of that."

Wilcox flashed his teeth beneath his ornate moustache, "I suppose so. "

"Well, maybe you don't have to worry about that too much longer," Wilcox continued. "Grant whipped the Johnnies at Shiloh last month, and he and his guns are on the way down the Mississippi even as we speak."

Whit shrugged, "Don't matter to me one way or the other. I a free man, now, do as I please."

Wilcox frowned, "You aren't exactly free just yet, boy. If things go bad down there, you'll be back in the cotton fields sure enough. In the meantime, you work for the US military. You better keep the hosses coming or we'll find something else for you to do that you know how to do."

Whit pressed his lips hard together, but held his peace. Whiskey was waiting for him somewhere, and a good meal. First, though, he decided to check in on Nila.

In mid-June, all of the horses had been broken except for the stallion, which Josh let loose out in the Red Hills. While they waited for the old man to return, Bev and Billy played mumblety-peg or whittled wood. Without the regiments and the Indians, there wasn't much to do or see at Fort Belmont. They talked about going after more horses, but the ones they had just brought back stood idle in the corrals, too. Plainly put, it was getting hot and there wasn't much to do.

Bev threw his penknife at Billy's boot, who hopped. "Hah," said Bev, "you lose! You do better if you not so jumpy, Billy boy."

"You darn near stabbed me that time, Bev. I'd rather keep all my toes than win."

"That true. But, I still need muh knife," Bev said, smiling.

Billy got down on his hands and knees, leaned over and turned his head to grasp the haft of Bev's knife with his teeth. He raised his head to pull it out of the ground, stood up, and handed it over.

"Go again?" asked Bev.

"B'god yes!" Billy said, "I want my revenge!"

"You gonna be waitin' a long time on your revenge, Billy boy, 'til the devil die of a chill."

They started again, taking turns throwing their knives as close as possible at each other's feet to make one of them flinch first. As they played, Wilcox rode up and dismounted. He walked up, but they ignored him, continuing to flip their knives.

"Pardon the interruption, boys, but I need to talk to you."

Bev whipped his knife down barely an inch from Billy's foot. "Go on ahead, talk," said Bev, not looking up.

Wilcox's face flushed, but he kept an even tone. "All right. You can see that the fort's pretty much emptied out. All the regiments are down in Baxter Springs, even the new Injun home guards. The rest of the redskins have been dispersed to different camps around the country."

As he listened, Billy grew uneasy, guessing where the sergeant was headed.

"This means that there isn't much need of new horses here at Belmont. In fact, we got more than we can handle right now."

Bev straightened up, his penknife resting in his hands, and faced Wilcox. "Say your piece straight up, Wilcox."

Wilcox hesitated. "Captain Gunby says there ain't much use for you around here either."

"Is that so?" Bev said, now resting his hand on the pistol he wore at his side.

"Exactly what he said," Wilcox stammered, "your services are no longer needed at Fort Belmont." He stared at Bev, whose demeanor hadn't change at all, solemn and silent as he stared back at Wilcox. The way this was going, Billy thought, one more unlikable word out of Wilcox's mouth and Bev might just gun him down on the spot and run. What'd Bev have to lose, considering what Wilcox just said? Mostly, the way he was saying it.

"Listen," Wilcox quickly said, holding held his hands out, palms up, "Captain Gunby figures you boys got three choices: head up to one of the other forts and work there, go to a contraband camp, or just move on down the road. Those're your choices."

Billy swallowed. If Bev, Josh, and Whit went to one of them contraband camps, where would he go? What would he do?

"Not much choosin' there," Bev said. "None of us goin' to work at no other fort or contraband camp. We free now to go where we want. Guess that's what we do when Josh gets back here."

Wilcox suddenly changed his tone, saying in a sly voice, "You might be able to do somethin' else. Captain Gunby told me that Congress is gonna pass a law maybe next month that will free slaves here from the Rebel states to serve in the Union army. If that happens, you boys could sign up, fight for your freedom forever, you and yours."

"This law ain't passed yet?" asked Bev. "They been tryin' to pass ab'litionist laws a long time. None of them ever been passed."

He turned back to Billy when Wilcox said, "Or, you could join up with the Injun Home Guard down in Baxter Springs."

"We ain't Injuns."

"No, but your friend Abraham is, a black Injun. He could put in a word for you."

"If he's still there," replied Bev.

"He most likely is," said Wilcox, "and anyway, you'd be welcomed by the regular cavalry there, too."

"Truly?"

Wilcox nodded. "All you gotta do is take the horses down there to them. They'd welcome you with hot skillygalee!"

Just the mention of the dish had Billy smelling the bacon and hardtack, his mouth watering. Bev looked skeptical. "I suppose we'd be taken these hosses down for free. We don't work for free no more. We'll just move on."

Wilcox said, "Now hold on a bit, there. Captain Gunby has authorized me to pay you a dollar each for the horses you escort down to Baxter Springs. Further, he will write you a military promissorynote requesting Colonel Weer to pay you another dollar for each horse that makes it there in good form."

Bev glanced at Billy, who was still shaken by the news. He returned his sight to Wilcox and said, "Two dollar a hoss. Guess we back in business."

The trip to Baxter Springs took ten days to travel the two hundred miles from Fort Belmont. Two horses were lost, one a mare breaking a leg in a groundhog hole. The other, a young colt, ran off to be killed by a wolf. Other than that, the ride had been easy and pleasant.

Billy thought that he could see some life coming back to Bev. Just being around horses, caressing and caring for them seemed to lift the man's spirits a little. It looked like he'd started up that long hill to feeling that even after losing Eli life could be worth living. Billy knew what it was like, he still kept the mourning portrait of his family in his bag. He'd take it out now and then, beat up as it was banging so much against the old Cochran handgun and powder box stuck down there with it. A line crisscrossed over his mama's neck, across Little Sister Bess's body. His daddy still looked okay, though rough treatment had faded his face some. His own face seemed like that of another boy, so much had happened since then. The shock in his eyes and his open mouth in the picture struck him as an impression of his younger self looking in fear at afuture that he was living now. He missed home and he missed Daddy, too. The ache ebbed gradually, he knew, but it was still there, not hard to dredge up. So, maybe Bev wasn't all that distracted right now.

Other things had changed, too. When Bev told Josh and Whit about Wilcox's proposal, Josh shrugged his shoulders, saying in an offhand way that Baxter Springs was fine with him. Billy figured anyplace was fine with him as long as he was out of the hemp fields. Whit almost roared with glee at the news, ready to kill every Grayback that snaked across his path. But Bev took issue with Whit.

"What about Nila?" Bev asked.

"What about her?" Whit snapped.

"Who'll look out for her when you gone?"

"She be awright," said Whit. Billy could see the muscles working around his jaw, sure sign that his water was beginning to boil.

"Awright by herself? Her people's gone, her daddy the chief gone! Ain't no one gonna be around here except a bunch of old Bluecoat hoss jockeys who can't help her, or won't help her, and might even do her some bad. And you say she'll be awright?"

"She be fine, anyone here mess with her, they answer to me," Whit said, pulling himself up in brazen defiance. "I blow their heads off, just like I'm gonna do to Massah Johnny Reb."

Bev shook his head back and forth, "Everyone know you can't shoot for shit, and you gonna take on a tussle of hoss soldiers or maybe five thousand deadeye Rebels. You crazy, boy, outta your mind."

Whit buttressed his lips. "I can shoot, shoot better 'n you."

Bev shook his head ruefully. "Everyone here can shoot better'n you, Whit. Even me, and I can't shoot. You oughtta stay home with Nila, she can protect you."

Whit took a roundhouse swing that Bev easily ducked while punching with his left hand. His fist thumped off of Whit's temple, sending him down on his backside in a heap. Bev leaned over and said, "You do what you want, Whit, what I care? But, if one bad thing happen to that girl while we gone, I will cave in your head for good."

"I'm goin'," said Whit, and he did.

For the ten days it took to catch up with the Blues at Baxter Spring, neither of them spoke to the other. It was enough to drive everyone mad, thought Billy.

They ambled up to the picket on guard outside of the encampment, all tents this time in a meadow between two woods. The guard let them through, directing them to the quartermaster, who corralled their horses. After giving them a receipt, they headed to the middle of camp to find the commanding officer's post. Another guard introduced them to Colonel Weer, a portly, florid man, short in height, with a vast scraggily salt-and- pepper beard cascading down to his breast. As he talked, between words he sucked deeply on a pipe stuffed in his mouth, exhaling moisture-laden clouds of smoke up toward the peak of the tent.

"So, you are the gentlemen that brought us another lot of fine horses. I thank you for your service to our forces and to the Union. I have instructed our quartermaster to honor the voucher you brought with you and to pay you one dollar each for the mounts that you've secured. We will make good use of the steeds in our upcoming reclamation of the Indian Territory. Is there anything else I can do for you while you're here?"

They all glanced at each other, then Bev spoke. "We ain't goin' back to Belmont. We wanna fight the Rebs."

Colonel Weer blinked in surprise. "Well, I guess I can understand your motivation in this conflict, and I applaud it." He took on a conspiratorial expression as he said, "In fact, we are planning an imminent incursion into the Territory where the renegades have been raiding regularly. I could use some scouts who know the terrain. Since you have proven yourself to be seasoned horsemen, I would be delighted to offer you posts as scouts for this campaign."

Bev replied instantly. "We be scouts, count on that."

"Thank you, I am indebted to you already."

The Colonel stepped in front of each of them to shake their hands. When he reached him, Billy almost stepped back himself from the sour odor of whiskey wafting from the Colonel's mouth.

"My orderly here will escort you to the guides' quarters where you can rest up. Believe it or not, we will be marching at the break of dawn, six thousand strong down the Neosho River."

"We know that river," Bev said flatly. "We can help you."

Chapter 16. Locust Grove

Near the lines where the cavalry horses stood tethered, the scouts bivouacked in a rough circle of tents. After they tied up and unsaddled their own mounts, Bev and his fellows meandered over to a campfire in the center of the tents. A tripod stood above a fire over which a black pot hung with stew bubbling up to its rim. A varied group of men sat on logs around the fire, talking and drinking, some eating from bowls. When Bev and Billy came into the light, one of the seated men jumped to his feet.

"Muh bruthuhs!" he shouted gleefully.

"Abraham Bowlegs," said Bev smiling. Billy grinned, "Long time, Abraham."

Abraham twisted around to the other men sitting by the fire. "Dese muh frens' frum Arkansaw, we waak all de wey frum de mountains tuh dey blue soldier forts. Den uh come heah tuh fight dem rebel debbles. Now, dey heah, too!"

"Hey all y'all," said Bev, "glad to meet ya."

They settled in to talk, telling stories and sharing a few pulls on the jug. Billy thought it tasted awful, but he drank a little bit of it anyway.

The next morning, the Bluecoats struck camp, piled the tents, chairs, and cookware into transport wagons pulled by strings of mules. Officers ran around yelling and cursing at the soldiers as they packed everything away, then assembled on parade. When they were ready to march, Colonel Weer and his staff rode up on their horses to take position at the front. As soon as they gave the order to move out, bugles blasted up and down the column.

The officers prodded their horses into a slow amble, and each regiment fell in behind them, four in a row, row after row, fifteen hundred rows in all. In their deep blue, woolen uniforms, the men were sweating already in the heavy late-June weather, even though noon was three hours away. Captains, lieutenants, and sergeants cajoled and poked men up and down the line to pick up their pace, keep going, save their water, catch up to the row in front of them. The last of them didn't pass for two hours, and they were followed by caissons and cannons, the supply wagons, and finally, camp followers, both men and women.

The scouts sat on logs and camp chairs in a line looking out on the long procession. As the troops passed by, they ate bacon-flavored pone while carrying on a constant chatter about this and that. They compared one regiment to another, their footwear and tunics, the insignias and banners identifying their states, and sometimes counties and towns.

"Bet you miss walkin' with all them other soldier boys, right Billy?" asked Whit, grinning wickedly.

Billy replied in a somber voice, "I don't miss it a bit, not one bit."

"Why, Billy, ain't you got no more soldiering in you? You don't want to kill Johnny Reb?"

Billy shook his head slowly, "I grew up with some of them Johnny Rebs. I seen enough of 'em face down."

"Just that one little bitty fight that one time? You seen ever'thing, seen it all?"

"I seen enough."

"Well, I can't wait," Whit barked gleefully with a rumbling laugh. "I wanna see as many of them white crackers dead on the ground as I can. I love to be the one who put them there."

"Do he look like anyone who own any slaves?" Bev said crossly, flicking his head toward Billy. "Likely none athem mountain boys owned one thing, never mind slaves. You got the proof right in front of you, Whit. Why you such a jackass 'bout Billy in all this?"

"'Cause I hate all them white boys keepin' us down. I wanna kill every one of them."

"Then, you gonna have to kill some wearin' blue, too."

"Hey," said Josh, "Here come them Injun soldiers."

The members of the Indian Home Guard regiment padded by, Delaware, Cherokee, Osage, Creek, and of course, the Estelusti with Abraham in the vanguard. Each soldier wore traditional garb mixed with various Union elements, a blue cavalry hat with a golden tassel, a short-waist roundabout closed with shiny brass buttons, or maybe long, blue wool pants, a gold stripe on the outside of each leg. Otherwise, impressive feathered headdresses, embroidered deerskin shirts and buffalo coats, leather leggings and beaded moccasins marked the finery of all the native people. They carried a mix of arms, some with Springfields, others with Enfields, a few long rifles, Brown Besses, shotguns, various handguns, and just a few with bows and spears. Chief Quacornowha, known as James Segondyne to the whites, spoke for the Indian Home Guard regiment.

When Quacornowha saw them looking at his men, he let out a loud cry, followed by a chorus of other yelps and howlsthroughout the Guard. Grinning broadly, the seated scouts jumped up and shouted out happy hollers themselves. After everyone but a few stragglers had passed, the scouts stood up and casually saddled and packed their horses. Once each man was squared away, without a word they all mounted in unison. Just then, a Union officer cantered up to the group.

"Lieutenant Asa Barber, First Missouri Cavalry. Colonel Weer has assigned me to be your liaison officer."

Barber wore a forage cap, a dark-blue shell jacket, light-blue jeans hugging his legs, and long, black riding boots. He had a .36 Navy Colt holstered on his left hip and a curved saber strapped to the right. Dirty blond and lean, the sharp gaze of his gray eyes belied the gentility of his features.

"The Colonel wants to know why in tarnation you men aren't up front, spread out to reconnoiter."

"We goin' tuh get to dat now," said Abraham, riding at the head of the party. He wheeled his horse around in a tight pirouette, another surprise for his old traveling companions.

Barber squinted as he parsed the unfamiliar dialect. At length, he said, "Well, all right. Follow me to the head of the column. From there, you'll be divided into units of two each to search for the enemy. If they are found, one scout will return to our main force to report while the other rider maintains discreet contact. That clear?"

The men looked at each other, mildly amused and skeptical. As soon as they arrived at the front, they split off in all directions, four to a group, with Lieutenant Barber shouting loudly at their fast disappearing backs.

Bev, Whit, Josh, and Billy rode together. Unlike regular army mounts, they rode Indian ponies without horseshoes. Although they increased the risk of a horse going lame or splitting a hoof, the men took the chance in exchange for stealth when they approached an enemy position. The ponies had been trained to hunt buffalo, which meant they made as little sound as possible snorting or snuffling to prevent spooking the game. This training worked equally well when the prey were men.

The trackers ignored Lieutenant Barber's orders because they had worked out their own strategy beforehand. Experience told them that two-man teams would not work. Instead, groups of four riders raced down the Spring River to its juncture at the Neosho, where they fanned out along its various branches and runs. Together, they searched an area almost a mile wide on each side of the main river. Traveling under the cover of darkness, they looked for campfires and other signs of a large body of men. Once a team found the Graybacks, one scout would stay to keep track of them, while another raced back to tell the Union brass. The other two riders in the group would take off in opposite directions back up the river to let any other scouting team they met know of their find. Those teams then would send out two of their men to run down the rest of the teams. The ripple effect meant that in a matter of a day or less, all of the scouts except for those shadowing the enemy would return to form up with the Bluecoats cavalry.

Sure enough, Bev and the rest had been out just three nights, lately going down and around Lost Creek when they heard a birdcall the next morning. Josh returned the call, and Hunka Ahgre, an Osage, silently walked ahead of his horse into their campsite. Tall and dark, the Osage warrior wore his people's traditional soft moccasins and stockings, a bow across the back of his deerskin coat.

"Grays found," he said.

"Where?" asked Bev quickly.

"Jus' 'bove Lake Hudson, said Hunka, "a supply train goin' south, mebbe ta Fort Gibson."

"How many days walk?"

"Three, five to Gibson."

Bev mulled the information over for a moment. Then, he said to the Osage, "Thank you, Hunka. We'll send out two men at dark to tell other scouts."

"I ride, tell some more," said Hunka, "you gimme 'nother pony. Dis hoss ti'ed."

Bev's head moved back, "You want to ride on to another team?" Hunka nodded, and Bev said, "Awright. Guess I'lllook for one myself."

He glanced at the other men and said, "Josh, why don't you take Billy and Whit here back to the main army. I see you there later."

Bev returned his attention to Hunka. "Say, who found them Rebs first?"

Hunak Ahgre said, "Abraham Bowlegs."

"Figures," said Bev.

When Colonel Weer learned of the Confederates' whereabouts, he called in his officers to form a plan of attack. After a good deal of

204

conversation and deliberation, the meeting was adjourned and the junior officers returned to their units.

"Weer thinks we cannot move the entire brigade fast enough to get to the Secesh before they make it to Fort Gibson," said Lieutenant Barber. "But, he thinks a smaller, fast moving force of two or more companies can get below them and maybe intercept them.

"Now, Abraham Bowlegs says the Reb supply train is made up mostly of rogue Injuns from the Five Civilized Tribes. So, we think the best way to fight them is with their own kind, the First Indian Home Guard with you boys in support, along with a detachment of the Ninth Kansas cavalry. You will guide this force, about 300 men in all, to a suitable position for an attack somewhere below Hudson Lake. Like before, you will travel at night, surveying both the movements of the Secesh force while also seeking out an appropriate salient. Any questions?"

Billy whispered to Josh, "What the heck did he say?"

"He want us 'n some other boys ta hightail it down south of the Graybacks so we'all can get the jump on 'em."

"Well, then why didn't he say so?"

"He from the north. They talk book talk up there, like the bible."

"I heard preacher talk, but nothin' like that."

"Yeah, wellmebbe preachin' different all over, mebbe."

The troops moved out at sunset, hewing close to the Neosho River while the scouts alternated in tracking the Rebel supply train and reporting back. As soon as Lieutenant Barber learned that the enemy force was on the east side of the river, he moved his regiments to the west side. They traveled faster than the Rebels, who were slowed by their laden ox-pulled wagons. In just a matter of a night, the Blue force slipped silently past the Rebels. The end of the second night put them below Hudson Lake well ahead of the wagon train.

In the new dawn light, Barber surveyed the land. He decided that the best position to take was on top of a small western ridge covered by locust trees that overlooked the Fort Gibson trail. Woods grew on each side of the road as well on level ground. Barber placed the Kansas cavalry and the scouts on both sides. Rather than get caught in a crossfire, the cavalry would fight initially on foot, then mount to ride down any Grays trying to escape. Once every soldier was posted, they all waited in silence.

Now into the first week of July, the heat of the day drained them. Barber had made sure that each man carried plenty of water. But, the wool uniforms soaked up sweat that failed to evaporate in the humid air. The deerskin outfits were no better, suppressing the heat inside until the men wearing them were forced to open up buttons and loosen strings for relief. After a few hours of waiting, the tired men started to drowse, so many so that the sergeants and corporals assigned watches to ensure that everyone would be awake when the Rebs arrived. Time dragged on, and the men suffered in their hot, damp clothes, even moreso when a host of green flies found them. The flies bit them so severely that several men had to clench their teeth to remain quiet.

After the morning drifted into afternoon, many of them started to wonder if the Rebs would come by at all. Maybe they had taken another route. Maybe they weren't on their way to Fort Gibson. The whispered conversations grew loud enough for the stripes to crack their riding crops a few times to shut them up.

Billy lay next to Josh, both of them awake, shifting their weight trying to get comfortable.

"How you think this will go?" he asked.

Josh pursed his lips thoughtfully. "If'n the Grays come this way, we got the jump on them, that's fo' sure. If they don't come, we go after them again. Either way, we awright."

Billy nodded, wanting to believe the wise old black man. But, his stomach roiled relentlessly, his mind glutted with terrifying memories of Fisher Creek, blood erupting from men horribly shot or hit by shrapnel, falling apart on all sides, front and back. How long before he would feel the searing pain of a bullet or a bayonet, one that he would know was final, his last feeling before death's black shroud descended? He shivered violently at the flood of unshakeable, dreadful thoughts recurring over and over.

"Y'all right, Billy?" asked Josh. "You shakin' like you cold. You got a chill, mebbe?"

Billy shook his head, his teeth chattering, "Naw, I'm fine, Josh. Feelin' bad for them boys we gonna shoot. Works me up a bit."
Josh nodded knowingly.

The word came down the line. A squad of riders had been spotted trotting on the road. They came into sight, glancing from side to side as they rode for any signs of Yankees being about. The men hiding on the roadsides froze, and the enemy scouts passed on. As they disappeared, Billy noted that many wore Confederate gray. But,with their elaborate headwear, most looked more like fellows from the

Bluecoats's own Injun regiment. Abraham had told him that the Rebel army was full of Cherokees and others from the Five Civilized Tribes. Now, he knew that the Black Freeman had been telling the truth.

A corps of horsemenarrived, followed closely by several wagons pulled by oxen and mules. The orders of the officers were to wait until the Rebels were in the middle of the road. The Union soldiers on the ridge would open fire first. When the Johnnies broke toward the woods for cover, the Kansas cavalry and the scouts would let loose their volley.

Billy could barely hold on to his rifle, his hands were so sweaty. Gorge rose in his throat as the road started to fill with wagons. Soon they were abreast of him, then past him until he couldn't see them far down the road. He chewed his lips, thinking soon, soon.

A tremendous roar of gunfire rocked the air; men on horseback and on the wagons immediately began to fall. Birds bolted from the woods into the sky as more shots reached a ragged crescendo after the second wave let loose. Billy couldn't bear watching, but an officer bellowed from the right, "Here they come!" Billy crouched low while everyone around him rose up and fired at the men running from the road toward them. Those in front fell as one from minié balls bursting through them. A second blast of fire came from the line in the woods followed by the Union troops on the ridge. The Rebels fell front and back from the barrage, the survivors dropping for cover. Suddenly, Billy and the rest heard balls whisking by them as the Rebs returned fire.

"Godda—!" shouted Barber, somehow just a few yards away. "Fall back! Fall back for cover."

Surprised, Josh said to no one, "We already got cover."

"Get to your horses!" yelled Barber.

As soon as they tried to move back, several of them fell, shot. Seeing their own men down, the others ran backwards, and more of them dropped, splayed out. Billy moved back some, but the flying bullets overhead stopped him short. The others followed suit, hiding as best as they could behind trees or fallen logs.

"Where the hell is our support from the ridge?" Barber roared. He screeched, "Return fire! Fire at will!"

Most of the blue soldiers cringed, while some started firing back. The fight settled into a sharpshooting match marked by solitary men gasping and dying on either side, one by one. Billy tried to burrow beneath the log in front of him, desperate to escape, all the while worrying that the Grays would charge again. Tears of fear streamed down his cheeks, and he clutched his rifle stock as close as he could, his hands whitening from the effort. The shots kept whizzing by above him, and he flinched at the sound of each one. Petrified, he cried silently with his mouth open wide, saliva stringing from one lip to the other joining the streams from his eyes.

A bugle sounded, and they heard exultant cries in the distance from the road. More fire could be heard, and voices shouting from behind the Rebels. The sound of shooting gradually lessened, then stopped completely. Barber stood up and gazed out in front. He turned and said loudly, "It's over, boys. The Rebs have given it up. Reload, and stand at your positions."

Slowly, the soldiers and scouts quickly reloaded their rifles and stood up. Without a signal, they started back toward the road. As they retraced their steps, they picked up their own, some wounded, others dead, and brought them back out to the road. They found it to be crowded with their Union comrades and at least a hundred Rebels who had surrendered.

The soldiers from the woods solemnly laid their dead in a row next to others who had been killed in the melee. The rest of the ground was strewn with distorted Rebel bodies left where they had died. When the two lines of Blues met each other, the men yelled into the air, "Huzzah!"

Lieutenant Barber called to the men. "It is a decisive whipping we handed to the Johnny Rebs, boys, we licked 'em real good." He pivoted around, searching the joyous men until he saw Bev standing next to a wagon, making a tripod with his legs and his rifle. "Mr. Bowman," said Barber, "I would appreciate very much you riding to tell Colonel Weer of our overwhelming victory. Chief Hunak Ahgre of the Indian Home Regiment and Sergeant Henry of the Ninth Kansas Cavalry will accompany you. Gentlemen, if you please," he finished.

The rest of the men were assigned various jobs. The scouts and a contingent of the Kansas cavalry galloped off in pursuit of the Rebels who had escaped. Other men were detailed to pull the dead Rebels to the side of the road. Sergeants and corporals began inventorying the large number of wagons captured while one detail watered and fed the oxen and mules.

Billy and Josh joined Whit on the crew charged with readying theUnion dead for burial, just sixteen men. They searched each body for personal belongings and for scraps of paper with their names and homes written on them. A sergeant collected themto write to their families. Many of the dead left nothing, including the few who were Indians. Billy came upon one with a burlap sack across his face. He lifted it, and sat back. Abraham Bowlegs stared past him with clouded eyes. A cascade of congealing blood coated his chin from his lower lip down to his neck, looking to Billy almost like some kind of tribal warpaint perfectly applied.

"M'lord," he exclaimed.

"Shot right through the gizzard," said a Kansas private. "Blood explode outtahis mouth all everwhere, poor bastard. "Still, looks like he was lucky," the private went on. "Better n' bein' gutshot. Now, that's a bad way to go.This fella must'a died pretty quick. Hell, the whole shebang lasted not even an hour."

Billy sat back, horrified, remembering back when Murray described the awfulness of it just before the battle at Fishing Creek. The private moved on while Billy hurried to rearrange Abraham's shirt collar to cover the seeping wound in his neck. "Josh," he called out, almost a wail, "Josh, it's Abraham, Abraham Bowlegs. Killed dead."

Josh stepped over and crouched, peering down. "That a shame," he said, "I sorry to see such a good man brought down so."

"He's shot dead and I never fired my gun even once."

Josh patted Billy on the arm, "No matter, Billy. He ain't gonna hold it against you. He knew you was a good man, too. Some's for shootin' men, some isn't. You a good boy, Billy, for sure, and the Lord knows it. You see old Abraham again someday up there where he's starin' at us now."

Weeping, Billy nodded while he closed Abraham's eyes.

Colonel Weer could not have been more pleased with the outcome at Locust Grove.

"Bully, that's just bully! A hundred Rebels dead, a hundred and ten more captured, along with sixty-four wagons full of goods vital to the South's cause. You fellows even reeled in the rebel colonel, Clarkson, the head of the whole train. All this the day before Independence Day. I am giddy with delight! Since it is July Fourth, Lieutenant Barber, I believe we should divide all the clothing among the soldiers and any refugees. The powder and shot can be requisitioned equally among unit heads. Now we can march on Fort Gibson and finish kicking the Rebs out of the Oklahoma Territory!"

"That really what he say?" said Whit.

"Every word of it," said Bev, "I heard it myself; 'Bully, bully, bully.' He's one happy Union braid for sure. He sure drink like it, anyway."

Whit dropped his shoulders skeptically. "I don't know 'bout all this."

"Why you think you wearin' new britches, man?"

"Maybe 'cause my butt hangin' out the old ones?"

All of them laughed loudly. The fighting was over for now. They all felt sad about Abraham, even Whit, and they buried him in a proper grave. After Locust Grove, Weer decided to march his makeshift brigade down to Flat Rock, less than fifteen miles from the Confederate stronghold Fort Gibson. If they could wrest that bastion from the Seceshs's grip, the South would be finished in Indian Territory.

The word had gotten out among the Civilized Tribes, too. Those Cherokee who had escaped Locust Grove to Tahlequah told grim stories of the Federals's might. Dispatches from General Curtis informed Weer that three new Indian regiments had been formed with defectors from the Confederacy. The tide had turned.

As Bev and the others rode down toward Flat Rock, they became uncomfortable.

"I ain't particularly tickled about goin' to a place we gave plenty of room when we first come up this way," said Whit as they mosied along on their ponies. "What if the Rebs beat the Yankees this time? We get caught, they send us straight back to Kentucky!"

For once, Bev kept quiet. Billy stared at him and said, "You think that could happen, Bev? You think the Rebels can beat us?"

Bev grimaced, "I don't know. They might could."

"And send us all back?" Billy asked, now alarmed.

"If they catch us, they send us back, Billy. Not you, maybe."

"Oh, no, they for sure put me back in the army or in jail."

"Well ... maybe that's true."

"We can't afford to lose, Bev!" Billy said.

"I know. Fort Gibson is a different thing from Locust Grove. I ain't sure Weer can let go his bottle long enough to think up a good plan. To tell you true, I ain't all that comfortable around here either."

"Food gettin' scarce, too," added Josh.

"True," said Bev. "It a long way from here to Fort Baxter. Maybewhat we done to them Rebs, this time they do to a Yankee supply train."

They rode in silence for a time, mulling over the risks staring at them. Finally, Bev said, "I don't think we want to play dice out here strung out like we are from places more safe to be."

"Then, what we gonna do?" said Whit.

"I think we ought to go back to Fort Baxter, then to Fort Belmont. Go back to what we know how to do, hosses and huntin', wait out the rest of this war."

Billy looked at Whit and Josh, then at Bev. "I believe we all think you right, Bev."

In Fort Belmont, they were welcomed back by the skeleton company now under the command of Captain Wilcox.

"So, you got you self a promotion," Bev said.

"I did. I am now in command of seventy-five of the finest, oldest soldiers in the United States cavalry." They laughed, then Wilcox said, "What about you?"

"We're fixin' on catchin' and sellin' hosses to the army, pick up where we left off 'til this war is done with."

Wilcox twirled one of his moustache handlebars, "Not too much call for more horses around here. Since Grant and his keep whipping the Rebs, they're moving further and further south. Now, if we had the railroad here, we'd take as many horses as you could get, buffalo, too. Back east, the Confederates are given us hell. Of course, they haven't run any rails out here yet. I doubt they will 'til the war's over one way or the other. You all are welcome to stay here as long as you want, but you might want to consider going back east."

"How's that?" said Bev.

Wilcox said, "Congress just passed the Confiscation Act. All slaves owned by the Rebels are now free. They put through the Militia Act, too, which lets you boys work or join the Army. You do that, you get paid for what you've just done for free."

The men exchanged glances. When no one said anything, Bev spoke. "We pretty much sure we don't want to go back anytime soon. Too many crackers ready to kill us soon as look at us. Or, put us back in chains."

Wilcox shrugged. "I don't know about that. Word is that Lincoln is working on an order to free all you slaves soon, north and south. The abolitionists are winning that war."

Bev nodded, "Yeah, well, 'til they beat down the last Grayback, we plan on keepin' movin' west."

Wilcox shrugged his shoulders again, "Suit yourself. You can stay here for a while, like I said. When you go west, you might want to head for Fort Larned in Comanche country. It isn't much bigger than ours, maybe smaller. But it's right on the Santa Fe Trail, used by a lot of traders. In fact, the boys in blue's job out there is to protect the locals from the Indians. It could be a good place for you to set up, sell some horses, shoot some buffalo, raise up some cows. Not a bad life."

"No town out there?" asked Whit.

Wilcox shook his head, "Not yet. Probably one'll spring up after the war."

"So, we have to make our own whiskey."

"I'm afraid that maybe so," said Wilcox, eyeing Whit wryly.

"That's awright, I got no problem with that," said Whit.

Bev wheeled around. "How 'bout you, Josh, Billy? Y'all wanna go down the Santa Fe Trail?"

Josh held his hands palm up as Billy said, "We keep our distance from the Rebels?"

"Sure you can," Wilcox said, smiling.

Chapter 17. On the Range

When he thought about it out on the Kansas plains, Billy found it mystifying to be so far away from home for so long, almost a year now. After reaching Fort Larned, they got right to work on making a living on the vast, flat land. They rested their horses and restocked provisions at the fort, then headed southwest to see what they could see.

The change of seasons colored the landscape with a blend of magnificent wild wheat browns, plum mauves, lavender and lilac blues, and muted greens. After meandering over long stretches of endless, level terrain, they came upon a river flanked by stands of autumn-colored trees.

"Must be the Pawnee," Josh said. "The major show it on his map at the fort. The river named after a Injun tribe from 'round here."

"Good to be seeing the river instead of them Injuns," said Whit.

"They could be friendly," Billy said.

"Yeah, just like you smart," Whit said.

Billy frowned, but he was ignored.

Bev moved his head around, surveying the area. "Water, trees, and no one else around," he thought out loud. He faced the other men, "This could be the place."

After that, they rode back to the fort where they bought a wagon and two mules, axes, cross saws and hand saws, wedges, planes, hammers, nails, shovels, plenty of rope, and other building tools. Bev used some of the money saved from their horse trades at Belmont for the materials. When they arrived back at the chosen spot, they set up camp and started looking for trees to fell. By then, they had learned that the stream they thought was the Pawnee in fact was the Saw Log Creek where the main river petered out. Further exploring turned up plenty of wildlife, buffalo and horses included.

In a month, Bev and Josh dropped enough trees to split into planks for framing a two-room cabin. At the same time, Billy and Whit dug up clay to mix with straw into sun-dried mud bricks. They used the bricks to close in the cabin walls, and split shingles to cover the roof. On the other side of the cabin away from the creek, they dug a pit and put up an outhouse. Once finished with these essential structures, they worked on building a corral for the horses and mules.

They also built them a lean-to, which they would convert into a barn before the winter came.

Two-day trips to the fort added cookware, blankets, and other odds and ends to the household. Nila made the meals for all of them, and kept the cabin in order.

Sitting on the Santa Fe Trail, the fort also supplied them with news, sometimes from traders passing through, other times from weeks-old newspapers read by Bev. One old report headlined a brutal battle fought near Sharpsburg in Maryland that left thousands dead on both sides. Lee and his boys had been forced to head back south, though they weren't really licked. Lincoln didn't care, he used the victory to put out a proclamation that would free the slaves at the beginning of the year.

"You believe that's enough for us to think about goin' home?" asked Billy.

Bev pursed his lips in a scowl. "No. They ain't done with the Johnnies yet."

"That's right," Whit chimed in, "just'cause they whipped 'em once don't mean they stay whipped."

Another yellowing paper reported that back in June, Memphis had fallen to the Federals. General Butler had swept up the Mississippi without much trouble and secured the important southern port with barely a shot fired. As soon as Bev read the story, he sat down and leaned back against a wall.

Memphis fell into Union hands not more than a month after they left. If they could have stayed put for just a little longer, they wouldn't have suffered so through the winter and spring, starving, freezing, hiding, and fighting. Instead, they would be celebrating their new-found freedom, making plans for the future, living and loving life. Mary Louise could retire from her two jobs working every day and allnight. Eli might still be alive. If only.

Mary Louise, he thought. Standing, he crumpled up the paper and tossed it aside, walking away to get back to the work at hand.

Whit seemed prophetic when news of several other Confederate wins came down the road, the massacre at Fredericksburg topping them all. The blood toll staggered the Union, and Bev and the rest stayed put. By winter they completed the barn and stable. To prepare for the spring, they fenced in more pastureland and constructed an outsized smoke house for room to cure multiple buffalo downed in one hunt. Billy and Josh took care of the hunting and the vegetable garden.

Digging the garden in the dense Kansas earth proved to be exhausting work, and much more so when they dug out a root cellar beneath the cabin.

Bev and Whit went after horses. Soon, traders learned of the black men's spread and began stopping at it as a way station. There, they could find fresh mounts, jerky, smoked meat, and various sundries. As usual, Bev took a good portion of the profits to squirrel away for future needs.

The winter had been long, cold, and boring. They had ample to eat but little to do except track wild horses and hunt when they could. Otherwise, they found themselves imprisoned in the cabin as the wind, sleet, and snow hit hard on the prairie. Visitors were few, and after being together almost every waking moment for a year, only the most irritating traits of each of them were left to learn. Spring brought blessed relief, but raw emotions lingered for a time.
Whit came into the cabin one April day, a sour look on his face.

"Not a nag in sight," he said, and threw himself down on a chair, his legs splayed out in front of him.

Billy sat in a corner doing his best to sew up a split seam on one arm of his gray tunic. He looked up at Whit and said, "Where's Bev?"

"Where you think?" snapped Whit, followed by mumbling, "Likely puttin' up the hosses as usual."

Not saying a word, Nila brought Whit a wooden bowl of stew and a clay cup of water. Billy watched her as she moved silently, gliding over the wooden planks as though riding a puff of wind. Her long black hair and deep black eyes fascinated Billy, though her lineless face appeared thinner now, drawn.

Whit took one look at the bowl, and pushed it aside. "This kinda livin' don't keep body and soul together."

"Josh and me plan on plantin' a couple of fruit trees," Billy said. "If we can get the seed to sprout, should be good eatin' in two, three years."

"Two, three years," Whit repeated scathingly. "Then, I suppose we gonna have a regular grove of apples, peaches, and pears just fallin' all over us."

"Not likely that much," said Billy, slightly abashed, "but somethin' like that."

"And we sell the bounty for real money," Whit said.

Billy frowned, "I doubt there be much left over to sell," he said.

"Unhuh. Instead of eating all them apples, we ought to make 'em into hard cider. Make a dollar or two sellin' that, that for sure."

"We ain't got no apples yet," said Billy. "Maybe a couple of years."

"Sure. And you see me waitin' around here a couple of years for some apples? 'Cause I don't. I'll be long gone by then."

Billy frowned again, his brow puckering as he motioned with his head at Nila, who stood at the sideboard kneading dough as though nothing had been said.

"Oh, don't you give me that face. We all be goin' our separate ways when the war over. I'm just the one sayin' so."

Glowering, Billy dropped his eyes to his sewing.

"Only thing is, to get anywhere, you got to have some money. The way things goin', we ain't never gonna have enough, especially with Bev holdin' out the way he do."

Billy didn't reply.

"What we need is some money maker, some kind of business," Whit said almost to himself, lost in a reverie. His eyes brightened. "Maybe it ain't such a bad idea to pick some apples. Maybe so!"

The next day, Whit took the wagon to Fort Larned without telling anyone why. He returned in two days with a large, company-size cast iron cooking pot, a couple of kettles almost as big, two sacks of sugar, all sorts and shapes of glass bottles, and several burlap bags of grain and potatoes. Billy was in the garden when Whit pulled the wagon up.

"Bev around?" he said.

Billy shook his head, "He and Josh rode out since you was gone."

"They out for hosses?"

"They are, and huntin'."

"Good enough, don't need them lookin' over my shoulder. C'mon, you can help me get this stuff into the smokehouse."

Puzzled, Billy decided not to ask questions since he knew Whit wouldn't answer them. Just as well to let it all come out on its own, he thought.

They had the mash simmering in the big cast iron pot in no time. Once it was heated, Whit added the brown sugar "for more bite and flavor," he said. After an hour, he and Billy poured the mash from the big cooking pot through a thin linen rag into one of the kettles scrubbed clean by Billy. Whit allowed the liquid to settle, added yeast, and sealed the kettle top with adhesive plaster he'd gotten from the fort hospital. Two days later, the kettle began to bubble up a bit out of the spout stuffed with a porous rag. "It be ready in two weeks," Whit explained. "Then, we strain it into that other kettle, and let it set for a month. It be clear and strong, ready to bottle and sell. Now, c'mon, we put this stuff and the kettle back in the corner out of sight. Don't want nobody to fuss with it 'til we ready. Go ahead, fetch ahoss blanket from the barn and throw it over everything."

Bev and Josh returned the next day, again without any wild horses. They traipsed inside the cabin tired and discouraged.

"Y'all come up empty handed?" Whit asked, his voice bright and warm. "No matter, get 'em the next time. Maybe we can get us some spring deer, they out feedin' their fawns, now."

Bev regarded Whit skeptically. "You in a good mood. What you do while we was away?"

"Not much," replied Whit, "this 'n that."

"This 'n that, huh?" Bev said sardonically. "I bet. This 'n that means you sit around all day, eatin', sleepin, and doin' nothin'?"

"Oh, I did some things," Whit said, "you gonna see."

"I be surprised if that true." He swiveled in his seat and said, "Billy, tell me what you did while we was gone. Just about everything around here, right?"

After two weeks, Whit begged off riding again and Billy went hunting with Bev. They returned with mule deer, two carcasses, which Whit volunteered to help Billy hang in the smokehouse. To Billy's surprise, Whit had managed to siphon off the first fermented batch himself. In a month, Whit said, the liquor, clear and delicious, would be ready to jar and sell.

Whit and Billy headed out to the smokehouse one early morning in April. Secure in knowing that Bev and Josh had gone out for more game, they lined up the Mason jars and other glass bottles for the final pouring of their first batch. Whit tipped the kettle over to allow the liquor to trickle into a tin funnel inserted in a bottle's neck. Billy held the bottle steady until it was full, then stoppered it with a wooden plug. Whit took the full-to-the-brim bottle from Billy and carried it to a small worktable with two cups on it. He poured from the bottle into the cups, corked it, and put it down. He picked up the cups and handed one to Billy, smiling broadly.

Billy nearly spit it out. He swallowed it quickly, burning all the way down his throat. Tears in his eyes, he said, "B'god, you poisoning me!"

Whit took a sip, coughed, and said, "You get used to it, you like it, too."

They had half of the bottles filled when Bev walked in with Josh behind him.

Looking like foxes caught in the henhouse, the two men squatting on the smokehouse floor instantly stopped moving.

Bev stood over them, legs apart, hands on his hips, elbows out. He shook his head, saying, "I knew you was up to somethin'. I should a known it be no good."

"Oh, it good awright, Bev, it real good. It gonna make us so rich, we don't have to be chasin' down anymore gamey meat. We eat high on the hog after this."

Bev swiveled his head again in disapproval. "Just make sure you don't burn the smokehouse down."

He walked away.

Within two weeks, they had bottled enough liquor to try selling it at the fort. They placed twenty bottles in the wagon bed, cushioning them with new, green prairie grass. Taking along some jerky and bread baked by Nila, they traveled the two-day trip to Fort Larned at a leisurely pace. In the evening, they made camp and ate something while sipping some of the spirits, which Billy learned to tolerate.Drowsy after each day's travel, they didn't have much to say to each other. Emboldened by the drink, that evening Billy spoke his mind.

"Whit, if you leave," he asked, "you takin' Nila with you?"

Lying on a blanket with one arm shielding his eyes in the dark, Whit answered, "Yes. No. Maybe, I don't know. I don't know if I'm leavin' at all. Or, at least anytime soon."

"You don't know?"

"Nope. Ridin' with a woman is hard work. I don't wanna do that. But, if we sell some liquor, maybe I won't have to leave."

"You don't like how we make a livin' now?"

"It hard work, boy. If workin' is easy, life is easy."

They reached the fort without incident and Whit drove the wagon around it until he spied the mess building. He moved the wagon behind it in a corner where it couldn't be seen easily from the various guard posts. He pulled the brake on the rig and stepped down, telling Billy to stay put. In half an hour, he returned with a sergeant and four privates. Whit pulled back the blanket covering the jars, selected one and lowered it down to the sergeant's waiting arms. The sergeant, a short, round-bellied bearded man of perhaps fifty years, yanked out the wooden stopper and held the bottle up with both hands. He took a hearty drink, and nearly dropped the bottle as he began a loud coughing jag. Two of the privates of about the same age as the sergeant saved the bottle from falling.

The sergeant turned to Whit and said, "That's some kind a juice you got there, boy. Take the hair off a wooden leg." He turned to his men, "Try it, boys, tell me what you think."

Each of them took a slug, until they all were bent over, hacking. This time the sergeant caught the bottle before it hit the ground. He looked at the men, then back at Whit and Billy, nodding, "I believe it has passed muster. How much y'got and how much?"

"Including the one you're holdin', I got twenty jars, five dollars apiece."

The sergeant frowned, dropping his furry brows almost over his slit eyes. "That's steep, boy, mighty steep. Hell, we just a bunch of broke soldiers stuck out here in the wilderness, we ain't got no five dollars apiece. We'll give you two bits a jar. That's it."

Whit scowled. "You takin' this poor Negra for a ride? I keep it, take it to Fort Belmont. They give me more."

The sergeant rolled his eyes, "They just as worn out and ill-paid as us. Only thing you'd be doing is ridin' far and wearin' out your horses just to get the same rate. You lose money in the long run."

Whit said, "I'll take my chances."

The sergeant sighed, his teeth clenched. He rubbed his salt and pepper whiskers in thought, then said, "Tell you what. We'll give you a dollar each for ten jars, and you can sell the rest to them Injuns over there waiting for their gov'ment treaty money. They don't know no better, they pay you the full five dollars per jar."

Whit wiped his face, thinking. "How come they pay that much? Where they get that money?"

"Like I said, from the federal gov'ment," the sergeant stressed. "They are paid for being moved off their land back east and endin' up out here. They come to the fort once a month to collect."

Whit licked his lips, his mouth open, calculating. "Awright. A dollar a jar for you, providin' the Injuns buy the rest for five dollars each. If they don't, you pay up the rest."

The sergeant scratched his head, "You drive a hard bargain, poor Negra. But, I'm sure the Injuns'll go for it, so I'll take the deal."

"Well, awright then. Get your money together and step up."

They sold ten jars in no time. As the sergeant was leaving, he turned and raised an index finger, "One more thing. You come back here to sell more white lightning, don't expect to sell all you got to Injuns and none to us. Do that, and I'll be telling the commandant about your business. Whenever you here, you have ten bottles saved for us at a dollar each. After that, I don't care how many you sell to the redskins."

Whit grinned and said, "Fair enough, but you got to save the empties for us for when we come back."

The sergeant nodded.

He hadn't lied about the Indians, they bought the last ten jars and bottles for five dollars apiece in no time. "We got to get working fillin' more glass," Whit said.

After buying more grain, sugar, and Mason jars, they searched the fort high and low for other empty bottles. While riding back to the spread, Whit said, "Next time, we make thirty bottles of liquor so we can sell twenty to the Injuns. We make a fortune," he went on, "but I ain't finished at that. Instead of spendin' all the money, we save it 'til we can buy the largest pot they is, maybe two, and a thumper, plenty of copper coil, and spigots, everything we need to make us a proper still. Cook up some fine bourbon, sell it for twice as much, get rich quick."

Billy gazed up at Whit, at his familiar light-mocha skin and aquiline nose, the thinness of his face and his long, lean frame. After being together for more than a year, this was the first time that Billy could remember seeing such ardor in the man, a passion that bordered onthe religious. Billy never knew such passionhimself and he was in awe of Whit's. But, he couldn't help himself when he said, "You sure, Whit, they all gonna pay twice more? You think they care if it bourbon or just shine they drink?"

Whit scowled, his eyes still fixed ahead. "Awright, maybe we get a quarter or two more."

The first problem with their liquor business arose from the drop off in doing their share of work around the homestead. In the beginning, it only annoyed Bev. Josh and Nila never complained, which aggravated Bev, who thought that the two moonshiners failed in simply beingfair. During the next couple of months, however, with the expansion of their liquor production, they neglected more and more vital work to everyone's survival. Finally, Bev felt he had to bring it up.

220

"You all ain't doin' your work," he said flat out. Whit and Billy sat together at the opposite end of the plank table they used for nearly everything in the cabin, including meals. Josh rested on a stool behind them in one corner of the cabin. Nila crouched on a stool in the corner opposite to Josh.

"We can't make it without everyone workin' around here," Bev continued. "Josh and Nila are picking you boys up most of the time, now.They don't complain, but they're tired and they can't keep up. Me neither. Y'all got to step it up."

He could see Billy's guilty expression as he shrank in his chair. But, Whit's reaction concerned him more. Sure enough, he watched as Whit's color deepened, his eyes growing wider, harder.

"We doin' our share," Whit said petulantly, "why you always on our backs?"

Bev sighed through his nose. "You ain't doing your share. We're low on everything, meat and staples, just one hoss to sell in the corral, and a garden full of weeds and no vegetables. We need to fence in more pasture, get feed for the animals to last the winter. We need you to get on it!"

Billy murmured, "I'll get back in and work the garden tomorrow," but without looking, Whit waved at him to be quiet.

"We give y'all a share of the liquor money," Whit said.

"That's nice, but it ain't enough," Bev replied. He headed Whit off before he could speak again. "We all know you plan to grow your business. That may be good, bring in more money for everyone, but no good for now. We need you to help us to get ready for the winter. Now's the time."

Whit said, "We do our work. We can get it all done before winter and still make more liquor. That liquor money gonna come in handy in case of emergency, too. The garden fail, the critters die, game go away, no hosses to sell, that money save us."

Bev shook his head, "Not if you plan on buying equipment for a still."

"We'll have enough money left over!" barked Whit.

Again, Bev shook his head, "I don't think so."

They paused, each tense, their tempers on the verge.

Whit started again. "Tell you what. You give me and Billy our share of the money you put aside. We buy the still now, earn some real money right away. That way, we give you more money from sellin' shinesooner, not later. And, we work harder around here to catch up."

Bev wiped his mouth. "You keep sellin' liquorlike you are and kick in all the money now. When fall come around, if we ready, you get the money to buy your still and cook all winter and next spring."

A sick smile crossed Whit's face. "You want all our liquor money now? Just like you take any other money we make, saving it up foranother rainy day. You one uppity nigger, Bev, you know that?"

Bev balled his hands into fists beneath the table.

"We work harder," Whit said. "We kick in more liquor money, keep the rest, buy our still now. That's it." He stood up and motioned to Billy, "C'mon, Billy, we got mash to check on."

The two of them left the cabin.

Bev released his hands and spread them to grab the table's edge, holding on to it as tightly as possible.

For a month, matters seemed to simmer down. Whit and Billy tried to keep up with their work. They attempted to schedule fermentation checks and bottling between horse roundups and hunting trips. But their work around the ranch itself lagged. Despite Josh taking on more and more of the building projects and caring for the animals, any thoughts of bringing in livestock and planting crops fell by the wayside. Nila tried to help, taking over the garden by herself, but she also fell behind.

At the same time, Bev took on as manytrips as he could for horses and game, though Billy and Whit rode out on rare occasion, too. Billy was too good a shot to keep him from hunting,and Whit still wanted to learn how to shoot. Most of the time, though, the two were busy at the ranch fermenting, which enabled them to contribute more money. The question remained of whether it was enough or not to offset the labor lost preparing for the deadly cold of winter in Kansas.

Bev tried to stay patient for the sake of what little harmony they could maintain, but he also wanted to strangle Whit and kick Billy in the shanks. He knewthat sooner or later he would have to speak out again and he despised the thought.

At the end of June, Nila spotted a body of horsemen riding down from the trail. The shimmering heat from the sun at their backs made them hard to identify. She ran away from the garden to the cabin, took out a pot and a ladle, and hammered on it in the doorway.

Whit and Billy had gone off on a hunt, a rare occasion for them, but Josh and Bev came running. During the past year, a few Pawnee braves tried to raid the place, but a few gunshots in the air drove them off. They kept coming back, however, and it seemed that someday they might pose a serious threat. Josh and Bev grabbed rifles and pistols, and took up posts on either side of the cabin. Nila held another handgun behind the table facing the door. The riders turned out to be soldiers from Fort Larned, not Indians.

Bev stepped out in front of the cabin. "Hello, Sergeant," he said. He nodded at the five other cavalrymen, "Howdy, fellas."

A burly man with a white-spotted black beard and a large girth leaned over his pommel and said, "I'm Sergeant Avery from Fort Larned. I'm guessin' you're Bev Bowman, that right?"

"That's me," said Bev.

Avery raised his eyes and looked around. "Well, I'll be. Guess you boys did turn into sodbusters. Who'd known?"

"We're ranchers," Bev said crisply.

Still surveying, Avery dropped his eyes to Bev and shrugged his shoulders.

"What brings y'all out here?" said Bev.

"Well, we got a little problem, Bowman, with some of your boys. One colored one named Whit, the other a scrawny white boy. He's Billy, I think. Is that right?" he said, turning back to one of the privates. The private nodded yes, and Avery came back to Bev.

"Seems these boys been sellin' moonshine at the fort. Ordinarily, we don't like to interfere with commerce, but we've been havin' problems lately."

The sergeant dismounted, and stood in front of Bev, coming up to just the middle of his chest. "You see, our men are fine with havin' a nip or two, it don't cause them any problems most times. Some get into scrapes, have to spend a few days in the hoosegow, maybe muck out the latrines. But, generally speakin', they all good soldiers."

He drew closer, which caused Bev to breathe consciously only through his nose.

"The problem is, your boys been sellin' to the Injuns. Now, everyone knows that your common Injun can't hold his firewater, and them around the fort are no exception. They lay about doin' nothin', pissin' off their squaws and the old chiefs who come complain to the commandant. Which, a' course, comes back down on us. That ain't the worst of it, though. A few nights ago, a couple of braves got a snootful, started yelpin' and shoutin', you know, regular war cries. The white women folk damned near fainted from fear. So's the commandant, he sends the captain out to stop all this carryin' on, and the captain comes to the sergeants, me included, to stop all this carousing and so forth. Long story short, if it can be now, we confront them unruly Injuns, they threaten us with blood curdlin' war cries and knives, and so we had to shoot 'em."

Bev stared plain faced at the sergeant, giving no hint of what he felt.

"Well, now the chiefs are up in arms, the squaws are cryin' rivers, and the captain and commandant are no happier than before. They conduct an investigation, that where they learned your boys Whit and Billy were the ones responsible."

He waited for Bev to respond. Hearing nothing, he continued, "Anyway, they sent us out here to pick the two of them up. So, where they be?"

"They ain't here, Bev said. "They gone for good."

"Gone for good? How's that, now?"

"We had us a fight. They quit on us, left for Mexico."

"A fight you say?" the sergeant said. "Over that squaw over there, maybe?" He jerked his thumb toward Nila in the doorway, "I can understand that. She purdy good-looking for a redskin."

"She my wife," Bev said.

The sergeant gazed up at Bev, "Oh. No offense meant."

"None takin'," said Bev.

"Well then, I'll report back to the commandant that the other boys has run off to Mexico. That ought to shut the door on this situation, if you and your boy over there don't plan on sellin' no more whiskey to the Injuns."

Bev shook his head, "They took the liquor-makin' stuff with 'em."

"Oh. Give cookin' up some tequila a try?"

"Maybe so."

"Okay then. We'll, if you don't mind, we'll be campin' out at your place, here, and leave tomorrow morning. That all right?"

"Yes. I have my wife bring y'all some supper."

"Oh, now, don't go to no trouble. She a good cook, is she?"

Bev nodded, "Meat 'n taters."

"That would be just luscious." He craned around, "Corporal Evans, have the men pitch camp near the creek." He returned his attention back to Bev. "We do appreciate your hospitality." He turned to go, then came back up close to Bev, "Say. You think those boys left any of that liquor around here, maybe?"

Bev said, "'Fraid not. They took it all with them to sell."

"Oh," said the sergeant, "shame."

Late that night, Josh and Bev sneaked out of the cabin past the sentry and headed out as far as they could along the trail. They put some distance between each other, and found places where they could hear anyone traveling toward the cabin and see anyone coming over the horizon at dawn. If Whit and Billy happened to show up that night or in the morning, Bev and Josh hoped to intercept them before the soldiers could. They didn't come back that night.

The next day, Bev waved languidly at the bluecoat cavalry as they walked their horses back toward the fort. As soon as they disappeared, Bev said to Josh, "Awright. Let's get to the smokehouse and get rid of all that moonshine nonsense."

Two days later, Whit and Billy rode back in, a dressed deer carcass strapped across the mule trailingbehind them. They pulled up in front of the smokehouse, dismounted, and proceeded to untie and haul the deer inside. Bev and Josh watched them from the front of the cabin.

Whit strode out of the smokehouse slamming the door shut and open on the rebound. He halted close to Bev, rage filling his face.

"Where the hell is my still? Where my shine?"

"Gone, Whit, done with. The blueboys showed up lookin' for you and Billy. They getting' ready to to take you in for riling up the Injuns with your liquor. Some of them Injuns got killed. I sent 'em away, but if they come back with all your stuff still in the smokehouse, they grab you up for sure."

"You take my still, my whiskey?" Whit arched his head closer to Bev. Billy stepped out of the smokehouse and immediately stopped, watching from a distance. Josh, leaning on the wall of the cabin, stood up straight.

"We took all that and threw it in the creek," Bev said, his voice rising. "Maybe them Yankees put you in the stockade, but we ain't goin' with you."

Nila came out and stood in the front doorway.

"You goddamn son of a bitch!" Whit said as he sprang at Bev. Bev was ready and hit him across his face, but the momentum of Whit's jump caused them both to go down in a tangle. Whit sat up and punched Bev twice in the jaw before Bev could roll him over. He hammered Whit with his fist four times, harder each time until Whit relaxed. Bev stood up and took a step away while Nila hurried past him and knelt next to Whit. She used the edge of her apron to wipe blood from Whit's nose and mouth. Whit slowly pushed her away.

"You think this the end of this?" he said. "You think it all goin' back the way it was? Bev tell everyone what to do, everyone do it. You think you God almighty, Bev, but you ain't. Hell, you ain't even who you think you is. Eli your stepbrother 'cause of your mama? Hell, no, you Eli's step brother 'cause of your daddy. That's right, old man Bowman cover some other black bitch, she birth you and die. She a real darkie, yessir, that why you as black as you is, not high yeller like Eli. The old man cover Eli's mama, she tell you she your mama, too, so you take care of Eli. You ain't got no mama, Bev, jus' old man Bowman your daddy."

Bev clenched his fists again and started forward, "You lie!"

Laughing, Whit shook his head, "I tellin' the truth. You know why I know? 'Cause your other brother tell me drunk one night. That's right, your old best white boyfriend Kyle tell me after drinkin' a snootful of my whiskey. Ain't that a laugh?" he said, laughing loudly, "Everybody know it at the Bowman farm, too, 'cept you. Ain't that funny?"

Bev glanced around desperately. He caught Josh's eye. "This true, Josh? This ain't true, is it?"

Josh hesitated, then slowly nodded up and down.

"How you like that, Bev?" Whit went on. "You own brother Kyle ready to string you up, maybe cut your balls off first. You knock him down 'cause he say you a no-good, skunk card cheat. You think you a massah, can knock anyone down? Not if you ain't white, nigger, not at all, can't even knock down you brother. And you know what funniest 'bout all this? I the one that cheat at cards. I cheat and you get blamed. And I didn't say one thing, not one word. How 'bout that?"

Bev roared and lashed out with his boot, kicking Whit in the chest hard enough to send him rolling back into the ground. Bev tried to rush forward, but Josh stepped in front and held him back in his embrace.

Whit scrambled to a crouch and pulled out a long, sharp dirk. He began to rise when Josh turned his head and said, "No knife, Whit. If you try, I take it from you."

Furious, Whit hesitated, staring at the calm old man easily holding Bev at bay while looking at him. Slowly, Whit tucked the knife in his belt behind his back.

Josh then returned to Bev. "That it, it oveh. Whit goin' out a heah fo' good."

"Me?" shouted Whit, back on his feet. "Me go?"

"You go, now, Whit. You done enough. You done mo' than that. You go now, don't come back."

Whit stared at the old man and Bev, who had stopped struggling. "That fine," he said. "I'm goin', y'all be sorry. I sick of all you cracker-lovin' niggers anyway. Nila, go get your stuff."

She disappeared back into the cabin. She came out with a bundled blanket across her shoulder and moved behind Whit.

"Nila, you don't have to go," said Josh.

She didn't reply.

"I takin' a hoss for me and for Nila. Don' try and stop me."

Still standing where Josh had been holding him, Bev said. "If I see you again, Whit, I'll kill you."

Whit smiled, nodding, "Awright. I wait for that."

He pivoted and headed for the horse barn. In fifteen minutes, he and Nila rode away. They left on July Third, the one-year anniversary of their fight with the Johnnies at Locust Grove. Later on, word drifted from down the Santa Fe trail that the Yankees had won a huge battle somewhere in Pennsylvania on the same day. A day later Grant presented Vicksburg to Lincoln to celebrate the Fourth of July.

Chapter 18. Leave Taking

With Whit and Nila gone, everyone had to do even more work. Josh took a turn at cooking, immediately reminding them all of the savory appeal of Nila's wholesome meals. Then, Josh recalled the wild hog that Billy had roasted in the Boston Mountains. They all remembered how the East Tennessee mountain boy had found salt to season the succulent pig. Before Billy could gripe, Bev and Josh elected him chief cook by acclamation.

That left Bev and Josh to track game and any horses that they might find. All work not considered vital to the spread ceased for lack of manpower. Billy had his hands full with tending the garden, feeding the horses, and mucking out their stalls on top of whipping together some kind of meal every day. He spent a lot of time alone.

After a few weeks staples ran low, and they decided that Billy would take the wagon to Fort Larned to buy what he could find. Bev rolled the money Billy would need in a square piece of leather and tacked it to the bottom of the wagon seat. Billy sat on it, his Enfield loaded and leaning barrel up next to him in case of any trouble. But, the trip proved to be uneventful, no Pawnees, no Rebel raiders or desperadoes, not even a passing traveler to camp with for company. The two-day ride left him alone with his thoughts, not a pleasant pastime, he knew.

He reminisced about his daddy, wondering how he was after more than a year since his only son ran off. Once again, Billy brooded over not knowing if he was even alive. Living alone among the ravenous Graybacks, it seemed unlikely that his daddy could survive. Maybe he did, maybe he had figured out some way to make a living, some sort of job in Maryville, maybe. If he was alive, he must feel lonely, too, with no family left around him.

Billy lowered his head ruefully. Here he was, a thousand or more miles away in a strange land with a bunch of strangers. Good fellows they were, but how much alike were they? Not much. All he had to remind him of the old life was his stash hidden away in the smokehouse, the family picture taken ofMama and Baby Sister, so long gone, and his daddy who might be gone, too. A corncob pipe he'd been given in Memphis, a few other knickknacks he'd picked up at the forts, and the Colonel's pistol that he kept for no reason at all.

Not much to show for a life, he thought, even one as short as his so far.

After all this passed, the war and everything, what was he going to do? Go back home? Somehow that seemed too far away, he thought, too far from where he was now. But, if Daddy was alive, how could he leave him alone by himself? What if he got back to Maryville and found that Daddy had passed. Then, what? He couldn't think of any answers.

He arrived at Fort Larned and steered the mules up to the commissary. Inside, he bought beans, lentils, flour, sugar, tobacco, matchsticks, paraffin candles, seed, and oats for the horses. He also bought horse shoes and shoe nails, but passed on a barrel of long wood nails since no one had time to build anything right now. Billy did buy a small bag of Smith Brother's cherry coughdrops, which he liked to parcel out to himself as a treat. Other than that, he couldn't think of anything else he needed to purchase. He stared at a small, brown bottle decorated by a white label printed with indecipherable scrawl in black ink. Billy couldn't read the mysterious markings, but he knew what it was from asking the clerk before: "Dr. Archer's English Elixir/Bitters to Cure All Common Ailments." He'd had a taste once, when Whit bought a bottle for his indisposition before they had started cooking moonshine. He remembered that it was bitter, but it did make you feel better. He wondered if he should purchase a bottle for the trip home. He decided not to, knowing that Bev would ask why there wasn't more change when he returned. Thinking that he had everything, he paid the clerk and left the store, ready to start the journey back to the spread.

After tying a canvas tarp over the supplies in the wagon bed, he stepped up to the seat and released the brake. Then, he clicked three times with his mouth to move the mules along. Passing down toward the lower bank of brick buildings in the fort, he was about to turn the corner of the one on the end when he heard a shout.

"Well, well, looky what we got here."

The voice was familiar even as Billy turned his head to see Whit leaning against the wall.

"How you doin', Billy boy? Look like you got a full load."

Billy nodded, pulling up on the reins to stop. "Supplies. We was runnin' low."

"I guessed that. Got anything good in there? Somethin' I might could use?"

"Sorry, Whit," Billy said, leaning over toward the lean black man. "Bev keeps a close eye on goods and money. I in big trouble if I come back short."

Whit spread his mouth in a grim smile. "Bev be Bev," he said ironically.

"Yeah, I suppose so," Billy said, then hurriedly, "So, how you been, Whit? You surprise me bein' here at the fort. I thought you'd be long gone from these parts."

"No, I still hangin' on. Make me some money playin' cards, doin' this 'n that."

His clothes looked dirty to Billy, like he had been sleeping in them, maybe on the ground.

"So, where's Nila? She takin' good care of you, I suppose."

Whit's grin burst into a full smile, "Naw, Billy, she gone. Her daddy Chief Chekilli come take her away up north to their camp near Fort Leavenworth."

"Really? She awright?" Billy asked.

"Oh, yeah, she awright. She got a big belly. I goin' to be a daddy myself!" he said with a loud laugh. Then, looking pensive, he said, "I guess I'll go up and see 'em one day. See my son!" he almost shouted, laughing again. "Ain't that somethin'?"

"That's somethin', awright," said Billy. "Really somethin'."

"Yes it is." Whit drifted off in thought. He started, and said, "So, what about you, Billy boy? What you up to these days?"

"Not much. Busy runnin' around the spread. Now I'm the chief cook 'n bottle washer, since Nila gone."

"That so? Well, I can't say I all that sorry 'bout things, the way they turned out. Sorry for you, maybe."

"Yeah, well …." Billy mumbled.

Whit snapped his head up. "Hey. You makin' any shine since I left? You got any with you?"

Billy shook his head, "'Fraid not. Bev won't have it for sure."

"Aw, why you care what Bev want or don't want? That a sweet little thing we had goin' there.* Made us some good money," Whit rumbled. Then, he said, "Say, you outta think about startin' up again. Wouldn't take much, you know what to do, and this fort still pretty dry. You make some nice money."

Billy winced, saying, "I don't think so, Whit. Bev wouldn't like it, and the braids here might come get me."

"Maybe. They leave me alone since I been here. Don't seem to care what I do."

230

"Yeah, well," Billy said, "I guess I don't want to take the chance."

"Oh," said Whit, "I see, I guess."

Billy searched his mind for a way to change the subject. "So, Whit, you got any plans you'self? You ain't goin' to stay here for good, right?"

"Oh, no," Whit replied quickly, "this just temporary."

"Right," said Billy.

Whit cocked his head, "You hear the news, didn't you? 'Bout the big battle down in Injun Territory? No? It happen 'bout a week ago, at Honey Springs near the Elk Creek. The Yankee Injuns met up with the Rebs and whupped their ass!"

"That so?"

"Oh, yeah, and some of them fightin' with the Yankees are colored boys. They join up with the Kansas Injun regiment and blow them Johnny Reb suckers up!"

"That right?" said Billy.

"That right. Open Injun Territory and Arkansas all the way up. Things changin' around here, yessir!"

"Mighty amazing," said Billy.

"Yeah, so that's my plan, to head on over to Fort Scott and join the regiment so I can kill me some crackers, you bet!"

"Now, that's a plan, Whit."

"Yeah it is! Jus' as soon as I can head out, I'm goin'."

"Good enough," said Billy, "I wish you all the luck."

"Why, thank you, Billy, I appreciate it."

"Yeah, well, I best be on my way," said Billy.

"Yeah, I see." Whit, seeming a bit unsure, said, "Billy, you sure you don't have any of that whiskey on you? You sure?"

"I am, Whit, ain't not a drop left."

"Oh," said Whit, rubbing his chin. He raised his eyes, "Then, what 'bout one of them cherry cough drops? You like them, I know. How about givin' me a cherry cough drop?"

Without a word, Billy pulled out the bag and tossed it to Whit.

"Well, thanks, Billy," he said, starting to cackle, "I know you love them cherry cough drops."

Billy waved silently with one hand as he snapped the reins to start the mules moving.

On the way back, Billy thought about what Whit had said. Living had become more difficult for everyone since the big break had happened. Whit didn't seem to be any better off. In fact, he appeared to be barely getting by. And, Nila was gone, back to her people with a child on the way. No more seeing her black hair and shining dark eyes, her supple form as she went about the business of keeping the homestead in order. No more the sweet smells of her cooking, the taste of her exotic, native dishes. Now, the cabin seemed darker, the fires burned lower, even in midsummer.

On the bank of the Saw Log Creek, Billy sighed, wiggling his toes in the cool water. Soon, he'd have to get back to the cabin to start the dinner fire. Before that, he needed to feed the three horses in the corral, then muck out their stalls in the barn, feed the chickens they just bought, pick some snap peas out of the garden, and bring in water for everything and everyone. A long day every day, Billy thought, with no end in sight. Now, Bev was talking about adding some hogs to their livestock. That meant that, aside from building a chicken coop, they'd have to put up a pig pen and more fencing. Constructing the pen had to be better and tighter since hogs could nuzzle their way out of just about any wood or wire barrier. But they all liked the idea of sizzling bacon for breakfast, pig knuckles and kale, even pork loin for supper once in a while. A lot of work, though, a lot of work, butchering, curing, and hanging in the smokehouse, then waiting.

A carp shot out of the water after some flying bug that Billy couldn't see. He'd like to get out his fishing pole and catch a few, but he didn't have time. Even sticking his fish-belly white feet in the cold water made him anxious. He could just see Bev and Josh returning to find him lolling about, dungaree pants rolled up, feet dangling in the creek. That made for a bad picture. Better to get going.

Another fish leaped out of the corner of his eye, and when he looked over, he saw something foreign in the water. He kept staring at it, but it didn't come into focus for him, a dark, round shape like a man's gut sticking out of the water rushing past. He stood up and gingerly walked over, avoiding sticks and brambles on the way. He drew closer, and at first still couldn't identify it. Gradually, its contours seemed familiar, until he finally figured out what it was. The waters swirled around it, a round, black island in the creek with a thin, black rod curving around it, divided by a slender, dark wooden handle. Billy knew then that he was looking at one of the old kettles that he and Whit had used for simmering mash.

He waded into the water and tried to pull it out by its handle. Too much silt had filled it, making it too heavy to budge. Billy stooped low in the water, soaking the bottom of his trousers as he held on to the kettle with one hand while sticking the other elbow deep in the water to dig out the silt. In short order, he pulled the kettle up and walked it over to the bank.

It looked no worse for wear since being in the water where Bev had tossed it weeks ago. Billy knocked on its sides, and found it to be sound through and through. He stood and gazed up and down the creek, but saw no other parts of the still in the rushing stream. Just this kettle had survived.

He sat down and thought about what to do with it. He knew that he couldn't rebuild the whole still. That would take buying a good deal of new equipment and he didn't have the wherewithal. Anyway, even if he could start it all up, it would only end the way it had before, with Bev throwing it out. Bev would be mad, too, real mad. But, the kettle seemed to be in perfect operating condition. With a few modifications in the process, Billy imagined that he could heat up some mash and turn it into a small amount of liquor. A taste, he thought, not for sale, but to soften the hard life a little bit. He had missed having a taste after Whit had left. It wouldn't hurt if he made just a jar or two. Except, even one jar would set Bev off. But, just a sip or two after a long day. Just a nip now and then.

Billy stood up, grabbed the kettle by its handle, and started back to the spread. He had sugar, grain, and even some leftover yeast. He could get that mash cooking in quick order and ready to ferment in no time. As far as dinner went for today, they all could eat cold cuts of venison and raw vegetables for a change. If they didn't like it, he'd be happy to switch places and let them cook. And, if Bev didn't like him taking a pull now and then, too bad. Still, he thought, he better keep this little operation to himself as much as he could. No need to make waves. Who knows who Bev might give the boot to next?

Further west, Josh had set up on a rise overlooking a long, flat stretch of prairie grass. They hadn't seen buffalo for quite a while, but this time in late summer should mark the herd's return, all part of their ongoing circular migration. If they were right, Josh could take down several before they bolted. If the timing was wrong and the big beasts didn't show, Josh might see a mule deer or something else that he could shoot.

In the meantime, Bev rode over to a copse of trees that topped another wrinkle in the flat earth. He tethered his horse and kept a look out for game. If the herd came along, he could mount up and drive them toward Josh. Otherwise, he would scan his part of the landscape for smaller game. If he saw any, he'd take a potshot himself. Not near the marksman that Josh had become, Bev still shot a rifle well enough to hit his spot. Anyway, splitting up provided a wider area to hunt, and it also gave Bev plenty of time to mope by himself.

Since Whit's banishment, Bev could not help himself from sulking around Josh and Billy every day, almost all day long. Between losing Eli, then learning that his mama wasn't his after all, that he'd never known his real mama,had leveled him. Black folks everywhere wondered where they came from, who their ancestors were, and why God had chosen them for such hard lives. Only a few had any notion about their grandparents, and great grandparents, passed down to them by their folks through cherished stories. Most slaves at least knew their own mamas who loved them, they knew that much. He didn't. His mama wasn't his mama, if what Whit had said was true. His mama didn't love him so much as she wanted him to protect her real son Eli. Only a cruel joke from on high had made Eli actually his half-brother. All his love and worry for Eli, his guilt for losing him troubled Bev now. Should he have been looking out for Eli all of these years?

He didn't know, he didn't know who he was. Half-brother to Eli and Kyle? He cringed at the thought. He could kill Kyle, and that hideous cripple, old man Bowman. He could murder Whit, too, for knowing and telling him all this after nearly getting him lynched or worse. Then, a thought came to him. Had Kyle given him a chance to escape because they were brothers? Yet, Kyle had made it clear that he wouldn't lift a finger if Bev had been caught.Kyle would have let him hang. So, how far does blood go? If he had known all of this before, Bev thought, would he have tried to save Eli, bring him to freedom? He had no answer. It didn't matter either way because he had failed Eli and his mother.

One thing Bev recognized for sure was that he didn't know who he was. Who were his folks? Who were his people? Why was he so alone? He ached with confusion, asking himself how he could love Eli and resent him all the same. He was furious at Mama, except he understood her reason, too. For all of those years, he had been special on the Bowman farm, an exception from every other slave there. He had always thought it was because of his close friendship with Kyle. No wonder Eli'smama tried to piggyback her son on Bev and his privilege as Kyle's lifelong friend. Little did any of them know that these relationships all derived from them being brothers, offspring of that wretched old lecher Massah Bowman. Bev had been betrayed by everyone he had ever loved. When it came down to it, even Old Josh admitted that he'd heard things in the past.

Consumed by misery, Bev sat in the thicket, his eyes on the ground. A flash of color jerked up his head. Antelopes bounded on the edge of the tree line, a small herd of five or six. He whipped his rifle around, fired, and missed every one of them.

"Son of a—!" he snorted out loud. The antelope did their jittery dance across the grass quickly moving out of sight. At least they were going in the right direction, Bev thought. Josh might have a shot at them.

He sat down to settle back into his mournful reverie.

Toward the end of August, they noticed that more homesteaders showed up at their doorstep. Men, women, and children gazed at them with eyes hopeful and hopeless, asking for water, food, andshelter if possible, while ready to cringe at the first harsh word snapped in their direction. They didn't offer much in the way of trade, but at least they broke the dulling sameness and solitude of the men on their homestead. So, the three former runaways shared what they could, and chatted with them about where they'd come from, where they were going, and if they had any news about the war.

Some of the white travelers were a bit standoffish, not used to the idea of seeing a couple of black men and a white-trash country boy tending land as if it was their own. Such visits went one of two ways. The white homesteaders relaxed and enjoyed the hospitality of their unordinary hosts, or they were sent on their way quick step. Of the many groups who stopped off at the cabin, they were surprised most by the wagon that pulled up with a black family aboard.

A dark black man slender of build handed the horses' reins over to the woman next to him and climbed down the front wheel to stand before them. He wore a farmer's slouch hat, braces holding up his bib-top dungarees, beneath that a light brown checked shirt. As soon as he alighted from the wagon, he thrust his hands into his pockets.

Bev noticed right off that the man sported a fine moustache, curving tight and sharp. He was clean, too, and from the look of the woman on top of the bench, they were a married couple. It'd be no surprise if some kids were tucked in the back of the wagon beneath the canvas cover.

"How do, neighbor," said Bev.

"Howdy, mistah," said the visitor.

"What brings y'all to our place?"

"Your place? That's mighty impressive," said the newcomer, "mighty impressive indeed. My wife and I hope to do the same someday not too far away."

"You plan on staking out some land?" Josh asked.

"Yessuh, as soon as we find the right spot."

"That impressive its own self. How you able?"

"We'all come from Cairo, Illinois. I was a barber there 'til business fell off. Earned enough money to buy some mules and this wagon. We sold our house and set out west. Before we left, I file for a homestead under the new law from President Lincoln. See here, here's the paper."

He pulled out a folded square of paper and handed it to Bev. Bev straightened it out to see that it was an official looking document with flowery type and a printed seal. The paper declared that *Wesley Wilson, Freeman and intended citizen, has fulfilled all requirements for the claiming of property in the Western Territory provisional to*—Bev glanced up as he started to refold the paper.

"Wesley Wilson, a freeman."

"That's right," the small man said. He turned and pointed to the slim, young woman sitting on the wagon bench. "This here's my wife Hermione." She nodded, smiling slightly. "We got three kids in the back of the wagon, two boys and a girl."

Wilson returned his sight to Bev. "We be mighty grateful if we could camp here for the night, maybe fetch some water for the mules and cow."

Bev craned his neck, seeing for the first time a Holstein tethered to the back of the wagon. "You welcome to stay. Bring your family in for supper. We always glad for company."

After the barber and his family had pulled out the next day, Bev spent a lot of time thinking about them and their plan to put down roots on their own land. Most black people would never be able to get together the money they needed to travel west and stake out property, even if the land was free. Yet, we already have a farm, Bev thought, me, Josh, and Billy. Only, we don't own it, at least officially. When the war is over and things change, more people might come out here to claim their own place. Some might get the idea of taking over thisspread, maybe thinking that three runaways couldn't be eligible for homestead ownership, two niggers and a cowardly Johnny Reb. Certainly they couldn't be free or have served nobly to preserve the Union. Most white people didn't need any more reasoning than that to take their property. Except they were free, more or less, Lincoln had freed them twice. And, they had fought for the Union at Locust Grove, including Billy, never mind his forced time in the Rebel army. Bev and his did qualify to own their farm. But, they needed some kind of proof. He kept thinking.

Over dinner that night, he told Josh and Billy that they had to talk.

"That barber Wilson, he won himself a homestead claim because he is free. He got a paper that says so and he ain't even turned over one shovel full of dirt. We got a proper farm right here, land growing things, livestock, buildings, a real homestead of ours already. Exceptin', it ain't ours by law. Blast it, if Wilson had a mind to, he could've claimed our property and we couldn't do a thing about it."

"I don't see us lettin' him do that," Josh said.

"'Course not," said Bev, "but white folks, those with guns, they a different matter. They can say we don't got aright to this property, they can say it illegal what we been doin'. They can take it all away from us someday, somehow, unless we do somethin'."

"We plan on stayin' here?" asked Josh. "We ain't never goin' back to Kentucky? Billy ain't goin' back to Maryville to see his daddy?"

They looked at Bev, their brows wrinkled. Bev swallowed and said, "Well, I don't know about that. Maybe we stay, maybe we go back. For sure we're stayin' if the Rebs win. Even if they do and we want to stay away from the South, people could still take our farm from us. And if we do want to go back to Kentucky," he glanced at Billy, "and Tennessee, we need to sell this place so we have some money to start ourselves up again."

Josh and Billy nodded together at the common sense of Bev's words.

"But, we ain't got nothin' if we don't own this place free and clear. Either way, we need to do somethin' to make sure it belong to us."

They exchanged looks and shook their heads in agreement again.

"Well, what can we do, Bev?" asked Billy. "How we gonna do anything that show this place is ours?"

Bev pinched his chin. "I think we need to go see somebody who might help us out."

"Who that be?" asked Josh.

"Some brass at the fort. Maybe hehelp us. If not, maybehe tell us who can."

The other two nodded.

Both Bev and Josh felt that Billy should go to provide a white presence in their request. Major Wilcox invited them in to his office as soon as they arrived. Their old lieutenant at Fort Belmont had been promotedfrom captain to major just a few weeks ago and given command of Fort Larned. He greeted Bev and Billy with gusto.

"Good to see you boys getting along so well," said Wilcox.

"Get yourself another promotion there, Major?" asked Bev.

"And another fort with a long experienced garrison," replied Wilcox. "That means old."

"Well, your moustache look the same."

"Pomade, Mister Bowman, discerning use of pomade and a delicate pair of trimming scissors. And, you look to be as clean-shaven as ever."

"Old habits die hard," said Bev, stroking his long beard, still growing since he'd left Memphis.

"Indeed. Well, I have not forgotten your fine service at Locust Grove on behalf of the Union. How can I be of assistance?"

Bev explained everything to Wilcox, who listened closely.

"I see no reason why you and your partners cannot file a homesteading claim to your property," Wilcox said."I'd be happy to write letters of introduction to the appropriate offices to speed your cause along."

"Thank you, Major, we're grateful for your help."

"Not at all. If you can wait a little bit, I'll have my orderly copy the letters for you to ward off any shenanigans."

"That be fine. C'mon, Billy, we'll go find somethin' to eat, then come back."

They left Wilcox's office and headed over to the commissary. On their way, they noticed that the usually relaxed soldiers seemed on edge, their rifles on their shoulders or held by the barrels in front of them. Bev cast his eyes around and saw that the usual guards at the perimeter had been doubled. "Lot of nervous bluecoats around here."

"I seen that myself," said Billy.

"Yeah, let's go on to the commissary, see if anybody tell us why."

In the commissary, they spied Sergeant Avery knocking a piece of hardtack on a tabletop. They sauntered over and Bev said, "Hey, there, Sergeant, how you been?"

Avery glanced up from his seat on the bench and recognized the men above him. "Why, hello, boys, surprised to see you. What brings you to the fort?"

"We come here often enough, so why you surprised?"

Avery said, "Well, I thought you'd be hunkered down at your place, considering what happened."

"Oh, yeah? What happened?"

Avery leaned in. "Quantrill and his boys ran through Lawrence the other day. Killed near 200 folks, maybe more. A lot of 'em were you people, slaughtered in the street. We been on guard since."

"My people."

"That's right, men, women, children, anyone they could find, they shot 'em or burned 'em alive in their houses. It was a genuine massacre. That cold-blooded killer rode right out a town, barely lost a man. No one knows where he is or what he's up to now."

Bev glanced at Billy, then looked back to Avery. He took his hat off and scratched his head vigorously. "Awright," he said, "thanks for lettin' us know."

"You may want to pick up sticks, think about findin' a safe place to hide out."

"How 'bout here at the fort?" Billy asked.

Avery pulled back. "I'm not sure that's such a good idea. There ain't many of us here, we might all get killed if they come for you."

"Uhhuh," said Bev. "Okay, thanks anyway."

They rode out that night.

After telling Josh, they all decided to stay close together at home for a while. If Quantrill and his raiders showed up, they would make a stand. They also kept three horses tied to a hitching post out back in case they had to run.

Billy wasn't all that pleased about the other two being around the spread so much. It constricted the time he had to cook up more mash, and he was starting to get low on his shine. As the days passed full of tedium and anxiety, Billy found himself looking forward more and more every day to a pull or two from the jug. Stuck together with the others now, he felt jumpier without knowing why.

August faded into September, the leaves of the creek trees going from drab green to burnt sunlight hues. With hunting and horse chasing curtailed, they did their best to find useful things to do. Worry lurked in the back of their minds that the fall had fled by fast and they had lagged in stocking the larder for winter. They knew, too, that the unforgiving, harsh winters on the plains would arrive soon enough. To keep such thoughts at bay, they worked hard on fixing up the cabin and other structures on the property. They finished the pig pen and the chicken coop, and started on another paddock for more horses. They did not work far from the house, though, and their rifles always stood next to them, propped up and fully loaded.

In mid-October, on a hot, dry day, Josh saw dust kick up in the distance, kicking higher as it drew closer. He immediately called out to Bev repairing harnesses in the tack shop, and Billy busy in the smokehouse. The two converged upon him, rifles in their hands, pistols and knives hanging from their belts.

"Dust on the line," Josh said, pointing in the direction away from the creek.

"You think's it raiders?" asked Bev.

"No way to tell right now," said Josh.

"Awright," Bev said, "let's spread out, get the angle on 'em."

Billy rambled over to a fence next to the barn while Bev took up a position opposite him behind the wood pile. Josh fell back to the center corral and dropped behind a log rolled over there for cover as planned.

They could hear the thud of hooves coming closer, and they each cocked the hammers on their rifles, looking to draw a bead on the first three in line. Then, Josh rose to one knee.

"They ain't Graybacks. They's Blueboys."

The three of them gradually stood up and Bev walked over to meet them, a corps of about ten or so riders. To his surprise, he realized that Major Wilcox rode at their head.

Wilcox raised his hand up, and the horsemen slowed to a walk, stopping when they were just a few yards from Bev.

"Major Wilcox, glad it's you."

"Yes," said the tall officer, "I imagine so. Have you had any trouble here?"

"No sir. Why, is some comin'?"

Wilcox nodded his head solemnly. "Quantrill and his cutthroats. They struck again at Baxter Springs. Caught General Blunt and his column off guard out in the open. Seems the Rebel dogs dressed in federal uniforms. They fooled Blunt and proceeded to cut his men to pieces."

"B'god!" murmured Billy.

"Blunt and a few of his made it to Fort Baxter, but a hundred others died. Meantime, another gang of renegades ambushed some of our troops on the Texas Road. They retreated to an outpost and held their ground despite being heavily outnumbered. After a harsh fight, Quantrill and his assassins finally decided to retire."

"That's a lot a fightin'," Josh said.

240

Wilcox shook his head in agreement, then suddenly dismounted. He closed in on Bev and said almost in a whisper, "I heard that many of the men killed were from the 2nd Kansas Colored Regiment. Word is..." Wilcox hesitated, "the word is that your friend Whit Mayo was among the fallen."

Bev froze, stunned. Seeing his shock, Wilcox placed his hand on Bev's shoulder for a moment, then withdrew it. "They say the colored boys fought valiantly, the reason that Quantrill left."

Bev lowered his head. "Thank you for tellin' me, Major. I appreciate it." He raised his sight back to Wilcox. "So, what now?"

Wilcox said, "I've ordered out some patrols to warn the homesteaders to be vigilant. Quantrill would kill them just as much as look at them. His lieutenant Anderson is worse, I'm told. It is likely that Quantrill went south to Texas to winter over. Still, I believe it's my duty to inform the citizens in these parts."

"Okay," Bev said. "Well, thank you for the warning, Major. Safe travels."

"Right. Take care, Mr. Bowman," Wilcox said as he slung himself onto his horse. He signaled to his men and they wheeled around and rode off.

"What'd he say to you, Bev?" asked Billy. "What'd he whisper?"

Bev faced Billy and Josh, and told them the bad news.

The very next day, Josh let them know that he was leaving.

Chapter 19. The Long Winter

Once Josh left, Billy and Bev spent most of their time together.

"I got to go back east to Kentucky," Josh told them, "mebbe futher south. It time I go. The world a changin' 'n I needs to do my part."

"What part?" asked Billy. "Ain't being free part enough?"

Josh shook his head, "They others need to be free, too. I can't stand aside, watch them struggle. I need to help them."

"We did help them, Josh," said Bev, "we fought them Johnnies at Locust Grove, beat 'em good. That helped a lot a people in Injun territory."

Josh grimaced, again shaking his head back and forth. "I got to go back home for my own. I got to find my wife."

Astonished, Bev and Billy stared slack-jawed at Josh. After an instant's beat, Bev said, "You never told us about a wife before."

Josh pressed his lips together. "It a long time ago. When I got whipped? They sell my girl down to Lou'siana, we just married, she just sixteen. I go mad like a mad dog. They beat me and whip me 'til I can't move. When I better, they beat me again. I give up finally, my baby gone." He smiled painfully. "So, all these years I go along to get along. Now, thing's different."

Bev and Billy exchanged glances. "We're sorry for you, Josh," Bev said quietly, "we sad about your sorrows."

Josh smiled self-consciously, and they fell into silence. After a while, Billy said, "You think you can find her, Josh? I mean, after all this time?"

Josh raised his hands and dropped them. "I don't know, Billy, but I got to try."

Bev sighed heavily. "It ain't safe, Josh, the way things goin'. Rebel hounds are killin' blacks outright if they catch 'em. They losin', but they still killin' out of spite, maybe more now than ever."

"I know, but I can't worry 'bout that."

They all paused again to think. Billy broke the silence, asking, "Then, what you plan on doing, Josh?"

"I gonna join up with the Yankees. Could be my best chance to find my wife."

Bev and Billy nodded silently. "That soundsright, "said Bev, "the boys in blue are pressin' the Rebs pretty hard."

242

Soon after, they all rode to Fort Larned to see Wilcox about Josh enlisting. Privately, Bev met with the Major to talk up Josh's ability to ride and fight, especially his dead-eye shooting.

"He sounds like he could be a good one and Lord knows the Army's starving for recruits. They're conscripting anyone they can get their hands on. The Micks in New York rioted, lynched a lot of you boys in the streets, even burned down an orphanage for black kids. Had to send troops in to restore order. Hell of a thing."

He gazed at Bev for an instant, who noticed gray strands in Wilcox's hair, in his moustache. "Anyway," the officer said, "I'll give your boy a letter to take to Colonel Williams. He commands the colored regiment at Fort Scott. I'm sure he'll be happy to add him to the rolls."

Bev lowered his head slightly. "I appreciate it, Major."

Wilcox dipped his head with a weary smile.

They sent Josh off with a good horse and the Enfield. He left from Fort Larned as part of the guard detail for a small wagon train headed east for supplies. According to Wilcox, they would stop at Belmont, then at Baxter where Josh would join up with the Kansas volunteers. Beyond that, future orders for the colored regiment had yet to be issued. For Bev and Billy, as soon as Josh passed out of sight from Fort Larned, they doubted ever seeing him again.

They settled into an uneasy routine. Their usual work suffered more than ever with only the two of them left to do everything. The winter struck hard, and the meat hanging in the smokehouse diminished fast, even with fewer mouths to feed. Cold took off most of the pigs, and they slaughtered the last two to cut their losses. They ran out of pork before the New Year. A fox broke into the chicken coop and killed all the pullets, which of course meant the end of eggs, too. Even the goods stored in the root cellar began to run out, which came as a surprise to Bev. He wondered out loud how that had happened, and Billy averted his eyes.

"We need to plan a long hunt, get somethin' hangin' in the smokehouse, enough to last the rest of the winter."

Lying on his cot, Billy cringed. "It's so cold out there, Bev. We could freeze before we find anything."

"Freeze, starve, what's the choice? I rather freeze with my belly full than starve nice and warm."

"I know, but I just ain't feelin' up to snuff."

Bev could see that. Billy seemed listless, out of energy. If he was sick, a hunt was out of the question for the time being. Billy was the best shot and besides that, no one could go out alone in this weather. Whoever did would never make it back, and the man left behind couldn't survive alone. With nothing left in the larder, at some point they would have to abandon the spread and head for the fort. In this weather, though, that wasno sure thing either.

They could slaughter a horse and eat it. Just thinkingof it made Bev pull a face as though he had tasted something awful. True, too, if they did decide to eat horsemeat, then ran out of it, they would have no chance of getting to the fort. They needed to do something else for sure.

"Okay, Billy, you rest now. We'll talk about it later when you feel better."

Billy nodded, drowsing off.

The next day, they ventured out of the cabin with the hope of seeing something close by to shoot, a rabbit, a crow, anything. A good eight more inches of snow had fallen, which made negotiating the white landscape slow, painstaking work. The overcast sky intensified the glare, causing both of them to cast their eyes downward, glancing up now and then to search for game. The entire exercise seemed futile, but they had no choice. They stumbled along for a while until Billy tried to forge through a large snow drift, tripped, and fell across it.

"This ain't just snow," Billy said, "there's somethin' beneath here, covered up."

"Huh," said Bev. His curiosity heightened, he started to sweep the snow away with his free gloved hand. He brushed until he hit something firm, then scraped the snow until a different color was exposed, reddish-brown.

"Billy, that's fur underneath there."

Billy laid the squirrel gun down on the crusted snow top and joined Bev in clearing the mound. Both men pushed away the snow as fast as they could, watching a form take shape as they worked. Finally, they had most of it free. They sat back to look at what they had found.

"It's a critter, all right, good size, too," said Billy.

"Got any idea what it is?" asked Bev.

Billy examined it closer, then said, "Some kinda steer or cow."

"It's too long. You ain't never seen it before?"

244

Billy shook his head, "Not really." He leaned over to what looked to be its head, and felt around its shape. "It's like a boot," he said, "with a big long bump at the toe." He stared up. "I do believe it could be a moose, Bev!"

"Go on," said Bev, "it ain't big enough to be any moose."

"No, it ain't big," Billy said, "Maybe it young, died from freezin'."

Skeptically, Bev squinted as he gazed down at the carcass, now taking a more specific shape as Billy continued to dig it out.

"It's still big," said Billy, "even the young'uns get big, I guess."

"You sure it's a moose? You ever seen one before?"

"No, not up close. But what else can it be?"

Bev shook his head, "Well, it's meat and it's dead. Can you get under to move it?"

Billy tried to hoist it. "Too heavy, and it's froze to the ground."

Bev nodded, "Awright. I go back, get some shovels. You keep an eye on it, keep an eye out for wolves. Here, take the heavy gun. If they show up, you ain't gonna stop none of 'em with a squirrel gun. Take out the big dog first."

Billy shook his head up and down, agreeing. After handing Bev the squirrel gun, he took hold of Bev's rifle, a Springfield he'd picked up after they gave Josh the Enfield.

Digging the young moose's body out of the icy snow and dragging it back to the cabin proved to be a lengthy, enervating task. Billy suggested getting a mule out to help, but Bev said no. "Hard work in the cold might wear it out, especially 'cause they ain't eatin' much either."

They brought ropes out of the horse barn instead, tied them to the back hooves of the carcass and pulled. They tugged at the heavy animal for four hours, heaving in unison, then sitting on it together to catch their breath. By the time they dragged it to the cabin door, they were spent.

"C'mon, we gotta get it in to thaw," Bev said. "Can't gut it frozen."

"I know, but I am so tired."

"You tellin' me?"

Another hour of jerking and yanking and they had the moose inside the cabin near the fire. After resting and eating what solid food was left in the larder, they used blankets to sop up the cold water gathering around the thawing body.

"Think we could get some shut-eye before cuttin' it up?" asked Billy.

Bev pinched his lips together. "I don't know. If we lucky, we dress it at just the right time, we can get most of its innardsout all at once. If not, we goin' to have a terrible mess on our hands." When he saw Billy's pained expression, he said, "Tell you what. You sleep a bit while I keep an eye on it. I wake you if it looks to be about time. If not, we can switch, make sure we're ready to gut it when it turns soft."

Billy corked off immediately while Bev struggled to stay awake. He stood up and paced the floor until he was too tired to walk. When he finally gave in and sat down, he jabbed a sharp stick in his thigh to stay awake. After another hour and a half, he checked the belly of the dead animal. Still pretty stiff, he thought. He woke Billy up and turned in himself.

Almost at once, Billy jostled him awake.

"How long I been out?"

"Two hours."

"Really? Seem like five minutes. Okay, your turn."

"No, no, I think it's ready. Its belly's slack."

Bev started slicing it open, while Billy followed with one of the wet blankets. The entrails fell onto it in a semisolid, gelatinous mass.

"Let's get it outta herebefore it stinks up the place," Bev said, grabbing two corners of the blanket. Billy grabbed the other two, and they dragged the steaming mass out the door, dumping it to the side of the house just a few yards away.

"We can store the rest in the woodshed for now, butcher it tomorrow."

Billy looked relieved, happy that they would have to drag it just to the lean-to attached to the back of the cabin instead of all the way to the smokehouse. They exerted themselves again and managed to pull it into the shed, which wasn't high enough for the carcass to hang. Billy cringed when he saw it, thinking that Bev would have them take it to the smokehouse right away.

"Prop it up," said Bev. "I too tired to fuss with it now."

Billy exhaled his relief. Eat first, sleep, then move the dead moose to the smokehouse the next day. "We got a little bit of soup left," he said.

Worn out, Bev agreed, half-noddinghis chin to rest on his chest. They ate, and after banking the fire, they fell into their bedding and into heavy sleep.

A haunting bellow distant from the cabin pulled them halfway out of their torpor. Like a ragged trumpet, the noise sounded again, closer now, jarring them awake.

"What the blazes is that?" Billy asked in the dark.

"Don't know, but it seem just outside, now."

A thundering, crashing blow hammered the cabin door followed by a deep-voiced shrieking wail. A second, thumping clout caused the men's remaining stupor to evaporate completely in alarm. A third strike buckled the door and Bev jumped up shouting, "Get the rifle, Billy!"

"It ain't loaded!" Billy cried and Bev barked, "The pistols, they loaded!"

Billy scrambled to the wall hooks where the handguns hung while Bev reached for his rifle and cartridge box. He started loading and the door collapsed inward from the surge of a giant, enraged beast howling in fury. Billy aimed and pulled the revolver's trigger, which misfired. The rampaging animal raised up, butting its head on the roof, and flourishing its oversize hooves at Billy. He ducked to the side of them coming down to trample him, while Bev swung his rifle by its barrel smashing the moose across its neck. Further infuriated, the huge creature pivoted to crush Bev.

Billy regained his feet and fired the .44 again and again, hitting the moose in its neck and behind its shoulder. The moose shrieked, ready to stomp Billy when Bev leaped forward slashing and stabbing with his Bowie. Caught between them, the moose stopped and Billy shot it point blank in the head. The moose whimpered once as its legs folded and it crumpled to the floor.

The two men stood suspended around the body, each taking in that it was dead.

"B'god," exclaimed Billy, "m'lord."

Bev heaved out a breath. "Where the hell it come from?"

Billy shook his head in confusion. They gazed at the dead moose, its brown fur roughed up high against the grain by the struggle, frozen snow still clinging to its back and shoulders.

"Look at its head," Bev said, "no horns. A cow."

Still holding the pistol in his hand down by his knees, Billy said, "The young un's mama. She come lookin' for him. He got lost and she come here, smell his guts outside maybe, maybe his body in the woodshed. No wonder she got so mad."

The cabin was in shambles, most everything knocked to the floor, two chairs splintered by the large quadruped's flailing hooves. Bev turned the intact chair near him upright and fell back into it, staring at the huge, steaming mound sprawled across most of the cabin floor. "We for sure lucky. The good Lord blessed us today. Now, we got more meat than we can eat, ever."

Billy looked for a seat, then leaned on the table. "What're we gonna do with all this now?"

Bev shrugged, saying, "Gut it, drain it, butcher it, hang it up in the smokehouse. What else?"

"M'god, tonight?" Billy whimpered.

"Good lord no! I'm tuckered all the way out, I'm goin' to sleep, deal with it in the mornin'."

"Thank baby Jesus!" exclaimed Billy.

Bev nodded, "Go on ahead and get in bed. It cold enough for that meat to last 'til tomorrow."

Billy got up and pulled together his blankets, rolling them around him as he dropped onto his broken bed on the floor. Bev banked what was left of the fire and wrapped himself in his own blankets, asleep almost as he fell into bed.

They spent most of the next day harnessing the mule to the moose's back legs and dragging it off near to the horse barn. Later that evening, they eviscerated the carcass, then used block and tackle to drag it inside the barn and hang it from a high beam to drain. The butchering could wait until the next day, and the freezing weather meant that for a time they could hold off on smoking the meat.

The brutal weather finally broke and the two men went back to their usual chores. They ate well, now, and the moose turned out to be delicious, especially the poor yearling.

"This is good," mumbled Bev over a full mouth.

"Yup," said Billy. "I heard at the fort there ain't that many moose around here no more. Hunted out, I s'pose."

"Well, then, we was really lucky."

"That true," said Billy, "but I wish we had a few spuds left, maybe a carrot or two."

Bev said, "Yeah, it strange how we run out so soon. Come spring, maybe we need to plant more."

Billy nodded, "Yeah, that's a good idea."

Christmas came, and though they no longer had to worry about the prospect of starving, the holiday seemed sad and dreary without Josh, and even Whit. Billy gave Bev a short riding whip he had woven out of strips of leather. Bev gave him a Lorenz rifle that he'd bought in secret at the fort the last time they were there.

"Bless me, this is a beautiful Christmas present, Bev! I thank you so much," Billy said as he held the rifle, looking up its length pointed at the ceiling. "So purdy!"

"'Yeah, since you give up the Enfield to Josh, I figure you had to have something to shoot, bein' the best between us."

"Well, thanky, Bev. I wish I got you somethin' better than that old whip. Don't seem near enough, now."

"Now, don't start that, I think it purdy. Maybe I use it to whip you into shape," he said laughing.

"No need, no need."

After their exchange of presents, they gradually lapsed into silence. When he had been around, Josh didn't say much, thought Billy, but somehow he seemed to warm up the cabin just by being there. And, heck, Whit wasn't all that bad when he was feeling good. He wasn't all that nasty all the time, and he did keep them laughing with his big talk. Billy missed him some, but if he ever returned Bev would kill him, probably. Of course, Whit was dead now, gone for good. Nila was gone, too, and only the Lord knew if she was alive with her baby. Despite all the ups and downs they all had, Billy missed being together with them, almost like he missed his daddy. Life on the property now just seemed to be work and silence. For all that, Billy took himself out to the smokehouse more often for a few pulls of bark juice from his cloudy jars.

Two days before New Year's, Billy thought of a way they might get out of the doldrums.

"Bev," he said as they sat eating opposite each other at the table, "it pretty quiet 'round here. There ain't that much to do that we couldn't take a break. Suppose we go to Fort Larned for the New Year, see some folks and have a little fun."

Bev thought for a moment, then said, "I don't know, Billy. That pot healer came through here said the fort was full of the flux, lot of them boys quick-steppin' it to the latrine. We don't want no part of that, now, do we?"

"No," said Billy glumly, "I suppose not."

The icy cold returned in mid-January, costing them one of their mules. They used the remaining horses to drag the poor animal as far from the homestead as possible to ensure that wolves and other predators kept their distance. The other mule, Beulah, became agitated at the loss of her stall mate and started to lose weight herself.

"She keep goin' like this," said Billy, "we gonna lose her, too. Now, maybe we have to go to the fort."

Bev shook his head, "She'll be awright. The hosses keep her company. We get another mule come spring."

His lips pressed into a frown, Billy nodded and trudged off to the smokehouse.

The wind blew that night into the morning, and the fire in the cabin almost died from the frigid air swirling down the chimney. Standing in front of the hearth with one hand holding his blanket closed over his shoulders, Bev stoked the flames back to life.

"Good Jesus, it's cold in here," muttered Billy, completely ensconced in his bedding withonly his face peeking out.

"Yes it is," said Bev. "While I do this, why don't you go get us some meat out of the smokehouse."

"Aw, Bev, we don't got nothin' left in here?"

"I believe we ate it all for supper last night. You didn't want to go then to fetch more for breakfast."

"Blast it all to dickens. No bread, not a heel?"

"'Fraid not."

"Doggone. Awright, I'll get up."

Billy worked himself free from the twisted blankets and sat up in his union suit shivering uncontrollably. He quickly pulled on socks and his boots, his wool shirt, and his overalls. He stood up, put on his shell jacket, and grabbed his heavy canvas coat. Hepulled it on, buttoned up, then stuck his slouch hat on his head, securing it with a linen scarf tied beneath his chin. He slipped some wool socks over his hands, and walked to the cabin door flapping his arms back and forth. He pushed it open against the fierce gusting wind, hunched over, and stepped out.

He trudged quickly to the smokehouse, slamming the door behind him as he boltedinside. Without a moment's pause, he padded over to the hidden jars and took a swig. He turned around then, picked up a hatchet, and hacked off a chunk of frozen meet from the hanging moose. They'd eaten all of the yearling, but plenty of meat still hung off of mama moose. He tucked the cut of meat under his armpit, buried the hatchet in a log, and pushed the door open to make the dash back to the cabin.

Billy ran two steps out of the smokehouse and stopped. Snorting clouds of breath, two horses harnessed to a wagon stood in front of him. A figure swaddled in blankets sat on top of the wagon bench, also heaving steam into the freezing air. Utterly surprised, Billy wondered if it wasn't anything but an apparition, a lost ghost wagon from the prairie.

"Hello?" he yelled. He shouted louder over the wind, "Hey, there!"

Without a word, the figure on top descended from the bench in stiff movements, dropping heavily to the icy surface. He turned to face Billy and unwrapped the thick, woolen scarf around his head beneath his nose. Once again, Billy stood amazed.

"Why, you the barber!" he said. "What ya doin' here?"

"We came back," said the man.

"But, it's the dead of winter!" cried Billy.

"We couldn't make it," he replied, shaking his head ruefully.

"What your name again?" asked Billy.

"Wilson. Wesley Wilson, with my wife, Hermione, and our three children."

"B'god. Praise the Lord you ain't frozen to death out there, Wesley Wilson." Billy paused for a moment taking everything in. Then, he said quickly, "Well, let's get y'all into the cabin. Bev gettin' the fire goin', and I got some meat here to eat. Darn good tastin', too, moose meat."

Wesley looked back to the cabin and Billy said, "C'mon, now, let's get 'em inside 'afore they all freeze. Diggin' holes ain't possible in this weather."

The two men helped Wesley's wife and children out of the wagon. Billy noticed then that their milk cow was gone. He led them to the cabin door, pulled it open, and stepped aside to let them in.

"Bev," Billy called out, "Guess what? We got ourselves a barber!"

Hermione Wilson followed her children into the cabin, and Billy whooped with exuberance, "And maybe a cook, too!"

Chapter 20. The Promised Land

"We just couldn't get anything to work," Wesley said. He and his family wasted so fast through the meat Billy had fetched that morning, he had to fight the elements again to get more. He made sure to chop off three times as much this time, and also took three more sips from his jar before leaving the smokehouse.

"We thought we found a nice piece of land, plenty of room to grow, good looking soil, all that. We got right to work building a dugout, since there wasn't enough wood around, and a lean-to for the horses, and a corral. We found out, though, that our stake was too far away from the creek. Just fetchingwater every day took a lot of work, firewood, too."

Bev remembered the barber as a neatly slender man, supple, with clear eyes. He looked skinny, now, his sight seeming haunted, stunned by unexpected failure.

"We was runnin' out of food, too, faster than we figured. Probably all the extra work we was doin'. Still and all, we was okay until a wind storm knocked everything to tarnation. I tried hunting and setting traps, but the pickins' were slim." He glanced behind him for an instant, where his wife and children sat resting at the table. "When the children stopped mewin', we knew we had to come back."

Bev observed the children, all of them skinny, their faces drawn with fatigue. Lucius, the oldest at thirteen or so, had a chestnut complexion that matched his mama's. His bony frame suggested that in a minute or so he was likely to be taller than his daddy. The girl Portia favored her daddy, smart-looking, delicately handsome. Her looks and her smooth, blemish-free walnut skin put her on the verge of breaking hearts everywhere. At seven, the youngest child, Tiberius, stood smaller than both of his siblings. He pouted and whined like most runts of the litter, but he possessed a sturdy frame and promised to be brawny if not tall. Bev could see some value in all of them to help around the place.

"So, where you plan on goin',now you turned back?" Bev asked.

"Fort Larned," Wesley answered in a somewhat apologetic tone.

"But we wereon the way, huh?" said Bev.

"It crossed our minds," Wesley admitted.

"Unhuh," said Bev. "Well, y'all are welcome to stay for a time. We got plenty to eat and can get more if we need to."

Smiling his relief, Wesley said, "Thank you, thank you. May the good Lord bless you, all of you. We were about at the end of our rope. And, we sure will help out here, any way we can."

"Yes, you sure will," Bev said smiling, and everybody laughed.

Before long, the Wilsons melded into the routine necessary for the farmstead to survive. The boys gathered firewood, fed and watered the horses, mucked out their stalls, and groomed them as often as they could. When the weather turned warmer, they helped clean out the garden. Billy took them to the creek to fish, though the water ran too cold to catch much at that point. Billy liked having them around and really enjoyed the help they provided. He found that he could steal away to the smokehouse more often now for liquid fortification.

Hermione, a reed of a woman who barely topped five feet, took command of the cooking and the garden. Billy watched her performing prestidigitation around the fire. He fixed on her gentle, comely features, her soft amber eyes peering out of that smooth, umber silhouette. As she worked, she kept up a lively exchange with Portia, whom she was teaching her magic. She tried to engage Billy when he was there, but he just sat silently at the table, daunted.

With the Wilson's pitching in, the new community took hold of new life. Bev and Wesley went after horses and on scavenging forays. They also capitalized on having two wagons by caravaning to different buffalo feeding grounds. During the first hunt, Billy brought down two, one that went into the smokehouse, the other to Fort Larned to sell. With all of the winter losses and the need to buy grain and other foodstuff, the bare planks of the common coin coffer began to show. Bev felt great relief that it was still cold enough to haul a buffalo to Larned to earn a few extra greenbacks.

On the trip to the fort that January, Billy joined Bev. He argued that he should go since he had shot the critter in the first place. Listening, Bev smiled wryly at the skinny, red-haired man standing fiercely before him, hands on his waist, elbows sticking out. Just a couple of years ago, he'd been a scrawny little sapling topped by a crop of carrot hair, the whitest white boy Bev had ever seen. Now, he looked a little fuller, an auburn stubble struggling to grow on his chin. After all they'd been through, he admitted to himself that sitting together with the little cracker for a day or so was kind of nice, sort of relaxing. The arrival at the fort jolted them quickly out of their tranquil state.

"Typhus, yellow fever, the flux, you name it."

Sergeant Avery had met them on the road just leading up to the fort. Fat as ever, he seemed propped up on his saddle rather than astride his horse.

"Some of the boys are doin' pretty bad," Avery said, "quick-steppin' it to the privies back and forth, and back. The sawbones has his hands full with a bunch of 'em just wastin' away. They can't hold any water in. When they start shrinking up like Egyptian mummies—I seen one, once, in a carny show in Memphis—they shrivel up and their skin gets tight as a drum, the Reaper ain't far off."

Wide-eyed, Billy said, "M'god, what do you do to not get it?"

Avery glanced at him, "They ain't much you can do. Stay away from the sick ones. Fill your canteens upstream from the latrines. Or, just absquatulate altogether."

"Ab what tulate?"

"Get your asses outta here."

Bev scowled, "We got buffalo meat to sell."

Avery blinked his eyes, unfazed. "I suppose the quartermaster might want some of that, though Lord knows it could last forever considerin' the boys we already put in the ground. You take your own chances goin' up there, but if you want to, go on ahead."

Avery turned his horse sideways to give them room. They glanced at each other, then Bev snapped the reins and the wagon slowly passed by.

Bev felt Billy twitch nervously next to him. "We get to the quartermaster, we sell the meat and clear out right away, right?"

They sold the buffalo for thirty dollars, and the quartermaster ordered six soldiers to unload the wagon. One man coughed, and Billy blanched. "C'mon," said Bev, "we'll go up to headquarters, see if Wilcox got some old papers."

Now a colonel, Wilcox was away from his office. But, his adjutant sent them outside to a woodpile where old newspapers lay stacked to use as kindling. Bev picked up the most recent ones, and began reading about the war. After losing at Chickamauga, the Yankees won a big fight under Grant at Chattanooga back in November. It brought Bev back to years when they were riding the train to Memphis past the smoke rising from Fort Henry, Grant's first big victory. That and his win at Fort Donelson opened up both the Tennessee and Cumberland Rivers for the Union army. Bev understood the importance of that, but mostly he remembered how the battles had distracted the Rebs from hunting runaways, giving him and the others a chance to jumpfree.From the newspaper these days, it looked like Grant was still beating the Johnnies like a tin can.

"We done now?" asked Billy, fidgeting. "I'll feel a whole lot more comfortable when we leave the fort behind."

After that, Wesley replaced Billy on supply trips to the fort. In February, the flux had run its course. "It's played out," Wilcox said, "but it cost us half our men. Most all the Injuns died."

It surprised Bev to see Wilcox showing some grey hair. They hadn't seen him on the last trip in February, and the scourge rampaging through the fort apparently had taken its toll on him. He sat in a camp chair behind a campaign table in a square tent, waiting for them to fumigate his permanent quarters, a weekly precaution against bad humors.

"I've been sent some replacements," said Wilcox, brightening up a bit as he said, "even a few striplings for once. Yes, the young replace the old, the old sadly giving up the mortal coil, as the Bard put it."
Bev didn't know what he meant, but he still paid close attention.

"Anyway," Wilcox said, "we got other problems coming on. It seems Quantrill's gang of murderers split into separate units so they can wreak even more havoc. I'm sending out details to warn folks to be vigilant, they might show up anywhere." He stared solemnly at Bev cockeyed from his camp chair and said, "You know what they did to your people at Lawrence and Fort Baxter." He took a sip of coffee from a battered tin cup, then said, "Did you know Quantrill's got a colored boy riding with him? Hard to fathom."

Bev remained silent, standing in front of the major's campaign table.

"There have been Indian raids, too. Comanche, maybe, or Kiowa, maybe Pawnee, I don't know which. Doesn't matter, it won't be long before we go after them. When the war's finished," he said. His expression became one of interest, "They hanged a bunch of them back in '62. Dakota on the warpath up in Minnesota. Minnesota! The natives are causing trouble everywhere these days, they see the writing on the wall. Abe Lincoln himself signed off on the execution, thirty-eight chiefs. Fifteen hundred troops were posted around to keep a lid on, right in the middle of the war. And here I am with just seventeen barely able men, poorly armed, mind you, and seven broken down horses." He raised his eyes again. "We cannot protect all the homesteaders out on their properties. You might be wise to pull up stakes and pitch a tent here for a time. Once all this is over, you can go back, you'll still own your land."

Bev shook his head, "We'll be awright. We'll get you some hosses, too."

Staring up cockeyed, Wilcox dipped his chin slightly as he said, "It's your funeral."

In March, Wilcox accepted two buffalo brought by Bev and Wesley. They used the money to buy a new mule to replace the one that had died, new chickens and a rooster, a cow for milk and butter,and as many cans of preserved fruit and vegetables that they could find, though exorbitantly expensive. They tried to buy a steer, but there was none to be had. Wesley persuaded him to buy some kernels for sweet corn and a supply of seed to try planting wheat later that spring. Theycould grow the wheat for bread or cut it early before it seeded to make hay for the livestock, if needed. He made sure that they didn't buy bearded wheat, however, which caused sores in horses's mouths from eating too fast.

Because of the cow trailing behind one of the wagons, it took them three days to return to the farm. As soon as they arrived, everyone ran out from where they were to welcome them, the boys from the paddock, Portia from the garden, and Hermione from the cabin, wiping her hands dry on her apron as she walked to the wagons. Billy came from the smokehouse, a wide grin on his face. Everyone greeted each other warmly, the children hugging Bev around his waist and chest. Their warm little bodies, delicate like birds, sent a pang through him, a feeling hard to comprehend.

They started to unload the stores from the wagons, all in a festive mood. Lucius and Tiberius ushered the milk cow to the horse barn. Portia balanced a stack of cans on her chest and meandered toward the cabin. Hermione followed her with a stack of her own, calling out behind her daughter, "Watch the front step, Honey."

Wesley guided the new mule to the barn while Bev and Billy muscled the crate of chickens over to the coop. They teeter-tottered the crate on a post where the fence had been tacked back together, this time run deep into the ground. They opened the wire lid and the chickens half flew out of the crate to land on the ground inside. Bev and Billy used their hands to shoo a couple of malingerers out, then dropped the crate to one side. Wesley approached with a smaller cage with the rooster in it, which he freed just above the coop fencing. The bird set off on an immediate crowing spate as it alighted on the top of the coop, stretching its neck feathers out as it screeched and screeched.

Holding his hands over his ears, Billy shouted, "Gal dang!"

Wesley said, "He'll give it up pretty soon. He's halfway mad, halfway happy to be free."

"And we gonna have fresh eggs in the mornin'!" Bev exulted. "Next trip, we get morehogs, one of 'em just for the eatin'. Bacon 'n eggs! Only thing missin' is grits."

Wesley and Billy grinned. Wesley headed back to the wagon to see if there was more to unload. He lifted the sacks of feed for the animals and the corn seeds out of the bed when Bev called to him. "Wes, why don't you leave the sacks for me and Billy. We'll get 'em."

Wesley glanced at him, shrugged, and said, "All right. I'll get the mules squared away."

He unharnessed the two mules and led them to the barn. His boys met him at the doors and held them open as he guided the mules inside. Bev motioned to Billy, and they walked over to pick up the sacks of feed and seed. Bev carried one stack to the smokehouse, and propped the door open for Billy. After they entered, Bev closed the door and hoisted his sack onto a shelf built into the wall. Billy followed suit, and turned to leave.

"Wait, Billy." Bev said.

Surprised, Billy turned around to face Bev. As soon as he saw the big man's expression, he stiffened.

"Come over here." Bev stepped straight back to where Billy hid his jars. He picked one up and held it out for Billy to see. Billy swallowed, his stomach falling down to his knees.

"You think I don't know about this? Of course I do. I come in here just as much as you. I know you been cookin' up liquor for a while, you can't get nothin' past me. "

Panicky, Billy began to stutter, "I, uh, I, uh I,—"

"Nevermind that, Billy, I ain't mad," Bev paused, then said, "yet."

Billy took a deep breath.

"You're doin' your part okay, you ain't messed up, and you're still the best shot around here, maybe in the whole territory. So, I let it go, look the other way. But, things are different, now. We got kids here, they got to be takin' care of different. I can't let you cook up all the grain and vegetables no more. We need to save them for the kids."

Billy's terror began morphing into guilt.

"And, it ain't good to drink around babies, they get ideas themselves. So, I'm asking you, Billy, to quit it. Don't cook up no more bark juice, don't be drinkin' no more. Can you do that, Billy, for the little ones' sake?"

Billy saw the imploring look in Bev's eyes, and he felt shame. He huffed out air and said, "Sure, Bev, I'll quit. I can do that."

"That's good, Billy, I knew you could." Smiling, Bev thrust out his hand and Billy awkwardly shook it.

"Okay, then, let's get to the cabin. I'm sure Mrs. Hermione whippin' up somethin' good for us with all the things we brung back. Eggs, Billy, soon we'll eat some eggs!"

Billy smiled, and Bev clapped him on the shoulder as they left the smokehouse.

Full blown spring arrived and was welcomed by everyone, common to all people since the beginning of time. Song birds returned from their sojourn down south and animals dropped their babies everywhere, followed by foxes, wolves, and wildcats. Once the weather had warmed a bit, Billy took Lucius and Tiberius out to learn how to shoot. He was happy to find that they were able pupils, soonknocking prairie chickens out of the sky straight to the supper table.

The relief from winter buoyed and spurred a surge of activity. Wesley tilled the prairie grass with one of the mules and a plow bought from some settlers on their way back to civilization. Though the returning folks had survived fairly well during the severe winter, they'd had enough of the country life and went back home. Wesley planted an acre of wheat further out. With the boys' help, he started building a fence around it to prevent buffalo and other grazing animals from trampling the seedlings.

Hermione and Portia tripled the size of the garden, working hard to enrich the unyielding soil with aged horse manure. They planted a cornucopia of vegetables, staggered for spring, summer, and fall harvest. Sweet corn from kernels brought back from the fort followed, and plans were laid for later plantings of winter crops to harvest in the cold weather. They built a fence around the garden beds, too, and set up a couple of scarecrows for good measure. The boys would help by watching for critters sneaking into the garden, which they would drill with the squirrel gun. Through their efforts, many a jackass rabbit and groundhog graced the stew pot.

On occasion, while Bev and Wesley rode out to forage, Billy took the children fishing at the creek. They headed up stream above a beaver dam to fish for crappies, catfish, and bass. As they sat in the warm sunlight watching their lines, a beaver suddenly scrambled from the woods on the other side of the creek. It slipped into the water and disappeared.

"Most likely, it swam under and up into its little hidey hole. See the bundle of sticks there in the middle of the dam? That's probably where it's lyin', snug as a bug. Someday, maybe we can trap him. The pelt makes a good hat, all the swells wear 'em in the cities."

"But, it's so cute!" Portia whined.

"What's a swell?" asked Tiberius.

Billy didn't mind spending time with the kids. He liked lollygagging around when Bev was gone anyway, and the little ones made him laugh. Otherwise, life on the property could be pretty boring, especially without a little white lightning to pick him up. He could never go against Bev on that, who was sure to find out anyway even if he tried. But, that didn't mean he didn't miss it.

Spring and summer passed quickly. The men built pens and a pigsty for hogs, which Bev and Wesley bought from a sutler on their June trip to the fort. On that trip, Bev found a newspaper from April sporting a big headline, "Senate Passes 13th Amendment Abolishing Slavery." A subhead stated that passing it in the House it was in doubt.

The paper also reported on a battle that month at Fort Pillow in Tennessee. Confederate General Nathan Bedford Forrest and his 2,500 cavalrymen overwhelmed the Union garrison there, which included 262 U.S. Colored Troops. Of them, only sixty-two escaped; the rest had been slaughtered inside the fort. After the massacre, Forrest and his men rode off, abandoning the fort after just one day.

Bev grimly folded the paper, twisting it into a tight baton. They had been free of the South for almost two years and the Graybacks seemed to be giving ground. But, they could never lower their guard, never, not until every single southern cracker had been put down.

On the August trip, Wilcox warned him of another Rebel threat. A Confederate general named Price with 12,000 riders was sweeping through Missouri. If he succeeded in winning the state back for the Johnnies, they could be looking to run right next door into Kansas. And, of course, Indians were always a danger.

On that trip, Bev and Wesley brought back another cow and two steers. The horses and buffalo had proven difficult to find lately, which turned them to raising more livestock on the farm. They had spent most of the previous two months building an addition to the horse barn for the new stock. Once the new animals arrived, they started preparing for harvest time.

Late in September, Billy and the boys took their rifles out to hunt for wood ducks, delicious eating and readily available during their migration. They headed off to the creek, this time fording it in a shallow spot. Billy then positioned them above the beaver dam behind natural blinds to wait for the birds to alight. He told the boys to be as quiet as possible, and when the ducks settled on the still water above the dam he would take the first shot. As soon as he fired, they would open up on the nearest bird next to the water.

Billy felt sweat dripping down the side of his head from beneath his slouch hat. It was hot, unseasonably so, but not as bad, he remembered, as when they were putting up the new pig sty and cow barns back in July. At the end of every workday that month, he felt like he'd been through a rainstorm in some place like a jungle in Africa. He used his forearm to wipe his brow, thinking, this was uncomfortable, but not like working in the fields.

In late afternoon, a flock of birds flying above started to loop down toward the pond. Wood ducks, he saw as they drew closer. Tightening his grip on the bird gun, he stilled himself as, one by one, they plopped onto the water's surface. Wait until the last one is down, he told himself, then plunk the first one that had landed.

The birds floated in an informal circle, quacking away. Billy raised his gun deliberately to sight in, when they all took off in a wild flapping mass. What the blazes? He saw them then.

A rust-colored man with a completely black face down to his neck pulled a lead rope on a pony, guiding it to the water. The pony dipped its head, and another man similarly painted followed with his mount, then another, and another. A few wore buckskin outfits, some of them bare-chested, with bows and quivers strapped across their backs. Others in worn dungarees carried lances straight up, and one had an old Kentucky long rifle. Each one displayed black paint on his face, his chest, arms, and other parts, heightening their fearsome effect. A war party for sure, Billy thought. Thank God the boys had held off firing like they'd been told. Now, they had to remain quiet, quieter than church mice. But, how could he let them know? How to make sure?

260

Slowly, carefully, he withdrew silently as though hunting the jumpiest game there was. He crawled on hands and knees to Lucius first, who stared at him, shaking like he was in a snowdrift. Billy raised his index finger to his lips, his eyes wide and stark. Lucius nodded his head. He did the same with Tiberius, then gestured for him to follow. They carefully crept back and sideways, until they joined up with Lucius. Billy silently cautioned them to remain still, and moved to a spot between them fronting the beaver pond. There, he took up a position behind brush that allowed him to watch the Indians.

They were joking and laughing quietly as they cleared out a space by the creek to tether the horses. They pulled up a few logs and sat on them, chewing on some jerky while they talked. They planned on staying, Billy realized. He hunkered down to wait for dark, hoping the boys could stay quiet for that long.

When night fell, Billy guided the two boys quietly away from the creek bank. As soon as he was sure that they were out of earshot, he hurried them to the edge of the tree stand. They ran as fast as Lucius could through the prairie grass downstream from the beaver dam. Eventually, they found the shallow spot and forded the creek. Then, they dashed to the farm.

"Injuns," Billy said breathlessly to Bev and the rest, "a war party for sure."

"What'd they look like?" asked Bev. "How many?"

"I counted eight, all painted black from head to their neck, some halfway down their chests. They all looked like they was wearin' shrouds, like they was goin' to a wake."

Wesley nodded, "Sounds like Pawnee. Definitely out to raid."

"I thought they was on our side," said Bev.

A brief grimace crossed Wesley's face. "Maybe most of them," he said, "but you can bet all of them hate homesteaders takin' their land. Or, maybe they're just hungry."

"Yeah," said Bev, "either way, they're bad for us. Get out all our guns and load 'em up. We'll tie the hosses and mules in their stalls in case the redskins lookin' to steal them. Wesley, you get in the cabin with your family. Put the boys at the windows, Hermione and Portia can reload. And, give the girls pistols, too."

Wesley nodded, and bolted to the cabin. Bev glanced at Billy and said, "C'mon, Billy, let's get to the barn, tie up the livestock good."

The two men ran off toward the barn, Billy still gripping the bird rifle in his fist. They threw open one of the doors and split up on either side, grabbing rope along the way. They were halfway done when the howls in the yard started.

"Damn!" spat Bev. He darted to the side door and cracked open the top half. The Indians had just ridden through, shouting heart-stilling cries as they pulled up, jerking their ponies around to ride back and forth. They drew closer and closer to the front door of the cabin, one of them throwing his lance into a plank where it quivered, the feathers at the end waving back and forth.

Bev turned to Billy, who stared, his mouth hanging open. "Shoot 'em, Billy, pick out the leader!"

Nervously, Billy raised his rifle and sighted. "C'mon, c'mon!" Bev yelled, "we got to draw 'em off the cabin!"

Billy aimed, and aimed, and lowered the barrel.

"Billy!" Bev cried, and Billy jerked up the rifle and fired.

The Indians yanked their horses to a stop. Wesley and his sons opened up and the Indians took off, yelling and yipping, fading into the dark.

"Didn't hit a darn thing," said Wesley, "but they ran off. I suppose they thought we were easy pickings."

"Don't matter," said Bev. "They thought they's in a crossfire. Smart thing was to get outta that."

The three men sat around the table, exhausted yet still tense. Tiberius and Lucius sat together on their bunk, both their eyes and mouths round. Portia helped her mother brew some tea since they were all up for the night. Loaded rifles were propped on both sides of the door and the handguns lay on the table.

Hermione leaned over Billy to set down a cup of tea, then stood behind him and rested her hands on his shoulders. "One thing is for certain," she said, smiling, "Young Billy here is a hero."

Billy's eyes shifted back and forth. Bev squinted at him. "We're all lucky, though. After this, we keep some firearms in all the buildings. Carry the .44s, too, wherever we go." He dipped his chin up and down and the others all motioned agreement.

The Indians never came back, and to discourage any that might show up, the lance in the door had been stuck through a pig's skull topping a post that they drove into the ground at the center of the buildings.

Everyone continued to work toward buttoning down for the winter. On trips during the fall months, Bev and Wesley brought back as much feed as they could find and also a full crate of masonry jars packed in straw. Hermione put up all of the vegetables, with the boys foraging for apples far and wide in the creek woods. She pressed them into service readying the preserves, which caused them to complain about doing women's work. Once the jars were full on the shelves in the root cellar, they turned to harvesting and shucking the wheat.

Billy hunted nonstop, packing plenty of deer on a mule back to the farm. He also bagged an occasional antelope, even an elk. He saw no buffalo or moose, but the smokehouse was full of game to eat through the winter. The sow had dropped a litter back in July, ten little piglets that thrilled the children. After a few months had gone by, Wesley made sure that the kids were down by the creek playing before dispatching one of the new pigs. Everyone enjoyed the ribs.

Bev tracked the progress of the war as much as he could. More than half a year later, Congess still had yet to pass the 13th amendment. Grant and his generals pressed the Confederates at every juncture. He suffered shocking losses in battle after battle while inexorably pushing the southern general Lee tighter against the wall. At the same time, Sheridan and Sherman won clash after clash and Lincoln won re-election.

Wesley and Hermione were glad to receive the papers, which they read to their children, then used to teach them to read to themselves. As he listened to each child parse the letters and words out loud, Billy gradually realized that soon he would be the only person on the farm who could not read. He said nothing about it, though, too proud to bring it up.

By December, they were ready for winter and happy to spend most of their time inside the cabin. After tending to the livestock, they would sit next to the warmth of the fire, the men whittling, the ladies sewing or knitting, and the boys playing games or wrestling around. Soon, it would be Christmas, and presents were in order. Wesley had carved some animals for Tiberius and Lucius, and a doll for Portia, for which Hermione had sewn the clothes. But, presents were required for Hermione, too, which called for a trip to Fort Larner to see what Wesley could find.

The weather held and the two men reached the fort in good time. Wesley left for the sutler while Bev rode the wagon up to the headquarters for the latest newspapers. He blocked the wagon wheels, hung feed bags on the mules, and walked over to the wood pile where the papers were stacked. As he passed by, Colonel Wilcox stepped out of the building and lit a stogie. He puffed as he watched Bev carrying a few papers back toward the wagon.

"Merry Christmas, Mr. Bowman," said Wilcox, puffing away.

"You, too, Colonel Wilcox. Hope you have a nice day."

"Oh, I intend to, what with the war nearly done. Won't be long now before Grant rolls Lee up. Then, we can all relax. And, since nothing is happening out here, we're already in a festive spirit."

"That's mighty good news to hear," said Bev, laying the papers in the well of the wagon's bench. "We pretty good ourselves, ready to fatten up over the winter."

"That's good, that's good." Wilcox paused, then said, "So, you don't have a hankering to go back home after all this is over."

Bev shrugged, "Never give it much thought."

"The war'll be over soon and slavery's finished. Just as soon as Congress passes the amendment."

"Maybe so," Bev said, leaning against the side of the wagon, "but they ain't done it yet. Besides, I don't have anything back there to go back to. Just some bad things to remember."

"I see. No family or folks." A light seemed to dawn on Wilcox, "Say, that reminds me! Maybe I have something that'll change your mind."

He darted inside the building, and quickly returned with a bundle. He unwrapped it and handed a yellowed cardboard envelope to Bev. "It got here just after you left the fort last month. I planned on giving it to you when you came back, and I near forgot. Anyway, there it is. It's old, it's been following you all around Kansas, Fort Scott, Belmont, and finally here."

Bev stared at the envelope, utterly confused. He examined it, turned it over, and gazed at the address again.

"You can read, can't you?" Wilcox asked, then said, chuckling, "Of course you can. If you can't why all the newspapers?"

Bev held it front facing him again. He read the address:

> To:
> Mr Beverly Bowman of Kentucky
> General Delivery
> The Indian Territory
> The United States of America

In the corner, he saw a return address:
> 826 North Second Street

Memphis, Tennessee
The United States of America

He stood stock still, completely stunned. Slowly, he opened the envelope and unfolded the letter inside.

May First, 1864
To Mr Beverly Bowman
Lately of the Bowman Farm, Kentucky
c/o General Delivery
Indian Territory of the USA

Dear Mr Bowman,

I hope this letter finds you well, and the Good Lord watches over you all the time. I wish your good friends Mr William McKenny Mr Joshua Bowman and Mr Whitman Mayo are well and good in God's good hands.

If you have gotten this letter, maybe you are surprised to read it. After we met, Mr Jacob Burkle taught me to read and write. I asked him to after I saw you read and write. Now, I can happily say I can read and write after two years of learning. I hope you are pleased and will write to me so I can write back.

Important, I have news about Eli. It is good, he did not drown in the Big Muddy. I know I saw him taken by slavecatchers. It is so sad I told Mr Burkle, he tried to find your brother. Mr Burkle tried to buy him back from the Bowman Farm people, but they said no. Do not be sad, after the law freeing slaves came, Mr Burkle tried again, the Bowmans said ok. The Bowmans asked a lot of money but Mr Burkle said any price is worth Eli and all slaves. Eli came to Memphis and he is very sour. He has lash scars on his body and is angry at the Bowman masters.

That is all I have to write. Please write if you want if you get this. I would like to read how you are.

Sincere Bless you,
Mary Louise Smalls

Bev read it, and read it again. Mary Louise. My God, he said to himself. My God.

Chapter 21. Posthaste

Bev read the letter several more times, then marched into Wilcox's headquarters and requested a telegraph to be sent with the mail wagon on its monthly trip to Fort Belmont. Wilcox made a half-hearted fuss about denying Bev's request given that they were still at war and telegraphs were restricted to military communication.

"C'mon now, Colonel, you just told me the Rebs are on their last legs," said Bev. He pulled a newspaper from his armpit and punched at the front page. "It say right here Price been driven out of Missouri and Grant's armies got Lee pinned down in Petersburg. One telegraph ain't gonna make a difference in the war and I got to get in touch with these folks now! It's important, damn important!"

Wilcox hesitated, fully taking in a passion within Bev that he'd never seen before. Finally he said, "I guess one won't hurt at this stage of the hostilities. That's providing you pay the going rate for sending a telegram."

Bev addressed the wire to Jacob Burkle:

> *Mr J Burkle,*
> *126 N 2ⁿᵈ St*
> *Memphis TN*
>
> *Received M.L.S. 5/1864 letter. If M.L. still in Memphis, will write posthaste.*
>
> *B Bowman*
> *c/o Fort Larned, KS*

Bev knew that his telegram wouldn't be sent from Belmont for two weeks at best and a reply, if any, could take as much as a month. He knew that the delay would drive him mad, but it was the best he could do. Nonetheless, that night he wrote a letter to Marie Louise to go on the mail wagon along with the telegram, hoping that she still lived on the Burkle estate. He felt keenly the futility of sending anything back to Memphis, which Union forces had controlled for more than two years. Since then, freeing slaves there likely took place in plain sight. In turn, Burkle must feel freed himself of his dangerous, covert operation. Knowing Mary Louise as he did, Bev knewthe first thing she'd do was search for her daughterno matter whereit took her. This meant that he might himself search high and low for Mary Louisein vain. Still, he had to write.

Miss Mary Louise Smalls
c/o Jacob Burkle
126 North Second Street
Memphis Tennessee

Dear Miss Smalls,

I received and read your letter with great joy. It is a blessing from high up to know that you are well, and that you and the most honorable Mr Burkle have saved my brother Eli. It grieves me to learn his sweet nature has been spoiled by the terrible brutality inflicted upon him by the Bowmans. May the Lord chasten them for their actions in this world or the next.

I am sorry for writing to you so late. Me and my companions have traveled far since I saw you last. Through Arkansaw into the Indian Territory up across Kansas. We have seen great suffering. I am sad to write that Whit Mayo died fighting as a Union soldier. Josh left to find his family in the Deep South. We know that many more in this vast land have seen such sorrows. But we are free, praise God, and we are well, Billy and me, we even own a farmstead on the Kansas plains.

Miss Mary Louise Smalls, I have often thought of you while traveling this far. I hold you in great regard and, dare I say it, affection. I pray that this is not too forward of me. I only wish you the best, that you and your daughter are reunited and live happy together. If in any small way you feel any little warmth or kindness toward me, if only as a friend, I will return to visit you and pay my deepest respect. May the Good Lord always be with you.

I remain your faithful friend and servant,
Beverly Bowman

The letter went out with the telegraph. Bev could not sit still, however. Waiting a month or two would be like waiting through all eternity. Now, every trip to Larned would be fraught, high hopes versus dread of that empty feeling when nothing had arrived, nothing had changed. Every disappointment condemned him to another month of waiting before he could repeat the maddening routine all over again. How many months of this torture could he endure before he gave it all up, surrender to the truth that nothing would happen? Where had this foolish hope come from after only a week spent with her nearly three years ago? His rational mind asked himself repeatedly how he could be so crazy. He was driving himself mad.

He tried to put the looping thoughts out of his mind by working harder. Billy and the Wilsons knew about the letter and Bev's attempts to reply. They watched him push himself around the property, wading in on every task along with his usual chores. He helped weed the garden, cultivate the field, tend to livestock, repair fences and outbuildings, anything he could do to speed up time without thought.

Wesley knew that for all of Bev's efforts, the big man's anxiety grew every passing day as the date of their monthly trip to Larned approached. He and Hermione's hearts went out to him, distressed to see such a formidable, active man diminish before their eyes. When Billy had told Wesley how Bev hadmet Mary Louise, the barber shook his head.

"It's hard to believe," said Wesley, "a strong fella' like him'd get so worked up over a woman he knew for such a short time."

"I don't know," Billy said, "I don't know much about women and men. She was nice, though."

"Yeah, well, I'm not sure I'm up to going with him this trip," murmured Wesley. "I hate to see him so disappointed when nothing shows up from her."

Billy gazed up at Wesley. "I could go this trip. I could take your place."

Wesley shook his head, "No, I can't have you doing what I should. I'll make the trip no matter what." He lowered his head, saying sorrowfully, "I sure hope somethin's there for him this time, a letter or somethin'."

There was no letter, no telegraph waiting for Bev. He and Wesley loaded up the wagon with flour, grain, and various other supplies. They tried to find some goats to buy, but there weren't any around the fort. Wesley bought some fabric for Hermione and three wooden buckets to go with the others back at the spread. They climbed onto the bench at the front of the wagon, andwithout a word, Bev snapped the reins lightly to put the mules in motion. Seeing the dark grief on Bev's face, Wesley didn't try to start a conversation. Instead, he started to read one of the papers that out of force of habit, Bev had fetched from the woodpile in front of Wilcox's headquarters.

Wesley read a couple of headlines about Sherman giving Savannah to Lincoln as a Christmas present and how Grant's huge army was on the verge of a breakthrough at Petersburg. Then, a headline on one of the papers stopped him. He raised his eyes to Bev.

"Bev, the House passed the Thirteenth Amendment on January 31. All black folks are gonna be free in America, Bev, everywhere. Just a matter of time, they say, before all the states ratify it."

Bev continued staring straight ahead. "It ain't happened yet," he said, then mumbling, "Too late for me anyway."

March rolled around, chicks were born, piglets, too, even a foal, the first one ever on the farm. The children were beside themselves with excitement. Wesley had brought two puppies and a kitten back from the fort in February, and they played endlessly with each other if they weren't playing with the boys and Portia. All living things seemed to be thriving and the weather was warming.

"Looks like we're gonna make it out of the cold," said Wesley.

Bev just nodded, still brooding silently most of the time. Billy said, "I can't wait for some fresh vegetables. And an apple, b'God! I do have interest in eatin' an apple!"

"Yeah, well that's a ways off, Billy," said Wesley.

"I know, I know," replied Billy, "but I could eat one if they was some around."

They watched the sunrise, then started to separate on their way to work.

Bev stopped Billy. "I need to talk to you, Billy," he said. "C'mon over here to the barn."

Billy's eyes showed concern. As he followed him inside he wondered if Bev knew he was drinking again. They both leaned on the side of a stall facing each other.

Bev gathered himself together to speak, but held up. He uttered a few indiscernible sounds, and stopped again. Finally, he pulled in a deep breath, exhaled, and spoke.

"Billy, I gotta go," he said, his features frozen, serious. "I have to go back."

Billy blinked, several times. "What? Where? Back where?"

"Back east. To Memphis. I got to find out, Billy, I got to know what happened—is she alive, did she get my letters, my telegraphs? Does she care to see me at all? I'm outta my head about this and I can't stand it anymore!"

"You're going back east?" Billy asked, confused, shocked.

"To Memphis. If she ain't there, then I'll go where else she might be."

"Back east, where all that trouble was. What it took us to get here, what we lost. You wannago back."

"I got to, Billy, I got to know!"

"Back over them mountains again. Maybe get in the way of them Reb raiders. Theykill us still, it don't matter what the law is."

"It's risky, I know."

Billy shook his head, "I don't see it, Bev. I don't see much left there to go back for. I ain't sure my daddy's alive, even. I kind of doubt it, in fact."

Bev pulled his head back. "You can't go, Billy. This is your place, now. You can't give it up, you worked too hard! You got to stay here, keep the property goin', help the Wilsons get along. I'm goin' alone, it's my stake. I don't know what is gonna happen, I don't how I'm gonna be if I don't find her. There ain't no good in this for you comin'. You need to stay put for your own sake."

Billy looked as though he might cry. "But, Bev, it's you and me. We all that's left."

"I know, Billy, and if things go right maybe I can come back someday. If not, this is your place anyway, and you got Wesley and Hermioneand the kids. They all our family now. We can't leave 'em high and dry, you got to stay."

Tears were running down Billy's cheeks now and Bev felt a blade in his heart.

"Listen, Billy," he said, "we'll go to the fort together, I'll get a telegraph sent back to Maryville, ask about your daddy. Most likely, he alive and doin' well. He find out where you are, he probably come out here to be with you. Shucks, he can ride the train almost all the way, they buildin' 'em so fast. How about that, Billy, your daddy ridin' a train here? How that sound?"

Billy's lower lip buttressed out, but he'd stopped crying. "You come back here someday, Bev?"

Bev nodded, "I'll try to come back sometime."

"Maybe bring Miss Mary Louise with you?"

Bev's jaw tightened. "I don't know about that, Billy. I hope. I will try somehow."

Billy nodded. "And, we'll send a telegraph to my daddy."

"That's right. You, me, Wesley, we'll take the wagon in for a supply run. I ask Colonel Wilcox to send the telegraph directly to your daddy. Then, I head east, while you and Wesley go on back to the farmstead."

Everyone gathered around the wagon to say goodbye to Bev. Tiberius glowered, but kept his peace while Lucius and Portia wept openly, inconsolably. Hermione brushed away dampness from her eyes, smiled brilliantly and said, "Lord keep you, Beverly Bowman. You are truly blessed in His eyes. Thank you for everything you've done for us, thank you so much."

She hugged him fiercely, kissed his cheek, then stepped back and away to hide her tears.

Looking stunned and still somewhat surprised at Bev's decision, Wesley said, "Well, I guess it's about time for us to go." He climbed up on the wagon, followed by Billy, who was wearing an expression of utter remorse. Bev smiled awkwardly, hugged the weeping children, and mounted his horse. Wesley flicked the reins and the mules slowly pulled the wagon, a pack mule trailing on its end, away from the house.

At the fort, Bev arranged for the telegram to be sent to the constable in Maryville. He also checked for a message or a letter for himself from Memphis without any luck. He shook hands with Wilcox, who wished him safe travel. Bev thanked him for his support, turned, and walked out of the Colonel's office.

Outside, he met Billy and Wesley. "Well," he said, "that's pretty much all of it. The telegram is gonna be sent to Maryville. I sent the letter I wrote to your daddy, too, just to make sure. So," he hesitated, "I guess I better ride on, now."

Awkwardly, he reached his hand out to Wesley, who shook it. At the same time, each man clasped the other's shoulder with his free hand. "God speed," said Wesley, and Bev nodded. He turned to Billy.

Billy stood completely disheveled, his body heaving as he cried open-mouthed without a sound. Bev enveloped him in a bear hug, whispering in his ear, "You take good care of yourself, Billy Boy. God be willin', we will see each other again, this life or the next." Billy moved his head up and down, still crying.

"Awright, then," Bev said. He mounted his horse, took the pack mule's rope from Wesley and tied it to the pommel of his saddle. He turned his eyes back to the two men standing below him and said, "Take good care boys," and rode away below the midday sun.

Bev left a big hole in the homestead after that, both in work and his missing presence. Billy liked Wesley enough, the barber always treated him as an equal, with respect. The kids were fun, too, birding and fishing, just shooting the breeze along the way as children do. Occasions like that grew rare, however, since he had to fill in for Bev on all the hunting trips now, and when they went out looking for horses. They couldn't find them anymore, or buffalo. They brought mule deer and the like home for the table, but the cash animals seemed to have disappeared. Existence on the homestead had become mostly a matter of sustenance these days. As far as Billy felt, the change meant more work and no money for Dr. Archer's English Elixir or Smith Brother's Cough Drops. Life was drudgery and boredom, and he decided to do something about it.

Before long, he had a good batch of mash fermenting in the smokehouse. He'd made a lot this time, enough to fill all of the mason jars he had on hand. In six weeks, he'd have more than enough.

While he waited, Billy went about his chores diligently. Slowly he and Wesley managed to catch up with the season. They had seed in the field by the end of April and were well along in mending fences and finishing off the new pens and sheds. Without horses to train, they could concentrate on the livestock while fitting in some hunting. Billy enjoyed that the most with the boys,who now brought in most of the geese, ducks, and other fowl. He planned on showing them how to fire the heavy caliber rifles next, confident that he could mold them into the best of marksmen. Like their father, he thought, who turned out to be a fair shot and brought down his share of game. The smokehouse and the larder were full, and Hermione made the most of them. For breakfast, they had ham and eggs, cornpone, fresh baked bread, porridge, sometimes biscuits and bacon, and in late summer, blackberries, raspberries, and cream. For lunch, it was often fish or jerky on thick slices of buttered bread. Dinner would be roast chicken, waterfowl, or some other meat with baked or fried potatoes and whatever other vegetables in season. But, the best thing of all that Hermione put on the table was pie.

Apple pie, black raspberry pie, peach pie, squash pies, and pies made with nuts, it was a heaven that Billy hadn't known since his mama died almost fifteen years ago. He felt guilty, too, of the knowledge every time he took a bite that Hermione baked better pies than his mama ever had. The lavish, sugary taste of that beautiful black women's pies condemned Billy to hell, and he didn't care one bit. Put a piece of pie and a glass of buttermilk in front of him, and he was happy to sin.

He watched her move around the cabin like a sorceress conjuring addictive stews, soups, and sauces, always with the most brilliant, warm smile on her face. With good humor, she cajoled her children to help her ready the table and serve the magic of her devising. She was more than a cook and housekeeper, though. She worked in the field, in the garden, and with the animals. Sometimes she dispatched one for dinner, soothing it with kindness and respect that made its demise fluid, almost a transition rather than a violent death. She helped with every physical project, too, unloading wagons, or holding planks, and joining in other labors with surprising strength. She could sing.

Wesley would come inside and fold her in his arms, and Billy would fall into a blue mood. Then, he would head outside to see how the mash was settling.

Finally, it was ready. Using a funnel, he filled all the mason jars, thirty in all. He took a long pull from one jar, hacking fiercely as the liquid burned down his throat. He capped it, and put it and nine others away in his hidey hole. He covered the rest with a buffalo rug and made his way out of the smokehouse into the front yard.

Wesley was in the stable working on shoeing a mule. Billy strode over to him.

"Maybe it's time for another supply trip to the fort," he said.

Wesley craned his neck up at him. "I don't know, Billy, we ain't got much to sell or trade. There's a lot of work to do around here, too."

"We can take some of the birds the boys shot, sell 'em to the Colonel. He probably ain't ate a goose or a duck in a long time. Fish, too. He might appreciate the taste of somethin' different. There might be news from Bev, too."

Wesley slowly moved his head up and down. "Might also get some news about the war. But, heck, Billy, we got a lot to do to keep everything goin'. I don't think I want to leave Hermione and the boys alone here while we're gone. Suppose the Injuns come around again? They can't be left alone to deal with them."

"That true," said Billy, looking serious in thought. Then, his expression changed as if a light had descended upon him. "Say, what if I take one of the boys with me? They both good shots, now, and you could stay here to watch over everything." Wesley seemed unsure, and Billy went on, "We only be gone for two days, we won't dawdle any, I promise."

Wesley smiled a pained grin and said, "I guess that'll work. Take Tiberius with you. I'll ask Hermione to put a list together of what we need."

Billy smiled, "Good enough, then."

Billy and Tiberius loaded the wagon that day, putting in a string of waterfowl and a basket of dried fish. Other than that, there wasn't much else to sell, so he threw in a buffalo hide, saying, "Maybe they need a blanket or a rug, maybe."

That night, he left the cabin for the outhouse. On the way back, he veered over to the smokehouse and started carrying jars full of the cloudy liquor to the wagon. He carefully placed them in at the front end of the bed, tucking scraps of leather and rags between them. Ten trips and he had them all loaded and covered with the buffalo hide. After finishing with the wagon, he made one last trek back to the smokehouse for a nice swig out of his own stash. Then, he returned to the cabin, conjuring up a story about how long his stay in the outhouse had lasted.

They made it to the fort without incident and instead of heading directly to the Colonel's quarters, Billy drove the wagon over to the mess tent. "Wait here, Ty," he said, "keep an eye on things, don't let nobody near the goods. I'll be back directly."

He went into the tent and asked one of the cooks where he might find the short, stout sergeant. The cook jerked his thumb over his shoulder and Billy hurried that way. He found Sergeant Avery sitting in his union suit on a camp chair, his coat draped over its back and his pants in his lap. Avery's tongue stuck out of the side of his mouth as he intently tried to aim a thread through the eye of a needle.

"Hey, Sergeant," said Billy, "how it goin'?" His voice was somewhat tremulous.

Sergeant Avery glanced up, and knitted his brows. "You from the ranch a couple of days out from the fort, that right?"

"Yessir."

"Yeah, you been here before." Avery smiled, "That's right, you 'n that skinny Negra supplied us with joy juice 'til the Injuns acted up. Shame about that."

"Yessir, well, I got some more if you is interested."

Avery suddenly looked alert. "That right? Where you got it?"

"In the wagon next to the mess hall."

The sergeant stuck the needle in the spool of thread, stood up, and tossed it onto the camp chair, saying, "Let me get my britches on and we'll see what you got."

Avery pulled his braces over his shoulders as they walked to the wagon. Billy whipped back the buffalo hide and pulled out a mason jar, holding it up proudly to the sergeant.

"Well, then, crack it open, let's have a taste," said Avery.

Billy popped off the top and handed the jar to Avery. Examining it, he hesitated, and said skeptically, "That's pretty cloudy lookin'."

Billy didn't reply. The sergeant took a drink and sprayed it out on the ground next to him.

"Blasted, that's the worst I ever had. You call this liquor? Drinkable liquor?"

"It'll get you where you want to be," said Billy.

"Maybe so, if it don't kill you first. You drink this swill?"

"All day long," said Billy.

"Then you must be a crazy man."

"Try again. You get used to it."

Avery took another sip and forced it down, coughing severely after swallowing. "I could feel the fire in it, all right, but it takes some doin' to get it down."

Billy shrugged.

"How much you want for it?"

"Dollar a jar, same as before."

"Hell's bells, it ain't worth no dollar! You should pay me!"

"If you want it, it's gonna cost," said Billy.

"Yeah, but not no dollar. I give you twenty-five cents a jar, that's it."

"Twenty-five cent! That ain't even worth it!" cried Billy.

"Take it or leave it. I be lucky to sell it to the boys at that myself."

Billy sighed. He'd brought it all this way. Finally, he said, "Okay. Tiberius, help me unload, will you?"

They moved the twenty jars of cloudy liquor from the wagon to the ground, and Avery peeled off five dollar bills. He handed them to Billy.

"Five dollars, it just don't seem worth it."

"It ain't worth it," said Avery, "but that's what you get."

Glumly, Billy folded it and put it into his pocket.

"Why don't you and that skinny black boy make the clear shine you used to? That stuff is worth the money."

Billy shook his head slowly, "Whit dead. Joined the colored regiment, got killed by Quantrill and his thugs."

Avery smirked and said, "Niggers never know when to keep their heads down."

Billy suddenly felt as though something was crawling over his brow across the back of his head. Without looking behind him, he thought about young Tiberius listening.

"Too bad for him, too, since the war's done with, now."

Billy squinted, "The war's done? What do you mean?"

"It's over. Lee surrendered to Grant back in April. Too late for your Negra friend. Lincoln, too, sort of, though he got shot afterwards. He got plugged the same day they raised the Union flag back over Fort Sumter. Imagine. Anyway, we don't have to worry about them Johnny Rebs no more. Now, it's just the Injuns."

The war's over, Billy thought.

"Say, why you don't take a crack at cookin' up some real shine?" asked Avery. "You must know how, you been around that friend of yours long enough, right? 'Afore he got kilt, I mean."

Billy stared at Avery, distracted. Then, he said, "I don't know. Maybe." He stepped up on the wagon, sat next to Tiberius and flipped the reins to get the mules moving.

"We'll pay you top dollar if you do," the sergeant called out as they drove away.

Colonel Wilcox greeted them warmly, smiling and offering to pay twenty dollars for the birds and the fish.

"I'm happy to see that you are well and still prospering," he said to Billy. "And, with the war over, your young man there is free!"

"He already free," Billy said absentmindedly. "Thanks for the twenty dollars, I know the goods ain't worth all that."

Wilcox smiled benevolently, "Call it a celebration bonus."

"Appreciate it, sir. May I ask, you heard anything from Beverly Bowman? Any news at all?"

"I have not, but I did receive a telegram addressed to him." Wilcox returned behind his desk and rummaged through the drawers. "Here it is, not terribly dated, sent on February 21st."

"Is it from Tennessee, Colonel? From Maryville?"

"It is from Tennessee, but from Memphis. If you like, I can give it to you now to save for Mr. Bowman upon his return."

Billy nodded his head and Wilcox gave him the telegram.

In the wagon, Billy opened it and handed it over to Tiberius. "Can you read that?"

Tiberius flattened out the yellow page and started to read out loud.

"To Mr. Beverly Bowman, little c, slant stick, little o–I don't know what that means," said Tiberius.

"Never mind. Read the rest."

Tiberius continued, "Fort Larned, KS. Dear Mr. Bowman, Message from M.L. Smalls. Welcome. Yours, Jacob Burkle." Tiberius looked up. "That's it."

Welcome. From Mary Louise Smalls. She welcomed him. By now, they could be together. They should be together by now, thought Billy. But no message from Maryville, no news about his daddy. Nothing.

He blew out his breath. "Okay, Tiberius, thank you." He took back the telegram, folded it, and put it in his pocket. "Best we get a move on," he said, snapping the reins. They left the fort and started on their way back to the farmstead.

Billy decided to cook up a batch of whiskey. He rummaged around the smokehouse searching for the elements used by Whit, and found the one missing kettle easily enough, but not the piping. Most likely, Bev had thrown it into the creek along with the other kettle almost a year ago. Since it was copper, however, maybe it hadn't corroded. Billy grabbed a fishing pole, told the boys that they couldn't go with him when they asked, and ambled off toward the creek as if he hadn't a care in the world. Once at the bank where he had found the first pot, he moved upstream, baited the pole, and secured it to a log, pointing out over the water. He cast the hooked line into the stream, then hiked back to search for the pipes. He cut a sapling down, and waded into the water, dragging the green branch back and forth in the stream.

At first, he moved randomly through the coursing stream, awkwardly scraping its bottom. Mostly, he tumbled river stones around with the makeshift rake. The water was cold, too, even in mid-June. After an hour of futile scouring, he climbed out of the frigid water to warm up and rest. He needed to do this in a different way, he realized, in some kind of pattern. Back and forth didn't make sense, since the weight of the pipes would have them settle on the near side of the creek where Bev had tossed them. If they were still here, they would be stuck in silt, too. Otherwise, they could have rolled down the stream who knew how far. He could be here for hours, days, even, without finding anything.

He sighed, then told himself he'd give it another hour or so. He'd cleave close to the bank, hoping that the piping had gotten caught in the mud, marking his pattern a rough two feet out. Bobbing his head up and down to himself, he eased back into the stream and started raking again.

An hour passed without any luck. He scrambled up the bank, shivering and swinging his arms to stimulate some heat. While out of the water, he heard a noise upstream, a sort of wood chaffing. He peered up and saw the fishing pole bent over, its line a taut u-shape flexing up and down. B'geez, he said to himself, a fish!

He ran up and grabbed the pole just before it worked free from the ground. Billy yanked on it and pulled hard, walking it back into the brush until he saw a silvery, arching creature flipping and flopping at the end of the line. Billy seized the line in one hand and dropped the pole. Hand over hand, he worked his way to the fish until he closed in on it. He pulled it back away from the bank in case the line broke, and stepped on it with one boot to hold it in place. He extracted his knife and clubbed it with the haft until it was dead. Then, he lifted it up still on the line. A six-pound carp, who would've thought?

Laughing, he extracted the hook, cleaned the fish, and tied a cord through its gills. Then, he hung it from a tree limb for safe keeping until he headed back. Without thinking, he stepped directly into the water where he'd caught the fish, and began trolling for the pipes again. Only fifteen minutes later he found them, stuck in the bank a few feet down the creek. Bev must have walked the parts up the side of the bank as he threw them in. Happily, he stashed the pipes away in the brush to fetch later. He gathered his pole and the fish and started his return to the cabin. Laughing all the way back, he marveled at himself. He'd even caught a fish for dinner.

Billy concocted the first batch very tenuously, carefully walking through the steps that Whit had showed him. Sometimes his memory failed him and he had to wait until he could recall what came next. If he couldn't remember, he followed his best guess. The initial readying of the mash wasn't hard, that's how he'd made his cloudy brew. The distillery presented a much greater challenge. Finally, after some meticulous trial and error, he thought he had it set up correctly.

The day he had the mash ready, he waited until nighttime when everyone was deep in slumber. He stole away to the smokehouse and fired up the still. After sometime, to his complete amazement, he saw

278

condensation form and drip at the end of the coiled copper. Once a spoonful had filled the receptacle, he switched it out and took a sip. It burned, but it was definitely liquor, not the cloudy mix he'd made before, but crystal clear, genuine moonshine. Billy almost clapped his hands, it thrilled him so.

Over the next few nights, he filled up his thirty mason jars. While he cooked, he drank his product, causing Wesley to wonder why Billy seemed so tired that week. He occasionally staggered around somewhat aimlessly, appearing ready to walk right into a barn door. Hermione worried that he was working too hard or maybe was coming down with something. Billy said it was just the weather turning hot.

After distilling his first batch, he knew that he would need more supplies and more jars. Like when he had cooked with Whit, he used much of the feed for the animals and other foodstuff for the mash. He couldn't keep doing that without raising suspicion, and he would need to sell more than twenty jars of his joy juice to stake his operation. This called for another trip to Fort Larned. Wesley agreed because surprisingly, they seemed to be running low on feed for the animals. Once again, Tiberius went along that August, since it had worked out so well before.

"Tiberius, here's a dollar. You go on up to the commissary and get your mamaa bottle of Florida water while I take care of some business. If there's any change, buy yourself some hard candy, for your brother and sister, too, if there's enough."

Tiberius ran off happily, and Billy walked over to Avery's tent. When Avery tasted from the jar, he exploded, "Now, that's what I call some genuine bust head. I'll give ya fifty cents a jar."

"A dollar a jar," said Billy, "take it or leave it."

He used the twenty dollars to buy extra grain and two boxes of mason jars, eighteen altogether. There would be plenty of liquor to sell on the next trip. Before leaving, he checked in with Colonel Wilcox, but no telegram had come from Maryville.

Toward the end of September, Billy had thirty jars of liquor hidden away in the smokehouse, not to mention his own reserve of ten. He was cooking up a batch for the last eight jars with another trip to the fort in mind for next week. This time, he'd get half as many jars along with more grain. Winter would be along before you know it, he thought, and travel would be harder considering the weather. It wouldn't do to leave the farm, either. At that time of year, Indians were more likely to make a try for their goods. In fact, more bluecoats had been assigned to Fort Larned. It was part of the buildup to enforce a brace of new laws in Congress that were likely to rile up the natives. That meant a lot more shine to sell, thought Billy, but that would have to wait until the spring.

Also, as of late Wesley and Hermione were becoming a lot more irritating. Wesley had found Billy sleeping in the barn more than once, and Hermione had smelled something on his breath. Both of them rode him about not finishing some of his jobs, which was setting them all behind for the winter. Wesley had been busy harvesting crops, Hermione putting up preserves, but Billy hadn't been out hunting for a while. They still had plenty in the smokehouse, he said, and he'd go hunting with the boys again soon, when his lumbago cleared up some. As the days passed, though, the Wilsons looked unhappier and unhappier.

That very afternoon, in fact, he told Wesley that he would be smoking some wild geese that Tiberius and Lucius had brought home. Wesley didn't say anything, but his expression was sour as he took a team of mules out to plant winter wheat. As soon as he was gone, Billy got the still fire going, then stretched out for a snooze.

When he woke up, the south side of the smokehouse was a wall of flame.

"B'God!" He jumped up and ran outside to get a bucket of water. Dashing back in, he threw the water haplessly at the wall. He heard voices shouting as he ran out again. Hermione and Tiberius were filling up buckets from the creek and rushing them over to toss at the smokehouse. Lucius ran to warn his father.

Billy, Hermione, and Tiberius formed a line from the creek to the smokehouse, dashing buckets of water on it with little effect. Then, Wesley rode up on a mule with Lucius on the back. They jumped off and joined in the brigade. As they continued to throw water, they heard glass cracking and sudden explosions, one after another inside the smokehouse.

"What in blazes is that?" shouted Wesley.

"Shine!" Billy cried out, mortified, "the mason jars are blowin' up, and the liquor is burnin', adding to the fire!"

Another staccato of bursting jars went off, the flames soared into the sky, until the entire structure of the smokehouse collapsed in on itself. Everyone stepped back, their eyes fixed on the fire still raging.

When the flames subsided, Wesley turned to Billy. "You've been making moonshine? All this time, you've been making liquor and drinking. Look what you've done, Billy! That's all our meat we got for the winter, gone! How we gonna make it now, Billy, with all that gone? How we gonna survive?"

He walked away, putting his arms around Hermione's and Lucius shoulders, with Tiberius trailing behind. Wesley halted, and stared back at Billy. "You got to go, Billy, you can't stay here anymore. Either that, or we got to go." He startedthe children back to the cabin. Hermione walked away, too, but kept her head turned, staring back at Billy with a look of horror on her face.

Billy stood still, stuck to the ground.

He said nothing for the next month. He lived in the tack shed, keeping warm at night with buffalo hides. From daybreak until nightfall, he worked nonstop building a new smokehouse. Once Wesley saw what he was doing, he joined in with Tiberius and Lucius, but they never exchanged a word unless it was about the construction. They finished the new smokehouse in two weeks.

After that, Billy took a horse and a mule out by himself onto the prairie with the Lorenz. Two days later, he returned with a mule deer. He left it behind, and took another horse and mule out. During the next two weeks, he brought in enough game to replace half that was lost in the fire.

On October 1st, 1865, he knocked on the door of the cabin. Wesley opened it carefully, thinking a stranger was looking for a place to stay that night. When he saw it was Billy at the door, he swung it wide open.

"C'mon in, Billy, set down and have some dinner."

Hermione came over, smiling slightly, and said, "We got plenty, rabbit stew."

Billy shook his head. "Wesley, you have paper?" Wesley nodded, frowning. "And ink and a pen?" Again, Wesley motioned yes.

"Then, write this down." Billy waited until Wesley was at the table, ready to write.

"'I, Billy McKenny, sign over all my property next to the Saw Log Creek to Beverly Bowman and Wesley Wilson. In return, I will accept a mule, the squirrel rifle, and some shot and powder.' You got that down?"

"Yes, Billy, but this ain't right. It's your place, you must keep it. I said things in haste, badly, and I am sorry. We want you to stay with us like we always was, a family. We're your family, Billy. Ain't that right, Hermione?"

"Yes, indeed, Billy, you're a brother to us, an uncle to our children." As Hermione spoke, Lucius and Portia wept openly, while Tiberius tried to hold back his tears.

Billy solemnly swung his head back and forth. "You was right. I need to go. You don't know me, and if I stay I will destroy this place. Now, sign my name." Wesley hesitated, then signed Billy's name. "Draw a line for my mark," said Billy, and Wesley scratched a line next to the signature. Billy reached over and took the pen from Wesley's hand and scribbled an X on the line.

He straightened up and said. "Thank you. Date it, please." Billy stopped at the door and said, "It has been very much a pleasure knowin' you all. I appreciate it."

The next morning, he rode off on the mule with the squirrel gun in front of him across the saddle.

Chapter 22. Silver City, 1875

Margaret "Maggie" White stood on the back landing of the house, a porch without steps suspended above the dwellings spread out below. She looked down the hillside at theirbricks and clapboards stained with grime, most of them empty since the Plum Minehad shut down. The sun sat low in the east, just peeking out over the mountains far in the distance. Another dawn, another day.

She wore a white chemise frilly on the shoulders and undone in the front, white crotch-less bloomers, and nothing else. No matter, she felt hot even this early in the morning. Of course, her avoirdupois would make her suffer the heat no matter what the season or weather. At age thirty eight, gone was her youth and with it her girlish figure. She wasn't massive, she knew, but any affect of a wasp waist was a wishful memory. She didn't miss the corset, but that's why the boyos didn't bother with her anymore, she thought, puffing daintily on her cigarillo. Of course, not many boyos around anymore, either, with the Virginia & Truckee railroad up and running. She held the cigarillo in her hand bent at the wrist, her elbow resting cupped in her other palm, supported by its arm stretched crossways just beneath her bodice. She would have to go back to work soon, but still, she waited, smoking.

There. As usual.

A scrawny figure crawled out from under one of the abandoned houses situated on the slope just above her house. He pulled himself up leaning against the clapboard sideand threw up, prodigiously, splattering his shopworn boots. He pushed his head out further and vomited again, this time missing his footwear. Once finished, he pulled a sleeve from his union suit over his hand to wipe his mouth. Then, he yanked the sleeve back and rubbed his belly. At the same time, he scratched his rear end.

What a fuckin' mess, she thought. Every morning, he came out and tossed his biscuits, daily proof that he drank all night every night. She shook her head. How long can this sorry wastrel last? Oblivious to the spy above, the gaunt little man slipped on a denim shirt from beneath the house. After buttoning it up, he brushed it off with his hands as though that made a difference, then ran his fingers through his oily red hair to comb it. He rubbed the stubble of his blondish-red beard, but gave it up since he clearly had no means to shave it.

Once he had pulled himself together as best as he could, he slowly descended from thefront of the house past Maggie's perchto the dirt road below. Off to earn his living, she thought.

Maggie turned around and opened the screen door quickly, so as not to let any flies in the house. Otto greeted her in the kitchen.

""'Mornin', Maggie" he said, without looking at her. He scrubbed dishes in a huge iron bowl. "Get your morning coffee, gonna be a busy day."

"Oh? The cavalry coming through?"

"No, nothin' like that. I just have a feelin' is all."

A feeling, thought Maggie, a sure thing. Otto greeted every day with a feeling. Things were going to change, a spur of the Comstock Lode would be found here, bring back the mines and the mills. All the railroad bridges to Virginia City would collapse suddenly, bringing back the freight wagons to Silver City. None of this was going to happen, but that grizzled old groundhog with his shock of wheat eyebrows woke up with new hope every day, only to go to bed every night with the same old disappointment.

Still, her job at the Pleasant Times Parlour House was to keep the bed sheets changed for the two fallen angelsupstairs. She swept out the rooms, dusted the delicate oil lamps, washed the dishes after lunch and dinner, and performed any other chore that might come up. That included bedding the desperate stranger whenever one came along. Thank Baby Jesus they sent the laundry out to Chung to wash, one of the last Chinamen left in town. The rest had moved on to Gold Hill, Virginia City, Pine Grove, and other towns still booming. Out of fifty saloons that once operated in Silver City, but two remained open. That was twice asmany watering holes in the town as livery stables and hotels. The fire house stood vacant, used rarely by volunteers if a conflagration broke out. Off in the distance rested mines and mills sagging and rusting. Only the cemetery was well populated these days.

They did have a jail, presided over by Sheriff Albert Hermann of stout German stock. He was easygoing, pleasant to meet on the street, but hard when somebody acted up, local or stranger. His place of business saw the most traffic in town, though he enjoyed a lot of down time, too. A widower of twenty years, he came over for a poke now and then for old time's sake. She didn't mind.

Better get to it, she thought, swallowing her black coffee in one gulp. Not much of a breakfast eater, she marveled at how she never wasted away, far from it. It must be eating lunch and dinner regularly, and the beer, of course. She passed by a looking glass hanging in the parlor and stopped in front. She still owned a cute little doll's face, if a bit long, with bee stung lips, though these days her curly black locks sported a few grey strands. Her eyes were still stark green, though, the only ageless feature left to her. She shrugged and moved on. Keep doing this job until it wasn't there to do anymore, she said to herself. Then what?

Upstairs, she stripped the beds, and took the bedspreads out on the front balcony to shake off the dust. She snapped one in the air, folded it, and hung it on the railing. She lifted up the other, and stopped. The gaunt, red-haired drunk meandered below, heading up the dusty street, his hands in his pockets, on his way to breakfast at the Silver Dollar. She shook her head and shook out the other blanket.

The sheriff stopped by in the evening. "What's your pleasure, Constable Hermann?" Maggie asked with a smile.

"How about a beefsteak and a thick slice of bread, Miss White, or should I say Mrs.?"

"Happy to oblige," she said. She tossed her head, "The 'Mrs.' days are long gone. Miss White will do fine." She said it with a bit of a bite. Hermann knew very well her situation after all these years. She shrugged, "So, canned peas, too?"

"And apple sauce, if there's any."

Maggie nodded and went in to give Otto the order. When she returned, the sheriff had pulled up a chair at the end of the trestle table, his black Stetson hanging on the back. A blond man turning gray, his gentle features suggested calm and reassurance, a demeanor attractive to most people, men and women alike. Twenty years her senior, Maggie found him just as appealing as the rest did. She allowed her eyes to soften a bit and said, "So, will you be staying the night?"

The sheriff's mouth tightened into a scowl, "I am afraid not tonight. I have a prisoner in the jail. Drunk and disorderly again."

"The red-headed boy, all skin and bones?"

Hermann nodded, "The town sweeper. I found him face down in the street, his feet up on the walkway. I thought I should bring him in, see if he was all right. He was, but ....." He shrugged his shoulders. "At least he'll get a meal and a place to sleep for the night."

"Yeah, well, the lad looks like he could use it for sure."

"Yes, but he's not much of a lad. Oh, he looks young, but he's older, I think. He has an old shell jacket from the war that he wears when it's colder."

"Oh? How long has he been here?"

"I'm thinking four, five months, perhaps. Could be longer, he just came to my attention about then."

"Huh. I think I've only noticed him for a few weeks. What's his name?"

"McKinney, William McKinney. He says people call him Billy. He's from the South, I believe, considering his accent. His tunic is gray, anyway."

"Is that a fact? Huh."

"Yes. Could you ask Otto to rustle up something for him to eat? I can take it when I'm finished here."

"Yes, of course, Sheriff. I'll get him now."

Maggie didn't give it much thought until she saw the wastrel again while she stood barefoot on the back landing. She risked getting a splinter, but she enjoyed the warm sun so much and wiggling her toes, she was willing to chance it. Again, smoking her morning stogie, she saw him emerge from the crawlspace of the house below. Again, he bent over and upchucked.

She sighed. What a sráide.

He straightened up and twisted around in her direction, standing as if in a daze. Maggie blew out air, and called down, "You, feller. Yes, you. Are you hungry? Thirsty?"

Startled, the gaunt figure placed his hand fingers spread open on his breast, appearing quizzical.

"Yes, you," she said sternly. "Do you want a bite of bread and jam?"

He hesitated, then bobbed his head up and down. "All right, then, come down around the hill up to the front door."

She met him at the door with a wet towel. "Here," she said, throwing the towel at him, "clean yourself up. And, take your brogans off before you come inside."

He ate manically, stuffing his cheeks with jam-covered bread so that he could barely chew at all. They sat in the kitchen on stools, a third one in the middle between his legs with the plate on it.

"Sweet Jesus, I thought you got a full meal last night."

286

"You mean in the clink?" he said in a muffled voice. He pushed the mound of food in his mouth to one side and said, "That lined my innards. This is fillin' 'em."

She nodded silently, holding her chin in one hand. "So, you're William McKinney."

He moved his head up and down as he cleared his mouth again, "Billy. That's what they call me."

"Who?" Maggie said. "You have kin around here? Where are you from?"

Billy swallowed a lump, and said, "Maryville, Tennessee. Actually, in the hills thereabouts."

"And, you're all the way here in Nevada?"

"Yes'um," he said. "I been a few places these past few years."

She watched him for a time. He was pretty white, freckled a little bit on top, and red in the face and neck from the sun. He had blue eyes and gazed at her like a true innocent. She noted that he was missing only a few teeth, an eye tooth on the right, and a lower one in front. She wondered if he was an idiot or something.

"How the hell do you survive here, Billy McKinney? The mine's gone, freighting's gone, there isn't anything around here but sage, gravel, dry hills, and cold mountains. The water's alkali, terrible to drink. How do you get by at all?"

He lifted and dropped his shoulders. "I don't tend to drink a lot of water." He burped, "'S'cuse me, ma'm. I do this and that when I can. Sweep a lot a floors, pick up scraps here and there. I get by."

Maggie shook her head ruefully, "I honestly don't see how. You look pretty well on your way to being dead, Billy McKinney."

His hackles raised a little as he said, "I been doin' okay for thirty years, now. On my own for the past thirteen."

Maggie put her hands on her knees and sat up, "Well, I for one am amazed. You must be much more resourceful than I imagined."

Billy didn't reply.

She swung her head back and forth ruefully. "You're an odd feller, Billy. I don't see much in the way of a future for you." She sighed, and thought for a moment. "Tell you what. You promise not to vomit tomorrow morning, I'll fix you breakfast again. If you lose last night's supper, stay away. You can lick it back up. What do you say?"

He shrugged again, "Sure. I can't make no promises, I do plan on drinkin' later. But, I'll see if I can ease up a bit. A good breakfast picks a man up for sure."

Maggie nodded, "All right. I'll be watching you, so don't try to hide anything."

The next morning, Billy stumbled out of the crawl space and spewed forth the night's intake. Maggie dropped her head, saying under her breath, "Eejit."

She went on with her routine, cleaning the house, making the beds, taking meal orders, guiding the girls, teasing Otto, and chatting up the sheriff. Several mornings later, she heard a knock at the door. Billy stood on the front porch, his wretched hat curled up in both hands, a look of contrition on his baby face.

"Hello, Ma'm. Just wanted to tell you I didn't puke this mornin'."

Maggie gazed at him frigidly. "No money for whiskey last night?"

He shifted uncomfortably and she relented. "All right, come in. I'll get you a nibble."

She put out some cold fried potatoes, a square of goat's cheese, and some beef jerky, which he tucked into as though it had all come freshly off the griddle. While he ate, she grilled him. Where're you from? Where've you been? What did you do?

Billy told her his sad tale, pressed into service with the Secesh even though he was a devout ab'litionist from the east Tennessee mountains. He mentioned running into trouble and having to run lickety-split from the regulators. He told her how he'd fallen in with a band of runaway slaves, how they ran west to Injun Territory only to learn the Redmen was in with the Graybacks. He described how they changed course into Kansas where they fought for the Yankees, then set up a farmstead out on the plains, breakin' horses and huntin' buffalo, antelope, even moose.

Maggie thought she'd never heard a more outrageous tale in her life. Then, again, his name was McKinney. She stared at the bony lout sitting opposite her, his scrubby little beard, stained teeth, and pushed-back greasy hair. His clothes were disgusting, wrinkled and filthy, and she could smell him from across the table. His expression mimicked that of a dog, soulful, sad eyes, cringing ready for the next blow. She shook her head slowly.

"I have work to do."

He smiled uneasily, and said, "Well, I gotta get on my way myself."

"Right. Same deal tomorrow. Come back if you're sober, I'll give you a meal. If not, don't bother."

"Yes'um. I know the rules."

"Yeah, well," she said as he moved to the front hallway, "see if you can't get a bath, too."

He was out the door.

Maggie fed him breakfast almost every day for the next three weeks. He arrived in the morning without fail for the first week, then missed a day the following week. He missed the first day of the third, but made it for four straight mornings after that.

"Out huntin' jackass rabbits," he explained.

"Oh. Get any?" she said.

"No," he said ruefully. "Come up empty. All I got is a couple of snares."

"Too bad," she said, "you must have been hungry."

At the end of a month, he managed to show up every morning in line with her rules. He still drank plenty, she knew, but tailed off at night to be presentable in the morning. He seemed to her to be less grungy. His clothes were still stained and grimy, but he looked as though he had scrubbed his face and combed his hair. Blessed Mary, she thought, she hoped he wasn't getting the wrong idea.

Over a breakfast of scrambled eggs, ham, and biscuits, Billy ate at close to normal speed. Maggie watched him, observing that he looked like he'd gained a few pounds. They chatted more, what little gossip there was about town, goings on at the Hardwicke House, the slender yield at the Welty Silver Mine. Welty was the last mine in Siver City still open, though barely. On her own, such subjects drove home to Maggie that these measurements of the town fading presaged the end of her current livelihood. She put it out of her mind when talking with Billy.

"So, how in God's name did you end up here in Nevada?"

"Well, the war wound down, then it was over. One by one, the black boys left to go back home, for different reasons, I guess. They was one family who stayed on the farm, made a go of it. I was kinda the square peg in a round hole, so I rode off. Went back into Oklahoma, shot buffalo for the army for a time. Hooked up with a bunch of black cowboys in west Texas. That went okay for a while, but they got a little mad with me for a few little slipups I made."

"Such as?" Maggie asked.

"Well, I fell asleep on night lookout a couple of times, and some of the steers wandered off. After that, me and them cowboys parted ways. I heard about the silver and gold finds in Nevada, so I headed up to Pueblo, sold my horse and bought a fare on the railroad. Caught the Denver Rio Grande up to Cheyenne, switched over and rode the Pacific all the way to Reno. Headed up to the mountains to find my fortune."

Maggie nodded, "That went well for you."

"As good as anyone, I suppose. Started like everyone did, placer prospecting, panning, the like. Found some gold, never could keep a hold of it for long, though. Everything is expensive in a boom town, you know?"

"I imagine Red Eye is, too."

"Yeah," said Billy, "I downed my fair share of that for sure." He toyed with his fork, pushing the greasy crumbs around on his plate. "I just couldn't find that vein. I moved on to Virginia City, see if I could find a blind lead near the Comstock. No such luck. I was busted out, so I signed up to work in the mine. Right under main street, thousands of feet below. We hammerin' away at the walls, throwin' ore into small cars pulled up top to be crunched up and melted for the good stuff. Our shift done, they hall us up on a car, we all cramped over 'cause of the low ceiling, give you a pretty good idea of what a man's last trip beneath the ground must be like. When we finally come out up top, it was dark outside like we never left. Next day, we go down again in the dark.

"We was so tired, we set out straight for The Office, get a glass of Triple X and a cutlet, paid plenty, too. We was too tired to wash up, looked like raccoons with dust all around exceptin' our eyeballs. The pay was good, but not all that good. The boys who owned the digs was the ones sportin' diamonds on their pinkies. We all just had busted fingernails.

"I would'a continued underground for longer, I guess. I knew the other fellas, we got along, enjoyed our company in the saloons. This one old guy, shorter than me but twice as heavy, he came all the way here from England. Cornish, he said he was. Worked forever in coal mines over there 'til they hired him to come here. 'Share the wisdom of 'is waies,' he said. I could hardly make out his words. He let me tag along, learned me a good bit about diggin' ore, how to pace myself, save my strength for all day, mostly. Said he was stayin' long enough to make a pile of money, then be off back to his kin in England. Eddie, his name was, Eddie Teague. Old enough to be my daddy but strong as any mule I ever saw. We was talkin' about nothin', him standing maybe five feet from me just on the other side of some timbers. Next thing you know, he's under maybe fifty tons of mountain, just one arm stickin' out, his one finger pointin' straight ahead.

290

"They was soundin' alarms and all, 'and we hightailed it to the closest car shaft, each of us climbin' in and shoutin' at them to yank us up. That was the longest trip I ever took in them movin' coffins. When we got up top, the entire mine collapsed. Lost forty-eight men. Never got a body out, not even Eddie's. Closed that shaft for good. Last time I worked underground, too.

"I worked for a few more months in a stampin' mill, soul-killing work. They had a battery of six stampers slammin' away day and night. We stood by breakin' up rocks with a sledge and shovelin' it into the battery. The heavy stamping rods pound 'em into dust, which mixed with a little water turns into silver paste. They didn't miss a trick, used to throw in quicksilver to catch the smallest specks of silver and gold. On top of that, we added salt and copper to keep the precious stuff and the quicksilver from stickin' together. Some smart science fellas figured this all out, but we was the ones who had to do the work. And at the end of every day, we had to clean everything, blankets, screens, and all that, then start it all over again the next day, dawn to dusk. Might as well stayed in the mines, get more pay. Anyway, I got sick of it pretty quick, and quit. That ended my minin' days."

Maggie already knew most of what went on in the mines and the mills, but she never really heard a firsthand account before. She'd seen hundreds of miners in her day, maybe thousands, but Billy's story explained why they all looked so haunted and worn out.

"So, what do you do now?" she asked quietly.

"To get by? Asa Jackson tosses a few dollars my way for tendin' his hosses, muck out the stalls, get 'em fodder, things like that. He let me stay in the stable last winter, I kept warm usin' a pile of hoss blankets. Other folks give me the odd job, Harry at the General Store has me sweep the walk, shovel snow after a fall. I pretty much sweep every floor in town. I go out to the old Plum Mine once in a while after a rain, see if any silver tailings show up. And, some people stand me for a meal once in a while out of their Christian hearts," he said, fixing his sight on Maggie, "like you."

Maggie averted her eyes, "I don't have a Christian heart. Just extra eggs and potatoes."

"Yet, I do appreciate your generous sharing."

"Yes, well, don't get too used to it."

They spent the rest of the summer and most of the fall meeting for breakfast, whenever Billy didn't go on a bender. When he did, the next time she'd see him, she acted snotty. She'd criticize him for his slovenly appearance or just not say a word as she slapped down the plate. Still, whenever he showed up, she never failed to serve him.

The first snow that winter buried Silver City beneath four feet, followed by a freezing rain that hardened the surface into a slippery, impassable shell. Everyone in the town hunkered down wherever they were, wrapped in buffalo robes and wool army blankets close to wood burners and fires. Swathed in every scrap of cloth they could find, Otto and the girls clung together next to the fireplace in the parlor. Maggie stood close by wearing a heavy canvas duster over three layers of dresses, shivering as she stared out the frost covered window. Peering out of the crystal encrusted panes, she searched for movement on the street. Before, she had tried to step out on the back landing to see if he was down below, but the treacherous ice and breathtaking cold forced her back inside. Next to the front window, she kept her chilling vigil, even knowing that no one alive would be out there, while anyone dead would be unmoving.

The two parlor house girls Jean and Sally Mae sang hymns in harmony. They practiced long hours together while waiting for gentlemen callers to visit the house. Tall and angular, with black hair and black eyes, Jean conducted their effort. Blond Sally Mae, young with big blue eyes and a baby-fat pudginess to her, followed her older companion. Every now and then Otto would join in with his ragged baritone, and the girls would swat him playfully on his shoulder to stop, telling him he simply could not sing. They would all laugh together, then the girls would start another gospel song. Maggie listened but never joined in. Why practice singing, she thought, when Otto was the only one among them welcome at the church services?

The fire started to die and Otto made a move to rise and throw on more logs.

"We're runnin' out inside here," he tsked. "I guess I'll see if I can get more wood off the front porch."

Maggie grabbed him by the arm. "Otto, do you think we could make it to the livery stable? Maybe pick-axe a path?"

Otto looked down on her with gentle eyes. "I don't think so, Maggie, I'm sorry. I doubt we could even get to the shed to get a pick, and the stable's a good half-mile from here." Her face dropped and he said, "Don't worry, that vagabond's been living in the mountains for a long time. He'll make it through this blizzard like he's done a hundred times before."

She dipped her head hopefully, feeling worried at the same time.

In two days, the melt began and Maggie badgered Otto to get a pick and help her bust a path through to Jackson's Livery. After several hours of cracking the snowcap and pushing aside the pieces, they managed to snowshoe their way to the horse barn. Asa, the only black man in Silver City, met them at one of the stable doors. He stood straight, bundled up in a fur-lined campaign coat left over from his days in the cavalry, his felt hat tied down over his ears with a scarf. When they reached him, Asa started by shaking his head silently.

"He ain't here. I kept an eye out for him, but the fall came too fast. I 'spect he holed up somewhere else close to where he was."

Horrified, Maggie immediately turned around to trace her steps back to the house. Otto had to move her aside to get in front so that he could cut a path when necessary. They made it back in a half hour, and Maggie had Otto smash the ice to the abandoned place across the road behind the Parlour House's back landing. Once there, he shoveled out the crawl space where they found Billy, ice-cold blue in his buffalo robe, but still alive.

As they walked him back up the hill to the house, she breathed in his ear, "For Christ sake, why didn't you come here first? We'd of taken you in, you fuckin' eejit!"

They brought him inside and started to warm him by the fire.

"From now on, you come to the house. Drunk or sober, you come here. I will not see all those breakfasts wasted, do you hear?"

Billy swept the path in front of the Parlour House to the street. After he finished, he would gather firewood for the stove and logs for the parlor room fireplace. Maggie would have breakfast for him by then, and they would eat before he went out to find an odd job or two to earn a few bucks. As he swept, he reflected on how lucky he had it, a place to stay and steady meals. He had bounced back from near freezing to death and he'd expected to go right back to fulltime scavenging. But Maggie wouldn't stand for it. "I've invested too much in you already, McKinney, Lord knows why. You stay here for the winter. After that, you're a free man in a free country and you may go off and kill yourself in any fashion you like."

As he swept, he saw her in front of him, her curly black hair that she brushed from her face all the time. Her pursed, red lips formed a cupid mouth that exploded into a full free smile when she laughed, her eyes flashing green and golden light. She laughed mostly at stupid things he did, which drove him to do more stupid things to tell her about. No matter how ridiculous he was, she always treated him well.

"There's a small linen closet that you can sleep in. Just move the sheets off the bottom shelf, remove the plank, and you should have enough room to bed down. If you have anything you want to store, you can keep it there."

He nodded and trekked over to Asa's to retrieve his knapsack. He carefully placed it on the side of the closet wall closest to his head when he slept.

"That's all you have?" she asked. "What's in it?"

"Not all that much," Billy said, "just a couple of keepsakes."

"Can I see?" Maggie said.

Almost reluctantly, he reached into the sack. He brought out the picture first, bent and broken in a few places with the corners worn off.

"This is your family?" Maggie askes softly.

He bobbed his head. "My daddy, my mama, little sister Bess, and me," he said, pointing at himself.

"You're so young," Maggie said, "such a baby." She studied the portrait, then said, "Your mama has passed, here."

Billy nodded again, "And little sister. Died of the croup."

Scrutinizing the image carefully, she bit her lower lip, murmuring, "I lost my two babies to diphtheria. My little darlings, gone."

"I'm sorry to hear that," Billy said. "I didn't know you was married, had children."

"Oh, yes, sixteen years old. Married to a lawyer in Philadelphia. He wanted to come west, establish a big practice out here in the silver fields." She glanced up at Billy for an instant. "You know, file claims, settle disputes, that sort of thing." She dropped her eyes back to the battered portrait. "Figured he'd start ranching, too. We were living on a small spread outside of Gold Hill when Henry, my oldest, became sick. He had a high fever, then started sneezing bloody snot. My baby girl Julie contracted it quickly after that. Then, I caught it. All of us were so sick. I tried to break their fevers but they left me just like that. I got worse, and my husband went to find a doctor. The doctor was able to save me, but no more kids for me."

She fingered the old photo while Billy tried to think of what to do, what to say next. "What happened to your husband?"

"Robert? Oh, he went to Virginia City on business one day, never came back. Shot dead playing cards in the Millionaires Club, can you imagine?"

"I'm sorry to hear that."

"He was a harsh man. I wasn't so much distressed at his passing as I was wondering how I was going to make a living."

"What'd you do?"

"I read in the *Territorial Enterprise* a notice for a schoolmarm in Silver City. I came here and taught in the schoolhouse for six years. It was a happy sad time for me being around all those kids just about the same age as my little ones. But, I loved them."

"So, why'd you quit?" Billy asked.

Maggie looked at him in a slightly puckish way. "I didn't quit. Silver City went bust, everyone with kids moved on, emptying the schoolhouse. There were none to teach, and the city couldn't afford to pay me."

"After that?"

She rolled her eyes in exasperation, "What do you think? I came here and joined the brides of the multitude." Billy scrunched up his brow, and she said, "You know, a daughter of desire, a soiled dove. A chippie." He still wasn't getting it, so she said, "I laid back and spread my legs."

"Oh," Billy said, staring at her in a different light.

"I haven't always been this ample. Back then I was considered a female divine."

Billy thought she still was.

"Oh, come on," Maggie said, "don't tell me you've never taken pleasure with a whore. All those years you rode with cowboys and soldiers?"

Billy dropped his head, a troubled expression on his face. "I did a couple times, I guess," he said, "I don't recall it that well. I ain't much with the ladies. Maybe I was too drunk."

"Maybe you were," Maggie said. She changed the subject. "So, what else you have in that bag?"

Billy reached in and pulled out his gray shell jacket, dirty and tattered. He unfolded it to reveal a bundle wrapped in oil-stained muslin. He carefully removed layers one after another until the contents were revealed.

"What in God's name is that?"

"It's a gun, a pistol."

"That's the strangest pistol I've ever seen. What kind is it?"

"It's a revolver. See? This flat chamber rests on top. It got seven chambers for seven rounds."

"Is it old? How did you get it?"

"It's old, back before the war. I got it from a southern colonel before I left the Grays."

"He gave it to you?"

Billy shifted uncomfortably. "Well, I sort of shot him with it."Seeing her incredulous look, he told her the entire story. "That's why I ran."

Maggie sat back in her chair, unsettled in her thoughts. She examined him for some time, then said, "It sounds like the colonel's death was an accident."

"None of them woulda seen it that way."

"Perhaps not.But that," she said, waving an index finger at the gun, "that isdangerous. Why keep it? In fact, why keep it hidden away if you see it as protection?"

Billy shrugged his shoulders. "I don't know. I've had it a long time."

Her expression became pained. "Billy, why didn't you go back home after the war? Why didn't you go back to your da'?"

Billy shifted his sight past her. "I don't know. I was afraid, I suppose."

"Of what?"

"I don't know. Of what I'd find, or what I might not find. I don't know."

She nodded solemnly, handing his picture back to him.

Another fierce storm swept through Silver City that night, and the wind knocked snow down the chimneys, dousing all the fires. Billy lay in the linen closet, sheets and blankets piled all around him. He was still shivering when the door opened, and he saw light from a candle. A voice came from the figure holding the candle. "Come with me," said Maggie. "It's too cold to sleep alone."

The first few nights, they simply slept close together. When the storm passed and the fires were lit, she still kept him in her bed. Eventually, she embraced him and moved against him.

He remembered her as being warm and wonderful then and after that. The best part was hugging close and talking forever. He told her how much he missed Bev and Josh, and the Wilsons. He confessed that he was afraid to return home because of what he had become. He also told her how puny he felt when everyone around him told him what they had seen in the paper, which he couldn't read. That was one of the reasons he never tried to go back to the farmstead in

Kansas or his daddy's farm. He just hadn't amounted to much of a man.

Maggie said in the dark, "Well, I can't fix your drinking, that's for you to decide. But, I do believe I still have some of my school books tucked away. We can work on that, we can get you started reading. It's going to be a long winter, after all. We'll be needing something to do."

He was learning, too, faster than he thought. But, he didn't have much to offer in return. Pushing the broom up and down all over town, brushing Asa's horses, all those small chores didn't amount to much. Nothing that he could bring to her, he thought. He wanted to take her away from Silver City, take her to faraway places, exotic places, bring her things she deserved for being so nice to him. But, how was he going to do that? How could he get what he needed so that she would stay with him? He needed to figure it all out, somehow, he needed to figure out something.

Chapter 23. Tailings

After staying warm throughout the winter for the first time in a long time, Maggie enjoyed the arrival of spring. Billy acted the child, cozying up to her in the way that her lost little ones had done this many years ago. She still welcomed the occasional visit by Sheriff Hermann and the updates on the town and its residents. Some boy had stolen a bundle of clothes from Sun and Chung, got caught immediately and was thrown into the hoosegow. The kid was so skinny, Hermann said, he managed to escape by climbing up out of the chimney.

Maggie laughed out loud and said, "So, did you organize a posse to run him down?"

Hermann shook his head, puffing on a stogie while scratching his belly through his long johns. "Isn't worth a penny's effort. Hell, there're plenty of desperadoes enough out there to keep us busy. Highwaymen at Devil's Gate just waiting to hold up some poor placer on his way to the Virginia City assay office. Those are the boys that get the law's attention, shoot you as soon as look at you."

Billy, on the other hand, offered the pleasure of asking the questions, ones she could answer easily enough. He also proved to be an apt pupil, learning to read and write well beyond her expectations for a southern hayseed. His progress had reached the point that she had to send him off by himself with some of her old books to give herself some rest. He still went off on his benders, too, disappearing on occasion for days at a time. When he showed up bedraggled and shamefaced, she sent him to the linen closet to dry out. He was barred from her bed until he took a bath.

As the weather warmed, however, there was no talk about Billy leaving the house, anytime soon at least. He usually spent mornings looking for day work and returning most nights at dinner time. He worked at the livery stable fairly often, but Asa couldn't pay him much. He slung ice at the Hardwicke House during the temperate months, and swept the floors at the General Store and at Donovan's Hospitality Saloon and the Golden Gate Bar and Hotel. Lately, he tried to avoid the latter two, since he tended to drink up his wages after work, given the convenience of the locations. After that, there was no point in going back to the house to suffer the unspoken disapproval of Maggie. Better to bunk out back on those occasions.

298

When nothing easy came his way, Billy would head up the road between the hills at the Devil's Gate into the adjoining ravine to the Plum Mine. The Plum Company abandoned the mine several years ago when the cost of extraction and milling outpaced its silver production. Heaps of tailings surrounded the rusting equipment near a looming, vacant stamping mill. Black entrances of abandoned mine shafts gaped open close by, and a sizeable pond lay just a few yards north of the entire complex.

The tailings had been worked over many times through the years, leaving the pond water a milky graphite color punctuated by gaseous slicks on its surface. Like many other down-on-their-luck prospectors, Billy used a shovel, two buckets, a pan, and a metal screen to sift through the mine residue for leftover granules of silver. After several hours of labor, he might accrue a small bag of tiny nuggets to exchange for paper tender at the assay office in Virginia City, another two miles away. There, he had plenty of drinking establishments available to quench his thirst. Such proximity usually delayed to the next day the five-mile return walk to Silver City. Sometimes, if the tailings were good, he didn't return for the next few days. More often than not, though, the hours he spent hardly amounted enough to pay for one drink. Then, he would stash the bag of silver grains and his tools in a shallow cave in a nearby hill. When pickings in Silver City were slim again, he would trek back up to the Plum Mine pond for another crack at panning hoping to fill the rest of the leather bag. These days, though, filling the bag confronted him with a decision. Head up to Virginia City and carry on, or tuck the bag away again for other possibilities.

This time, Billy hid a full bag away. He knew well that his resolve might easily fail him on the very next trip, or any trip after that. In fact, he was sure of it. He shook his head dejectedly. Saving was not his strength, which meant that he needed to make more money faster. Maybe he would have to go to Virginia City and go back into the mines. The thought nearly made him sick.

"You have progressed so well," said Maggie, "you might even write a letter."

"A letter?" Billy said. "Who to?"

They lay side by side in her bed, fully clothed, reading together by yellow lamplight while waiting for Otto to hammer the iron ring for dinner. Maggie turned onto her side. "You could write me a letter," she said.

"Now, why would I do that?" said Billy. "You're right here."

"Well, for practice."

"You make me practice all the time. I don't need no more practice.

"Anymore practice. Okay, then," she said, thinking, "how about to a friend? How about to your friends on the farm back in Kansas?"

Billy shook his head, "I ain't got nothin' to write them about. They don't need to hear from me."

"Oh, come on, they would be glad to get a letter from you. I'll bet they wonder where you are all the time, what you've been doing with yourself."

"That take maybe two sentences. That's all I can write anyhow."

"Oh, don't be so pitiful. You've had many exciting adventures they'd enjoy reading about. You could fill an entire journal with them."

"Naw," Billy yawned, "I don't think so."

Maggie laid back. She thought for a moment, then turned to Billy again.

"All right," she said, "then, how about your friends from Kentucky, the ones you escaped with?"

Billy stopped, then said, "I have no idea where they are. I don't think Josh can even read."

"The other fellow can. You told me he could read. What was his name? Beverly?"

"Bev. Bev Bowman. No one calls him Beverly. It Bev, and he can read."

"Then, write him a letter. "

"Where would I send it? What would I say?"

"Tell him where you are and what you've been doing. Tell him you would like to know how he is. Ask him if he found his lady friend and his brother. There's a lot you could write."

"That is a lot. I don't know if I could do that."

"I'll help you, Billy."

"But, where would I send it?"

"Send it to your farmer friends in Kansas. If he hasn't come back to them, they might know where he is. They can forward the letter to him. Send it to the gentleman in Memphis, too. We'll make two copies. If your Kansas friends—"

"The Wilsons."

"—if the Wilsons don't know where he is, your friend in Memphis might."

"Burkle, Mr. Jacob Burkle."

"It's worth a try. With two letters going to your common friends, one of them is bound to reach Mr. Bowman."

"Maybe," Billy said. He fell silent, his mind going back and forth from the past to the present. "What would I write?"

"Write and tell him that you want to know how he is. Tell him that you miss him."

Billy looked Maggie in the eyes. "I do miss him. That I do."

Dear Bev Bowman,

This is your old friend (I hope) Billy McKinney. I hope you remember me. I have learned to write and to read. This may surprise you. You know me as a real huckleberry, I bet. I have a friend who has taught me how. Maggie makes sure I am right in what I am writing. We live in Silver City Nevada. I have not struck it rich. But I eat regular.

I would like to know how you are, if you do not mind telling me. You can write me. If I can not understand what you write, Maggie can tell me what I do not know. She is very honest so you can tell me the truth. I hope you are well and found Eli well and Miss Mary Louise. Tell me where you live and what you do.

With great friendship, may the Lord bless you.
William (Billy) McKinney

Maggie helped him copy the letter and address each one "in care of" the Wilson Family, and Mr. Jacob Burkle.

"C-slash O," said Billy, gazing at the front of one envelope. "'In care of.' That what it mean, huh?"

"It saves space," said Maggie. "There. Now, all we need to do is go to the post office and mail them."

The U.S. Post Office stood in the center of town, a single-story, wooden structure with three rooms that ran front and back like railroad cars. The first room was relatively large, with a long, pinewood wall stretching from one side to the other, topped by a small ledge and a screen all the wat to the the ceiling. Two small, half-oval windows in the screen allowed the exchange of mail between the civil servants and the town citizens. Behind the postal workers, Billy could see stacks of envelopes and packages piled on top of desks withbulging canvas bags resting against them on all sides. Adoor in the back opened on to another room where he spied a wood-burning stove and some chairs. Beyond that, he couldn't see anything else, although he supposed that the last room served as quarters for the postmaster and his kin.

Maggie stepped up to one of the windows and handed over the two letters, asking that appropriate postage be affixed. While she waited, Billy gazed at the walls outside of the cage covered with various handbills and notices. Some with pictures on one wall caught his attention.

The first was for Black Bart, $1,000. The Sonora Stagecoach Company out of San Francisco had put up the reward. Billy looked at the etching of a grizzled old man with a gray, handle-bar moustache and thin, gray hair. Another flier from Wells Fargo offered $300 for the same desperado dead or alive. Billy read one for Andrew Jackson "Big Jack" Davis, $500, also for robbing stages, this time right here in Nevada. The most amazing poster declared a $4,000 reward for John Wesley Hardin, murderer, sighted in Texas, Alabama, and Florida.

The entire wall was festooned with similar indictments, none offering less than $100. Another from Nevada caught his eye, John Heaney, for rustling, horse theft, stage robbery, and murder, $1,500, dead or alive. Seen in parts of California, Nevada, Utah, and Arizona. Heaney's sketch showed a cold-eyed expression and lean, curled lips beneath a broad cavalry hat with braid tassels. Below, he wore a checkered shirt buttoned at the neck. Surrounding him were handbills of other men, known members of his gang.

"The letters have been posted," Maggie said behind him. "Are you ready to go?"

Billy quickly glanced around, then back at the wall. Nick Worthington, New Mexico, Colorado, horse thievery, murder in cold blood, $600 dead or alive.

"Billy?"

He followed her out the door as she cautioned him not to get his hopes up too high about receiving a reply very soon. Depending upon Bev's whereabouts, most likely the letters would have to be forwarded at least once. Then, his friend would have to write a letter back, and just its delivery could take a considerable amount of time as well.

Billy listened to her, half paying attention. If he could capture just one of those outlaws, he would have enough money to do anything he wanted. Then, he remembered the pictures he had just seen, the menace in the expressions of those men. He also remembered how it felt going into battle and the stark dread that had consumed him. He clenched his teeth, wondering if going back into the mines wasn't a better alternative.

He relocated to a boarding house in Virginia City. Maggie was against it, furious that he would even consider leaving after all she had put into minding him. He understood, he felt deeply beholden to her, he said, but he needed to begin earning his own way.

"For what?" she snapped. "For my sake? To be worthy of me? A sporting woman whose best time was far away and long ago? Just what kind of dumb yokel are you? There are lots of other ways to make a buck than burying yourself a thousand feet benath the earth."

"Not as fast, though," he said.

"Fast? Who cares about fast? Slow and sure, the philosophers say, and I'll add 'alive.'"

"I'm sorry, Maggie, but I can't live off you forever. I got to make my own way."

"All of a sudden, now? All right, then, you stupid eedjit, run off to Virginia City, bury yourself crazy. But come winter, don't expect to be sleeping in the linen closet, never mind my bed!"

She left the parlor. Eventually, he left as well.

Billy lasted a week in the mine. Every morning and every evening, he felt the dim darkness folding around him like a black shroud. Every night, he emerged from the hole with sick relief overridden by abiding dread of the next morning just hours away. The tension sent him straight to the Delta, the Gold Hill Saloon, and any number of other watering holes in Virginia City that might dull the shrillness of his fear. He stayed out as late as he could, buying rounds to keep the other groundhogs from leaving for bed. No matter how much Who-Hit-John he drank, the night ended, and he forced himself to straggle back before dawn to the mine head. By week's end, he was out of the boarding house, broke.

He thought of working in a stamping mill, but knew that every penny he earned there also would make its way into saloon registers. He'd find himself out on the streets again soon enough. He sighed, back to sweeping the town, back to bedding down in the crawl space. He threw his knapsack over his shoulder and started walking the five rugged miles separating Virginia from Silver City.

The trudge took him through Gold Hill and into the rocky, dry hills defining the canyons flanking the Devil's Gate. Before he reached it, however, he came upon the cut that led up to the Plum

Mine. When he reached the notch's opening, he wondered if he should climb up to get some water, given the heat of the day. He also realized that his buckets and panning tools rested in the cave up there, too. Since he was here, he might as well try his luck with the tailings.

The pond was about a mile up the rocky hills covered by sage and other scrub. The noon sun beat down upon him and perspiration dripped from his brow and cheeks. As he climbed, he wiped the sweat periodically off his face with his sleeves, alternating each arm.

The slate colored pond drew into sight and the clear running spring that fed it lay just beyond on the far side. Billy usually skirted the pond to the spring that fed it, drank his fill, topped off his canteen, thenstopped by the shallow cave for his tools. This time,as he closed in on the near edge of the pond he noticed something odd, some kind of anomaly in the terrain by its shore. He drew close to see what it was.

A body. Sprawled out in front of the pond, its head near the water. Billy halted at once. He'd seen a few corpses through the years. One couldn't help it, life being hard in the wilderness. The sight of a dead person, though, still arrested him. He breathed in and stepped over it.

The fellow was young, younger than himself, Billy figured. His hair was black and thick and his eyes were open, blue, but opaque from the glaze of death. His mouth hung wide, as though forming a word, also frozen before it could be uttered past his yellowing teeth. He wore a rumpled green and black checkered shirt, pulled apart as though the poor fellow had tugged at it in his mortal throes.But, this unfortunate human's arms lay spread out on either side of his body. Deep, claret blood had formed a halo around the unfortunate's shirt at his breastbone. He'd been shot, all right, or stabbed, in the heart.

Billy surveyed the rest of him, noting his dungarees belted tight and his high riding boots. The boots were quality, which made him think that the poor fellow had not been killed to be robbed.

He sat back on his haunches. What should he do? Probably, go into town and let Sheriff Hermann know about the dead man. But if he left now, the coyotes might make short work of him. He couldn't carry the body to Silver City, it looked to be too heavy, and the way was rough and rocky. Maybe he should bury him to keep the scavengers off. He had his shovel in the cave. The rocky ground would make digging hard though, thought Billy, and it might take all day into the night. So, what to do?

While he mulled the options over, he stared at the corpse. Something caught his eye. The shirt, he realized, it looked familiar. Why was that? He peered at it, trying to cipher it out. A checked shirt, pretty common, except these checks were pretty large, kind of unusual. Black and green, what did that mean? He thought and he thought, and couldn't get it. He smacked himself on his brow, damned head! He stood up, looked down, and it came to him.

Checked shirt, its squares big, black and green. He'd seen a shirt like it, big squares, black but gray, not green. Except, he'd seen that shirt in a black and white picture on a poster. On thatposter, John Heaney, the notorious desperado, wore a shirt with big black and gray squares. Except, Billy thought, green squares could look gray in a black and white picture. This was John Heaney dead here?

Billy lifted his head, his eyes now roving furiously around the shore of the pond. There it was, he thought, in a sage bush a dozen yards away. He hopped over and pulled it out, a cavalry hat with gold tassels in front. John Heaney's hat.

"B'god!" he said, "B'god." Murderer John Heaney, wanted dead or alive for $1,500. Here he was right in front of him, dead as a doornail. "M'god!"

All the money Billy ever needed here for the taking if he could get John Heaney's corpse back to Silver City. But, how? He could go ahead and bury him, but someone else might find the body, or the coyotes and birds might dig him up. Or, maybe the men who killed him were bringing the law back right now to collect their reward. He needed to get the dead outlaw away from here and run to Silver City himself, or they might shoot him, too.

Billy bent down and rolled the cadaver half over. He noticed an empty leather holster big enough for a heavy handgun on the corpse's hip. In the dead man's back pocket, he sawa billfold. Billy slipped it out as he gently allowed the body to roll back down. He opened the billfold and saw that it was empty except for a small, squared scrap of paper. Billy unwrapped it to see some scribbling.

Carroll Polk Esq.
If I am dead tell
　Henry Polk Oklahoma City
May God rest my soul.

Carroll Polk. The dead man was not John Heaney, unless he had stolen the billfold before getting himself killed. The $1,500 seemed to float away in Billy's mind. How did this Polk fellow end up dead here near the slag pond? He perused the body again, closely examining its face. The open, fixed eyes revealed nothing to him of coldness, only distance. From what Billy could remember of the poster, the dead man could be Heaney, or not. He couldn't tell from his features one way or another. Then, Billy suddenly realized that he could make sure no one else could tell the difference, either.

Billy refolded the paper and slid it into his shirt pocket. He turned the stiffening body again and slipped the empty billfold back into the dead man's pocket. Then, he moved around to grab it by the armpits. He tugged it parallel to the pond's edge and dragged it up to the small cave where he stashed his tools.

To make enough room to fit the body in the small crevice, Billy had to hide his tools behind some sage brush. Even so, he was forced to double the corpse over to shove it all the way inside. Then, he stacked large stones at the cave's mouth to conceal it and also keep predators at bay. Before closing up the cave, though, he took the bag of silver tailings and tucked it into his trousers. When he was sure he had everything secured, he stood up, stretched, and started quickly down the path to Silver City.

Billy reached town two hours later and marched directly to the general store. Bobby Evans stood behind the counter stacking cans of peas in a pyramid. When he spotted, Billy, he showed his surprise.

"Billy, where you been? I got some serious sweeping for you out front." In his mid-forties, Bobby Evans stood about five-eight high on a firm frame that he always draped in a wool suitto signify his station as chair of the town council. He sported a moustache joined to a goatee,with round, wire-rimmed glasses adding the finishing touch to his professional demeanor. Because of the heat, however, this afternoon he worked in his shirtsleeves, rolled up and secured by garters. His suit jacket covered a tall stool behind the counter for quick access in case a fellow town dignitary entered the store.

"I been minin', Mr. Evans, up Virginia City ways. Got some tailings for you all."

He pulled out the small leather bag and handed it over to Evans, who pulled up a set of scales onto the counter. He carefully poured the silver bits on the scales and watched the needle bounce up and down, settling on the half-moon weight gauge. After scrutinizing the results, Evans said, "I'll give you four dollars."

"That ain't much, Mr. Evans," Billy said. "Can't you spare a little more?"

Evans pulled a handkerchief from his pocket, removed his glasses, and proceeded to rub the lenses. "I suppose I can give you five dollars—" he said, concentrating on his polishing.

"That be good," Billy said.

"—if you sweep the front walk."

Billy said, "Awright, but I can't right now, I have somethin' else I gotta do."

"Really? Well, that's a problem, isn't it."

"Looky, Mr. Evans," Billy said, "I promise to sweep the walk later—"

"Oh, I don't know about that," said Evans.

"—and I'll spend the whole five bucks right here, right now."

"Right now? I guess I could front you a fiver, then."

"That's great, Mr. Evans, thank you, thank you so much."

"So, what can I get you?"

"I need some .38 paper cartridges."

Evan pulled his head back, his face scrunched up skeptically. "Paper cartridges? Nobody uses them anymore. All the cartridges are brass cased now. What do you need paper cartridges for?"

"I have an old pistol from the war. I want to take it with me while I'm prospectin' up in the hills, chase off varmints that might come along."

"What kind of pistol is it?"

"A turret gun."

"Huh. I don't believe I've ever seen one of them."

"I'll bring it around one day, show it to you," said Billy. He started shifting his feet back and forth, beginning to worry about time and the body up in the cave.

"I'd like to see it." Evans rubbed his head, "I suppose you could take some powder with you and some cigarette papers, make your own. You got balls?"

"I do," nodded Billy, "and caps, too. All I need is the gunpowder and the papers. And some gun oil, a brush, and a swab."

"Okay." Evans rummaged around behind the counter and in the back room. He returned with several items and a small linen bag. "Here's a can of powder, the tools, and a packet of cigarette papers. I threw in a tub of lard, too, so's you could seal the chambers. You know, misfires."

"Thank you, Mr. Evans," Billy gushed. "Uh, is there any change to be had?"

"Not a penny," said Evans, "and don't forget to come back to sweep that walk."

After leaving Evans' store, Billy headed directly to Asa Jackson's livery stable.

"I have a favor to ask you, Asa."

The tall, bony black man peered down at Billy, his head pulled up warily. "What you want, Billy? I ain't got no work just now."

"I know, Asa, that's fine, that ain't it. I need to borrow one of your mules for a little bit."

Asa wrinkled his thick gray moustache. "Now, what in blazes you need a mule for?"

Billy shared a secret smile, "I got somethin' to bring back I found up in the hills. It could be pretty valuable, I think."

"Is that so?" said Asa wryly. "Hit the jackpot, did you?"

"Well, maybe close to it." Billy gave Asa a conspiratorial look. "Tell you what. Loan me the mule, and if I do get somethin' out of this, I'll pay you back for the rentaltwice what you generally charge."

Asa nodded, "Give you a mule now, you pay later. Now, how could I pass on an offer like that?" He went back into his stable and in short order led a mule outside. He handed the reins to Billy as he said, "I want her back in twenty-four, no later. She better be in good shape, too. Make sure you get her plenty of water. It's hot out in prospectin' country."

"You brung me Annie?" Billy said in delight. "She a good old girl," he said as he patted her gray muzzle. "I'll take good care of her for sure, Asa, you can count on that."

"Just bring her back," said Asa, "and cash, too, if you do hit it rich."

"You betcha, Asa, cash on the barrelhead."

"Yeah, that's rich, comin' from a drunk like you, Billy."

Billy made it back to the Plum Mine in an hour, thanks to Annie. When they arrived, he dismounted and guided her up to the spring that fed the pond. Annie drank fully, then turned to scrounging for food in the scrub. In the meantime, Billy slid down the slope and opened the cache where the body lay. Everything was as he'd left it.

He pulled out the corpse, much stiffer since being laid away. Billy dragged it down to where he had found it originally and rolled it over, belly down. He yanked the corpse around head first tothe water's edge. Then, he gathered up some nearby rocks and constructed a small pyramid in front of the corpse. He lifted it by the torso and positioned itwith the dead man's chin propped up on the pyramid as though he rested while looking out on the pond. Billy stepped away, moving quickly forward again when he thought the body would fall off. But, it stayed in place.

Billy brought Annie down and tethered her to a sage bush far from the pond's shore. He removed his old knapsack from behind the saddle and dug into it to bring out the oil-stained, muslin bundle. He unwrapped it, and inspected the old pistol. No pitting, no structural damage that he could see. Billy lubricated the pistol, swabbed out the barrel and its peculiar horizontal chambers, and brushed clean all of the working parts. Then, he took out his old cartridge box from the sack and extracted one .38 lead ball and one brass cap. He laid them aside and pulled out a slip of cigarette paper from its packet, and rolled one end tight to form a cone. He twisted the end into a tight tail, and carefully held it on end on top of a flat rock. He then put the makeshift cartridge into a chamber tail first. Then, he positioned a ball on top and tamped it into place with the pistol rod. He repeated the process six more times. Once he had situated the cartridges and balls in the cylinder, he gingerly laid it on top of the flat rock. He placed seven percussion caps on ther nubs below each loaded chamber, then set the horizontal cylinder back onto the gun frame and locked it into place. He was ready.

Billy hesitated and breathed in deeply. The gun hadn't been fired for a decade and a half, and that time it almost killed every living creature close to it, including himself. He'd oiled it now and then through the years, but never fired it in all that time. The risk was high, he realized, but the payoff could be sky high.

He knelt down on one knee ten feet behind the body, raised the gun with both hands, squinted his eyes almost shut, and fired. The ball ripped through the corpse's head knocking it forward hard enough to scatter the pile of rocks beneath it. Billy looked around, felt around, and realized that the handgun had worked perfectly. Quickly, he got to his feet and rushed over to the splayed-out corpse. He saw a round, bloody hole right at the knobby part of the head just below the crown. When he turned it over, he dropped it suddenly and crawled over to heave into the water. The man's nose and mouth had been blown apart and outby the force of the heavy round, leaving a mass of congealing blood, bone splinters, and teeth fragments in a huge, open crater below his placid blue eyes. Billy stretched to reach the body and gently pushed the eyelids down.

He rubbed his mouth with the sleeve of his shirt, staring at the ruins of what used to be a face. He gathered himself, saying silently, no one could say the dead man wasn't John Heaney now.

He struggled to get the stiff body up over the saddle, but managed, making sure that it stayed put by tying its hands and legs together underneath the mule's belly. When everything looked to be in order, he started walking down the cut to the main road back to Silver City.

Billy reached town an hour before sunset and marched directly to the jailhouse.

"Sheriff Hermann!" he shouted, banging on the door. "Sheriff Hermann, open up, I got somethin' to show you, please."

Hermann came to the door and said, "Billy McKinney, you're making quite the commotion. What's the matter?"

"Come here, Sheriff, I got somethin' to show you." He led the sheriff to the mule, and flipped the burlap sack up to expose the dead man's head and trunk.

Hermann stepped back. "What the fuck? What's that, Billy, what'd you do?"

"I killed him, Sheriff, I shot him dead. That there is John Heaney, the murderin' outlaw. I seen his poster on your wall, and I seen him up in the hills and killed him."

Sheriff Hermann's mouth fell open. Incredulous, he said, "You, Billy, you shot John Heaney."

"I did," said Billy, grinning proudly, "I got 'em good, twice."

Hermann stared at the ravaged head of the body, then at Billy. "I can't hardly believe you, Billy. You sure this is John Heaney?"

"I am, sir. Look at his shirt—checked, just like his picture."

"There are a lot of checked shirts worn by cowboys out here."

"Maybe, but that's him in that shirt, I recognized him from the poster."

Sheriff Hermann frowned. "Now, Billy, you're a good boy, you never cause trouble even on a bender. You're telling me you shot and killed the worst outlaw around these parts and brought him in?"

"That's the truth, Sheriff."

Hermann twisted his head back and forth, dubiously. "How'd you do it? Where'd you find him?"

"Up at the Plum Mine, camped out by the pond. I was hiking back from Virginia City before dawn, when I decided to go up and see if I'd get lucky with the tailings. There he was, sittin' by a campfire almost burned out. I knew it was him right away. I pulled my gun, crept up to him Injun style, stepped back and told him to get up, he was caught!"

"You did? Then what?"

"Oh, he was cold-blooded, all right. He come at me and I shot him."

"You shot him."

"In the chest. He turn and run, and I shot him again, right in the back of his skull. Near blew his head clean off."

Hermann leaned back. "So, Billy McKinney shot John Heaney. I didn't know you had a gun, Billy."

"That's right, sir, here it is," said Billy, pulling the turret pistol from his belt and handing it by the barrel to the sheriff. Hermann examined it closely, smelling the chambers to confirm that it had been fired recently. He held it up to the fading light, turning and flipping it around to see it at different angles. He dropped it to his waist, and said, "This is one strange weapon you have here, Billy. I have to admit, I've never seen one like it before."

"Neither'd Mr. Evans," Billy said. "I got the powder and stuff from him."

Hermann slowly raised and lowered his head, "I see. All right, let me ask you this. Where were his boys, his partners in mayhem in all this? Joe Lister, Nifty Bob Owens, Dick Pritchard? All of them are wanted, too. Where were they? Why didn't you shoot them? Or, more likely, why didn't they shoot you?"

Billy swallowed, but said quickly, "They was there, all of 'em. But, I got the drop on Heaney, and when I shot him, they all took off like jackass rabbits. I'd of shot them, too, but I was too busy finishin' off Heaney. He was most dangerous, you know."

"Oh, I know all right. But you shot him dead and his fellow killers just ran off," Hermann said sardonically. "And this poor blown-up fool across a mule is what's left of the bloodthirsty John Heaney."

"I got more proof," blurted Billy. "Take a look at this," he said as he circled the horse and came back. He thrust the broad brimmed cavalry hat with golden tassels at Hermann. Hermann held the hat, fingering the two gold tassels in the front. For the first time, he appeared to be unsure. Just about everybody knew that Heaney rode with Bloody Bill Anderson in the war, he thought. It was said that

Heaney started as a Yankee until they shot his brother for desertion. Then, he joined the Rebels, though he kept his Union cavalry hat so that the Yankees would know who was killing them now. Heaney never would have parted with that hat, so the story went, unless he was dead.

By this time, half a dozen folks stood in a circle around Billy, Hermann, and the mule draped with the grotesque body. After Billy finished telling his tale, they all began to murmur while other distant figures walked toward the jail to see what was happening. Seeing them and holding the hat by its brim, Sheriff Hermann came to a decision.

"Well, Billy, it's starting to look like you maybe did bring in the dangerous John Heaney. I'm not sure that means you shot him."

"Does it make a difference?" Billy said sharply. "The poster says wanted dead or alive."

"Maybe so," Hermann said, "but maybe someone else deserves what reward there might be." He paused for a moment's thought. "To be truthful, I can't be sure that you shoot all that well, Billy. You've been in the bottle for a long time."

"I can shoot," Billy said.

A voice in the crowd spoke out, "What the hell's the difference, Sheriff? He got Heaney, give the boy his money."

Others yelled, and Hermann raised one hand palm. "All right, all right. Give me some time to sort this all out. We'll get some ice from the Hardwicke House and lay the body out, see if anyone identifies it otherwise."

Grumbling still could be heard from the crowd encircling them, and Hermann continued, "In the meantime, I'll telegraph Wells Fargo and see how they want to proceed in rendering the reward."

A shout went up and Billy beamed.

Propped up on pillows against the headboard of Maggie's bed, Hermann said, "The poor fellow is on display at the General Store. Bobby Evans insisted. It would take a miracle for anybody to recognize him, there's nothing left to recognize. They had to cover what was left of his face, for God's sake."

Maggie leaned against his chest the entire time he told the story. "So?" she said quietly, "now what?"

He turned his head to her, "Not much choice in the matter. Hell, the entire fucking town watched him describe his feat of bravery. It sounded like a dime novel. Evans was there, who knows who was watching his store? Asa Jackson was there to get his mule." He gestured to Maggie with his head, "Your Otto was there, jaw almost on the ground. Ayers and Donovan, too. Everyone watched with big eyes while Billy McKinney crowed."

"And?"

"He had the hat, the checked shirt. I told Billy I'd telegraph Wells Fargo and let them know I had circumstantial proof of John Heaney's apprehension. That the reward should be bestowed on William McKinney of Silver City, Nevada."

"You didn't!" she said, smiling widely. Hermann gave her the gimlet eye, "I did. Everyone within earshot cheered, of course."

"Brilliant! How much might he earn?" she asked.

He twisted his mouth, "The reward was for $1,500."

"Jesus in heaven, he's won himself a fortune!"

"If he gets it." He paused, silently weighing the odds. "I suppose he will. The evidence is powerful enough."

"I wonder what he'll do with it," Maggie said.

"Why, drink it up, of course!" thundered Hermann. More reflectively, he said, "He could have made a lot more if he'd blasted the other three. They're rewards on all of them, altogether another thousand dollars, I believe. That is, if Billy could shoot that good. Hell, if he can shoot at all."

Maggie said quickly, "Why, of course he can! He was in the war, you know. He showed me that gun, he kept it because he killed a Rebel colonel with it. He told me so! After the war, he shot buffalo for the army. So, he can shoot."

Hermann stared back at her. "How well do you know him? Why do you care?"

Her face reddened slightly. "I know him well enough, better than most."

He moved back to look at her again. "I must admit, I am surprised." He shifted his eyes, staring into the dark. After a while, he said, "So, Billy McKinney can shoot and he has a gun. No way of knowing what he'd do with it on a binge."

Chapter 24. The Wind Up the Flume

Billy became the cock of the walk in Silver City. George Ayers, owner of the Golden Gate, offered him a room and a bar tab on the cuff. Donovan ran a tab at his saloon as well. Bobby Evans advanced him credit for any sundries he might need. All of the other Silver City citizens showed him new found respect as well. The drunken town sweeper was now the toast of the town, reason enough to get drunk. He bought a bowler hat and wore it pushed far down over his forehead for strolls up and down the streets.

"It's going to take a week or more for the money to be wired here," Hermann had told him. "Proper channels and all that horseshit. Be careful of your new friends. You don't want to spend it all in one place all in one day."

He didn't have much faith that Billy would follow his advice. While they waited for the reward to arrive, Hermann had to deal with the deceased's mortal remains. The pine box would be paid for out of the town's discretionary fund, since itinerants passing away was not an unusual occurrence in a mining town. The council might balk at laying to rest an unrepentant murderer, but that's why they staked out a potter's field in the cemetery. Hermann had secured the plot and Heaney's body rested in the coffin, but the sheriff had yet to find someone to bury him. Digging graves in Potter's Field had been one of Billy's jobs. Now, he was too busy relishing his current celebrity to stoop to such work. Hermann rubbed the bristle on his jaw. Maybe he could find an Injun or a greaser to dig the hole for two bits.

Hermann stared at the holster and the billfold on top of his desk. The highwayman would be buried in his britches and his ruined checked shirt, but not his boots, stolen by someone during his exhibition at Evans. The circumstances of Heaney's death still nagged at the sheriff. He decided to keep the holster and billfold just in case. He put them in the bottom drawer of his desk along with the cavalry hat crushed to fit the space. Now, he thought, he better go find someone to stick Heaney in the ground before the ice melted and he started to smell worse than he did.

Billy had a snootful, which gave him the courage to do what he'd had in mind from the first. He climbed the front stairs to the Pleasant Times Parlour House and knocked on the door. Even though he waited patiently, the door's sudden opening startled him. Otto stood in the entranceway, still holding the door's edge.

"Hello, Otto," Billy sputtered.

"Why, it's you, Billy. I'm surprised to see you here."

"Yeah, well ...," Billy trailed off. "She inside?"

Otto shook his head sympathetically. "I'm sorry, Billy, she ain't, she went off to Evans for some cooking goods."

"Oh," murmured Billy. "That's too bad. Sorry I missed her."

"Yes, well, maybe it's for the best," Otto said. "I don't think it'd be a good idea for you to see Maggie the way you are right now. You're lookin' a little worn out, Billy, and I can smell you from here."

"Yeah," said Billy, "you probably right."

He turned to leave and Otto said after him, "You want me to tell her you stopped by?"

As he started down the steps, Billy threw over his shoulder, "No, that awright. I'm just goin' to go."

"Well, all right then," Otto said. After a moment, he closed the door gently behind him.

Billy ran into her out on the sidewalk. He stopped and didn't say a word. Her expression flashed surprise and a smile that immediately hardened as she halted in front of him.

"Billy McKinney," she said, "the Hero of the Nile." The contempt of her tone stung him. "What brings you to the Parlour House? In search of a pleasant time? I understand you've been enjoying yourself all over town since you slayed the dragon. So, why not here as well?"

"No, I ...." Billy mumbled. A beat went by before he said, "You keep track of what I been doin'?"

Maggie's face reddened slightly. "Hard not to, considering your notoriety."

"Oh. Well, I didn't come here for a pleasant time."

"Is that so? Shame, Sally Mae and Jean would love a visit by a champion such asyourself. Why they might even give you a two-fer, considering your illustriousness."

"Maggie, please," he said plaintively, "I just come by to see you."

"And, why would you do that? You don't need to settle for the likes of me anymore."

"But, I did it for you!"

"Me? Why would you do anything for me? To take me away from all this? You could have just stayed instead. You were coming to something, pulling yourself up for sure. And, now look at you! The smell of you!" She pushed past him, "Do for yourself, Billy McKinney, don't be doing anything for me."

She walked into the house.

Billy stared after her for a time. "B'god," he muttered, and walked back down the street to Donovan's.

Asa Jackson sat quietly on a bale of straw inside the livery doors. Outside, the sun's heat seemed to transform the earth itself, washing out all color in favor of searing white. Look at it long enough, and a shimmer would dance in front of the eyes followed by tears forced from the glare. Inside the livery, the air was not as warm, but still without much circulation between the open doors and windows of the stalls. The horses and mules snorted now and then, but mostly slumbered in the enervating heat.

Asa waited patiently as he observed the crumpled form doubled up in the stall in front of him. While he waited, Asa smoked, occasionally glanced out at the empty street, then back to the supine shape lying on the soiled straw. He waited for the buckled man to stir, whether it took hours or happened in the next five minutes.

At last, the sleeper sat up. Rubbing his eyes, then his stomach, Billy said, "Where am I?"

"You don't know? Not in a hotel, that's for sure."

"Huh? Oh." Billy muttered, "Ayers tossed me out of The Golden Gate a couple a days ago. Said I was too drunk, and the way I was spreadin' money all over town, once the reward came in he wasn't sure I'd pay up. So, I figured I'd step on down to my old amigo Asa, he'd put me up, I said to myself."

Asa nodded, took another puff on his pipe, and said, "Yeah, I don't expect to get paid by you anytime soon either. So, once you pull yourself together, you can muck out the stalls, water the animals, feed 'em, and brush 'em down. Then, we square on your accommodations last night."

Billy frowned sickly, "I don't think my innards is quite up to that burden right now. Can you give me a few hours?"

Asa squeezed his lips together in a knowing expression. "What choice I got?"

Billy blew out air and sat still. He said, "You got any coffee I might get a cup?"

Asa stood up. "I'll put that on the bill, too. And, don't expect any extra medicine in it, either."

Billy held up both hands, "God forbid."

316

"I be back an hour or so. I'll take my breakfast first, 'case you're wonderin'. You might wanta surprise me then, get a head start on them chores."

Billy didn't replyand Asa left. Billy smacked his dry lips, taking his time before he tried to stand up. His struggle centered on opposing urges, to stay put versus the growing need to urinate. Finally, the latter won out. He dragged himself to his feet, holding on to the stall's gate for stability. When he felt more confident, he started to walk to the back of the stable, pulling himself along hand over hand on the stall doors and railings. At last, he made it to a corner of the building where a pile of manure stood ready to be moved. Billy opened the buttons on his trousers and began to pee gloriously in a volume close to that of his equine companions.

Blinding pain at the back of his head sent him sprawling into the manure. A kick in his rear end followed, and a kick in his ribs. Billy rolled over to see a stocky figure of a man looming over him ready to line up another kick. He kicked him in the ribs again, which caused Billy to howl from the pain.

"Hello, hero!" the man said, kicking Billy again in the legs curled up around him. "Shot any more outlaws lately?"

The man readied himself to strike again when Billy held up his hands defensively, "Wait, wait, please don't."

His assailant, round-faced with a three-day stubble and fury in his eyes, laughed. He half-turned to several shadow figures behind him, silhouetted black by the sun at their backs.

"Hear that, boys? A cry for mercy." They all laughed harshly. The man's head had been completely shorn, his hat hanging on his back suspended from a leather draw cord around his neck. His dark-green shirt lay open in a valley down his chest that allowed bristly hair to push out, gray mixed with black. He wore a thick, brown belt around his waist with a heavy pistol holstered on one side and a large Bowie knife sheathed on the other. His corduroys were tucked into a beat-up pair of cowhide boots with dulled spurs on the end. Billy had no idea who he was.

"You don't know me, do you? You don't remember shootin' me? Boys, this scoundrel don't remember shootin' me 'til I was dead." They all laughed again.

Bewildered, Billy tried to scoot away, but there was no place to go except the back wallboards of the stable.

"Oh, don't you try to get away, boy. Here, maybe this will jar your memory."

He reached into his shirt to pull out a folded piece of thin cardboard and flipped it at Billy. Billy tried to catch it, but missed. "Go on ahead, friend, take a look."

Billy picked up the cardboard and opened it. Inside, he read the large letters "Wanted." Below it, he saw a sketch of a man wearing a hat. He glanced up, confused. Looking back down, he read beneath the rendering, "John Heaney, rustling, horse theft, stage robbery, and murder. $1,500 Dead or Alive."

Billy gazed up, trying to fix the visage above him with the image in the flier. Gradually, the realization settled upon him. Despite the differences of the flesh and blood figure and the printed, black etching brandished in his hand, the two were the same. Heaney had shaved his beard off, wore a solid-colored shirt and a new hat, but he still looked out of the same remorseless eyes.

"That's right, pal, you're looking at the infamous John Heaney, standing right over you." His lips curled, "And you thought you killed me." He looked back at the others and said, "Why I ought to drop him right now just for his bad intentions. The idea of you going after me."

"I didn't," moaned Billy, "I found a fellow up at Plum Pond dead already dressed in a shirt like yours and a hat. It was an accident that I found him."

"Ah!" He glanced back at the other men, now more distinct after drawing closer. Three of them, one tall and thin, wearing a full, gray beard. Another dressed much like Heaney, though he was a smaller, swarthy man. The third dressed in a black preacher's suit with a black vest and a gold watchchain looping from one side pocket to another. He wore a thin bow tie around the neck of his white shirt. Atop his head he displayed what looked like a wide-brimmed black bowler with a crease down the middle.

"The switch worked, boys," Heaney said. "That dumbfuck rube come to kill me, he served a good purpose." He stared coldly at Billy again, "And you took the credit."

Panicked, Billy gasped, and said "Listen, it was just ...."

Heaney waited for him to finish, but Billy fell silent. Heaney said, "Yeah, I know about that. You parading all over town, bragging on how you shot the horrible John Heaney dead. That's a crime itself. So, what do you think, men? Shoot him or slice him up?"

Billy cried out, "No, no!"

Heaney grinned, and his men guffawed in the shared joke. "Calm down, there, boy, I ain't gonna lay you low. You did as much a favor for me as that poor fella. You almost deserve the reward," he said, pausing, "except I believe I do, since I got killed for it. I feel it's only right that you hand it over to me. So, hand it over."

Billy blanched. "I ain't got it. It ain't come in yet from Wells Fargo. They draggin' their feet. It ain't been delivered to me yet."

"Shit," snapped Heaney, "just like 'em. One reason why I rob 'em." He eyed Billy sternly, "You sure you ain't lyin' to me, boy?"

Billy furiously shook his head, "I ain't, Mr. Heaney, not at all. Sheriff Hermann's waitin' for the telegraph. Supposed to come in any day now."

Heaney's expression turned grim. "That's not good. You sure about this?" Billy nodded repeatedly. "Then, we need someplace to stay while we wait. Someplace quiet, nobody bothers with. Can't stay here waitin' for that nigger to come back. So, you—what's your name?"

"Billy. McKinney."

"Billy McKinney, from the old country. How about that? You think you can find us an out-of-the-way place to stay? We like to be close to you, Billy McKinney, 'til our business is done. You think of some hidey-hole we could use 'til the reward comes in?"

Just then, a voice sounded from the front of the stable. "Billy, I got you Arbuckle's here." Asa was back from breakfast. "You finish mucking out the stalls?"

Heaney pulled out his gun, a massive Walker Colt with a leather loop around the barrel and the loading lever. He whispered to Billy, "If you don't want that nigger laid out, you best come up with some place now."

Billy strained to think of a place.

"Billy? Where are you boy?" Asa called out, his voice growing closer.

Billy hissed back to Heaney, "Follow me!"

He led them out the back door and around the side of the stable away from the town center. They could hear Asa still calling as they skirted around the livery's wooden walls. Billy peeked out front from the corner of the building. No one was out in the intense heat. He motioned to Heaney, who mouthed quick instructions to the other three men. One by one, they casually crossed the main street and strolled up the hill toward the higher road behind the first row of houses. Billy guided them carefully until they stopped behind the rear of the abandoned house where he'd lived months ago inside the crawl space.

Heaney sent the tall, gray-bearded man, Joe Lister, up to the back door. With practiced skill, Lister broke the doorlock and disappeared inside. He returned immediately and waved them up. The rest of them climbed the stairs warily into the kitchen. Dark and musty, the room smelled of rat droppings, stale, spoiled food, and a general deathlike sourness. Faded flowers decorated wallpaper rolling in curls up the damp wallboards, and jagged two-by-fours lay on the floor, broken off from the collapsing ceiling above. A few pots and pans caked with grime sat on the stovetop next to a rickety kitchen table, and refuse covered most of the floor except for the path that Lister had made to the front room.

In short order, the four outlaws sat around on broken furniture in the dank darkness of the sitting room. The room's filthy front windows faced the backside of the Pleasant Times Parlour House.

"It ain't the Ritz," said Heaney, "but it'll work for now. Okay, Billy boy, time for you to go out and do what you always do on a regular day. Start by tellin' that darkie livery man that you went off to get somethin' to eat. Make sure he ain't suspicious. Then, do what you do. Just be sure to stop by the Sheriff's office sometime today, see if that reward money's in. And, don't you worry, one of us will be watchin' your back for you. Bob, why don't you keep an eye on our new friend here this afternoon. Dick here will relieve you after a while. Make sure you keep your distance from him. We don't want the lawman to get suspicious."

The man in the preacher's outfit nodded and sidled up next to Billy, who noted that even the grips of his guns were black. Nifty Bob Owens, he realized.

"All right, then, get along little Billy. We'll see you later on today."

He didn't know what to do. Too stunned to think, he felt his nerves screaming at a pitch over and over again. If ever he needed a drink to soothe his battered body, today was the day and now was the time. But, he was broke. The Golden Gate wouldn't spot him, neither would Donovan's. He could walk up to Gold Hill, maybe even Virginia City. That was a long hike, he thought, considering how he felt after last night and the beating he'd taken this morning. Also, Nifty Bob might not understand it if he left town just to get a drink.

He decided to go back to the livery stable. If Asa wouldn't front him a few bits, maybe he would pay him after he cleaned the stalls and tended the stock.

Asa took one cynical look at Billy and said, "Well, if it ain't lazybones. Thought you skipped out on me."

"No, just amblin' around, tryin' to clear my head."

"I don't wonder. Full as a tick you was last night."

"Yeah, well," Billy mumbled. "Anyway, I clean out them stalls, feed the stock, you see your way to loanin' me a few coppers?"

The big black man smirked, "Loan, huh? That and all the past money I loan you, you owe me near a hunnert thousand dollars."

"Aw, c'mon, Asa," Billy moaned.

"You think it less?"

"I don't know," Billy muttered. He threw himself down on a hay bale and cupped his head in his hands.

"What the matter with you, boy? You don't seem quite right to me."

Billy quickly stood up and shook his body. "Nothin', nothin' at all. Just dragged out is all."

Asa seemed doubtful. "Awright. You see to doin' the stalls, straw and all. Wash, brush, water, and feed them quadrupeds, I give you four bits."

"Four bits? That all?"

"That what you worth to me, deadbeat."

When Billy finished, Asa gave him a dollar.

He headed up the street toward Donovan's, every now and then looking behind him. Without fail, Nifty Bob strolled fifty yards to his rear, making sure he was seen yet unseen. When Billy stopped, Bob stopped, pretending to look at notices tacked up outside the post office, or looking over some goods in Evan's store window. But, when Billy came abreast of the sheriff's office, Bob stepped out into the middle of the street and waited, his fingers resting on the grip of one of his handguns.

Billy knocked on the door and stepped inside.

"Hey, there, Billy," said Sheriff Hermann, "I'm surprised to see you." He squinted his eyes, "You look a sight, boy. Somebody clean your plow?"

"Just a little bit of difficulty I had at the Gate last night. Nothin' to worry about."

"Okay," said Hermann, stretching the word out doubtfully. "What can I do for you?"

"You gonna ask me every day, Sheriff? You know why I'm here."

"I believe I do. Not getting too anxious, are you?" Billy pouted, and Hermann said, "Well, it isn't here yet. I told you, these things take time."

"But, dang it, Sheriff, it's past a week now, and I need the money!"

The sheriff held his hand out, "Easy, Billy, easy. It's gonna come. You seem a bit agitated, boy."

Billy forced himself to be still. "I know, I know. It's just, I got bills to pay, you know?"

"Sure, all that high living you been doing. Maybe it's for the best that you can't spend it all up before it gets here."

Morose, Billy said, "Don't have to worry about that. Nobody's runnin' a tab for me no more."

"Too bad, but it's better for you in the long run."

"I guess," Billy said.

He left the sheriff's office to find that Nifty Bob had been joined by Dick Prichard. As soon as they saw Billy emerge from the jail, Bob jerked his head slightly for a sign. Billy solemnly swung his head slowly back and forth no. The two men stiffened and Nifty Bob pivoted to stride back toward the house. Dick leaned against a porch post outside of Evan's General Store. Billy sighed and walked the other way toward Donovan's.

"That ain't good, Billy," Heaney warned. "You need to do better, get an exact date. We can't be hangin' around here too much, people might get suspicious. The sheriff might start thinking things. That wouldn't be good for anyone."

"I know, Mr. Heaney, I know. I'll see if I can get a more specific day from him tomorrow."

Heaney nodded, "That'd be good. I wouldn't want to have to box your ears if I thought you was slackin'. The boys might wade in, too. Do better tomorrow, Billy. Get the reward and we'll be on our way, leave you in peace."

"I will," said Billy, a bit shrill. "I get the sheriff to tell me exactly when."

"All right, then. Let's all turn in now."

Billy led his morning shadow Joe Lister over to the Golden Gate Bar. George Ayers sat in the dining room eating his breakfast and Billy approached him about working for some pocket change. Ayers agreed, but only if Billy promised to drink in the Golden Gate when he had a thirst. Before long, Billy stood in front of the Golden Gate sweeping the wooden walkway, making sure that he was in plain sight of Lister. He swept for three hours until lunchtime.

While he swept, he thought furiously about the squeeze facing him. He couldn't tell Sheriff Hermann what was happening, he might throw him into jail for lying to get the reward. Even if he did tell, Heaney and his thugs would kill him outright. Ice ran up his spine at the thought. Billy realized suddenly that if he went along with Heaney and gave him the reward money, the cold-eyed outlaw would kill him anyway. Heknew that he was the only one who stood between Heaney being thought dead to the world instead of being hunted wherever he ran. The sooner that money arrived, Billy thought soberly, the sooner he himself would be in the grave. Some unmarked grave, he supposed, while the story would spread that he had run off to spend his money, in San Francisco, maybe. He felt so sad, so pitiful in light of the fate awaiting him.

To blazes with that! he shouted in his mind. He would run, run now, and to tarnation with the money. He would run all the way to San Francisco where fortunes were found every day. They would never catch him, and he'd only come back when Heaney was in the ground for sure and forever. That would serve the snake! Hah!

But, he could never come back. The sheriff still might put him in the calaboose, maybe for killing the unknown fellow he'd found at Plum Pond. Even if he could explain his way out of that, Maggie would have nothing to do with him ever again for leaving. If that were true, he might as well let Heaney kill him now. He sighed deeply. Life without her was unthinkable, and he'd gotten himself in this fix only because he wanted to do better by her. Funny that she didn't care about that so much. Yet, it was important to him, and now he would be gone and she would not be a bit better off.

He swept, mulling and mulling, churning everything in his head, over and over again. Finally, he decided that he could do one thing at least before he surrendered to the inevitable. Lunchtime rolled around, and he leaned the broom against the wall of the Golden Gate. He made a show of stretching his arms high above his head, spying Lister across the street sitting on a barrel in the shade of the Hardwicke House. Then, Billy sauntered inside between the swinging doors of the hotel.

He quickly walked over to the front desk and said to the clerk, "Hyrum, can I borrow a piece of paper and a pen?"

Hyrum, a skinny balding man in his mid-thirties said, "Cost you five cents for the paper. I'll lend you the pen, but you gotta give it back."

"Five cents? For a sheet of paper? Put it on my tab."

"Now, Billy, you know you're cut off. Sorry, but no tab."

"For a nickel? Blast all, Hyrum!" He dug into his pants pocket and produced a dime. "Here's a dime. How 'bout throwin' in an envelope?"

Begrudgingly, Hyrum gave him the paper and an envelope, "Same price."

Billy took the paper and envelope in one hand and the pen in the other. "Where can I write? This is private."

Hyrum frowned, "You can write, huh?" He pointed, "Over there at that little sitting table next to the armchair. Sit on the end, please, we don't want you to soil the fabric."

Billy gave him a dirty look, then grabbed the ink well and headed to the chair before Hyrum could complain. He sat down and thought about what he wanted to write. Then, he wrote, a full fifteen minutes.

"Hurry up, Billy," called out Hyrum. "I might need that pen and ink shortly."

Billy looked around in a broad gesture. "I don't see the Israelite host crowdin' your doors."

He finished writing and blew on the paper to dry the ink. He folded it and slipped it into the envelope. Then, he put the envelope in his back pocket and brought the ink and pen back to the front desk. Dropping them off without a word, he continued past through the small dining room into the kitchen and out the back door.

"You still got my knapsack, Asa? You know, the one with my goods in it?"

Asa went back into the side addition to the stable where he lived. Waiting at the door, Billy could hear him poking around. Asa emerged and handed over to Billy the beat-up old sack he had been carrying around for years. Billy took a quick look inside—there was the old Rebel shell jacket he still wore in chilly weather, fall and spring, and the Colonel's pistol wrapped in the oily muslin. He pulled out a small reticule where he kept the old picture of his family, cracked and fading. He took the envelope from his back pocket and placed it gently next to the old collodion print and placed them both into the small purse, which he slipped back into the knapsack. Then, he held it out to Asa.

"You don't want to take it now?"

Billy shook his head, "Maybe later tonight or tomorrow I come back for it."

Asa nodded, and Billy left for the back door of the Golden Gate. He went out to the front porch and began to sweep again until sunset, then headed over to the jail, now with Dick Pritchard tailing him not too far behind.

"I'm sorry, Billy, that' just the way it is." Sheriff Hermann seemed genuinely apologetic as he continued, "Those big deal city outfits do things on their own timetables, including pay. I remember one time Ayers came in with a rustler, a $100 on his head. The cattle company took six months to pay his reward."

Billy swallowed. "Sheriff Hermann, I really need that money."

"I know, Billy, I'll try to nail them down, I promise. But, I just can't tell you what I know might not be true. I'll try to push them, Billy, I swear."

"Thank you, Sheriff, appreciate it." Just then, he wished he had that dime back.

"Sheriff says July 10th, the money comes in." Billy told Heaney looking him straight in the eyes.

"Damnation, that's near two weeks." Heaney squinted and stared at Billy. "You ain't bullshittin' me, are you? 'Cause that wouldn't be good for you," he said, raising a fist.

"No, no, that's what the sheriff said. Listen, Mr. Heaney, I just want to be done with this. I'm happy just givin' you the money to let me be. I wish it were here today."

Heaney pulled back, half-convinced. Then, he said, "Well, awright, Billy, don't worry, now. We be outta your hair soon enough," clapping his hand on Billy's shoulder. He finished with a squeeze just short of painful.

The next day, Billy returned to the Golden Gate and picked up sweeping the front boardwalk again. "You just did it yesterday, it don't need it no more right now," Hyrum said.

"That's awright, gives me somethin' to do," said Billy.

"Yeah, well, you ain't getting' paid," Hyrum said, "and don't expect it to go against your account."

"You're a big-hearted river, Hyrum, you know that?"

Billy pushed the broom back and forth, curling his head down now and then to spy on his spy. Today, it was Nifty Bob again, looking more than bored as he sat by the post office beneath one of the few trees in town. Billy kept on sweeping, hoping that Bob didn't

325

notice how little dirt flew off the boards. Then, at midday, Billy propped the broom again and entered the hotel.

He scurried behind the buildings on the main street toward Asa's stable. Doubling over in front of the door, he hammered it with his fist. Asa opened up, took one look at the gasping little redhead bent over before him and went back inside. In just a few seconds later, he returned with Billy's knapsack. Billy took it from him, nodded, and sped off toward the Parlour House.

The house stood up on the opposite slope of the street, and Billy recognized that there was no way he could get there without crossing in plain sight. He debated whether to crouch low and move fast or just walk casually in a way that might not draw attention. After more deliberation, he grit his teeth, straightened up, and started ambling as though he belonged exactly where he was. He didn't see Nifty Bob standing up the street, watching him from the firehouse.

Billy stepped up on the porch and knocked on the door. He could hear footsteps approaching from inside until the door swung inward. Looking surprised, Otto said, "Why, Billy, I thought you headed back to Virginia City."

Billy shook his head. "Is she here?"

Otto said, "No, she's not. Went to the post office. Do you want to come inside and wait?"

"No," said Billy, "I want you to do me a favor. Take my knapsack here, and stick it in the linen closet for safe keeping."

"You sure you don't wanna come in? She'd be glad to see you, I think."

"I don't think she would. But, if somethin' happens, if I don't turn up for a while, give her the knapsack, will you?"

"Something happens? What would that be? What're you talkin' about, Billy? You in trouble?"

"No, no, nothin' like that. I just might be leavin' town for a while like you said. Find a place with better prospects. Maggie's been good to me and all, so I want her to have some things with my thanks."

Otto pursed his lips, eyeing Billy suspiciously. "You sure you don't wanta give 'em to her yourself?"

"No, that's awright. It ain't a bigdeal. Thanks, Otto, you been good to me, too. I appreciate it."

He turned and started down the steps and out of the yard. He dawdled as he walked, heading in the direction of the post office, hoping he'd run into her along the way, then hoping he wouldn't. Before he could decide either way, he met her on her way back.

326

"Hello, Maggie," he mumbled.

She gave him a hard look. "Hello, Billy. What brings you here?"

"Oh, I just asked Otto to take care of some things of mine for a bit."

"Really? Why would you do that?"

"Well," Billy said, hesitantly, "I'm thinkin' of leavin' town for a while. You know, greener pastures."

"Oh. I see. All right, I hope you find a good situation." She started to pass by and he ached at how wonderful she looked. He called to her back, "Yeah, if I'm gone long, I left you a couple of things I thought you might like."

She stopped. "You did?" Then, warily, she said, "Just where are you going, Billy?"

"I don't know. Maybe Carson City."

"And you plan on coming back?"

"I hope so," he said, trailing off. "I want to …."

"Billy, come inside and we can talk about all this."

"No, I can't," Billy replied. "Have to go back to the Golden Gate. Sweepin' up again, you know."

"Billy," she said impatiently, "tell me."

He hesitated, anguish etched all over his face. Finally, he spoke, his voice high, "I didn't shoot John Heaney." She looked surprised, then resigned as if she had known all along. Billy went on, "I found the body up near the pond already shot through the heart. Heaney must've killed him, put him in his shirt and left his cavalry hat so the dead man'd pass for him."

Startled, Maggie said, "Well, why didn't you say so in the first place? Why didn't you tell Sheriff Hermann?"

Billy mumbled, "'Cause I wanted the reward money." She appeared confused, and he said, "I shot the dead fella in the head to make sure no one could make out who he was."

"You did what?" Maggie said, pulling her head back in utter repugnance. "God almighty, Billy!"

"I know. But, I wanted the money so bad so you and me could go on together. I was afraid you'd boot me sooner or later if I didn't show you I could fend for us both. I couldn't stand thinkin' about that. That's why I did it. Only now, I wish I hadn't."

Maggie let loose a long sigh. "All right. You should tell the sheriff, Billy."

"I can't, Maggie. I just can't. But, I wanted you to know before I went away."

"He'll understand, Billy. Just tell him. Albert's a compassionate man."

"I'll be seein' you, Maggie." Billy said as he spun away.

"Where are you going, Billy?" she called after him. But, he didn't answer.

When night came, Nifty Bob escorted Billy from the Golden Gate back to the deserted house to join the others. They arrived to find the other men taking large bites out of sourdough and beef sandwiches, washing them down with warm beer. Bob sidled up to Heaney and whispered in his ear. Heaney shifted his eyes to Billy, then returned to his sandwich.

Bob made himself a sandwich and joined the rest lounging around the front room.

"Help yourself," Heaney said.

Billy slapped together two pieces of thick bread around a thick slice of dried beef. He was famished. He ate so fast that he swallowed enough air to produce a cacophony of burps. Heaney and the rest laughed, surprised by the rapid-fire eruption.

Past sunset, they kept one kerosene lamp at a low glow in the front room to make sure that no one knew that anyone was in the dilapidated house. Dick and Joe played cards close to the lamp, while Heaney lounged on the broken down settee. Nifty Bob used starlight and the bright moon to stare out the front window at the quiet town below, searching for any signs of night life. All of them were growing weary of their confinement, but Bob especially, since he was known as one who enjoyed the city lights. He gazed out the window for any kind of life, though mostly in disappointment. This night, he stiffened to attention.

"Hey," said Nifty Bob, "look out there."

They peered out of the front sash window cloudy with grime. Across the slope of the hill, on an overhanging terrace on the second floor, a woman stood at the railing. She leaned on her spread hands into the fading light, squinting to see into the abandoned house above and across the back yard.

"Holy shit," said Bob, "that's one well-fed woman. I'd like to share my pork 'n beans with her."

She retreated into the house and returned with a kerosene lamp. She stretched the lamp into the twilight toward the house, searching.

"Dick, kill the lamp," Heaney said quickly. Pritchard turned the lamp down until the flame went out. The bright starlight still offered them plenty to see. They watched her searching in their direction.

"She's fine as cream gravy," said Bob softly.

"I do like somethin' to grab hold of on a woman," Lister said.

"Quiet!" whispered Heaney. The men fell into silence staring at the woman on the terrace. Then, he murmured, "Nice curly hair there. Think she a widow?"

"Don't know about that," Nifty Bob said, "but I do know she's one fat tart." He twisted around to look directly at Billy and said, "That your girlfriend, Billy?"

Billy remained still, terrified at what he was hearing.

"I saw you two together this afternoon. Thought you were gonna grab her right then and there."

"She your girlfriend, Billy?" Heaney asked. When Billy didn't answer, he said, "Looks like you got more staked out in this game than you thought."

Chapter 25. The Plum Mine

Billy got drunk on the Fourth of July, though it just as well could have been any other day. Every day since Bob Owens had said he'd seen him with Maggie, Billy drank until he fell over. The Independence Day celebration in Silver City merely increased the number of elbows he rubbed in the town's saloons. Many of those tossing down shots of red eye were not hailing the nation's birthday, however. As veterans of the Cause, they bitterly cursed the Union and its perfidious aggression. Fights broke out between opposing veterans, with lifeblood sometimes spilled. As tight as he was, Billy still possessed sense enough or perhaps enough instinct to slip away before things became dangerous. This July Fourth, tempers reached the boiling point in Donovan's at noon.

Outside, Billy shaded his eyes from the brilliant light, gasping at the hot summer air. Water would do him better at this point, he told himself, but he ignored his own advice and headed towards the Golden Gate Bar. If a fracas started there, then he really didn't know where he would go to drink. No matter, wherever he drank his problems went
with him.

He had less than a week left before Heaney and his gang expected him to hand over the reward money. He quaked at the thought of what would happen if he showed up without it. Far worse, though, he feared for Maggie and what these murderers could do to her. Every time he thought about it, he felt sick to his stomach. And he thought about it all the time. No matter how much he drank, the horror in his head remained.

People started to assemble along the main street to watch the holiday parade. Since a good number of the town's residents marched, those standing along the street seemed more like picket lines than a crowd. Billy saw Chun and his family standing on the roadside along with a few other Chinese. He also saw Asa in front of his livery, and up the street, Hyrum at the Golden Gate. Donovan stood out in front of his place, his hands in his pants pocket. George Ayers and Bobby Evans weren't in sight because as mayor and town council chairman respectively, they would strut proudly at the head of the cavalcade.

The parade itself wasn't much. Virginia and Carson cities put on the big shows, Billy recalled, with plenty of spirit, not to mention scores of saloons. Last year, he traveled up to Virginia to get his bark juice, where he never ran out of watering holes. He couldn't go this year, though. They were keeping a close watch on him and what he was doing. So, he swept the boards, ran errands, and worked at Asa's to earn that day's drinking money. He also ran around to keep Heaney's henchmen's eyes on him, not Maggie. He had to think of something, work something out during the next week before all hell broke loose. Maybe he could run, he thought, but where?

"Hey, there, Billy."

Sheriff Hermann stood facing him, the sun at his back. Billy held his hand up to block the glare. "Hey, there, Sheriff, how you? Enjoyin' the parade?"

"It's nice to see folks have a good time," said Hermann.

"Yeah, 'til they start the fireworks. That right?" A brief frown crossed Hermann's face and Billy smiled. "So, any word about my money?"

"I'm surprised it took you so long to ask. As a matter of fact, I did get a message. A promissory note will be sent to the Virginia City Bank over night. I'm supposed to go up there with you to sign off on it. Soon as that's done, you can draw on it wherever you like. I don't recommend the Golden Gate, however."

Billy stared at him. "The money's in?"

"Just about. If you want, we can go up to Virginia tomorrow and pick it up."

Billy barely heard Hermann. Up across the street, Maggie had emerged from theParlour Housetrailed by Jean and Sally Mae. The folks already in line made room for Maggie at the road's edge. She folded her arms across her breast, settling in to watch the procession. Looking excited beyond belief, Sally Mae took the spot on Maggie's right. Jean moved next to her on the left, sidling over to make room for Nifty Bob. Grinning, Bob shifted around Jean to stand between her and Maggie. He lifted his eyes above the parade, his smile fixed, and stared at Billy. Then, he leaned over and put his arm around the taller Jean, who lowered her head to hear him whisper in her ear. Smirking, she took him by the hand and led him back into the house.

"You hear me, Billy? Virginia City, tomorrow?"

Without moving his sight from the street, Billy said, "I can't tomorrow, Sheriff. Supposed to help chop wood for the parson tomorrow."

"Is that right? After bothering me every day for the past two weeks, you can't put that off a day? I never knew you to be such a churchgoer, Billy."

"He's payin' me."

"He is? Don't he know you'll use it to buy liquor?"

"He says it's my choice." Billy shrugged, "I promise him I won't use it to drink, I tell him I'll get somethin' to eat instead."

Hermann shook his head ruefully. "Okay, Billy, let me know when you're free to travel." He turned on his heel and walked up the street. Billy didn't notice that he had left.

He chopped wood for the parson for a full day, and he did order some beef stew with his beer. At the end of the night, he staggered up to the abandoned house. Heaney was there, along with Prichard and Lister, but not Bob Owen. Billy told Heaney that he would be working in the stable the next day. Heaney nodded, and Billy curled up in a corner of the sitting room.

The next morning Billy left early for the stable. As soon as he arrived, he threw himself down on a bed of straw in an empty stall. An hour later, Asa greeted him with a tin of coffee.

"I need you to go up to Evans for some more oats. Here's five dollars. I will count my change."

Billy fretted all the way up to the general store. He knew that one of Heaney's watchdogs was out there somewhere spying on him. Just the idea of it made him cringe inside. He arrived at the store and stepped up onto the wooden walk. Lifting his head to go inside, he was dismayed to see Sheriff Hermann leaning against the open door.

"I'm trying to figure you out, Billy." Hermann stood opposite Billy in plain sight, which made him very nervous.

"Nothin' to figure, Sheriff, I just been busy."

Hermann pressed his lips into a fine line of exasperation. "Billy, you've been all over me every day about your reward. When I tell you it's there for the taking, you disappear for three days. The only reason I could find you is 'cause Asa sent you here to pick up some grain. Now, why don't you tell me what's wrong?"

"There ain't nothin' wrong, Sheriff, I swear."

Puzzled, Hermann squinted. "Is it one of the ladies? I saw that dapper dude with Jean during the parade. Is that it?"

Billy snapped, "'Course it ain't," his lower lip jutting out defiantly.

Hermann said, "Who is that fellow, anyway? I've seen him and a couple of others now and then. You know them?"

"No," said Billy, "not at all. They's strangers to me."

"Well, then, what's going on?"

"Nothin'. Nothin' to do with Jean, or that guy, or nobody at the Parlour House."

Hermann cocked his head. His features relaxed as it came to him. "It's Maggie. You're upset about Maggie."

Billy didn't answer.

"She stopped talking about you, too. I knew she was pissed. I didn't know it ran so deep." Hermann seemed a bit wan now, despite the heat from the red hot sun. "Well," he said, turning to leave, but he paused. "Whatever's going on, Billy, I'll help you. That's my job. And, we need to go get that money soon, or Wells Fargo might balk. Like I said before, let me know when you're ready to go."

Heaney smiled as he said, "Just a couple more days, Billy, and we'll all be rich. Oh, you think I'm gonna bilk you, do you? Naw, I'm cuttin' you in, you're doin' all the work, right?" He slapped Billy on the back, "So, relax. You get us the dinero, we'll split it up and we all go our own way. Is that right or ain't it?" He looked around the room and Lester and Prichard both nodded vigorously while Owens simply smiled.

Billy understood that Heaney lied to keep him steady. His bluster did the opposite. Billy was frantic to find a way out. But, he couldn't think of anything. Maybe he would have to go see Sheriff Hermann for his help. Sighing and shaking his head, he left the house on his way to the stable, thinking to himself, what a mess.

"Take care of the animals," Asa said. "I'm goin' for breakfast."

Billy nodded, sitting on the floor of the stall, his legs bent in front of him. He slowly tried to gather himself for the day. Then, he stretched out on the straw. Almost before he closed his eyes, he was asleep.

The horses snorting and winnowing awakened him. He jumped up and peered out of the stall, gingerly looking up and down the length of the stable. Apparently, Asa was still at breakfast. Billy quickly left the stall and headed to the rear of the barn where he relieved himself against the back wall. Then, he fetched two buckets of water from the small spring up the hill and brought them down to parcel out among the horses. After that, he gave them each a few forks of hay and a bowlful of oats. Then, one by one, he rotated them to an empty stall so that he could clean each of the stalls out. After he had them all back in place, he strolled over to the front doors. Peering outside in the morning sun, he glanced up the road.

Still no Asa. He lifted and dropped his shoulders sighing, then picked a currycomb off the wall inside and started to brush the horses.

Asa returned close to noon.

"I thought you died and left me the place," said Billy.

"I do that, God wouldn't let me in heaven."

"The meek don't inherit the earth?"

"You ain't meek, you just a misery."

Billy twisted his mouth. "That true," he said, still combing the horse.

Asa watched him blankly for a time. Billy said, "So, where in the nation were you? Bring me anything to eat?"

"There's a bread crust and some preserves inside. I get 'em for you."

"Why, thank you Asa."

Asa didn't move. "You know," he said, "I met a new fella come into town up at the café. Me and Albert Hermann eatin' some grits and bacon, a couple a eggs, coffee. You know the sheriff, he always interested in new folk comin' to town. So, he invite the fellah to sit down, join us. He sit down, order steak and eggs, spuds, coffee. So, we get to talkin', and Albert ask him what bring him to Silver City, silver, gold? The young fellah—he' ain't no more 'n twenty-five, thirty—he say he ain't in town for that. He come lookin' for his brother been missin' for a while."

Billy felt a qualm. "He think his brother come here to work the mines?"

Asa shook his head, "His brother come to hunt outlaws, he say. His brother read about 'em in the papers and dime books. Figured he'd win some reward money n' get famous on the way."

Billy's gut began to roil, which he knew wasn't from last night's drinking. "That sounds mighty cheeky to me."

"They from back east, Pennsylvania or somewhere," Asa said dismissively, "what you expect?" He paused, rubbing his white whiskers. "Then again, the one tellin' the story was pretty well strapped, so maybe they know what they doin'."

"What'd this fellah look like?" asked Billy.

Asa pursed his lips, "Not tall, not short. Pretty white, like you. Lanky boy, narrow in the hips. Yellow hair, not much beard. Blue eyes, real blue. Like I said, carried a big gun on his hip, a decent knife on the other."

"He tell you his name?"

Asa nodded, "Yup, he comin' down here later with his horse. Wants to talk more with the sheriff, first."

"So, what's he called?"

"Polk. Henry Polk. From Pittsburgh, or Pittstown, someplace like that. A nice enough boy, he comin' down here later, put up his horse. After he finish with Albert."

Billy put his hand to his mouth. He mumbled, "Gotta puke. Too much beer last night," he said, and ran off to the back of the barn.

He tried to slip around corners during the day, taking only inside jobs while he kept a look out for the new man in town. He found little to do since summer usually meant working outside. The best he could do was run back to the livery stable where Asa would throw a few coins his way. He would work, then wait for nightfall to sneak back into the old house with Heaney and his gang. To his great dismay and distress, he realized that he couldn't go to his usual haunts. It was likely that the new man would go there to search for news about his lost brother. The anxiety and fear without the numbing comfort of drink made the passing of the next few days for Billy hell on earth.

Two more days before Heaney expected the money to arrive. Two more days, thought Billy, without seeing any way out. What would he do? What could he do? The only thing he could think of was to explain everything to Maggie and ask her to run away with him. His deep fear, though, was whether or not she would go. She seemed to hate him now. Maybe if he told her that her life depended on it and that as soon as they were safe somewhere else, she could go her own way. It seemed like the most likely way to persuade her to leave. But, then, she would leave him, too, sooner or later. He sighed heavily, figuring that really, she had left him already.

"Hey, you," a voice said from the front of the stable. Billy shook himself out of his sad stupor and looked up front. A slender man stood silhouetted between the half open doors. Billy said, "You need help? The owner's away right now, if you need a horse or mule."

"No, I'm just here to drop my nag off. Rode up to Gold Hill to look around." The figure stepped inside, tall, blond-haired, wearing a short-brimmed hat, a patterned flannel shirt, and canvas trousers with a large revolver holstered on his right side. He looked to be thirty or so, and taken altogether, his appearance suddenly made Billy's stomach drop.

The stranger stopped, his stance wide. "You know who I am?" Billy shook his head vigorously, no. "My name is Henry Polk. I'm looking for my brother Carroll who came to this territory a month ago." He turned away to tether his horse to a support beam."You heard of him?"

Billy stammered, "No, I don't believe so."

Polk slowly lowered his jaw, his mouth open. His fair skin was gently tanned, his eyes bright blue. He had good teeth, and would be thought handsome in mixed company. Here, though, his features were tight and severe. "I've been looking for Carroll for a couple of months, now. Took the train from Pennsylvania all the way up to Carson City. Hired a horse and rode here. Talked to every lawman along the way, including your sheriff, Mr. Hermann."

Billy swallowed, his mouth cotton dry.

"I told him my brother was after John Heaney for the reward. He says Heaney's been brought in already, dead. Shot twice, once in the heart, once in the back of the head. Mr. Hermann says Heaney was brought in alone. Now, this all seemed funny to me, peculiar. Heaney rode with a gang of cutthroats. Where'd they go, I wondered. The sheriff said the man who shot Heaney ran the others off. You think that's true?"

Billy stood nailed to the floor, holding the currycomb in both hands, twisting them around it, panicked. "I, uh, I don't know," he said.

"Well, I'll tell you what I think. I think that wasn't Heaney that was shot. I think someone bushwhacked my brother. Shot him in the chest, then the back of his head while he was trying to crawl away. While rifling his pockets, the cowardly bastard saw that no one could recognize poor Carroll anymore, his face blown away, and had the bright idea of passing him off as Heaney. That's what I think."

He swiveled back to his horse to take the saddlebags off.

"It was easy enough to do, hell, lots of checked flannel shirts to be bought. Put it on Carroll's body, soak it up with some of his blood, who would know? Well, I knew. I recognized Carroll's holster, we bought our guns together, .45 Walkers—see mine?" He gestured down at the huge handgun in its holster. Billy realized that it looked like the same gun that Heaney had hanging from his gunbelt. Slowly, he grasped that Heaney had taken the pistol from Polk's dead brother, maybe even killed the man with his own gun.

"I tried to tell the sheriff," Polk continued, "but he wouldn't listen.Showed me Heaney's hat, but the ambusher could've found one of them, too, you know? Why not? The sheriff said he couldn't do anything no matter how I tried to convince him. He just wouldn't listen," Polk said, gazing at Billy. "So, now I've got to find out myself."

He threw the saddlebags across his shoulder and said, "When the owner returns, tell him I'm back and I'll be stopping at the Golden Gate, will you? Thanks."

Polk walked away out of the stable.

Billy slumped on a straw bale, stunned. How long would it be before this Polk fellow found out that he was the one who'd brought in Heaney's body—his brother's body? He was surprised that Sheriff Hermann hadn't told him already. Now, what was he going to do? Too late to undo it, too late for anything. Why hadn't that money come sooner? Why couldn't he have left town before Heaney found him? Left town with Maggie. He blew out a long breath. What could he do now?

He thought about it over and over. If he got the money, Heaney and his would leave town, probably after killing him. But Maggie would be safe. He'd tell Heaney he would have the money late tomorrow afternoon.

That afternoon, Billy drank at Donovan's Saloon without getting drunk. When he was sure he was fortified, he took himself over to the rundown house where he found Heaney and his men finishing off a roasted chicken.

"Billy boy, come on in and eat some fine chicken. Joe picked it up at the general store, plucked it, spitted it, and cooked it right behind the house. It's pretty good!"

Billy said, "I got news, Mr. Heaney, bad news."

Heaney's face immediately hardened, his eyes slit and cold. "What bad news?" he asked, his hand on the grip of his gun.

"A stranger come to town. Says he's lookin' for his brother. He went to see the sheriff and after talkin' to him, swore that it weren't you dead, it was his brother killed."

Heaney pressed his lips together and snarled, "Fuck!"

Without warning, he hit Billy with a roundhouse that knocked him to the floor. "Did he talk to you? Did you tell him something?" The three others stood up and crowded around Billy sprawled on the floorboards, each also holding their pistol in their holsters.

"No, no, I swear on the good Lord's bible!" Billy cried. "Asa Jackson, he owns the livery stable, he come and tell me this guy's in town. Says the feller talked to the sheriff. Then, this feller, Polks's his

337

name, shows up at the stable, all worked up about his brother and how you're still alive, how he gonna take care of you hisself."

Heaney loomed over Billy, "Maybe you know too much anyway."

"I don't want no trouble," Billy said. "I'll get the money tomorrow—the sheriff and I are goin' to Virginia City for it. I'll come right back and give it to you, be done with it."

Heaney's sharp eyes dimmed. "You're goin' tomorrow?"

"We are. I'll bring it over here just as soon as we get back."

"I don't know about that," Heaney said, rubbing his jaw. "That other guy might find out it's you gettin' the reward. He might trail you right back here to the house. I can't get into any scrapes now, now that I'm dead. A fight might bring the sheriff down on all of us."

He reached a hand down to Billy, saying, "Get up."

Billy rose to his feet, still shaking.

"A change of plans. You go with the sheriff tomorrow, get the money. Only, instead of meetin' us back here, we'll meet up at the Plum Mine. That way, we don't have to worry about that other jackass followin' you to the house, raisin' a ruckus. So, you go sleep somewhere else tonight. We'll light out of here before dawn, meet you at the end of the day at the mine near the pond. Got it?"

Billy nervously nodded while thinking that he had to see the sheriff, tell him that he was ready to pick up the reward.

He found Hermann in his office, reading the paper.

"Sheriff, I thought about it, and I think we should go on up to Virginia, get my reward now."

Hermann glanced up at Billy, then fixed eyes on him in a stare. He laid the paper down on the desk and said, "Billy, this rider came in the other day looking for his lost brother. Polk's his name. Said his brother was tracking John Heaney. I told him about Heaney, and he didn't believe me. So, I showed him the shirt, the hat, the holster and billfold. That's when he told me they were his brother's. Not the hat or shirt, but the holster."

Billy opened and closed his mouth, not saying a word.

"This fellow swears that someone murdered his brother and made his body look like Heaney's. He asked some good questions, questions I couldn't answer. Like where was Heaney's gang in all this." Hermann pushed himself back deeper in his desk chair. "I think it might be a good idea to hold off awhile on the reward, Billy, until I can look into this some more."

338

Appearing shocked, Billy stuttered, "But, Sheriff, I been waitin' a long time for this reward money."

"I know—"

"I owe people!"

"I understand that Billy, but this has become a dicey deal, here. I'm afraid if Polk finds out it was you getting the reward, he might cause trouble." Hermann raised his hand and pushed it downward, "Let's let it sit for a while. Maybe Polk will get tired, go off and search for his brother elsewhere. For now, though, I think we should wait." He nodded, affirming his decision.

Billy stumbled out of the jail and down the street, thinking that the fires of hell were about to consume him. Where could he go now? Still dazed, he headed for Asa's out of habit.

When he reached the livery stable, he found Henry Polk inside, leaning against a stall, his hand resting on his pistol. "Hello, Billy. Billy, right? Billy McKinney? Funny how you didn't tell me your name before. Your old pal at the Golden Gate, Hyrum, he told me. Funny, too, because he told me your name when he was tellin' how you were the one who brought in Heaney strapped over a mule. You do that?"

Billy slowly nodded and swallowed, "Yes."

"So, you gunned down John Heaney. That is funny, considering—and I don't mean any offense by this—considering that you're pretty well known as the town drunk. No offense, but the sheriff said you've never done anything like this before, ever. That true?"

Billy shook his head again.

"Well, I guess we know the real story, you and me. You killed my brother," he said, "so I guess I'm going to have to kill you, you son of a bitch!"

Billy raised his hands, "No, no, that ain't it, that ain't right!"

"Sure it is," Polk said, drawing his gun. He held it straight out and took aim at Billy.

Billy dropped to his knees, his head turning away while holding his hands outstretched in front of him. "Wait! Wait! It ain't what you think! Lemme tell you, please!"

"Why should I? Why shouldn't I cut you down in cold blood, the way you did my brother Carroll?"

"Because I didn't kill him! I didn't kill no one! I didn't kill John Heaney!" Polk hesitated, and Billy spoke quickly, "John Heaney is still alive. He killed your brother."

Polk dropped the .45 lower. "How do you know this? You bullshitting me?"

Billy pulled his hands back and rested them on his thighs. "I ain't. I found your brother dead wearin' Heaney's shirt with his hat nearby. I figured Heaney had left him like that 'cause the law was hot on him and his gang. That's, uh, that's when I thought up the idea of collectin' on Heaney's reward."

Polk's face twisted in grief and anger. "How do I know you're not sending me up?"

"I can prove it." Billy reached around his back with his right hand, and Polk whipped his pistol back up. "Hold on!" cried Billy, "I need to show you something from my back pocket. I ain't heeled."

Polk hesitated, then wiggled his gun barrel up and down. Billy slowly reached into the back pocket of his dungarees and pulled out a small square of paper now wrinkled and stained. He unfolded it and held it out to Polk. Polk kept the gun on Billy, while raising the paper up to the lamp light over his shoulder. He read.

Carroll Polk Esq.
If I am dead tell
Henry Polk Oklahoma City
May God rest my soul.

Tears broke from his eyes, pouring down both of his cheeks. He cried silently, wiping snot away from his nose with the back of his hand.

"This was with the body you found?"

Billy solemnly moved his head up and down.

"So, it was Carroll. My brother is dead after all."

The anguish on Polk's face shamed Billy. He wished he'd never found his poor, dead brother, or that he'd started this huge mess in the first place.

"So, you say you didn't kill Carroll," Polk sneered, "you'd rather pass it off on John Heaney."

"He did it, I know he did it!" said Billy.

"How's that?" asked Polk.

"He told me so hisself."

Polk's face hardened again. "You talked to John Heaney?"

Billy tucked his head low. "He snuck into town and braced me. Said he wanted the reward for him being dead now."

340

Polk's jaw dropped, his mouth open. "Why, that snake. There isn't nothing he won't do."

"He is a curly wolf, that for sure. Said he kill me if I didn't go along with it."

"So, where is he?"

"Up the street in a deserted house."

"Tell me which one. I'm going right there and kill him."

"You can't do that. He's holed up there with the rest of his gang. They all cold as ice, they gun you down right on the front walk, they don't care."

"Neither do I," barked Polk.

The sound of his voice rang out in the stable, reverberating dully as it faded into the following silence. Billy worried that the racket would wake up Asa. He gestured with his hands to lower the noise as he rose to his feet. In a calm quiet voice, Polk said, "Maybe I can surprise them somehow, slip into the house while they're asleep."

Billy shook his head again, "That ain't gonna work. They put a man on watch every night. They know you're here lookin' for your brother, so they be extra careful."

"How do they know I'm here?" Polk asked.

Billy swallowed quickly and said, "Everybody knows. Silver City's small, a stranger come to town, people know it, includin' Heaney." He paused to watch Polk's reaction, then continued, "Anyway, he and his crew are lightin' out just before dawn. They don't want the sheriff to get wind of them, so they clearin' out."

Polk said, "I thought you were going to meet him tomorrow with the money. How you going to do that if he's leaving in the morning?"

"I'm supposed to meet him outside of town."

Once again alert, Polk said, "Where?"

Uneasy, Billy said, "The Plum Mine."

"The Plum Mine?"

Billy nodded, "Where they shot your brother."

Polk slowly lowered his chin as he recognized the significance of the site.

"How far is it from here?"

"No more than a couple miles, just past Devil's Gate."

"So, I could get there before them."

Billy's eyes grew. "Hold on, there, you can't go up there by you'self! They's four of them and they killed lots of people, lots! Look what happened to your own brother. I tell you, you cannot get the drop on them no how!"

Polk grimaced, "Then, what?"

Billy took a deep breath and released it. "I ain't goin' to Virginia City tomorrow. Sheriff Hermann's startin' to think I didn't shoot Heaney. He wants to wait on gettin' the reward." He pouted and said, "We can go to the sheriff, I tell him the truth, everything. Tell the sheriff where they are, and where they headed. He could get a posse together and bring them all in. They all hang for sure for what they done. Blazes, folkshang 'em twice if they could."

Polk wiggled his head, "No. If they smell a posse, Heaney and his assassins will run. They've been good at running and hiding from posses for years. And, I want to exterminate them myself, all of them. So, I'm going up to wait for them at the Plum Mine." He holstered his gun and turned, saying to Billy over his shoulder, "Come on, you can tell me how to get there while I fetch my horse."

Chapter 26. Reckoning

Billy could not sleep. Thoughts roiled through his mind about what tomorrow would bring. He didn't give Henry Polk a rat'sass chance of taking down Heaney and his gang. But the eastern boy could spur Heaney to run again, never mindany reward money. Polk was sure to be killed, but Billy would be off the hook at least for tomorrow or longer if he wanted to cut and run himself. Polk's peril was his own choosing, he thought, not his doing. Except, he'd drawn Heaney and his to Silver City in the first place. If he'd just left it alone, brought in Polk's poor brother's body and leave it at that, none of this would have happened. He had gotten greedy and now Henry Polk's life and his own were on the line. Maggie's, too.

He should go see Sheriff Hermann and lay it all out. He'd take his lumps, but Polk and Maggie would be safe and maybe Heaney would be brought down for good. Maybe if he joined the posse the sheriff mustered up, he might share in some of the reward money. Then, memories of his stark, white fear at Fishing Creek, Locust Grove, even the Pawnee raid on the farmstead jerked him up short. Nearly nauseous at the images called up, he decided to tell the sheriff everything and leave the fighting to him. Billy knew,though,that after all this, one way or the otherhe would have to leave Silver City. Already known as the town sweeper, the town drunk, the town's biggest fraud would be added to his name. They would despise him, especially once they found that he' shot Carroll Polk's lifeless body in the back of the head to pass him off as the notorious John Heaney. He couldn't survive that. He would have to leave.

Better to get on with it, he thought, dawn was just a couple of hours away. He pulled himself up from the straw bedding in the stall and pulled on his boots. Hestuck his hat on his head and stood up. As he walked to the front doors of the stable, a horse snorted. He gave it a pat on the nose to keep it from waking Asa. Then, he silently opened one of the doors a crack and slipped through.

At the sheriff's office, Billy knocked several times, but no one answered. Nothing stirred inside. He stepped back. After a moment's thought, he decided to ask about the sheriff at Donovan's. He'd go to blazes first, he thought, before asking at the Golden Gate, the way that idiot Hyrum gossiped like he did, just like a woman. Donovan's was just a few doors down, too.

Once inside, he looked around and saw Jimmy Donovan sitting at a table in a back corner, surveying his establishment. Donovan was big and brawny, perhaps the biggest man in Silver City, maybe in the territory. His hair was burnt red aboveimposing sunburned features. Sharp, gray eyes peered out of half-closed lids surrounded by laugh wrinkles. He dressed well, but was renowned for his easy manner and grand hospitality, characteristics that keyed his success. Billy walked over, and before he could open his mouth, Donovan said, "Well, if it isn't Finn McCool, the giant-killer himself."

"Huh?" said Billy.

"Never mind. Have a seat, lad, take a load off." He waved to the bartender, twirling his finger in the air, then pointing it down at the tabletop.

"So, what can I do for you, Billy? Haven't seen you in a while."

"I been busy with work."

"Really?" Donovan laughed. "That's fine, good for you."

"I'm lookin' for Sheriff Hermann. He ain't at the jailhouse."

"Oh," murmured Donovan, his mood tempered almost imperceptibly. He said no more, so Billy asked him, "You seen him, Jimmy? He around? I need to talk to him bad."

Donovan raised his head slightly, his expression one of mild regret. "He's away just now, Billy. If you can wait 'til tomorrow, I'm sure he'll be back in his office."

"I don't want to wait," said Billy, "it's real important."

"You don't say?" Donovan said. Just then, the bartender arrived with two shot glasses brimming with rich, auburn liquid. "Ta', Tommy."

Donovan pushed one over to Billy, "Irish whiskey." He watched Billy hesitate. "On the house, a couple of boyos toastin' the old country." He lifted his glass and waited for Billy to follow suit. Billy picked his up, the two men clinked them carefully together and downed them in unison.

Billy put his glass on the table. "Thanks, Jimmy,that was awful good."

"Get it shipped from New York. Pretty penny, it is."

Billy smiled quickly to show his gratitude. Then, he asked again, his expression serious once more. "So, Jimmy, can you tell me where Hermann is?"

Donovan signaled to the bartender, who quickly came over with the bottle and poured out two more shots. After they drank them,

Donovan said, "I'm sorry, Billy. Hermann's at the Pleasant Times, visiting a friend."

Billy dropped his chin on his breast. "Yeah," he mumbled. "Of course. I should a thought that before I started botherin' you. My apologies, Jimmy."

Donovan grabbed Billy's arm on the table, "C'mon, now, lad, they've been friendly for a long time. Doesn't mean all that much."

"No," said Billy, "I guess not." He remained head down, staring through the tabletop.

"Yes, well," Jimmy said, trailing off. "I have to make the rounds, now, Billy." As he stood, he called out toward the bar, "Tommy, a pitcher for Billy, here." He turned back to Billy and said, "On the house. Stay as long as you like, 'til you're ready to go."

After Donovan left, Billy nursed his beer, wondering how he could ruin things so much in such a short time. Here he sat, feeling sorry for himself, knowing that it was all his own fault. Maggie was with Hermann, a good man whom she had known for a long time. Hermann was someone she could count on, not the town sweeper, the town drunk, and now the town scoundrel. Knowing that Hermann was better for Maggie caused Billy to taste bitter bile, feeling jealous rage and utter hopelessness. He drank.

Donovan's had emptied mostly. The proprietor had disappeared and the bartender seemed impatient. Suddenly, Billy realized that dawn was imminent. He rose up and stumbled toward the doors. Once outside, he lurched to the edge of the boardwalk, leaned over, and regurgitated.

He straightened up and rubbed a sleeve across his mouth. Tiny ribbons of pink light bordered the low, stony mountains around Silver City. Sunrise, just minutes away. Heaney soon would be gone from the empty house if he hadn't left already. Polk would be waiting for him up at the Plum Mine, but Billy had no confidence that the easterner could hold his own against the savage murderers. Sooner or later they would kill him just like they'd killed his brother.

Too late to go for Hermann, Billy decided, maybe too late to do anything. But, he couldn't let Polk just die up there. What did he have to lose, anyway? Cold ice waves suddenly raced through him. He saw himself sprawled on the rocky edge of the pond, life blood oozing out of an indescribably painful wound, followed by a slow ebb toward a black night. It all seemed so inconceivable, yet sure to happen if he went up there. He knew that any thought of death petrified him, but none more so than the idea of having it right in front of him, that day, that hour, that minute, that second. But, what choice did he have?

He hobbled as fast as he could over to the Parlour House. He skirted around the front to the kitchen door, and knocked quietly. Otto came to the door.

"Otto," he whispered, "I don't want to wake anyone, but I need somethin' out of my knapsack."

Otto stood motionless, his monumental eyebrows pulled together in thought. Without saying a word, he stepped aside and opened the door. Billy thanked him quietly and tiptoed up the back stairs to the hallway on the second floor. Carefully, he opened the linen closet and retrieved his knapsack.

He opened it, and pulled out the old shell jacket, laying it aside. He dug around until he located the oilcloth bundle at the bottom. Digging a little more, he found the box of cartridges and the bag of balls. He piled them on the floor, put the jacket and reticule back in the sack, and placed it on the closet floor. Billy stuffed the bullet bag in his back pocket, tucked the muslin bundle up tight in his left armpit, and slung the cartridge box by its strap over his shoulder. He stood up and started to leave the closet silently, but stopped for a moment's thought. He knelt again, opened the reticule, took out the envelope addressed to Maggie, and left it on top of the jacket. It was time, he thought, time to go.

Maggie awakened in the dim early morning to an empty bed. Albert apparently had left stealthily to avoid waking her. She smiled a little. He was nice, she thought. They'd enjoyed each other's comfort through the years. Early on they had discussed getting married, but they never did. She wasn't really sure why, though she understoodreally that she felt no hurry or need herself. During the many years she and Albert had spent time together, she figured that he wasn't that keen on it either. It wasn't a matter of propriety with him, everyone knew he spent many a night with his maturing, painted lady. Residue from past complications for each of themsimply blunted anything beyond what they enjoyed right now. For Maggie, she knew it was Billy McKinney. Sometimes, she found him to be detestable and at others endearing. Sometimes she felt both feelings at the same time.

Lolling her head at her ridiculous self, she swung her legs out of bed. Sitting on the side of the mattress, without looking she reached under and removed the bedpan from beneath. She stood up and quietly padded out of the room and down the hallway to empty it out the back window. Just as she neared the end of the hall, the linen closet door opened. Out from behind it stepped Billy McKinney.

"Billy. What in God's name are you doing here? Spying on me are you?"

Solemnly, slowly, Billy shook his head. "I came to get a few things. Otto let me in." He paused, then said, "I got 'em, so I'll be goin'."

She saw the bundle under his arm and the black, leather box hanging from his shoulder. "What do you have there? What's going on with you, what's happening?"

He looked at her, her brilliant green eyes, her fair skin, her long black hair loose and curving around her shoulders. Beneath her linen nightgown he could see the roundness of her body, her feet bare, always the way she preferred to walk inside the house. He said, "I got business at the Plum Mine."

"What business? What sort of mayhem are you up to, now, Billy?"

He huffed. "Henry Polk, the brother of the dead man I brought in is headed up there to ambush Heaney and his men."

"What? Heaney?" She cried, "He's here?"

Billy pursed his lips and nodded. "Up at the Plum Mine, waitin' for me to bring him the reward money I was gettin' for killin' him." He barked a harsh laugh. "I told Polk that Heaney bushwacked his brother. So, Polk's gone up to the mine to corner Heaney when the outlaw comes to meet me. But, Polk don't have a chance. I got him into it, I gotta try to get him out. So, I gotta get up there now and make Heaney leave him be."

His voice quivered as he heard himself saying such things, lying again.

"So, please let me go now."

"By God, you stupid, stupid boy!" she shouted. "You let that man go up there alone to face those murderers? How could you, Billy, it's despicable! We'll be putting him in the ground right next to his brother!" Her eyes flashed her anger at him. "Why didn't you tell the sheriff in the first place? You need to tell him now, at once!"

Billy stood in silence, his eyes hardened.

"Billy! You'll both be killed! You have to tell Hermann, it's the only way, Polk's only chance, your only chance!"

"No, Maggie," he said. "There's no time to do that. I got to go now."

He left down the rear stairs and out the back door. Otto closed it after him and watched the slight, fair-skinned, red-haired figure hurry north toward the Devil's Gate.

Maggie sped to her room, lit the lamp, and threw on her dressing gown and shoes. After tying them, she stood up and buttoned her gown, ready to dash out of the house and run to the jail. Before she moved, though, a thought occurred to her. She quickly lifted the lamp and darted back down the hallway to the linen closet. She opened the door and placed the lamp on the floor. Quickly, she pulled open Billy's knapsack. She found the shell jacket, a few other sundries, and the reticule. But, no bundle. Billy had taken his old pistol with him.

"Oh, Billy," she cried, "you are a fool of fools. Oh, Billy," she keened. She leaped to her feet andblew out the lamp. She set it on the landing and bolted down the front stairs and out the door, racing to the jail as fast as she could.

Maggie pounded on the locked door, pounding even when she heard movement inside, pummeling the thick wooden planks until the door opened. Hermann stuck his head out, his eyes still sleepy, his blond hair a thatch of wild wheat springing from his head.

"M'lord, Maggie, what's wrong?" Hermann asked.

"Albert! Billy McKinney's gone off to fight Heaney and his gang!"

Confused, the sheriff said, "Heaney? He's dead."

Maggie whipped her head back and forth, "No! He's alive with his bunch up at the Plum Mine. The dead man Billy found is another boy murdered by Heaney. The boy's brother's gone up to the mine for them and Billy's gone up to save him. Billy's taken that stupid old gun of his with him!"

Utterly mystified, Hermann said, "You're going to have to slow down for me, Maggie. Tell me the story so I can understand it."

Maggie stopped, took a deep breath, and let loose, as deliberately as she could as fast as she could. Slowly, Hermann's face drew longer and longer until she finished.

"It's all fallen in place," he said. "Henry Polk's out to avenge his brother. All right, do this for me. Run down to Asa and ask him for a horse while I get my guns."

"What about a posse, Albert?" Maggie cried. "You can't go up there alone!"

Hermann shook his head, "Not enough time. Go on, run down to Asa's. After that, you can fetch the mayor, tell him to get some men up there."

Stark fear lighting her eyes, Maggie tore off toward the livery stable.

Hermann pivoted back inside the jail and rushed to his sleeping quarters. There, he yanked on his boots and vest, and took his holstered revolver off of the bed post. He pulled out the handgun, flipped open the chamber and spun it to make sure it was loaded. He thrust the gun back into the holster and belted it on. Hermann grabbed his hat and hurried to the front office.He unlocked the gun cabinet and lifted out a double-barreled shotgun. He thrust some shells into his vest pocket and raced out the front door.

Before he could make the turn down toward the stable, he came to a full stop. Sitting on a horse, holding the reins of another, the dark silhouette of a man loomed over head. Hermann squinted hard trying to make out who it was. Stone-faced, Asa Jackson looked down at the sheriff. Hermann stared for an instant at the tall, black man sitting in the saddle before him, a horsesoldier carbine balanced in front against his saddlehorn. Hermann jerked around to see a pink morning glow cresting the eastern hills behind him. He turned back to Asa.

"Let's go," said Asa.

Without a word, Hermann promptly mounted the other horse. The two men wheeled around and galloped off north toward the Devil's Gate.

At the cut leading up to the Plum Mine, Billy searched for a good stand of sage bushes to hide behind. Once he felt he was out of sight, he unwrapped the Cochran and removed its horizontal cylinder, exposing its metal nubbins for attaching the firing caps. After carefully laying the pistol frame aside, he opened the cartridge box and extracted seven brass caps. He seated them on the nubbins and placed the cylinder down next to the other part of the pistol. Billy wrapped balls and powder in cigarette paper, producing seven cartridges. He retrieved the cylinder and inserted the cartridges into its chambers, carefully aligning them with the brass capped nubbins. Then, he inserted the loaded cylinder onto the pistol and snapped it into place.

Billy carefully climbed the slope up the cut several yards to the right of the worn path, doing his best to use the sage for cover.

Slowly picking his way up the incline, he found himself noting the reddish-brown rock of the hill and the dun-green, weathered branches of the brush. How lovely it all seemed with the morning sun bordering the mountains all around. He'd seen these everyday desolate markers for years, thinking of them only as road signs for a hardscrabble life. Never once had he recognized their sparse beauty until now. A remarkable display, he thought, designed by the good Lord to bring lovely order to the bare necessities of existence. Or, so Billy thought, wistful that he hadn't appreciated them before, yearning now for time to treasure such wealth. The closer he came to the top of the rise, the more forlorn he felt about what he might miss after today. Maggie.

Just before he crawled to the top, he stopped. He wished he had a beer, or better, a glass of whiskey. He sighed and inched up to peek over the crest. Cautiously, he peered down at the Plum Mine pond. He saw nothing. There was nothing there. A flight of birds flew overhead. Grebes cawed their dissatisfaction with the pond's water, too spoiled to alight. Then, quiet. Billy found the silence to be unnerving, as if he could be more unsettled, he thought.

He kept looking, searching for signs of life, wishing he had field glasses to scrutinize the whole area. Then, he saw life that caused his stomach to drop past his feet. Turkey vultures, sitting as high as they could get atop sage, occasionally flapping their wings once or twice as they waited. They stared down toward the ground and Billy followed their sight.

There it was, he thought, sick inside. A pile of crumpled clothes stretched out next to the water's edge just a few yards from where the vultures perched. Billy slipped down beneath the hilltop. He didn't need to look closer at the clothes to understand that something lay in them, someone. He wiped his mouth, took in a deep breath, and exhaled loudly. Then, he slid up over the top and skidded down the side, his pistol held high.

He reached the floor and crouched, darting glances around the gully in a full circle. He scurried over to the shape on the ground, which sent the vultures flying high. Billy paid them no attention, his eyes fixed upon the form below him, a body. He lowered himself to one knee and used his free hand to tug at the body, struggling until he managed to turn it over. Henry Polk stared past him with dead blue eyes.

Billy slowly rocked his head, his whole body. Too late, he thought. A wave of sorrow and shame swept over him. Henry had been shot in the chest and back, through and through, two enormous holes from what must have been a heavy round. What blood remained slowly leaked out, the rest soaked up by the gravel.

"Well, boys, look who's showed up for the party."

Dread quivered through Billy as he turned to leap up holding his gun out to shoot. Pain flashed through him and he dropped like a sack of rocks. Dazed, he stared up. Standing over him smiling with a scowl stood Nifty Bob holding a rifle he had crashed into Billy's jaw. Behind him on either side stood Lister and Pritchard, also grinning like ravenous wolves. Billy's head lolled to the right where he saw Heaney squatting down.

"Why, looky here," he said, holding the Cochran, "a toy pistol. Where'd you get this fancy firearm, Billy? Looks pretty nifty, wouldn't you say so, Bob?"

Holding his rifle aimed down at Billy, Bob raised his head and smirked.

"Anyway," said Heaney standing up, still holding the gun at the side of his leg. "We got things to talk about. So, Billy," he said, gazing around absently until he focused directly on him, "you bring the money?"

Billy wiped his mouth with the back of his hand, which he then noticed was bloody. "There ain't no money. Sheriff Hermann wouldn't get it. He didn't believe I killed you." He spoke in flat tones, his fearnow level with his resignation.

Heaney's face slowly burned red with fury as he realized what Billy was saying. "Fuck, you little fucker! I should'a known." Heaney bellowed. "No one'd ever believe a shithead like you could do me in." He kicked gravel at Billy, who reflexively cringed. "Well, then, that's that. No reason not to teach you a lesson now, lush." Heaney glanced up at the others. "All right, boys."

Without warning, they closed in on Billy striking with lightning quick, vicious kicks, again and again, causing him to bleed from his nose, mouth, and ears. Once they started pummeling him, he curled up into a ball like a baby, trying to protect himself as best he could. The outlaws surrounding him adjusted by kicking him more in the ribs, the spine, the crotch, and his head. They paused to rest while Heaney stepped on Billy's ankles, precariously shifting all of his weight up on the joint. Billy howled and moaned.

"This is what you get for keep comin' up empty-handed."

Heaney stepped off to crack another boot into Billy's face, lost his balance, and stumbled back. Billy cried out again.

"You little fuckin' mudsill," Heaney said, "it's almost worth losin' the money just to put you down." He bounced another blow off Billy's thigh. "All right, boys, let's get him up and be done with this."

Lister and Pritchard pulled Billy up and held him, standing.

Heaney brandished the gun, gesturing to Polk's body below. "See him? Bastard tried to dry gulch us. So, I plugged him good, blew his heart right outta his back. Used his own brother's gun, that Walker .45. Fires a hefty load, I tell you, perfect for me." He shifted Billy's gun to his left hand and pulled out the revolver at his hip. He held it up, and Billy tried to lurch out of the way.

"No point in movin', Billy. It's your time to leave. Heaven or hell, it don't matter to me."

"No!" sobbed Billy, "please!"

"Oh, I like that, Billy, you yellowbelly cocksucker. I fought on both sides of the war, never saw a coward to meet the likes of you."

Billy bawled openly, now, tears falling.

"Tell you what, Billy," Heaney said, holstering his gun, "I'm not gonna shoot you with my big gun right now."
Billy stopped crying, hopeful for an instant.

"No sir, I'm gonna shoot you with your own fancy gun. Let's see the look on your face!"

Lister and Pritchard moved away as Heaney raised the Cochran and held it at arm's length pointed straight at Billy.

"No, no!" screamed Billy, holding his hands out.

Heaney fired.

Riding hard to the top of the ridge, Sheriff Hermann and Asa Jackson arrived just in time to hear a volley of shots fired. Oh my God, thought Hermann.

They flew over the hill and down the slope as fast as they could gallop, reaching the edge of the pond in seconds. One man stood staring down until he heard the horses. He pulled his gun, but Asa shot him with his carbine, knocking him over on the ground, stilled. Hermann urged his horse up to a ring of bodies, one sitting hunched over. Holding his side, Nifty Bob slowly raised his gun. Hermann blasted him with the scattergun. The load of shot slapped the outlaw back into the water where he floated, face up. Hermann jerked his horse to a stop, dismounting on the run. He ran over to the bodies, his revolver drawn and cocked.

Heaney was dead. So was Pritchard. Asa had killed Lister, a shot in the chest, one in the head. Another body was stretched out near

352

the water, and in front of it, legs bent and arms on his chest, lay Billy. When Hermann reached him, Billy looked dead, too.

"Oh good Lord," said Hermann, "Good lord!" He knelt beside the body, wondering how he could tell Maggie, even knowing that this was likely the way it was going to end. He grabbed him by the arms, and Billy flinched.

"He alive, Albert," said Asa. "He got a bullet in his heart and he still alive."

"It can't be in is heart," said Hermann, "or he would be dead." Hermann grabbed a kerchief out of his back pocket and pushed it over the bleeding hole in Billy's chest. "It's near his heart, but it didn't hit it. That doesn't mean he's going to live. We got to get him to a doctor. C'mon, let's get a litter together to carry him out of here."

Hermann took his vest off and tied it tight around Billy's wound while Asa hastily picked up some rails from an old fence near the mine shafts. He lashed them together into a rectangular frame with lengths of leather cut from the reins of one of the outlaws' horses. Then, he pulled the saddle off of the horse and grabbed the blanket to stretch over the form as a makeshift hammock. At the same time, Hermann had taken the blanket off another mount and wrapped Billy in it. The two men eased Billy onto the litter and gently strapped him down, using other reins to secure him. Asa cut his rope and loosely tethered the horses together, leaving a length at the end to loop around his wrist. The two men hoisted the litter up as gingerly as they could, and started down the cut path with the two docile horses in tow.

"When we get down to the road," said Hermann, "one of us is going to have to ride like hell to Gold Hill for a doctor. I volunteer you, Asa. While you're gone, I'll keep dragging Billy in that direction."

Asa replied, "No. They pay more attention to you, Sheriff, not me. Sawbones think I talkin' about a hurt colored man, he maybe drag his heels."

Hermann didn't say anything, recognizing that Asa most likely was right.

In twenty minutes, they made it down to the road. Hermann stooped to check on Billy, and rose up. "He isn't doing too well," he said somberly. "He's breathing heavy, it's labored work. I don't think we can get him there in time."

He was interrupted by a racket coming from south around a curve in the road. The men gazed in that direction just as a carriage came into sight, its two horses running hard until suddenly they were held up. Inside the carriage sat Jimmy Donovan holding the reins, with Maggie White next to him.

"Thank God!" Hermann uttered. He called up to them, "Billy's been shot. He's in bad shape. There's a doctor in Gold Hill. We need to get him there right away."

Maggie hurtled from the carriage to Billy's side. Hermann saw her stark anxiety as she hovered, moving her hands without knowing what to do. "Don't fret, Maggie, he's a tough little firecracker. If anyone can pull through, it's him."

Maggie gave Hermann a quick, stark look, and returned her sight to Billy. His ashenface andslow, shallow breathing scared her. "Let's move him to the carriage right away," she said.

Asa and Hermann cautiously picked up the stretcher and transferred it onto the back seat of the carriage. Maggie climbed in and sat on the floor. She gently started to pat one of Billy's hands, whispering softly to him.

Hermann turned to Donovan. "You driving?"

Donovan nodded his head, "The mayor couldn't be found. I'll get'im there, though, faster than Ayers could."

Hermann climbed up into the carriage as he called out to Asa. "Can you go back for Polk?"

Asa lowered his head silently. He said, "What about the others?"

"Leave them to the buzzards. Let's go, Jimmy, schnell!" he said.

Jimmy cracked his carriage whip, and the horses took off.

The only doctor in Gold Hill did his best to stem Billy's bleeding without moving him from the carriage. Instead, he nervously urged them to take the wounded man to the hospital in Virginia City. Hermann gave him a cold look as Donovan snapped the reins again.

In Virginia City, they hurried Billy into an operating room to be seen by the hospital's best surgeon, courtesy of both Sheriff Hermann and Jimmy Donovan's reputations. Maggie sat on a bench against the pale green wall, twisting her hands in her lap, her head bowed in worry. After an hour, Donovan repaired to a nearby hospitality house for a drink, one which he raised to Billy. Hermann sat next to Maggie.

Two hours after they arrived, the surgeon, Dr. John Everett from Boston, came to them still wiping his hands dry with a white linen towel. A man of average carriage with hangdog features, Dr. Everett's dark eyes flashed with awareness and intelligence. He sat on a stool opposite Maggie and Hermann.

"We stanched the bleeding as best as we could. I probed for the projectile but, unfortunately, it's too close to the heart to extract. So, we sutured the wound. If he survives, he can live with the bullet where it is, though there's a risk of it moving and also of blood poisoning as the lead gradually disintegrates. Still, he's lucky to be alive at all."

The doctor moved in, "His condition is grave. The loss of blood concerns me. In good conscience, I cannot encourage you that he will survive."

"Dear Lord," Maggie breathed, tears brimming. Hermann grasped her hand, listening fiercely.

"There is a procedure that we can try, a blood transferal through a tube attached to a volunteer. This, however, is also a very chancy process with a significantly high mortality rate. We don't really understand why. Sometimes, though, it works."

"What are the odds, Doctor?" Hermann asked.

Dr. Everett took a breath and said, "One in three. Perhaps four."

Maggie buried her head in her hands. Hermann said, "No. We'll take our chances."

Everett sat back, his hands on his knees. "All right. We will do what we can to reduce the chance of infection, and hope for the best." He reached into a pocket of his vest and brought out a dazzling, gold pocket watch. "I must go. Leave the address of your accommodations so that we can contact you if matters change."

Maggie and Hermann glanced at each other, daunted by the idea of even being just five miles away. A disembodied voice called out, "Miss White will be staying at the Ritz Hotel across the street." Just back for the tail end of Everett's remarks, Donovan continued, "For as long as is necessary." When Maggie and Hermann looked at him in surprise, he said, "Surely Billy will need a devoted nurse." He shrugged. "When he's back on his feet, he can reimburse me out of his reward money. Isn't that so, Sheriff Hermann?"

Billy did not die, but he remained asleep for a long time, days turning into weeks. Maggie sat by his side, reading the paper to him, wiping his brow, and cleaning him up when necessary. To everyone's relief, infection did not set in. The narrow scar on his chest turned pink and healthy. Maggie still worried constantly, but Dr. Everett said that every day that Billy lived increased his chances of survival.

Hermann came up almost every day himself, though sometimes law enforcement duty kept him away. Asa often joined him, and occasionally rode up by himself. Donovan appeared once a week, and Otto made one visit. The mayor and the chair of the Silver City Board of Trade never found time to make the trip.

After three weeks, Billy woke up. He had nothing to say, but Maggie laughed and cried, grasping his hand almost too hard. He drank some water and some broth, then fell asleep again. Two days later, he talked.

"What," he said in a hoarse whisper, "happened?"

"You were shot, Billy. You almost died." Maggie nearly wept as she said the words.

"Oh? Huh." He drowsed off.

Over the next few weeks, he grew stronger and stronger, sitting up, taking solid food, later ravishing his vittles. As he improved, Maggie told him what she knew of what the folks up and down the Comestock Lode called The Showdown at Plum Mine.

"After hearing the noise, Albert and Asa rushed over the hill to find everyone knocked to the ground. He said it was as if a stick of dynamite had gone off right in the middle of them."

Billy winced, trying to remember. "Oh, yeah. Heaney was shootin' me with my own gun and it blew up, balls and metal flyin' everywhere. Happened to me once before," he said starting to drift off, "with Colonel Dixon. This time I got hit. Forgot the lard, misfire."

Maggie's brow furrowed as he dozed off. Lard? Misfire? She couldn't figure it out.

Hermann understood. "Using old handguns, they'd seal the chambers with lard, which kept a spark from one discharge setting off another. A misfire usually meant the gun would explode, likely killing the gunman." He scratched his head as he looked down on Billy napping. "Billy's old turret gun blew apart all right, but it must have fired off all seven bullets at the same time, too."

Maggie suddenly remembered searching through Billy's bags. She'd yanked out all sorts of odds and ends, while looking for the pistol, impatiently tossing each aside, including a small tin of lard. In his own hurry then, Billy overlooked the lard, and almost got himself killed.

Chapter 27. Running West

By early autumn, Billy was well enough to move back to Silver City. Maggie brought him back to the Pleasant Times Parlour House, putting him in her bed once again. She and Otto cared for him while he improved, becoming a bit stronger every day. Soon, he was propped up against a pile of pillows, reading the newspaper. Maggied had brought it to him to stifle his complaints about boredom. He gained weight for the first time since Maggie had thrown him out of the house. She thought he looked almost normal. His accelerating recovery, however, fed a growing restlessness. Billy's easy-going nature known to everyone in town turned into crankiness in confinement. Along the way, the change nourished a sense of uneasiness in Maggie.

Mayor Ayers finally showed up at the Parlour House to see Billy, who sat on the back landing enjoying the dry, fallair. Otto ushered Ayers up the back stairs, and Ayers maneuvered his substantial girth onto the small porch. His chubby red face leaked sweat from the climb, but Ayers shook it off. He stood in front of Billy and thrust toward him a bucket of beer.

"To one of my best customers," Ayers said. "Thank the Lord you didn't expire. The Golden Gate has stepped back from the brink of insolvency now that you are hale and hearty again."

"B'god, I never thought I'd live to see the day," said Billy as he grabbed for the bucket with both hands. He lifted it to his mouth and poured, sudsy beer spilling over onto his shirt. After he'd taken a long swig, he lowered the pail unsteadily, still lacking the strength.

"There's more where that came from," said Ayers with a grin.

"Thanks, Mayor Ayers, thanks so much," Billy gushed. "Can I offer you a drop?"

"Why, don't mind if I do," said Ayers, taking back the bucket. "Mighty warm coming up them stairs, never mind the intolerable heat outside." He helped himself to a few gulps, then passed the remaining beer back to Billy.

Maggie stood in the doorway. As soon as he saw her, Billy tried to hide the pail on the other side of his chair. He realized that she'd seen it and set it on the floor.

"Why, Miss White, how are you?" Ayers asked.

Maggie ignored him, her eyes boring straight into Billy's. Billy whined, "Aw, Maggie, don't be mad. It's just a little taste, to even me out. I'm goin' crazy, here, sittin' around."

Seeing the lay of the land, Ayers smiled stiffly at Maggie and said, "Well, I guess I'll push off. Plenty to do, you know, official town business and running a big establishment." He shifted his eyes to Billy, "Anyway, glad to see you perking up, Billy m'boy. As soon as you're up and around, let me know. There's plenty of sweeping to do at the Golden Gate. Take care, now."

Ayers swiftly sidled by Maggie and rumbled down the stairs. Maggie turned to Billy.

"So, Billy," she said, "is this the way it's going to be? Because, if it is, you can pack up and leave, get back to your important sweeping and the rest. But, I'll have nothing to do anymore with a fall-down drunk. Be quick about it and make up your mind."

Billy stared into her flaming green eyes, genuinely afraid. After a moment, he said, "Of course not, Maggie, it's just a taste to lift my spirits. I'm done with it, I promise, I'll have no more."

"Good," she said, her voice flinty, "then you won't be needing the rest." She reached out her hand and Billy reluctantly passed the bucket to her. She dumped its contents over the railing without ceremony while Billy morosely looked on.

Into October, Billy felt well enough to help Otto around the house. Silver City continued to fade away as more and more residents moved north to Gold Hill or Virginia City, while others went south to Carson City. Business at The Pleasant Times fell off a cliff. Jean was the only parlor house girl left. Sweet Sally Mae had married a placer trying to make a go of it prospecting up north.

After the Showdown, that same day Asahad returned to the Plum Mine to round up the Heaney gang's horses. Not much later, he moved his mules, buggies, and other gear to a new livery in Virginia City. The old stable stood empty, abandoned like so many structures in Silver City. Billy strolled down to the livery occasionally on his health walks. He would wander around inside and think about the work he was missing, and also Asa. For as close-mouthed as the blacksmith was, Billy discovered that he missed him in spite of all his mean cracks. Asa had come through for him, especially at the end.

"Things are changing around here fast, Billy." The voice came from the stable's front doors. Sheriff Hermann stood leaning against the open one. "Think you might move up to Virginia City to work with him there?"

Billy shrugged. He and Hermann were friendly after Plum Mine. Before all that, Billy'd thought the sheriff was a fair fellow, even when he put him in a cellnow and then. Since the shootout, though, he and Hermann shared some unspoken tie together—like with Bev and Josh, Billy recalled. How far away he had traveled from them and all that. Hermann made him feel it again a little bit. Part could be that since Billy had been recovering at the Pleasant Times, Hermann no longer stopped by the house to see Maggie anymore. That suited Billy just fine.

"You don't have to go up there and work, you know."

"I know," said Billy.

"No, you don't, really. You can go up and visit Asa, but you don't have to muck out his stalls anymore, or anybody's. You don't have to sweep boardwalks or floors either."

"What do you mean, Sheriff? I got to make my way once I'm strong enough."

Hermann shook his head, "Not now." Seeing the bewilderment in Billy's face, he said, "The reward. For Heaney, and his gang for that matter. Maybe at first you tried to fob off that poor dead boy as Heaney, but you made it right in the end. So, fifteen hundred for the murderer himself and another five hundred for Dick Pritchard. Asa and I split the reward on Nifty Bob and Joe Lister, since we shot those bastards. Asa shot Lister dead with his carbine riding full out. Hell of a shot."

"He was in the cavalry," murmured Billy, "Buffalo soldier Injun fighter."

"Right. His share of the reward and selling the gang's horses was enough for a new livery in Virginia City. Anyway, two thousand for you, Billy. I locked it in the safe in the jailhouse while you were healing up. I didn't want Ayers or Evans, any of that lot to get wind of it, figuring they would probably find a way to make a claim. Maybe your outstanding bills."

His mouth shaped in an O, Billy tried to take it all in. He was dumbfounded, one astonishment after another.

"So, I have it in cash up there waiting for you. I know it's a lot to absorb, but there it is." He reached into the breast pocket of his jacket. "Now, I recommend that you take some time to think about it before you come to pick it up. Make up your mind what you want to do with it, first. In the meantime, here's ten dollars to try out."

Billy held the bills in both hands, wide-eyed at the miracle of it all.

"All right, then. I'll see you soon, Billy."

Billy counted the dollar bills over and over. All the pain and fear he'd suffered through, maybe it'd been worth it. Maybe. He thrust the money in his back pocket and walked out of the stable as quick as he could muster. Stopping off to rest several times along the way, Billy finally made it to Donovan's Saloon.

Maggie sat in the armchair opposite her bed. Billy hadn't been back in the house for two days and nights. She didn't have to leave the premises herself to know what was happening. One of Jean's visitors had told her about Billy's celebration at Donovan's, then the Golden Gate, and back to Donovan's again. No one knew where he spent the first night, but Hermann had provided accommodations for the second. Maggie knew there was some reward money, but agreed with Hermann that it was best to keep it private until Billy was himself again. Well, he certainly was now, she thought.

She took a sip of her tea and placed the cup on its saucer on the side table. Then, she pulled out a cigarillo and lit it. Usually, she smoked out on the back porch, but that night she could give a damn. Puffing, she thought what an arse he was. Couldn't wait one day, had to go out on a bender. She clenched her mouth in a hard grimace, squeezing her tongue between her teeth and upper lip. Now that he was fit again and out and about, he could die for all she cared.

She sighed. She should have known better. Drunks are drunks, sops are sops. Only religion sometimes seemed to change their ways, but God knows, Maggie laughed harshly to herself, she was not religious and certainly could not show him the way. How she had become ensnared by Billy McKinney she would never fathom. He was a boy in a man's body, but so were they all. If that burnt-skinned, burnt-haired country bumpkin hadn't turned up with his innocent blue eyes and wondering ways, she would have been better off by far. Albert and she could have gone on the way they had for years, maybe even life. But Billy McKinney had to throw up in back of her house.

Well, Maggie said to herself, it was done now. She won't blink an eye, won't waste a tear when someone finds him dead in the street from drink. It's foreordained and she need have no part of it in her life.

"Maggie," a muffled voice called from outside. "Maggie." From back of the house. "Maggie." Who else could it be? She continued her smoking.

"Maggie!" the disembodied voice shouted, sounding like some sort of specter. Soon enough, she thought.

"Maggie, let me in."

Maggie left her room and strode down the narrow hallway, holding up just inside the landing.

"Walk on, McKinney," she yelled down into the dark night. "I'm through with you for good. Go sleep in some crawlspace somewhere else, you utter deviant."

"Aw, please, Maggie," Billy cried out. "I couldn't help myself, I came into some good luck. I had to celebrate and I got carried away a little bit."

"You always do, fool. Go on, get out of here. Don't come back."

"Maggie!—" She slammed the back door shut and went back to her bed to roll sleepless through the rest of the night.

The next day at noon, she sat over another cup of tea, now cold. Her head pounded as though she was the one who'd drank whiskey all night. She decided to strangle Billy McKinney if he ever showed up on her doorstep again. Otto tried to interest her in something to eat, but she had no appetite.

A knock came at the front door. Maggie glanced up, obviously distressed, so Otto said, "I'll get it."

He was gone for a good five minutes. Annoyed a little for no good reason, Maggie wondered what was keeping him. Eventually, he stepped back into the kitchen looking tentative.

"What is it, Otto? Spit it out."

He bit his lip, hesitant. Then, he said, "Billy is at the door."

"Oh, for the love of might—did you tell him to get lost?"

"I told him you didn't want to see him, but he said he needed to, one last time. Then, he swore he wouldn't bother you again, ever."

"Jesus, Mary, and—where's your billy club?" Otto frowned and she barked, "Get it! I'll billy him."

He handed her the cudgel he used to discourage unruly guests, and she marched out to the front porch. She slapped open the door to see Billy standing back near the steps, holding his hat rolled up in his hands, complete contrition on his face. She stopped in the doorway and said, "What did I tell you?"

He lowered his head abjectly, gazing up at her with wide eyes. "I know, and I know I did wrong. I can't expect anything. But, I want you to have this. It's all I can do to say I'm sorry, and to thank you for all you done for me."

He pulled out a thick leather packet from his back pocket and held it out to her. "It's what I promised you before. Now, here it is."

Leery, she tucked the short club in her armpit and took the pouch. She untied it and looked inside to find a huge wad of money. Startled, she raised her eyes to Billy.

"It's what you deserve," he said, as he wheeled around to go down the porch steps and down the sidewalk.

Confused, she remembered the dark morning when Billy had gone off to Plum Mineafter Polk. Searching for his pistol in his knapsack, she'd tossed aside an envelope addressed to her. She'd read it later while he was recuperating and laughed at it. Typical Billy, leaving her everything he owned, nothing. Now, he had given her all he had in the world and just walked away.

Maggie counted it that night, more than two thousand dollars. A stunning amountthat she couldn't keep,of course. Still, what would Billy do with it but drink it up, especially after she'd thrown him out? She might as well keep it. Considering that it was better tended by her hands, and also that Silver City was on its last legs, it made sense for her to keep it. But, she sighed, she couldn't just keep it from Billy either.

She puzzled out the situation until nightfall. Then, she dressed herself and went downstairs to the kitchen.

"Otto, can you bring a couple of buckets of water to the back door and leave them there? I'm going out for a spell."

She didn't bother with the Golden Gate, and instead walked directly to Donovan's Saloon. Once at the swinging doors, she knocked on them until the bartender came to greet here. Before long, Jimmy Donovan appeared in front of her.
"Is he here?"

Donovan looked her up and down. "You look quite fetching tonight, yourself, Miss White." He grinned broadly and said, "If you mean Billy McKinney, the man who bedded down John Heaney and company for good, he is inside imbibing a hearty beverage courtesy of yours truly."

"Can you ask him to come out?"

"I can and I will, of course," said Donovan.

"Thank you, Jimmy."

When Billy showed up, before he could say a word she started in."You can come back, Billy," she said, "if you're of a mind to. Conditionally."

Abashed, Billy asked, "How's that?"

"Number one. You will do your level best to control your drinking. Now, I cannot insist that a grown man quit a habit. That would be infringing on his God-given freedom. But, I can ask you to corral it. Fair enough?"

Billy hesitated, then nodded.

"Two. Regardless of whatever you do any given day or evening, you will return to the house before midnight. Yes?" she said.

"Yes," he replied.

"And three. I will control the money, all of it."

Yearningly, Billy said, "Can I get a few coins once in a while? Enough for just a tasteonce in a while."

Maggie reflected, then lowered her head, "Yes. A small allowance would be permissible."

He smiled happily.

"That's all, then. If you're willing to abide by these conditions, you can come home with me to the house now."

He looked as happy as a puppy, she thought, and walking ahead of him, she smiled a little to herself.

They walked back to the house. Inside the kitchen, Maggie reached over the sink and grabbed a bar of soap. She tossed it to Billy.

"There are two buckets of water out the back door. Give yourself a good scrubbing," she said as she turned to go up the stairs, "then come to bed."

The arrangement succeeded. Billy didn't stop drinking, but he kept the benders down to a minimum. Much of that control was imposed on him by Maggie doling out his spending money. After she had settled his bills, she informed every merchant in town that no credit for Mr. McKinney would be honored. Hence, both Ayers and Evans would not run tabs for him, which meant that he often ran out of resources before he ran out of thirst. On the other hand, Donovan often gave him a few drinks on the house simply because he loved having the celebrated hero in his saloon. So, there were a few occasions when Billy came home with a snootful. But, his curfew helped, too, a stricture that surprisingly he found suited himself as well. He made it home every night without fail. The arrangement meant, too, that his fortune remained substantial.

"That packet you gave me," Maggie said one night in bed, "there was more than two thousand dollars in it. I thought the reward was for just that."

"Hermann gave me ten bucks, which I used to drink and also to play faro," Billy explained, lying next to her. "I won! Can you believe it? I ain't never won a thing in my life! It was a big night for me. 'Course, I almost lost you 'cause of that night, too."

"You did lose me," said Maggie, "the money brought me back."

They both smiled looking straight ahead.

Silver City continued to fade away. Billy missed Asa, but when Maggie asked him if he wanted to move to Virginia City, he said no. Too big and noisy. She asked him if he'd like to go back east to find his father, and he shook his head sadly. After all these years, he was sure in his own mind that Daddy had passed. Then where?she asked. After his part in the Heaney shootout, Albert Hermann was the sheriff in Carson City now.Aside from Otto, the only person in town whom they liked was Jimmy Donovan, and he looked to be moving to Virginia City himself. Even Chun had pulled up stakes, taking his family to San Francisco, so they said. Billy didn't do much, no more sweeping, no more mucking out stalls. He also possessed not a bit of interest in working the tailings up in the hills. In some ways, then, their lives together were as idyllic as they'd been when they had first met. In other ways, they felt like they were marking time instead of imagining what they could be doing. Then, the letter arrived.

20 March, 1878
To: Mr. William "Billy" McKinney
General Delivery
Silver City, Nevada

From: Mr. Beverly Freeman
Paris, Arkansas

Dear Billy,

I hope this letter finds you well and happy. I was so surprised and glad to receive your letter of a while ago. I am surprised you learned to read and write. I never thought you would and I would never hear from you again. Life is hard, and I expected it to be hard for you like everybody. Now, I write to you with my spirit lifted, my heart flush because I know you lived when so many others have passed into the arms of the Lord.

I did not write back sooner because I did not receive your letter for months later. You see, I have been all over since the war ended. I can tell you a lot has happened. Going back after the war tested me deeply.

I witnessed ruin and death wherever I went. Farms were wrecked and abandoned. Bodies and bones lay about everwhere, soldiers in the field, common folk in cabins and the side of the road. Old and young, women and children, milk cows and horses. I thought what we saw at Fort Row was most terrible. Now, I know the worst happened all over. I'm not sure why, or whether the good Lord punished us for our past sins with this great war, or punishes us now for causing so much pain and misery amongst ourselves in those hateful four years.

I went to Memphis to find Mary Louise Smalls. I tell you, Billy, the closer I got, the sicker I felt wondering how she is, still alive God willing, but maybe not so glad to see me after all these years. Recall, she did have a husband lost down south, Lord knows where. And a daughter just up the road who might as well been in China the way things were. Mary Louise had a life of her own and I was away too long, I figure. Why hope she might see me again as more than a friend. But, she did.

I found her still with Mr. Burkle at his home. He is a great man, I am sorry to say he passed just a few years ago. He was real glad to see me, and called for Mary Louise to come to the door. When she did, her smile made me fill no time had passed at all.

Mary Louise and I got together and went to find her daughter Ruth at the Pritchers place. Going there, I made sure to tuck my pistol in my belt. The Yankees won the war and saved the Union, but a lot of Johnny Rebs were left alive and mad with guns. They sure didn't cotton to black folks walking around free, never mind dressing like white men. I was ready for the worst.

Praise the Lord, we found little Ruth there, six year old. She was in a cabin with an old mammy who took care of her. When Lincoln freed everone and the black folks left, the Pritchers moved out themselves. The only ones there still was the old folks. Mammy was happy to see Mary Louise back with her little girl, but sad to see her go and leave her alone. It was hard.

As soon as we got Ruth, we went to the Bowman farm to find Eli. All the Bowmans was gone, too. Kyle got killed in the war. It hurt me to think about it even after he nearly got me hung.

Some of our people stayed on at Bowmans and worked the land, all they knew how to do. But other white folks say they own it and they pay the free folks for what they grow and harvest. It ain't much, makes you wonder just what changed after all the fighting and killing.

We found Eli all grown now. But he changed, Billy, he is a bitter man. He was beaten regular by the Bowmans for running, whipped and made to work hemp. He is a sour soul, I think, and he feels we left him on his own to the slave catchers. No matter what I tell him, he thinks it. He broke my heart because he wanted no part of us. We went back to Memphis without him.

After, I thought we would settle down to start a new life. But, God Bless Her, Mary Louise felt a duty to go look for her husband John. I can't lie, it made me shake inside with a fearful fear. If Mary Louise warmed to me after many years, I worried to death how she would feel about seeing the father of her child again. I trembled inside thinking about it day and night. What could I do? I had to go with her to watch out for her. If the Almighty willed Mary Louise to rejoin with her rightful husband, in faith I had to accept it. But I did not like it all the way down. And I also thought we might find Josh too.

We took trains to Louisiana to look for Mary Louise's husband John and for Josh. Sad, but we did not find them. I pray they are still all right. Things for black people in Louisiana looked worse than Tennessee and Kentucky, like the war never ended or even happened in the first place. I should tell you, too, after seeing black people everywhere down so, I changed my name to Freeman. Mr Burkle helped me make it legal.

Back in Memphis, Mary Louise and I jumped the broom, except a minister married us, too. Mr. Burkle found him, Reverend Adams from the north, a hater of slavery always.

Once we married, Mary Louise and I packed up and left for Kansas. I had in mind you still could be there with the Wesleys. They built trains in Kansas since we left, making it pretty easy to get to Fort Belmont. Mr. Burkle gave us some money, so we bought horses and a wagon to ride to the farm. We figured on joining you and the Wesleys, stake out our own home. But when we got there, you and they were gone. The buildings down, the fields grown over. It was all done in, so we left too. We did not go back to Memphis, we went to Arkansas near Fort Smith. I started helping with the horses, Mary Louise, too, and we bought a small piece of land nearby a little town they call Paris after the one in France. Now we raise and sell horses and do pretty well by it. We got four children, Ruth, a grown woman will marry a nice boy from around here. We have three little boys, Beverly after me, Josh, and Billy, after you. They are good boys and are learning about horse raising and how to read and write.

That pretty much is it. We are happy here and will be staying, God willing. We are so happy to know that you are all right. We invite you to come down if you want and live here. We all run together *way back, Billy, and we can live together again. You, Josh, Eli, and even mean old Whit are my brothers and always will be. For the rest of my living days. So come someday, Billy, so we can remember them who are gone to the Lord's arms, all of us as free men.*

May the Lord bless you and your loved ones too.

Your friend and brother,
Beverly "Bev" Freeman

Billy shifted his sight up to Maggie, who had read the letter over his shoulder.

"B'god, Maggie, Bev, Bev Bowman—Freeman, now. My Lord." He shook his head back and forth, amazed. "And he misses me. Ain't that somethin'."

"It is, indeed," she said. She dropped to one knee next to him, her hand on his arm. "So, what do you think? Do you want to go to Arkansas, start new there?"

He looked into her glorious green eyes, her lovely round face framed by black ringlets with just a touch of grey in them now. Somewhat wistful, he said,"Naw. They got their life there, don't need to make room for other folk."

"Then what?" Maggie asked.

Billy shrugged. "How about San Francisco? Lot goin' on in California."

"San Francisco," she said thoughtfully. "San Francisco would be all right."

"Well, all right, then," grinned Billy.

Maggie looked at him somewhat askance. "If we go to San Francisco, are you going to quit drinking?"

"I guess, maybe. I guess I ain't going to drink no more," he said, "but maybe no less either."

She cuffed him on the top of his head and wrapped her arms tight around   him.

Acknowledgments

Writing a novel can be a very enjoyable and gratifying activity. Turning it into a story that others might like to read, however, requires a great deal of work and different perspectives from many kind people. This book benefited from a host of big-hearted supporters who contributed an enormous amount of their time and labor.

First, I must thank my wife Ivey, the love of my lifewho simply does everything to help me all the time. I also must thank those who read the manuscript, offering genuinely constructive criticism and enthusiastic support: my brothers George and Pat, my best friend and other brother Jim O'Donnell, and my sister Lucie Brown. Aside from helping me with the narrative, Lucie also bore into perform a superb job of copyediting, extremely vital to any successful writing.I also wish to thank my daughter Molly who exercised her mastery of myriad arts to create the cover for this book.

Finally, I would like to express special gratitudeto Stephen Brown. During one long discussion deep into the morning, Stephenrelated to me howa black man regardless of who he is can consider any encounter with the police as a potentially lethal situation. His candid conversation inspired a great part of this novel.

Select Sources

The Watermen's Song: Salvery and Freedom in Maritime North Carolina, David S. Cecelski, The University of North Carolina Press, 2001

Silver & Sawdust: Life in the San Juans, Keln Reyher, Western Reflections Publishing Company, 2005

Adventures of Hucleberrry Finn, Mark Twain, Penguin Books, 2014

Roughing It, Mark Twain, Peruse Press, 2015

The New York Times Disunion, Ted Widmer, Editor, Black Dog and Leventhal Publishers, 2014

Online Research

Wikipedia

Google
Gullah bible
Gullah: a study of language. - FreePatentsOnline
http://www.freepatentsonline.com/article/Reading-Improvement/90925090.html
CochranTurrets
https://www.americas1stfreedom.org/articles/2015/12/29/turrets-big-and-small/

About the Author

Dan Wallace worked in book publishing for 37 years, most of them at Gallaudet University Press. In 2014, he turned to writing full time. He has written five novels including *Tribune of the People: A Novel of Ancient Rome*. He also writes short stories, essays, and poetry that can be read online at his writing exchange *In the Wallace Manner* (inthewallacemanner.com). He lives in the Washington, DC, area with his wife Ivey and two black cats, Star and Moon. This book is dedicated to his daughter Molly and son Conor, both who constantly inspire him in myriad ways.

Reviews of Dan Wallace's Most Recent Novel

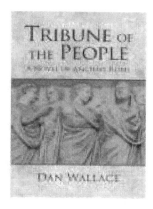

Publishers Weekly—Wallace's epic novel triumphs with a vivid historical account of ambitious elite Roman politicians and generals

Library Journal— This thoroughly researched novel is as dramatic and gory as any swords-and-sandals epic and demonstrates how educational historical fiction can be. A wide cast of characters including soldiers, senators, slaves, mothers, and wives expand the reader's understanding of life in this time.

Midwest Book Review—A deftly constructive, exceptionally well written, and consistently compelling read from beginning to end, "Tribune of the People" is a truly impressive novel of the old Roman Empire by Dan Wallace. This is the stuff from which block-buster movies are made!

The US Review of Books: Professional Book Reviews for the People— Wallace's epic tale vividly depicts the opulence and grandeur of the ruling classes while simultaneously detailing the sights, sounds, smells, and squalor of those not born to wealth or position. His battle scenes pulse with excitement as he couples the weapons, tactics, and strategies of war with the carnage they wreak. No less compellingly does he describe the deceit and scheming in the porticos of power as well as the intrigue and hidden agendas in intricate familial relationships. RECOMMENDED.

The Historical Novel Society—A most timely novel; the characters are engaging and well-formed and the story well told. The novel gives you a feel for ancient Rome in the last years of the Republic.

Tribune of the People: A Novel of Ancient Rome
By Dan Wallace
ISBN 9780828326049 Trade paperback, $19.95
ISBN 9780828326056 Kindle E-Book, $9.95

Order your copy at BrandenBooks.com or at Amazon.com.

Made in the USA
Middletown, DE
19 August 2018